STORMS

By Reba Stanley

Published by Westview, Inc.
Nashville, Tennessee

© 2008 by Reba Stanley. All Rights Reserved.

No portion of this book may be reproduced in any fashion, either mechanically or electronically, without the express written permission of the author. Short excerpts may be used with the permission of the author or the publisher for the purposes of media reviews.

ISBN 978-0-9819172-6-9

Second Edition, September 2008

Cover design and illustrations by Landon Earps

Edited by Bob Allen, Judy Allen and Sue Ergle, Author's Corner, LLC;

Printed in the United States of America on Acid-Free paper

PUBLISHED BY WESTVIEW, INC.
P.O. Box 210183
Nashville, Tennessee 37221
www.publishedbywestview.com

Dedication

To my loving momma; the one person this side of heaven who has always loved me and been there for me all the days of my life. I thank you for your continued support and never letting me give up.

Preface

Sitting at her husband's gravesite, Joyce McIntosh's world has been turned upside down. Will she ever be able to make it on her own? Joyce must learn a new way of life; one she and her five children won't find enjoyable.

Through the struggles of life, Joyce learns she must pull herself together and support her family. Trying to keep everything as normal as possible for the children, she learns the hard way that her church friends aren't what they once appeared. Or was she looking at them through an easy life's eye?

All at once he walks into her life; now she must figure out what to do with this man. Does she want to go down the path of romantic relationship again? Can her heart belong to another after more than twenty years of marriage? Can she bury one man after a lifetime of loving him, and then fall for another so soon? Or will she stay in her comfort zone just enjoying the solitude of being a single mom.

Joyce had always thought her faith in the Lord was strong, but through these trials she realizes she has much to learn about herself, and her God.

You will love this romantic story of loving, losing, heartbreak, and loving again.

Acknowledgements

Special thank you to those who have helped me along the way, each of you have been a blessing and I could not have accomplished this task without your help.

Marilee Wilkinson – without your words of encouragement from the beginning, I doubt I would have continued this project.

Tara Byrd – you are such a blessing to me; you have been a major player in getting this book ready for publication. Thank you sweetie.

Crystal Zaragoza – you too were a blessing to work with. I thank you for your words of encouragement and your long hours of work.

David – always remember 1-4-3.

Bob and Judy Allen – a special thank you to you and your staff for all your hard work and for having lots of patience.

CHAPTER ONE

Joyce sat in the first seat offered to her by her eldest son, Timothy, at the gravesite of her husband of almost twenty-two years. She didn't seem to notice the cold, crisp January air; she felt absolutely numb over the events of the past week. It had all seemed to be part of a bad dream; she wondered when she would wake up. In a way, it seemed just like yesterday when Joyce put on a beautiful white wedding dress, was escorted down the church aisle, and married the man she truly loved. She was so happy to become Mrs. Paul McIntosh. Through the years they had a fairly happy marriage; after all, every one had their rough spots every now and then, but for the most part they were happily married; now it was all over. Paul had suffered a major heart attack at the age of forty-four, and now he was gone.

Joyce and Paul had made their home in Garland, Texas, from the time of their wedding. Joyce was born and raised in Athens, Texas. She was very pretty with her dark hair, almost black, and sky blue eyes. Paul was from Oklahoma City. He stood 5'10" and had light brown hair and brown eyes. The two met during college at The University of Texas. It was there that Paul earned his engineering degree, while Joyce worked towards a degree in Art.

They married two years before Joyce finished her schooling. Even though neither one of them was originally from Garland, this is where they started out as a married couple. Paul had received a job offer in his field that was hard to turn down, so he took it; and eventually Garland felt like home to the McIntosh's.

It was hard at the beginning, but they were the typical newlyweds, spending much time alone and relishing in that alone time.

Paul's career was moving forward and, as time went on, the young couple became tied down to the responsibilities of married life. Work hours were longer; bills were not getting paid on time, and at times, Paul would become overbearing toward Joyce. After awhile, Joyce just assumed it was the stress from his work.

Joyce remembered a Sunday School teacher saying one morning in class while she was dating Paul, "You may have difficulty at the beginning of your marriage, and you might struggle trying to figure out who will be the boss." With her parents there really wasn't a "boss." Her father treated her mother with love and respect, not like someone to be ruled over. Joyce dismissed the thought completely that morning and never thought of it again until a few years after marriage.

Little things that didn't have much meaning caused Paul to yell at his young wife, such as paying too much for an item at the grocery, or not having a certain shirt pressed. To Paul, anything that was not to his liking was a good reason to yell, and yell he did. Eventually, she learned to live with his angry ways, and her reactions became the norm. She loved her husband, and she was certain that he loved her.

Paul and Joyce were very blessed with five children. Timothy was now twenty and in his second year of college in Wisconsin. At 6'2" with dark hair, hazel eyes, he was very handsome. Joyce missed her son, and was happy that he was half-way through school. She hoped that he could find work somewhere much closer to home.

The second of the McIntosh children was seventeen-year-old Elise. She was a petite, beautiful young lady, with light brown hair and blue eyes.

Samantha, or Sam as her siblings called her, was fifteen and just starting to turn all the boys' heads. She would hate them one day and talk about them non-stop the next. She had auburn hair like her Aunt Karen, and hazel eyes like her big brother.

The last of the McIntosh children were 10-year-old twin boys, Mark and Michael. No one could tell them apart, except the imme-

Chapter One / 3

diate family of course. The boys had brown eyes that were a carbon copy of Paul's. Joyce wanted to cry every time she looked at her sons, with their light brown hair and brown eyes; they both were very cute little boys.

Joyce sat in her bedroom chair, staring at the TV; not even focusing on what was on, remembering those first years of marriage. She felt she was spending too much time thinking of the past, but could not keep herself from doing it. Everything reminded her of Paul or of something in the past.

As she sat crying, her husband gone, she felt scared and alone. How would she get by? How would she continue to raise the children alone? They were sure to miss their father, playing basketball together out on the driveway, helping them with their math when he had the time. How would she handle that?

Paul had never allowed her to make very many decisions on her own, but now there was no other choice. Paul had actually crippled her from being able to stand on her own. She so badly wished he was there to put his arms around her and tell her everything would be all right.

Joyce's children noticed she was not doing well. She had become thin and her face drawn; she had dark circles under her eyes, and didn't seem able to take care of the children like she always had done. She just wanted to lie around the house; she stayed in bed much later than she had ever allowed anyone who was not sick, and found herself watching television more than she used to. However, she did make herself get up and get ready for church on Sunday mornings. Elise felt that calling their grandparents and asking them to come and help would be the answer to this problem. That is the action she took as soon as she could get the phone call made without their mother's knowledge. Joyce was happy and relieved to have her parents come and help with the children, but she still felt so alone.

After about two weeks of utter depression, Joyce made a decision; "That is enough!" She got mad about the whole situation, even at her late husband. "After all, Paul did not cherish me. Yes, we loved each other, and I miss him terribly, but he could be so loud and overbearing at times. He has caused me to be afraid of what the future holds. Now it is time for calm, quiet living!" Joyce said out loud to an empty room. Hoping this little pep talk would snap her out of her depression, Joyce took on a new attitude.

The next day Joyce sat the children down and spoke to them about how things were going to be from now on. "We have had a major shock and loss in this family, but we'll be alright. The Lord told us in His word that He would never leave us, nor forsake us. Each of us is going to have to hold on to that verse. You can't each deal with this in your own private way like I've been doing; we all have to deal with this as a family. Our hearts are hurting right now, but we will heal, we will stay together."

They all sat and listened to her with tears not only coming to Joyce's eyes, but the eyes of her children as well.

"So, if you need help, need to talk, come to me, okay? Please?"

"We will Mom ... won't we guys." This came from Elise, who was taking on her responsibilities as the eldest sibling at home. They all nodded their heads in agreement.

"That went well." Joyce told herself out loud as the kitchen had cleared out, and the children went their separate ways in the house. Joyce only hoped she could keep up her end of her little talk.

"I'll get it, honey," Joyce's mother replied, referring to the doorbell that had just rung.

"Hello Pastor Jones, Mrs. Jones, please come on in. I'll let my daughter know you're here," Elizabeth said to their guests. "Joyce," she called, "Pastor and Mrs. Jones are here."

"Oh, thanks Mom, I'll be right there." Joyce took a few

moments to smooth down her hair and straighten her clothes and to get her emotions in check.

"Pastor, Mrs. Jones, how good to see you ... can I get either of you anything to drink?"

"Oh no, thank you," Mrs. Jones replied.-

"We just stopped by to check on you and the children; we want to help you in any way we can, so please if there's anything we can do for you, let us know."

"Thank you really, but we are doing okay right now, I can't say we are fine, but we're staying afloat. There are many adjustments being made, but all in all I think we'll be fine. It will just take some time." Joyce said more strongly than she felt. The adults talked awhile, and she thanked them again for their concern before they left.

After the children went back to school, Joyce continued to keep a close watch on them, talking to each of their teachers and telling them her plan of action. Timothy had returned to college, and that in itself was a struggle. He wanted so badly to stay home and help his mother and siblings.

Joyce tried her best to keep everything in their lives as normal as possible, but there were days she just wanted to stay in bed.

Joyce's parents had come and stayed with them for two weeks. Their help to Joyce and her children was immeasurable, but it was time for them to get on with their lives as well.

"Mom, Daddy, I really am thankful for your visit, it has been invaluable, but we'll be fine; we will survive this storm." It was hard for Joyce to tell her parents that she needed them to go home so she would lean on God and not them. She knew they were there for her, and she could always count on them at anytime.

"I need to get things back to normal for the children and for myself."

"We understand Joycie. Your mother and I are just a phone call away, don't ever hesitate to call," Jason said to his daughter as he hugged her tightly. Jason and Elizabeth hated to leave, but both of them knew they had to let their little girl stand on her own feet. Within two days and many tears Jason and Elizabeth went back to their own home in Athens, Texas.

⌒

Joyce and the children continued attending the same church, staying involved in the various activities as they normally did. It was hard in the beginning, with Paul not sitting beside her, but it was something she told herself she would have to get used to. On Sunday mornings she had to make herself get out of bed and get the family moving to get to church on time.

The Pastor and his wife Libby visited often, making sure Joyce and the children were getting along well. But as normal and hurtful as it was, people started to forget. After a little while, it was almost as if Paul had never been a part of that church. In one way Joyce felt it best for it to be that way; in another way it was very hurtful. She felt jealous at times because others got to forget and go on with their lives while she and the children had to continue to live in and deal with the loss every moment of every day. She found it difficult to believe how quickly some had forgotten. After one morning service, before Joyce got out of the building, a man she and Paul had known for years approached her.

⌒

"Hey, Joyce, what's your hurry?" Diane, her lifelong friend, spoke loudly from across the parking lot.

"Oh, hi, Diane, Ron, I just need to get out of here," Joyce said to her friends in the parking lot after the morning service.

"Joyce, you look a little upset, did something happen?" Ron asked.

"You are not going to believe this, but Jim Richey just asked me out. Can you believe that? Paul has been gone just a few weeks and someone at *my church* of all places, asked me out."

"Yeah, that's pretty bad." Diane replied with a look of shock on her face. "Try not to let it get you too upset; men can be jerks at times."

As Ron heard this bit of news, he looked around the parking lot, thinking he would have a little talk with Jim. "Ron, what are you thinking?" his wife asked, a very concerned tone in her voice.

"I'm going to have a talk with Jim; I mean, how could he be so insensitive, honey?" Joyce has been a widow for barely a month, he knew Paul; now he tries to swoop down on his wife. That burns me, Diane!" Ron replied as he was trying to keep himself under control.

Joyce kindly explained to Ron how much she appreciated his concern and desire to protect her and the children.

"I really don't want the children to know anything about this. Jim needs to be told how wrong in so many ways he was, but not here, and not now." Joyce explained.

Ron agreed this was not the best time or place to deal with this issue, so he did as Joyce asked. "Besides, it may lead to other problems. If he does that again, I'll let you take care of it, okay?" Joyce told her dear friend with a loving smile. His grin in return was all that needed to be said.

The three adults waited for the children to come to where they stood talking, and then Ron invited them all to join him and Diane for lunch, his treat.

This is just what I needed Lord; You know just how to take care of me, Joyce thought to herself as she looked around the table seeing how everyone was enjoying themselves. She decided then and there to avoid Jim Richey at all costs, and if he did approach her again, she was going to punch him right in the nose.

"Mom, may Samantha and I go to the movie?" Elise asked.

"What are you planning on seeing, dear?" Joyce asked her eldest daughter.

"We're not sure yet, we'll have to see what's playing. I just want to see a movie, and I don't want to go alone." Elise replied.

"Alright, but be careful what you see."

"I know Mom; we won't see anything we couldn't all see as a family." Her daughter said in a frustrated singsong tone.

"Thank you. Now, do you need any money?"

"No. We both have our own to get in and maybe enough to share a bag of popcorn."

As the two girls went to the movie, Joyce went outside with her twin boys to watch them ride bikes. She was determined to enjoy the remaining childhood of her twins, especially now that she was doing all the parenting alone. They rode to the park and back, and Joyce decided to ride one of the older children's bikes with them. It was then that the boys wanted to race. Joyce told them they could, but not with her. They had plenty of energy; she, on the other hand, did not. They were at the park for a few hours, when Joyce decided it was time to head home.

———

One of Samantha's classmates saw her from across the theater lobby. He was excited to see her and walked toward her.

"Hi, Sam, whatcha doin'?"

"Hello, Kenny." Samantha replied in an irritated tone. "It is quite obvious I am going to see a movie."

Elise was at the candy counter and noticed her sister talking to a boy from school. Samantha was a beautiful young girl. It seemed like boys just couldn't help but stare and wanted to be around her, but Samantha wouldn't give them the time of day.

"Robert and I are seeing the same movie. You could sit with me and we could watch it together," he said with much hope.

"No thanks, I came with my sister. I'm going to sit with my sister and leave with my sister. And speaking of my sister, I'm going in the movie now, just me and my sister," Samantha told Kenny, making sure he got the point.

"Kenny, maaan she shut you down bad," said Robert, another classmate, and Kenny's best friend. Robert couldn't help but laugh at Kenny and the shocked expression on his face.

Chapter One / 9

"Come on dude, let's go on in." Kenny said with a face that said he was not giving up on Samantha so easily.

"So, what was that all about?" Elise asked Samantha when they found their seat in the theater. "Oh Kenny, he's in my class at school, and he's a creep. He wanted me to sit with him." Samantha said in a disgusted tone.

"What did you tell him?"

"I told him NO!" she said with a little rise in her voice.

"Is he here at this movie, or is he seeing the other one?"

"I don't know, and I don't care."

"Okay," Elise replied. *I can't believe it, my little sister has boys falling all over her, and I can't get one boy to even look at me. This just stinks,* Elise thought to herself.

Samantha didn't give Kenny another thought as she sat with Elise and watched the movie. When it ended, everyone exited the theater as instructed. As the sisters were walking out, Sam heard someone beckoning her once again.

"Sam!"

Samantha heard her name called from across the room, and she turned to look to see who it was.

"What, Kenny?"

"So, how did you like the movie?"

"I liked the movie fine; I thought maybe you would have left during the scary parts." Samantha took a jab at her classmate. Robert, who was standing with Kenny, started laughing.

"Ha-ha, very funny," Kenny replied sarcastically.

"Come on Kenny, I think I'd better get you away from her before she hurts you." Robert replied as he took Kenny's arm to lead him away.

"Sam, you were pretty rough on him weren't you?" Elise asked.

"No, not really. If I had let him sit with us, he would have gone back to school and told everyone we were out on a date, and possibly other things that didn't, and wouldn't ever, happen. Like I said he's a creep."

"Mom, we're back," Elise spoke quite loudly, so her mother could hear her from any room in the house.

"I'm in the kitchen, honey," Joyce replied. Samantha went on upstairs to her room as Elise joined her mother in the kitchen.

"How was the movie?" Joyce asked as she put some dishes away.

"It was fine. We saw a clean one, so don't worry, it was a bit scary, but clean," Elise said with little sarcasm in her voice.

"Where are the boys?" Elise asked.

"They're up in their room doing something." Joyce told Elise about their time of bike riding and the fun she had with the energetic boys.

"Mom, I don't think you should let Samantha out of the house alone."

"What?" Joyce replied with a strange look to her daughter.

"Well, I mean, we were at the movie and two of her classmates came up to her. One of them was flirting and asking her to sit with him during the movie. She shut him down cold, which I'm glad; I wouldn't have let her sit with him. I felt bad for him at first, but then Sam told me what kind of person he is, and I'm glad she told him in so many words to leave her alone."

"If she told him no, and didn't lead him on or flirt back, what's the problem, dear?"

"Mom, she is fifteen! I'm seventeen and no boy comes up to me like that," Elise sounded hurt.

Her mother felt a little hurt for her daughter herself, and lovingly explained how boys really didn't make any sense at times. Every girl either has gone through the phase of feeling as if no boys are paying attention to her, or they will go through it.

"Your sister will too when she starts liking the attention," Joyce continued to explain. "Just be thankful you're not the boy getting rejected. It does sound like I need to speak to Samantha about the way she spoke to that boy."

"No, Mom, please don't. I don't want her to know I told you. She'll get upset with me and then I won't have anyone to go to the movies with."

Elise then left the kitchen with cookie in hand.

Joyce and the children thought it would be a good idea to get away for the weekend. They went to Athens to visit her parents. She let Diane know they would be gone so that she wouldn't worry.

"Joycie! Hi! How's my girl?" Jason Arnold asked as he hugged his daughter tight. He had called her 'Joycie' since she was a very small child. He loved all his children and didn't play favorites, but there was something about Joyce that touched his heart.

"Hi, Daddy, I'm doing a lot better these days, thanks."

Jason then went on to hug the grandchildren. He adored each of them.

"Hey, after supper what would you say to some ice cream?" Jason asked the children with big eyes and a grin on his face.

"We'd say yes!" Mark replied with his eyes wide and his face happy. This started everyone in the room laughing at both Jason and Mark.

"Joyce, honey, you're here. I'm so glad," Elizabeth said as she entered the room and hugged everyone. "So, how is everybody?"

"We're doing fine, Mom." Joyce asked about her parents and siblings as the boys were in the kitchen with their grandpapa.

Elizabeth talked of how Jason still had his hand in the car business even though he was retired. He couldn't seem to stay out of it. Jason had begun doing a little wholesaling to make a few extra dollars. He said he loved the chase of the car business.

"Good for Dad. I guess cars are just in his blood." She joked.

Jason had been in the car industry as long as Joyce could remember; he loved that business.

The two women continued to catch up on current activities of each other, and realized it was getting pretty close to time to eat.

"Joyce, Sam, Elise, come on in the kitchen, and let's get the food on the table, I have it warming in the oven."

"Yeah, I'm hungry," Samantha said.

"You're always hungry," Elise told her younger sister as they were walking toward the kitchen.

There was a shocked look on Elizabeth's face as she went into the kitchen and saw that Jason and the twins had put the food on and set the table.

"Oh my! Look at this. Thank you, boys. Jason, I'm so surprised," Elizabeth said, stunned.

"See, I told you." Jason told the twins to where only they could hear. "Now, when we get ready to go out for ice cream there is no way your grandmomma can say no." The twins just looked at their grandpapa as if they had been told the secret to life.

After supper was over, and the kitchen was put back together, Jason felt it was the right time to play his hand.

"Elizabeth, I'm taking the kids to get some ice cream. Would you and Joycie care to go with us?"

"Oh no, dear, thanks. Joyce, if you want to go that will be fine."

"Dad, you go ahead. I'll stay here and talk with mom. Have a good time. Elise, honey, don't let your brothers eat too much will you?"

"Alright."

"Let's hit it," Jason told his grandchildren.

"Yeah, let's hit it!" replied Mark.

Elizabeth was always happy to see her daughter and grandchildren. Lately she couldn't help but worry about how Joyce and the children were managing.

"So, Joyce, how are you really doing?"

"Mom, I'm doing better. The kids are settling down and that's a big help. Samantha is still acting out with her mouth, though. Her words sometimes come out very hard. As for me, I'm lonely at times, but it is getting better."

Elizabeth advised Joyce to get out more, do more things with Diane. She knew it wasn't as if the two of them were single young girls anymore, but Diane and Joyce had been the best of friends all their lives. She knew Diane could help her daughter.

Chapter One / 13

Joyce was trying to stay active at church, and a few men had asked her out, but Joyce was not interested. "I'm not into that scene and may never be. I just don't want to go through all that again. I especially don't want to put the children through it. One man from my church asked me out just a few weeks after Paul passed away. Can you believe that, Mom?" she said with a little hurt in her voice.

Indeed Elizabeth was shocked. She knew men could be dumb about such things, but that was really dumb.

"Honey, some men just aren't too bright; you have to look over them."

"I know, Mom, but I really miss Paul." Joyce said with a sad look on her face.

"I know you do honey. I can't say that I understand, because I haven't been where you are, but it has to be hard."

Elizabeth was a good person to talk to, she never gave advice she didn't take herself. She didn't gossip, and she certainly didn't judge people.

Joyce's brother, Doug, planned to visit with her that evening; Joyce looked forward to seeing him and his family. She didn't get to visit with her siblings as much as she wanted, so she cherished the times when she did.

Doug was the oldest of the Arnold children. He was a bit of a joker, so Joyce knew it would be fun. Jason and Elizabeth had four children: Doug, Karen, Joyce and Chad. Their daughters had married men that took them away from their home, but their sons still lived in Athens, not too far from their parents. They all tried to keep in touch, but at times it was hard.

Karen and her husband and four children lived in San Antonio, Texas, so the family didn't see them as often as they would like. Doug and Chad visited not only their parents, but also each other often. Even though Karen and Joyce were miles away from them, they still kept in touch with one another.

The evening was a fun one. Doug, his wife Faye, Joyce, her parents and all the children sat in the living room and played a board game. It was so much fun; Doug had almost everyone in stitches. He told stories of his siblings when they were just children themselves. The story itself wasn't all that funny, but it was the way he told it. Later, he was most amazed as his six-year-old daughter won the board game.

"I taught her everything she knows," he said with a big smile as he picked little Lori up and gave her a big kiss on the cheek.

"Okay everyone, upstairs and get ready for bed." Joyce said.

"Oh, Mom! Do we have to?" Michael whined.

"Michael, if you didn't have to, I wouldn't have said to." Joyce kindly, but firmly explained to her tired son, that it was time for bed and that was the end of it.

Faye agreed with Joyce, it was late and time for them to leave as well. With this Doug, Faye and their children said their good byes and were headed for home.

CHAPTER TWO

Months later, Joyce decided she would have to go back to work. The thought frightened her some, but she had bills to pay, children to put through school, not to mention food to put on the table and clothes on their backs.

Once again, Joyce sat looking at her bank records, trying to figure out how to make the money go as far as possible. She had made budget cuts here and there but it just wasn't enough. Joyce knew how to take care of money, but in the past she never had to because Paul did it.

Dealing with the finances really caused her to be stressed, and at times just plain worried. Paul had left things in fair shape, but not good enough if the sole provider was no longer there. The decision was made whether she liked it or not; she would have to go back to work.

Paul had always been the one to take care of their business affairs, paying the bills and keeping the bank records balanced. Right now, Joyce was really struggling to make heads or tails out of them. She wanted to kick herself for not making Paul explain things to her more clearly. *Thank the Lord the house is paid for, at least I don't have to worry about losing our home,* she thought to herself. This thought brought to her mind what the Lord says about worrying. *Joyce, you know worrying is a sin so just stop it; besides, it isn't helping not one bit,* she thought. Matthew 6:26 came to Joyce's mind. "Behold the fowls of the air; for they sow not, neither do they reap, nor gather into barns; yet your heavenly father feedeth them. Are ye not much better than they?"

Come Monday morning I will just have to hit the work world again, but where? Doing what? Her thoughts continued as she kept looking over her financial books as she lay in bed. She had been a housewife and mother for over half of her life; it had been over twenty years since Joyce had actually held a public job. Now lying in her bed all alone and missing her husband terribly, these questions kept coming into her mind. She found herself becoming angry at Paul for never talking much about their finances; now it was all on her shoulders. After a few hours of tossing and turning, sleep finally came.

After weeks of interviews and filling out applications, Joyce didn't know how much more she could bear, but she had to keep on until she found something that would help feed and cloth her family. She felt the loss of her husband more and more each day. She longed to talk with him, touch him, just be with him; she now knew the real meaning of loneliness.

The absence of Paul was also very much a real part of the children's lives. Many nights she would hold and comfort Mark or Michael as they cried in their sleep or awakened from a bad dream. She saw how Samantha was dealing with it, and not in the best of ways, by often being unkind with her mouth to her family. Joyce had to keep on her about this, almost constantly, and it seemed as if she was not getting through. The older two children were handling it fairly well. They didn't talk about Paul much, but they were doing well in their studies and going out from time to time with friends. What Joyce didn't know was if it was because they *were* handling it well, or if they were hiding it to be strong for their mother.

"How's the job hunting going, Mom?" Elise asked as she came through the living room to find her mother going over the want ads from the Sunday paper.

"Fine, it would be just great if I were twenty years younger and had an actual degree in something." she said with aggravation in her voice. "At my age there isn't a job for my experience."

"Mom, why didn't you finish college?" This came from

Samantha who was usually too busy worrying with her hair and clothes to hear any conversations going on around her.

"Well, it really is pretty simple. I met your father; we fell in love, got married and then babies started coming. Next thing I knew I really didn't feel the need for it anymore. I was busy raising you kids, and your father really didn't want me to work outside the home. I just didn't see the need of going back. Now... well, now it's too late."

"It's not too late, Mom," said Elise. "Lots of older people go back to school. You could too."

"Thanks, Honey."

"When I get out of high school, I'm not going to college, twelve years is enough!" said Samantha. "I'm gonna take my first year after graduation off, just kick back and relax. After that year is up, then I'll look for a job in a clothing store. That way I can get a discount on any clothes I buy."

"Yeah, that sounds like a winner," Elise said in a very disgusted tone.

Joyce then thought about Elise going off to school next fall. It looked as if she would have pretty much a full scholarship, for which she was thankful, but Joyce was not looking forward to another one of her children being so far away from home. The University of Oklahoma is where Elise wanted to get her education, and it was a fine school; so Oklahoma it would be.

"I'm gonna be an astronaut." Michael's remark broke into Joyce's thoughts. He and Mark were in the living room floor watching a re-run of *Star Trek*. Joyce was amazed they were even listening.

"I'm gonna be a race car driver and win the Indy 500 when I get big," said Mark.

"No matter what each one of you wants to do when you get 'big' you must have a college degree in something. I don't want you to find yourself one day in the situation I'm in right now. It's time to start dinner. Samantha, Elise come help; boys clear and set the table."

As they all were headed to the kitchen, the doorbell rang, "Kids go ahead and get started, I'll get the door," Joyce said.

"Diane, come on in." The two women hugged for a moment.

"How is my oldest and dearest friend?" Joyce asked in a light-hearted voice. The only people on earth that knew these two women better were their mothers. Their friendship went back way before first grade.

"How goes it?" Diane asked.

"Alright I guess, come on in the kitchen while I make supper. Children, you all can go watch television while Diane and I talk."

"Alright. Diane, thanks, come anytime." Samantha said in a singsong voice.

"No problem kid." Diane replied in the same tone.

Joyce told Diane the truth about all the job searching and how she felt almost defeated.

"Exactly what type of work are you thinking about?" Diane inquired.

"Anything I can do that someone will pay me for."

Diane told her she had many talents and should be able to find something, but not to take just any old thing. She advised her to make sure the pay is worth her time, and that she would need good benefits.

Joyce thanked her friend and reminded her that the last job she had outside the home was before Timothy was born. Joyce worked as a secretary in a lawyer's office, and didn't know if she could even do that now. Things had changed so much in the world, Joyce didn't feel qualified.

Joyce invited Diane to stay for supper, but she declined since she needed to get back home. Diane reminded her dear friend that she would be here if she needed her, day or night. The two hugged. Diane talked a little to the children before she left. She loved Joyce's kids, and the children loved her in return. She treated them as if they were her own nieces and nephews. She teased with them, spoiled them just a little, and they knew they could always count on her.

When Diane got home to her husband, she gave him a hug and a big long kiss as soon as she walked in the door. While at Joyce's, she was reminded just how uncertain life really is. In actuality, she didn't know how Joyce was holding it all together. Having kids to raise alone, men hitting on her before the flowers on Paul's grave were even wilted, bills to pay when money was tight, and now having to look for a job after being a housewife for twenty years.

Michael ran through the living room to turn on the TV. When the phone rang, he answered it, since he was the only one in the room.

"Mom! Telephone!" He yelled from the living room.

"Thank you, Michael, but you really didn't need to yell... Hello."

"Hello, is this Mrs. McIntosh?"

"Yes it is; may I ask who is calling?"

"Yes, my name is Rick Cummins; I am with the Lone Star Supply Company. We received your application and résumé and would really like to set up an interview with you at your convenience. Are you still available for work?"

"Yes," Joyce replied. *Oh my yes, I can come right now,* she thought to herself. "How about tomorrow morning?"

"Tomorrow is fine."

"Let's say ten o'clock then?"

"Yes, ten will be just fine. Just ask for me or Don Miller at the front desk and our receptionist will take care of you."

"Alright, thank you, see you tomorrow then."

"Goodbye, Mrs. McIntosh."

"Goodbye, Mr. Cummins."

"Oh my, another interview, I hope my nerves will hold up, after all this is only the eighth one in a month," she said aloud.

Joyce took that moment to pray. She prayed to her Heavenly Father for wisdom and strength about this interview.

The stress of being both mother and father and dealing with their finances had caused Joyce to lose weight. Diane had noticed and had asked her a few times if she was all right. Joyce assured her that she was fine and that her nerves were keeping her from eating as much. "The hardest diet plan I've ever been on," Joyce joked with her friend.

As Joyce was looking through the closet for the right outfit to wear to her interview the next day, she was at a loss. Things didn't fit her as well as they once did.

"Elise! Samantha!" Joyce called out loud for her daughters.

"Yes, Mom, what is it?" Elise replied.

"Honey, get your sister; I need the two of you to help me find something to wear for tomorrow's interview. Seems I have lost some weight and things are looking a little baggy on me."

"Mom, did you call for me?" Samantha asked.

Elise answered before Joyce had a chance to; she informed her sister that they would be helping their mother pick out an outfit for her job interview.

"Cool, I've always wanted to get into mom's closet and work it." Samantha said with a gleam in her eye.

"Now remember girls this is not a fashion show, I need to look professional, business-like." Joyce told her girls.

"Sure, Mom, no problem," Samantha assured her.

The girls went way back in Joyce's closet and started pulling out clothes with a vengeance. They found things that Joyce had forgotten were in there, things that she had outgrown, but now could wear. The two girls put together not only an outfit for the interview, but also five other outfits that were suitable for the work place.

"Thanks girls, I could have never done this without you." *Diane will never believe this one*, Joyce thought to herself.

"Wow, that was fun," Samantha said. "Let's do your closet next, Elise!"

"No way, kid, keep you eyes and hands out of my closet," Elise told her very firmly as she walked out of her mother's bedroom.

The past interviews Joyce had were more learning experiences. She put in applications all over town for any position she thought she could possibly do. It seemed like there was always someone younger, better qualified, or the job was filled. Joyce tried to keep the attitude that the Lord had something better waiting for her, but each day it got harder and harder. She was starting to become discouraged, but tried not to let it show on her face to her children.

Tuesday morning, Joyce was up at five-thirty, dressed and ready for the day. She read her Bible but honestly had a little trouble concentrating on the words. The kids didn't have to be at school until eight, but she just couldn't lie in bed awake any longer. She had enough nervous energy to run to that interview and back again.

"Good morning, Mark."

"Morning," he said in his gravelly morning voice.

"Are your brother and sisters up?"

"I'm up already" said Samantha, coming in closely behind him, and speaking in a not so kind tone. Samantha was not a morning person, and kind words first thing in the morning were not easy for her.

"Watch your words and tone, young lady. That is not the way to start the day." Joyce said firmly.

"Good morning, Mom. What's for breakfast?" This came from Michael in a very carefree voice. He and Paul were always the morning people of the family.

"We are having muffins, fruit, and milk, want some?" His mother replied.

"Yeah, I'm hungry."

Joyce had Michael's plate of food in route to him as he sat patiently at the table; the phone rang as the other children awaited their food.

"I'll get it," said Michael. "Hello? Hey, Tim, what's up?"

"Hey little buddy, how are you this morning?" Tim replied. Just hearing his little brother's voice made him miss his family all the more. Being so far away in school never seemed to bother Tim before, but now that his father was gone, it bothered him a lot. Tim weekly counted the days until graduation.

"I'm fine; we're having breakfast, how about you?"

"I've already had my breakfast and am about to run through the shower and then to my class. Hey is mom near the phone?"

"Yeah," Michael replied and then simply handed the phone to his mother.

"He must need money since he's calling this early in the morning." This tidbit of information came from Samantha in her sleepy grumpy morning mood.

"Good morning, Timothy, how are you?"

"I'm fine, Mom, and tell Samantha I'm not calling to ask for money. I just wanted to say hello and wish you luck on your interview today."

"Thanks, Son, I need that. Don't mind your sister; she is really asking for a spanking before she heads out to school, she just doesn't realize it yet. Do you have an early class today?"

Tim answered his Mother's questions about his classes and other matters of his college life; she then filled him in on the day's plans. Tim really felt the need to talk to her a little longer, but knew she needed to go and get his siblings off to school. Actually he needed to get moving himself or he was going to be late for his science class.

"Alright boys, Samantha, Elise let's hustle up, we've all got places to be. Samantha I want that mouth of yours controlled today, do you understand?"

"Yes," Samantha answered her mother with a frown on her face.

Joyce pulled her vehicle into the nearest parking space that was available, at the Lone Star Supply Company, hoping she wasn't taking the space from someone. Taking one last look in the mirror, she got out of the car and walked into the office building.

"Good morning, my name is Joyce McIntosh; I have a ten o'clock appointment with Rick Cummins. I know I'm a little early." Joyce said with a kind smile.

"Just have a seat and I'll let Mr. Cummins know you are here. Would you like a cup of coffee, Mrs. McIntosh?"

"No, thank you." *The four cups I had before 9:00 a.m. were totally enough*, she thought to herself.

Joyce sat in the waiting area of the beautifully decorated office.

The expensive looking flower arrangements were carefully placed in just the right spot; Joyce felt the yellows and greens added energy to the room. There were also several oil paintings of different landscapes by what seemed to be a local artist. Joyce got up to view the paintings closer, remembering that at one time she was preparing to be an art major. The paintings were breathtaking; for a brief moment she wondered what it was like to sell a piece of artwork and have your work displayed in someone's home or office. The thought brought a slight smile to her face.

"Mrs. McIntosh," the receptionist said breaking into her thoughts. "Mr. Cummins will see you now."

"Oh, thank you." The receptionist led Joyce back to Rick Cummins' office.

Rick Cummins was the office manger of the Lone Star Supply Company. His office was very elegant as well. *Boy, nothing around here is half done*, she thought to herself as she looked around the office.

"Good morning, Mrs. McIntosh, how are you?" Rick said kindly, as he extended his hand.

"Good morning. I'm fine, thank you," she replied. Rick was a very business-like, nice looking man; he seemed to be very professional.

"Mrs. McIntosh, first of all let me say it's a pleasure to meet you. I hope you feel free to ask any questions you might have. Two other managers have looked over your résumé and feel you may be right for the position we have available." Rick continued to explain the job duties that Joyce would have if she were to have this position, along with the benefits and pay wages.

"I see," said Joyce, "Ah, Mr. Cummins, what are the hours for this position?"

"Seven to four. Would that work for you, Mrs. McIntosh?"

"Well, actually no, it wouldn't." The job sounded fine, to Joyce and she would love to try her hand at it, but she had to be totally honest with him, as she hoped he was being with her.

"I would be here when needed, and do the best job I could possibly do. I consider myself an honest and responsible person, and try to live by 'the golden rule', but Mr. Cummins, I have five children, one in college, and two come the fall. My husband died almost a year ago, so whatever job I do take, I need to be where I can get them to and from school each day. It's also important that I be home when they are home, especially since I'm now a single parent."

"I understand Mrs. McIntosh. I truly do," said Mr. Cummins, "But I don't know if we can change these hours. I will be honest with you as well. We do have other applicants to interview, but I will speak to the other two managers about the hours, and who knows, maybe we can work something out."

After talking about the position for another thirty minutes, all questions were asked and answered. Joyce knew that the hours would not work for her, as did Mr. Cummins; she also felt that working at the Lone Star Supply Office sounded wonderful. Everyone she talked to there was so friendly and kind. Answering phone calls and filling supply orders didn't sound hard at all to Joyce. Mr. Cummins on the other hand, felt this was a good person to hire, but the hours would just not work for her and her family.

"I'll be in touch, Mrs. McIntosh," Rick kindly told her.

"Thank you for your time, Mr. Cummins, I look forward to hearing from you again."

Rick knew there was something about Joyce McIntosh, but he didn't know what it was. Was it her honesty, maturity? He didn't know, but he did know he would try to get this woman hired at the Lone Star; he would talk with the other men and see what could be done.

⁓

Samantha had just gone into the kitchen to ask her mother if she could go to Shelly's for the afternoon when the phone ringing stopped her.

"I'll get it," said Samantha, "Hello?"

"Hi, Diane." It was Diane calling to check in with Joyce about her interview. Diane had been waiting all day, somewhat patiently to hear the result. "Mom, phone!" Samantha yelled through the house.

"Thank you, Samantha, but you really didn't need to yell. Hello?"

"I hope this is not a bad time. Samantha said you weren't busy."

"I'm not really. I was just looking through the job listings for the millionth time, but I always have time to talk to you, Diane."

Joyce and Diane talked about the interview; she told her it went well and how friendly everyone seemed to be. With disappointment in her voice, she also told Diane she didn't think she would be offered the job due to the hours that it involved.

"There has to be a job out there for me somewhere, Diane."

"So, what's your next step?"

"I honestly don't know. Timothy wants to drop out of school and help support the family, but I told him he was to finish school and that was it. I won't have it, Diane!" By the tone in Joyce's voice, Diane knew she meant what she said.

Joyce and Paul had been raising their children to know they must go to college and earn a degree, even if they never used it. Timothy was being torn over being at school and feeling a need to be at home helping his family. In his heart he knew his father would want him to finish school. Timothy also knew the job opportunities would be much better with a degree, but it was still hard to stay focused.

Diane and Joyce finished their conversation about the interview and Joyce's next step in finding a job. Diane left her friend knowing she was praying for her and encouraged her not to give up.

Rick was on his way to drop off some mail for the receptionist, when he passed Sean in the hallway.

"Sean, can you come to my office this afternoon around three? I need to speak with you about the position we are trying to fill."

Don and Sean Miller ran the Lone Star Supply Office. It belonged to their father, Brandon Miller, but the two sons ran it, and did so very well. Brandon had started them out working Saturdays and during the summers. Both boys took to the business very well, Brandon made sure they knew how each department worked. With the help of Rick Cummins, who had worked for Brandon for several years, and other dedicated workers the company had been successful.

"Sure, no problem. Any luck with the applicants?"

"Well, we have this one, but we really need to sit down and talk about it."

Rick wanted to fill Don and Sean in on the interview he had with Joyce, and how he couldn't shake the feeling this woman would be a great asset to the company.

At three o'clock on the dot the three men, Don, Sean and Rick, sat down in Don's office to discuss the possibility of a new employee.

Don Miller was the Senior Manager of the company, and his brother Sean was under him, but he always consulted the other two men when hiring a new employee, or making any changes in the company.

"So, if there is a problem with this one person, hire the other one if they're qualified." Sean spoke.

"The person I really think is best for the job has five children, and she has to get them to and from school. Her husband has recently passed away, so the hours are a serious thing."

As Rick spoke about each applicant he kept coming back to Joyce and the fact that he honestly felt she was best for the job. He went on to explain how honest and calm Joyce seemed to be, and how he really couldn't put his finger on the main reason he felt she was the best one, but he knew she was.

Don and Rick had worked with one another since Don began working at the Lone Star on the weekends when his father was running the office, and Don knew he could trust his judgment. As the three continued to talk about the applicants and the position, they knew it was not going to work for Joyce and the hours she needed.

"Let's go ahead and hire the other person, however, we do have another position I think Mrs. McIntosh would be right for," Don replied. "I'm in real need of a mature, efficient, reliable assistant and since you, Rick, are so sure Mrs. McIntosh would be good for the company, what are your thoughts on this?"

Both men looked at each other and wondered why Don was asking the question. Don had needed an assistant for a long time now, but just never admitted it.

"I think it's about time. To be honest with you, I feel Mrs. McIntosh is right for that position, hire her," Rick said with much conviction.

"Yeah, Don, hire her," Sean said to his brother.

As the two men answered Don's question honestly and quickly, Don decided now was the time to go ahead with this idea and if it worked out, maybe he could get home for supper every evening.

"Leslie, please get Mrs. McIntosh on the phone and see if she is still interested in a position here at the Lone Star; if so, set up an appointment for me to talk with her, and then let me know."

"Yes, sir," the receptionist replied.

"When, or if, Mrs. McIntosh comes in for an interview, I want both of you here for that; this is a major position and I want both your opinions."

"Will do," Sean said, and Rick agreed as well.

Joyce couldn't wait to call her parents after she received the good news. She was so thrilled she could barely talk.

"Hello, Daddy, I have good news. I got the job, and I start Monday morning."

"Oh, that is so good to hear. I'll tell your mother when she gets back from shopping."

Joyce was so happy to tell her dad about her new job. She let him know of her concerns for how the kids would deal with it, but they needed the money, so the family would have to pitch in and help make this situation work. It had all turned out well, and the hours would not be an issue after all. Joyce would still be taking the children to school, and picking them up in the afternoon, and would not be working on the weekends. Jason was happy for his daughter; he knew how worried she had been over her finances.

Jason was thinking way ahead and asked Joyce what she

intended to do with the children during the summer months.

"Oh, Dad, we will just have to cross that bridge when we get to it. I really need this job; the money Paul set aside has just about run out. I really didn't know what else to do."

"Now Joycie, don't you worry, we won't borrow trouble. I'm sorry I mentioned it; of course, you know your mother and I will always be here to help in anyway we can."

Jason felt awful for mentioning the summer months; he knew Joyce could handle it, why he said what he did was beyond him. He just hoped his wife didn't find out or he would get the sharp end of her tongue.

"What's the position; what will you be doing?" Jason asked.

"I will be an assistant to the boss. I will have different duties, but mostly helping him with his scheduling and workload."

"Sounds interesting."

Joyce was nervous just thinking about being an assistant to the boss, but she planned to give it her best shot.

"Well, sweetie, Monday morning you just walk in that office, do your best, and know your mother and I are behind you a hundred percent, as always."

"Thanks, Daddy that really means the world to me. Well, I gotta run, supper is about ready, give my love to Mom."

"I will."

"Bye, Dad."

"Bye, Joycie."

As the weekend went on Joyce, Elise, Samantha, Mark, and Michael all talked about the changes that would be taking place. Joyce really wanted things to stay as normal as possible. The kids were settling down and dealing with the death of their father a little better each week, and she didn't want to upset the progress they all had made. They talked about not taking on too many after school activities and how they would handle the workload at home. Joyce made sure they knew that each one of them would have to pitch in and do their share. Of course they should have been doing this all along, but with Joyce being at home all day every day, it gave her a way to keep from thinking about Paul.

Everyone agreed to pitch in and help around the house. Therefore, after talking with the children, Joyce felt a little better about the situation. She was still nervous about the new job, but at least now she knew where everyone stood on the matter.

Elise, being the oldest child at home at the time, spoke first. She let her mother know her getting a job was fine, and they would all help around the house. She didn't want her mother to worry about them with this new change in their lives. Mark and Michael were a little confused about their mother not being home during the day. They really weren't sure what that meant; after all, their mother had never had a job before or at least one where she left the house. The twins looked at each other, listened to the conversation going on around them, but said nothing.

CHAPTER THREE

Sunday morning, the McIntosh's scurried around the house getting ready for church, in order to be there on time. Everyone was ready except for Samantha; why it took her so long no one knew. Joyce had always hated going anywhere late; she remembered how Paul, at times, would get them wherever they were going right at the last minute, and it would drive her nuts.

Finally, Samantha was ready; they all piled in the vehicle and off they went.

"Good Morning Joyce, Mark, Michael, Samantha, how is everyone this morning? I didn't see Elise come in, is she here today?" Pastor Jones said as he greeted Joyce and her children.

"Yes, she's here," said Joyce.

"Yeah, she's over there talkin' with her friends; that's all they do is talk, talk, talk, talk," answered Mark with a voice that told of his confusion with girls and how they loved to talk. Pastor Jones laughed at Mark's thoughts on girls. Joyce gave Mark a very stern look for his comment.

Mark frowned his brow and said out loud with a confused look, "What?"

The Song Leader led the congregation in a few congregational hymns, and then the pastor took over the service.

"Good morning everyone; I hope you all are as ready as I am to dig into the Word today. This morning we are going to be speaking about Paul. Now, as you remember, Paul wrote a lot of the New Testament books. He teaches us a lot about the church, and brotherly love, repentance and salvation. He is a very bold person."

"Paul goes on his missionary trips, he preaches unpopular teachings, and he gets incarcerated for his preaching of the Word. Now let me ask you, have any of you been thrown into jail this week for preaching the Word? I didn't think so.

"Let's turn to Romans 1:16 "For I am not ashamed of the gospel of Christ: for it is the power of God unto salvation to every one that believeth; to the Jew first, and also to the Greek."

"Paul spoke boldly and loudly; he did not whisper so he would not upset those around him that may not have wanted to hear. This man told the plain facts. Let's look at those facts shall we?"

"Fact one: Christ died for our sins, all of us, not just the big, bad ugly man in jail, but also for the sweet little child that is back there in our nurseries this morning. He hung on a rugged old cross; shed His blood for you and me, *and* the old ugly, big mean man in jail. But we don't stop there, there is more, so much more.

"Fact two: He rose again the third day. We read about this in Luke Chapter 24. He lives today; death could not conquer Him, the grave could not hold Him down. He is sitting on the right hand side of the Father as we speak. Think on that for just a moment. Again, there is more.

"Fact three: He will be coming back again. Revelation 22:20 tells us this, as do other passages of scripture. We don't know when. Paul didn't know when, but he knew that he needed to be ready; he knew he was supposed to tell everyone he met to get ready. We, here today at this moment need to be ready. Are you ready? What would happen to your soul at this instant if you died? The Word tells us you will at that instant be in one place or the other – Heaven for the believers, Hell for the non-believers.

"All we have to do is humble ourselves and pray asking Jesus to come into our hearts, confess our sins with our mouth, believe in our hearts that He died for us, and that He will come in our hearts at that instant and live forever."

As Joyce listened to Pastor Jones' sermon, she thought about her own life at that point and time. She thought about her late husband, and was glad he had accepted Christ's love and salvation when he was a young boy. Then her mind came to the present. *Were the*

Chapter three / 33

people she would be working for Christians? Would they be able to tell from her life that she is a Christian? Then she found herself thinking about whether or not she would be able to handle the job. Satan was certainly using this new job to keep Joyce's mind off the sermon.

People seemed to stand around talking after the sermon was over. Joyce looked for her children; she still felt awkward standing around without Paul. While looking around for them, she heard someone speak to her.

"Hello Joyce."

"Oh, hi Bill, how are you?" Joyce replied.

Bill Winston had been coming to the Garland Community Church for many years. He had never really talked much to Joyce, but knew her and her children. Bill was in his early fifties and had been divorced for about eight years, but it was recently he had really begun to notice Joyce.

"Joyce, there are several people going out to eat this evening after church, would you like to join us?" he asked in hopes she would say yes.

"Aah, no, I don't think I can make it. But thank you for letting me know about it. I wasn't aware there was an activity this evening." Joyce thought she needed to get away from Bill and get away now. She kindly excused herself and went in search of her children.

When is this going to stop? She thought to herself. "Samantha and Elise; get your brothers, please, and let's go."

Joyce was so frustrated at this latest invitation she thought she may never come back. It was then that she silently prayed for strength to handle this situation correctly. In all honesty she didn't know if Bill Winston was hitting on her, or just being polite with his invitation. As Joyce headed for her vehicle, she felt as if she could scream. *I think I will just stop coming for a while, or maybe I'll start going somewhere else.* Joyce's thoughts were getting the best of her so she pushed them aside and took her family home.

"Hello, Ron, is Diane available?" Joyce asked over the phone that Sunday afternoon. She really felt the need to speak with her dear friend.

"Yes, she is. We looked for you after church, but you were gone. Is everything alright?"

"Yes, Ron, thank you, I just needed to get on home."

As Ron was talking with Joyce he reminded her that he would be coming to her house to check the kitchen pipes she had asked him about. The two agreed on a day, and Joyce told him if they were not home to let himself in with the key she had given him and Diane. It was then Ron gave the phone over to his wife.

Diane was glad to talk with Joyce; she had wondered why she had left so quickly after church. Joyce let her know it was Bill Winston this time that made her run like a scared rabbit.

"I may not be at church for awhile Diane." She said sadly.

"Why, what's wrong Joyce?"

Diane was a little upset by the explanation she received for Joyce keeping her self out of church. She kindly but firmly let her know that was wrong and Joyce knew it. Joyce knew very well that not only was it the wrong thing to do for herself, but a bad example to her children. After an hour of conversation, Joyce realized she was wrong in her thinking and thanked Diane for being there for her to keep her straight.

"There must be a sign on me, Diane, one that says, 'hey I can't live without a man'." Diane was laughing at this one.

"I'm sorry Joyce, but the way you said that..." Joyce giggled a little at herself too.

"Joyce, you should be thankful that men find you attractive. I mean after twenty-two years of marriage and five children, don't you find it a little flattering?"

"Not right now, I don't," she responded rather quickly.

The two talked a little while longer about Diane's life now. In all reality, Joyce was glad for the focus to be on someone else for a while. So they spoke of Diane's two girls, Mandy and Erin, and how they were doing in college.

"I gotta run, there is a lot of noise coming from the living room.

Hey, thanks Diane."

"No problem, Mrs. Attractive," Diane teased.

It was a warm Monday morning; Brandon Miller had a lot of work to do, and wondered how he would get it all accomplished in just one day. Lorna, his housekeeper of almost ten years, prepared him a delicious breakfast. Brandon only wished he had time to sit and enjoy it. Instead he gulped his coffee and downed a few pieces of bacon so fast he didn't even really taste it. He was out the door in no time and headed into Dallas to do some banking business, and then he was off to the Lone Star Supply Office to visit with his boys, then back to the ranch.

"Hi, Dad, what brings you into town and in the office today?" said Don.

"Oh, I had some business in town and finished way earlier than planned, so I thought I would stop by and see if you boys of mine had time for lunch."

Brandon found the day going a little strange; at first he was running a little late and had to hustle to get things done; now he had time to slow down and take his sons out to lunch.

Brandon let his two older sons run the business in town while he ran the horse and cattle ranch that was about twenty miles away. Richard, his youngest, was in his last year of college and helped on the ranch when he was home.

"It will have to be just you and me today, Dad," Don replied. "Sean said he had some errands to run."

"That's fine," Brandon told his son.

"I'll even let you buy," Don said while looking up at his dad with laughter in his eyes.

"Oh, how nice of you."

"Yeah, it is, Mom always said I was a good boy." They both laughed over this silliness.

Brandon Miller was a tall Texan if there ever was one. A handsome, well-built, dark haired man, dark eyes, and slightly tanned. He was a very successful businessman as well; owning the Lone Star Supply Company for fifteen years, now he shared it with his sons. Brandon figured if his sons ran it and helped keep it growing into a profitable business, they should own part of it as well. Brandon also owned and operated the Southern Star Cattle Ranch, a passion of his. He loved horses and loved being outdoors. The fact that he had made both businesses into profitable investments made it worth the challenge.

Both businesses were doing very well; each man kept up with the other and if any help was needed, help was given with no complaint. Brandon was very pleased with his sons; he and his late wife had raised their boys to be responsible and kind to one another. At times they teased one another unmercifully, but it was all in fun; everyone got what they gave and no one seemed to get hurt.

Brandon couldn't remember how many times they had the boys recite the verse, Ephesians 4:32 "And be ye kind one to another, tenderhearted, forgiving one another, even as God for Christ's sake hath forgiven you." There were days when Brandon thought it was just not sinking in, but in the long run, it had; his sons seemed to love and respect each other.

Don, the eldest son, mostly ran the Supply Company, and Sean was his right hand man. These two worked well together, and each did his share. They had both started working full-time at the supply office when they graduated from college, while their father still ran the company.

Richard really didn't like office work, as he was more interested in the ranch and being out of doors. He found every part of it thrilling and rewarding; he couldn't wait until graduation when he could work with his father on a day-to-day basis. He found being outside in the sunshine and seeing all the land kept his mind from getting cluttered. He especially liked working with the horses; to Richard, they were the most amazing animals. They were beautiful and could be gentle, but still a very powerful animal that must be taken care of properly and respected.

Richard was also the one who usually named the livestock; no one knew how this started, but it had, and had stuck. One evening a calf was born, and the next day when Richard saw the calf, he named her Juliet. When asked by his father why he named the animal Juliet, his reply was that he was thinking of the play *Romeo and Juliet* at the time he saw the calf.

Richard had worked summers with Brandon, but soon it would be different. He would have more responsibilities and could really enjoy being at home and on the ranch. Even though each Miller son had a position waiting for him when they grew to manhood, Brandon insisted they get a college degree. For the most part there was no complaining, but Richard was very happy to see the end of his school years in sight.

Rick started Joyce's day off by introducing her to other employees. The receptionist was his first stop.

"Mrs. McIntosh, this is Leslie Stevens, our receptionist. She is here to help you with anything you might need; don't hesitate to call on her," Rick kindly advised Joyce.

"Yes, please, Mrs. McIntosh, anything I can do for you, just let me know."

"Thank you, I will." Joyce told the receptionist.

Rick then directed Joyce to her office.

"As you can see it's not very big, but it has a lovely view of outside. I hope you don't find that distracting, but feel free to make it your own."

The office was occupied by a medium size desk and chair, matching filing cabinet, two office chairs that sat opposite the desk and a few pictures on the wall. The room itself was painted a very light mauve on the bottom, with light wallpaper on the top, and chair railing to divide the two. Joyce thought a few things from home would add to the décor, maybe a rug for the middle of the room, some photos of her children, and a plant or two.

"This will do nicely, thank you, and I love to be where I can see outside."

Rick left Joyce to her new office after telling her that Leslie would be filling her in on any other necessary information.

It was only moments until Leslie came to Joyce's office with some paper for her in hand.

"Mrs. McIntosh, here is a listing of all the phone extensions here in the office, plus, a few home numbers you may need. The supply closet is just down the hall for most of your office supply needs. Is there anything else I can do for you while I'm here?"

"Yes, Miss Stevens, there is. You may call me Joyce, I believe you and I will work very well together, and I want you to call me Joyce."

"Alright, and please call me Leslie."

"Okay, Leslie, thank you very much; I'll call for you if I need anything else."

Leslie met Don on her way out and informed him that Joyce had been shown the layout of the office, and she was now returning back to her desk. With a big smile, kind face and what sounded like lots of energy, Don welcomed Joyce to the office.

"I hope you are finding everything alright," Don spoke.

"Yes, Leslie has been very helpful, as well as everyone here. I think by tomorrow morning I will be ready to plunge right into things."

"Okay then, I won't keep you; call me if there is anything I can help you with."

"Yes, sir, I'll do that; thank you, Mr. Miller."

As Don was leaving he stopped just short at the door, and kindly let her know they were all on first name basis and she was welcome to do the same.

There were several people that came in Joyce's office at what seemed like all at once. As one would leave, another would appear, each welcoming her to the office and asking if they could be of any assistance. Joyce was happy to find herself in an office full of helpful people, but also wondered if this was the norm, how they got anything done.

When everyone had left her office, and she was alone, all Joyce could do was fall down into her chair. Her chair! The sound of that made her feel very nervous and good all at the same time.

Chapter three / 39

The warmth of spring made it hard to stay indoors; Joyce knew the warmth would give way to heat before long. She noticed the weeds in the flower beds as she was driving up to the house, she knew come Saturday she would need to take care of that or it would get out of hand. Her next thought was if the twins helped her, it wouldn't take that long.

Joyce heard the doorbell as she and the twins were putting away the groceries, Samantha had just walked into the kitchen and heard the sound as well.

"Samantha, would you get the door please?"

"Sure."

"Tim!" Samantha said with such happiness and surprise. "Oh Tim, you're home! Please, say it's for good." Samantha said as her arms locked around her big brother's neck, holding him like she would never let go.

"Yes, I'm home, but only for the summer," he said in a voice that sounded as if he were being choked.

"Tim! Tim!" the loud yells and squeals came from Mark and Michael who were very excited to see their big brother as well.

"Hey guys!" The boys both jumped toward their brother, and almost knocked him to the floor, but Tim loved it. He had missed his siblings and his mother more than he would let on.

"Boy, are we glad you're home!" Mark said with much conviction.

"Yeah, there are too many girls in this house," replied Michael. Timothy just laughed.

"Hi, Timothy." Joyce couldn't wait for the others to let her have her turn for a big, long hug.

"Hi, Mom." Joyce was so relieved her son was home. To her, it made the house seem more complete.

"Hey, where's Elise?" Tim asked.

"She's out shopping with a friend. I told her to be home by supper."

"Good, then I can surprise her." Timothy motioned to his brothers to help him gather his belongings and get them to his room up the stairs.

"Okay." They both answered. Timothy couldn't help but laugh as the boys were grunting and pulling to get the duffel bags up the stairs, bumping into and falling over each other, laughing as they went. "Watch it guys, you are supposed to be helping, not having a good time."

When Michael saw Elise pull up in the driveway, he told everyone. Timothy hid in the pantry, wanting to surprise his sister.

"Hey, looks like I'm right on time." Elise said as she saw food being taken from the stove on the table. She pulled out a chair and was about to sit down.

"Aah!" she screamed as Timothy grabbed her from behind and gave her a big bear hug. With a shocked expression, she turned around to find her brother, the brother she missed so very much.

"Tim! I'm so glad you're home. I thought you weren't coming home until Friday?"

"I got things done early and boom! Here I am."

"Mom, why are you crying? Aren't you happy?" asked Mark, who noticed tears starting to form in his mother's eyes.

"Yes, Mark, I am very happy. It's just so good to have all of us at home together again."

If Daddy were here, it would be perfect, thought Samantha, *but it will never be perfect again.*

It had gotten late, and Joyce had let the twins stay up a little past their bedtime. Now the fun was over, and it was time for them to be done for the day.

"Okay, boys, time for bed. Make sure you brush your teeth."

"Oh man!" Mark said with disappointment in his voice. "I wanted to stay up and watch some TV."

Joyce watched as the twins made their way up the stairs and then turned to face her older son.

"Now Timothy what are your plans for the summer?" She asked

"Well, I plan on catching up on some much needed sleep; I've already talked to Mr. Jenkins about some summer work. I really wish you didn't have to go back to work, Mom."

"I know, Honey, but that's the way it has to be right now. Besides, it's been good for me to get outside the house. We'll just have to trust God in this thing," Joyce said to her son. "School will not be out for the kids for another two weeks, so you'll have the house to yourself for a few days. I'm sure you won't mind that at all." Timothy just smiled.

Elise informed Timothy and her mother that her shifts at her job would be changing when school let out for the summer. Mr. Woods, her boss, had met with her and talked about a promotion. He said Elise had done very well and thought she was ready for some additional responsibility.

Elise had worked for Jerry Woods at Your Choice of Chicken after school and on Saturdays for the past year and a half.

"Well, congratulations Elise, that is very good news!" Joyce said. She was very proud of her children. *I wish I were as together on the inside as they appear to be,* she thought to herself. After talking with her two oldest children for another hour, they all went off to bed for a good night's sleep. Joyce, for one, certainly needed that.

"Finally! The last day of school. I don't think I could take another day of it," Samantha spoke from the kitchen table as she was spooning sugar onto her cereal. "That Miss Kimberlin is getting on my last nerve."

"Samantha!" her mother said in a shocked voice.

"Well, she is. All she does is stand in front of the class and look down her nose at all of us, just watching to see who she can chomp down on for any little reason. And the homework! It's never ending! The woman loves homework. I don't know what she'll do during the summer break with no homework to check and no students to make miserable. I can see why she's not married. Who in their right mind would want to live with her?"

"Samantha Diane McIntosh! That is enough. You will not speak of your teachers in such a disrespectful way; do you understand me, young lady?"

"Yes, ma'am."

"Now, all of you hustle up, or we all are going to be late for the day." Within a matter of about ten minutes everyone was grabbing lunch bags off the table and heading out the door.

CHAPTER FOUR

Joyce had been very focused on her work at the office all morning; she hadn't even noticed the time when Leslie called her on the phone to let her know she had a very handsome guest asking to see her. Joyce, confused by this information, let the receptionist know she would be right there. As she was walking to the lobby, she couldn't help but wonder who could be there to see her.

"Timothy, what a lovely surprise! What brings you into town?" She said as she hugged her son.

"I just thought I would take my mother out to lunch."

"Wow, now I can deal with that. Give me just a few minutes, and I'll be ready to go. Oh, where are my manners?" Joyce quickly turned and introduced Leslie to her son.

"It's very nice to meet you, Miss Stevens." Timothy told the receptionist.

Leslie couldn't help but notice Timothy's good looks and his manners. It saddened her to think she was too old for him. Leslie was a very pretty young lady in her late twenties and still single. Moments later, Joyce and Timothy were out the door heading for a lovely lunch at the O.K. Café.

The two ordered fairly quickly and talked of how Timothy was enjoying his free time. Knowing that his "free" time, all two days of it, wouldn't last long, he let his mother know he was going to make the best of it. He spoke of how William Jenkins, his former boss, had offered him his old summer job back, and he would be starting on Monday morning. He let Joyce know in a kind, but firm tone, that he felt it was his responsibility to help the family financially.

When Timothy's parents were his age, they had to move for his dad to have a good job that was in his field of study, but that wasn't Timothy's plan. He didn't have a wife to support, so he figured he had time to wait for the job he desired.

"Son, that is so sweet, and I do appreciate that, but you have your own life to live." The waiter chose that moment to bring their food to their table. Joyce let Timothy know things had gotten much better now that she had this new job; the house seemed to be much calmer these days. "It is all taking a little time, but we are making it."

This seemed to put Timothy's mind at ease, but he was still going to help out, and that was the bottom line as far as he was concerned.

"Sorry I'm late, Leslie; time just got away from me. I have a meeting in about twenty minutes; will you please call me to make sure I don't forget?" Joyce asked Leslie as she was rushing past her to get back to her office.

"Yeah, sure, no problem."

Joyce sat down in her chair, picked up her pen and began to collect her notes for her meeting when the phone rang.

"Joyce. Mr. Cummins, Mr. Miller and his father are in the meeting room, if you're ready," Leslie informed her.

"Aah what happened to my twenty minutes? Tell them I am on my way," she replied hurriedly.

"Yes, ma'am."

"His father?" Joyce spoke out loud to herself in her office. "Why is his father here?" This confused Joyce and made her feel nervous at the same time. She had never met Don's father and could not imagine why she would be meeting him now.

After Don filled Brandon in on his new assistant, he told his father that Joyce had been with them about two months and had proven herself to be very valuable to him. He went on to explain about Joyce's family and how she came to the Lone Star Supply. At that moment, Joyce entered the room.

"Joyce, hi," Don said as he and Brandon both rose from their chairs.

"Hello, gentlemen."

"I hope I haven't called you away from your desk at a bad time," Don said.

"No, this is fine; I have your schedule for next week ready for you to look over when you have the time." Don smiled at her as he took the schedule.

The meeting was about adding a supplier to their client list. Don always had his father sit in on meetings that he felt most important.

"Before I go any farther, let me introduce you to my father, Brandon Miller. Dad, this is Joyce McIntosh. She has been with us for a few months now and doing a great job. Joyce, my father, Brandon."

"Hello, Mr. Miller, it is a pleasure to meet you," she spoke as she extended her hand.

"Very good to meet you, Mrs. McIntosh." While Brandon was shaking her hand, he couldn't help but think to himself, *would you look at her and those eyes? I could get lost in that beautiful face.*

Joyce was not a short woman, but she wasn't tall either; she was very beautiful, but not to herself. She felt she was too rounded in some areas, a few strands of gray in her hair that she didn't want but refused to color. In all reality, you would never be able to tell that Joyce had birthed five children. Running around and playing with her children was the best exercise program there was. It was also in her budget, and, in the long run, it had paid off.

As Joyce was sitting there listening to Don speak to Brandon about her, it made her a little uncomfortable. He told him not only had she done very well at her job, but seemed to be very efficient. For some reason the older Mr. Miller was making her a little nervous as well, and for the life of her she could not figure out why.

Joyce could tell Brandon spent a lot of time outdoors, and whatever he did from day to day caused him to be in very good shape and very muscular. When he stood to shake her hand she noticed his height, he was sure to be over six feet tall and spoke with a very deep and alluring voice.

"We are giving you a raise, starting on your next pay period," Don informed her. Rick then spoke up and told her they all felt she had earned it. At the Lone Star Supply Company, they tried to make sure their employees were happy, and in return their employees would make them happy.

"Oh, Rick, Don, thank you very much! I certainly do appreciate it." Joyce thanked the men for her raise and good words of praise, and felt a little heat come to her face. She was not used to compliments, but did let them know how much she loved her job, even though she hadn't been there that long.

"You are more than welcome Joyce, and it's *us* who want to thank *you*," Don replied with a smile on his face. While the meeting was going on, Brandon sat there listening and watching. It seemed he did not have control over his own eyes; they kept drifting to Joyce.

As Joyce left the room and entered her own office, she let out a sigh. *Thank you Lord*, she said, but not out loud. Joyce then went back to her desk and began the work that she had left to have lunch with her son. As she was thinking of her son, she remembered she had forgotten to ask Timothy to take the boys to get a haircut this evening, but it would wait until she got home. When she got home she would tell her family her good news of her raise, something Joyce had never experienced before.

Samantha ran into the house, dropping her jacket and purse on the hallway table. She couldn't wait to tell her mother what had happened.

"Mom! Mom! Where are you? I got a job, I got a job!" Samantha said excitedly.

"I'm in here, in the kitchen," Joyce responded to her daughter's voice.

"Mom, oh, Mom, I got a job working with Elise at the Your Choice of Chicken."

"Oh, honey, that's wonderful, but I didn't know you applied."

"I applied last week, I thought I told you. Anyway, being Elise's sister gave me a little extra pull, and I start Saturday." Samantha was so excited she could barely contain herself.

Elise came in the kitchen as the conversation between Samantha and her mother was going on; she listened as her sister explained how it all came about.

"Yeah, just think Sam, not only do I get to tell you what to do at home, now I get paid for it," Elise said with much amusement. Samantha narrowed her eyes at Elise.

"Alright you two, none of that. We have good news to enjoy; let's not ruin it."

"Elise, I need to speak with you and Timothy after the other children are in bed, please."

"Okay, sure."

Elise and Samantha just looked at each other and shrugged their shoulders.

Supper was over, the dishes done, the boys were in their beds and Joyce had to have a serious talk with Samantha about why she had to be in bed at ten thirty.

"All my friends stay up to whenever they want."

"They wouldn't if they were my children." Joyce spoke to Samantha firmly. Samantha mumbled something as she went past her mother on her way to her bedroom.

"Samantha!" The tone in Joyce's voice let Samantha know that was the end of it.

When Samantha left the room, Joyce went to the kitchen to get herself a cup of tea, and then back to the living room to speak with her two older children.

"We have a small situation that will need all of our efforts."

She explained to them with her working all day, Timothy and Elise working pretty much full shifts, and now Samantha working as well, that left Mark and Michael home alone. The two boys were too young to be left to themselves.

"Children that are left alone long enough find things to do, and not good things." she explained, and then asked if either Timothy or Elise had any ideas.

"Don't worry, Mom; we'll work something out," Timothy

spoke, rubbing his chin as if this would help him come up with an answer.

After the three had sat and discussed the issue a little while longer, Elise did come up with a solution they all three felt would work.

"Tim and I could get our schedules together and fix them to where one of us will be at home when you're not," Elise said with an eager look.

"Hey, yeah that is a good idea; Sam can help out also, she won't be working full days or every day either," Timothy replied. He told his mother not to worry but to leave the situation to him and his sisters. Elise then spoke saying they would both talk to their bosses as soon as possible. Joyce went to both of them, gave them each a kiss on the forehead, and thanked them for their help; she just hoped it would work.

It was late and Joyce finally climbed into bed, thinking it had been a long and full day. As she thought back over the past months and how far they had come, she could only thank her God. After all, He had calmed the storm that they were in. With the loss of her husband, being a single parent, and needing to go back to work, it was clear God was taking care of her and her children just as He said He would. For that Joyce was very thankful.

Two weeks later, it was a different situation altogether, when Mark woke his mother in the middle of the night.

"What is it, honey?" Joyce heard the tears in his voice as he tried to tell her. She figured he had a bad dream; she was correct. She tried to get him to talk about it, but Mark was too upset. He sat on the side of her bed for a few minutes when he finally told her the dream was about his father.

"Why did he have to die?" Joyce just pulled her son close to her and let him sob. She thought Mark's bad dreams had stopped, but not this night.

"Here, get under the blanket with me, and we'll talk," She told her son. She was careful with the words she chose, wanting to not only comfort Mark, but also help him understand as best she could. Joyce reminded him how much each member of their family missed Paul, and maybe his dreams were a part of the healing process for him. The reason for his father's death was not easily explained, after all how do you explain such a thing to a child?

"Mark, we never know why the Lord takes someone away in death; we're really not to question God by asking why." She went on trying to explain as best she could; after all, she wondered why at times herself. "Mark, the only thing I can tell you is that God never makes a mistake. He is in control, and we have to ask Him to help us and give us the strength we need to deal with such a hurt." She cupped Mark's chin in her hand and simply said, "Remember, Mark, your daddy will always be in your heart, and you know where daddy is right now don't you?" Mark shook his head yes, and told Joyce that his father was in heaven, because he had asked Jesus into his heart when he was just a little boy, like Mark was now. This seemed to calm Mark and he hugged his mother and scooted down farther under the cover.

"Can I sleep in here with you for the rest of the night?" he said with his sleepy face.

"Sure, but only if you don't snore," she teased.

Mark giggled. "I don't snore; Michael does." Now they were both giggling. It wasn't long until both mother and son were sound asleep.

Don sat behind his desk, while Brandon sat on the other side holding his coffee cup, but not saying much. Brandon had come to pick up some supplies that were needed for the ranch, before he, Sean, Don and Joyce went to the ranch for lunch.

"Dad, are you alright?" Don asked his father who seemed to be a little on edge this morning.

"Yes, why do you ask?"

"Well, you've picked up that cup of coffee four times now and haven't taken a drink yet."

Brandon didn't realize his being preoccupied was obvious.

Don had invited Joyce out to see the ranch and to stay for lunch. This was something he had done with all his employees when they were new to the office. He then realized he never asked Brandon if that would be all right with him. "Oh no, Dad, I am so sorry I never even thought to ask you." Don said with a apologetic look on his face.

"Ask me what?" He replied with confusion.

"If you mind Joyce coming with us to the Ranch for lunch today. If it's a problem I…"

"No!" Brandon nearly spat at him, "No, no problem at all. Everything is fine, Don, you worry too much."

In truth, Brandon was looking forward to spending some time with Joyce. He had found her so attractive and fascinating. He didn't think she had even noticed him. But what if she had and didn't like what she noticed? What if she thought him to be a big dumb cowboy? Way too many of these negative thoughts were coming in on Brandon and way too quickly.

"Hello, gentlemen, how are the two of you today?" Joyce said as she entered Don's spacious office.

Brandon stood and both men responded to her; he appeared to be much calmer than he really felt. He couldn't help but watch her. Joyce appeared to be smooth and confident as she came in and sat down across from the two of them.

"Would you like a cup of coffee, Joyce?" Brandon asked.

"Yes, please."

As Brandon walked to the coffee pot that sat on the other side of the room, Joyce and Don discussed a little business.

"Sugar?"

"I beg your pardon," Joyce said, looking strangely at Brandon.

"Do you take sugar in your coffee?"

"No, just cream please."

Brandon kindly prepared Joyce's coffee to her liking and gently handed it to her, accidentally touching her fingers as she reached for the cup. He thought he would melt; her fingers were so soft and pretty.

It was at that time Leslie called and spoke with Don, telling him he was needed in Sean's office. Don politely excused himself and left the two adults alone.

While Joyce and Brandon were in Don's office alone, they began to make small talk. Brandon asked her about how her job was going, and teasingly asked if his sons were treating her well. After a small laugh, Joyce affirmed that she enjoyed her job and working with his sons. There were only a few minutes of silence when Joyce thought to ask about the ranching business.

"I hear you run a cattle ranch, is that right?" Joyce asked.

"Yes, I do. I have horses and beef cattle and, of course, a few bulls and..." Don came in the room cutting Brandon's words off.

Don apologized to the two of them as he explained he would not be attending lunch at the ranch. Sean would be, but there was a problem in the docking area that needed his attention.

Joyce asked if another day would be better, but both men agreed that it would be fine to go ahead without Don.

Sean came in at that moment and let them know he was ready if they were, so off Joyce, Brandon and Sean went to the Southern Star Ranch for lunch. As the three walked out, Joyce insisted they take her vehicle. She figured she might feel a little more comfortable if she were in control of something.

"I'll try not to spill you." Joyce laughed as she turned and walked toward her vehicle.

As long as you're the one mopping me up, you can spill me anytime, Brandon thought uncontrollably. He then silently scolded himself, hoping that would do some good.

"Here, it's the black Jeep. I know it's not the lap of luxury or anything you may be used to but, hey, I like it and, more importantly, it's in my budget." Joyce's jeep was kept in remarkable condition, not only clean on the outside, but on the inside as well, and with children that was not an easy task.

Sean laughed a little as he explained to Joyce the vehicle his father was still driving. Here was a man who was very successful but still drove an old, outdated truck.

"Yes, Joyce, really, you ought to see the truck I drive around the ranch. It's seventeen years old, needs a paint job, but runs well. Needs a few minor repairs every now and then, but honestly, I just can't seem to get rid of it. I love it," said Brandon. Sean laughed to himself at the thought of that old truck.

Hearing Brandon talk about his truck made Joyce more comfortable with him. It was then she asked him about his family.

"How many children do you and Mrs. Miller have, Brandon?"

"Three. And Mrs. Miller has been deceased for over ten years now."

"Oh, I'm sorry I didn't mean to pry."

"No apology needed, really it's alright." He went on to explain that Don was the oldest, and then Sean and last but not least was Richard. Brandon then returned the question to Joyce as she was zipping in and out of traffic, shifting gears like a woman on a mission.

"I have five children," she said proudly.

You sure don't look like a woman that has birthed five babies, he thought to himself. "What are their ages?" Brandon asked. Joyce answered his question and told about each child trying not to sound like the overly proud parent.

"You, Mrs. McIntosh, are one busy lady. How do you handle a big family and work too?"

Joyce explained to Brandon that she hadn't always worked outside the home. She told him of her recently becoming a widow and needing to go back to work to support her children. Not really meaning to, she also told of how it seemed as if it has been a lifetime since Paul died. This time it was Brandon who apologized for prying.

The two of them seemed to become more and more comfortable with each other as they rode toward the ranch. Brandon told Joyce of his deceased wife, Stacey. He and Stacey had been married eighteen years when she died; he had worked hard at raising their three boys alone, but gave God the credit for getting them through such a stormy time.

It was after Stacey's death that he hired Lorna, his housekeeper. He knew the boys needed a clean house and good meals to eat, and he couldn't give them that. The first two years after Stacey's death, Brandon missed her so much; at times he thought he was going to die himself. In all actuality, it was his sons that kept him going.

Joyce listened to Brandon as he talked of his family, and it took her a little by surprise when he spoke of God. *Oh, he must be a believer,* Joyce thought, but kept the words to herself.

"I do find myself depending a lot more on God these days, that is for sure." Joyce responded.

She must be a believer, Brandon thought. He would have been surprised to know the same thought had just crossed Joyce's mind about him. The conversation was cut off when they were getting closer to the ranch. Joyce figured she might need to pay closer attention.

"Turn right at the light. I'm sorry; I forgot you have never been to our Ranch before." Sean now spoke. He had been riding quietly while the other two adults talked. He didn't feel left out; he just enjoyed the ride.

"Does your ranch have a name?"

"Yes it does. It's the Southern Star," Sean replied.

Brandon bought the ranch a year after his wife died. It was great therapy for him, and the boys loved it as well. The ranch had turned out to be a very good business investment and a wonderful home.

Sean, continuing to give directions, and Joyce, listening closely, slowed the vehicle down so as not to miss anything. The scenery in this area was beautiful.

"Oh, I see your sign now. The Southern Star," she said out loud.

As Joyce pulled up to the big ranch house she was so taken in by its beauty, it was simply breathtaking. It was a two-story white ranch house with black trim and shutters, including a spacious front porch with a swing. Joyce had always loved a front porch with a swing. It brought back memories of her childhood at her parents' home. The house was huge. *I wonder how many rooms that thing has*, Joyce thought to herself.

The yard itself was even beautiful. Maple trees lined the long lane that led to the house; several other trees were planted here and there, and a few white dogwood trees were in the front. There were also lots of flowers in beds running around the outside of the house. Someone had their work cut out for them with the landscaping, and they did a very good job. Joyce just wanted to take in the beauty that she saw, and she hadn't even been inside yet.

Joyce parked the Jeep and they all got out. Brandon couldn't help but notice how taken in Joyce appeared to be with his home.

Brandon tried not to keep looking at Joyce, but she was so beautiful. It was not only her outward beauty that had captured him, but her inward beauty as well. She was sweet and kind and he wanted to get to know her better. How he was going to get through this lunch without making a fool of himself with this vision of loveliness at the same table, he didn't know.

"Would you like a tour?" Sean's voice broke into Joyce's amazement a few moments after they stepped inside the spacious foyer.

Joyce happily agreed, and off the three went to view the beautiful ranch home.

As Sean led the way inside the house, Joyce could feel the warmth in the home. The colors and decorations that were chosen made everything look so inviting. The front door walked right into the spacious living room. It had wood flooring and was decorated with a beautiful rug with the most interesting design. There was a big leather couch and matching chair and some other chairs that were so full and fluffy that Joyce could almost hear them beckoning her.

The wooden stairway was one of the first things you saw as you stepped through the front door; it alone was breathtaking. The color scheme in the house was masculine, but not overly so, with its navy, greens and woods. The large fireplace in the middle of the large living room, paintings, and a few floral decorations made the room welcoming and beautiful.

The next room they viewed was the kitchen.

"This is Lorna's domain," Sean said with a little laughter. About that time Lorna walked in the kitchen to get a pitcher of iced tea for the table.

"Lorna, this is Joyce McIntosh, Don's new assistant at the Supply office. Joyce, this is Lorna, our priceless housekeeper, and much more."

"Oh, stop it, Sean," the housekeeper replied with a small grin.

"Hello, it's good to meet you, Mrs. McIntosh."

"It's good to meet you, and please call me Joyce." After the introductions were over, Lorna went on about her business, and Sean continued being Joyce's tour guide. Brandon had a phone call to take, so he politely excused himself.

"Your Dad can't cook, huh?" Joyce asked with a soft chuckle. It had taken her only a few minutes after seeing what all Lorna prepared for lunch and how Brandon and Sean appreciated her to figure this one out.

"That's right. Dad can grill almost anything, but put him in the kitchen and he can burn water." Joyce found this so funny; she now seemed to be a lot more at ease at the ranch with the Miller men.

Sean continued to show Joyce every inch of the house, while Brandon was taking his phone call. They visited the second floor that had four bedrooms, a game room, and three and a half baths. Afterwards, Brandon met with Sean and Joyce, and let Sean know Lorna wished to speak with him.

"Please, Joyce, allow me to continue showing you around." Brandon said. "Would you care to see the stables?"

"Alright, I've never really been around stables or horses." The two of them walked outside and toward the stables.

Joyce thought the stables were quite impressive, clean and spacious. It was all painted white with a cement walkway, and dirt floors in the areas that the horses stayed. Joyce smelled the aroma of hay in the air when they entered inside.

"Oh, how pretty! What is this horse's name?" Joyce asked as the horse came right to her and nibbled at her blouse. "Oh, oh my," Joyce was startled as the horse seemed to be looking for something, and in a very personal area at that. The horse did not frighten her, but took her by surprise.

"This is Biscuit. Here Biscuit, stop that." Brandon now scolded the horse and then reached into his pocket and gave the large animal a peppermint. Joyce found this very amusing.

"Yes, I know he is a big spoiled baby. Every day he comes to me looking for a treat. He must have taken an instant liking to you for him to come right up to you like that," Brandon explained.

"Who named him Biscuit?" Joyce asked laughing as she rubbed Biscuit's face.

"Richard. He said the name just came to him, so Biscuit it is. He will be finishing college this coming spring."

"Who, Biscuit or Richard?" Joyce asked in a silly, playful tone. Brandon just chuckled.

"Don is your eldest, Richard is your youngest, and Sean is in the middle?" Joyce inquired.

"Yep, that's it." Brandon went on to explain the rest of his family, the older two sons being married to lovely wives, and how it was his hope that one day Richard would too.

Brandon looked at his watch and suggested they return to the house; he figured Lorna should be about ready for them to sit down to eat. Brandon, being the gentleman that he was, politely guided Joyce back to the house, but he could not ignore the feeling of how much he had enjoyed talking with her.

Time flew by as the three of them ate and talked. Lorna had prepared a most delicious meal - roast beef, new potatoes, baby carrots, green beans, homemade bread and sweet iced tea. Dessert was a fresh baked apple pie. Now full from the fine meal, which Joyce had thanked Lorna for, Sean and Joyce headed back to the office. As they were getting back into the Jeep, Joyce thanked Brandon for the lovely time, food, and the tour.

"It was all wonderful and, with a meal like that one, I doubt I will be worth anything for the rest of the day." Sean laughed at her comment.

When Joyce and Sean arrived back at the office, Don went into talk with Joyce and apologized for having to stay behind and help Mac in the loading dock. Joyce thanked Don for the invitation to the ranch. She told him of her tour of the house, land and stables. As Joyce thanked him again, she couldn't remember when she had such a thrilling lunch. It also didn't hurt that her host at the Southern Star Ranch was a very charming man.

CHAPTER FIVE

Joyce, carrying a load of laundry, realized no one was going to answer the phone that sat ringing. With her arms full, she shifted the load and answered the phone with her free hand.

"Yes, she is, may I ask who is calling please?" Joyce asked the person on the other end of the phone.

"Scott. Scott Parsons," the young man replied.

"One moment, Scott. Elise, you have a phone call, dear."

Scott Parsons was a young man Elise had met at 'Your Choice of Chicken'. He comes into the store at least twice a week just to see her. Most of the time she waits on Scott because he always tries his best to be in her cash register line.

The two of them had had brief conversations while he ordered his food at the counter, and there were a few times when business was slow that he had talked to her before he would leave. After weeks of working to get up his nerve to ask for her phone number, he decided it was time to call Elise and ask her out on a date.

"Hello?" Elise answered.

"Hi, Elise, this is Scott, how are you?"

"I'm fine, and you?"

"Oh, I'm fine. I was calling to see if you were busy tomorrow evening?"

"Aah well, no I don't think I have any plans."

"Would you like to go out, maybe to dinner and a movie?"

Elise was so excited that Scott called, but did not let him know of her excitement. She had talked to him many times at work, and come Friday night, she would go to dinner and a movie with Scott Parsons.

"I can't believe it! Scott Parsons just asked me out!" She spoke out loud after hanging up the phone.

"Who is Scott Parsons, Elise?" Joyce asked her daughter.

"Oh Mom, he is the guy that comes in the store a lot. I always wait on him if I'm not busy with something else," she explained excitedly.

"Are you two going out somewhere?"

"Yes, he is picking me up tomorrow at six o'clock and we are going out to eat and then to a movie."

"You do know I want him to come in. I want to meet him," Joyce said very firmly, but in a kind tone.

"Yes, Mom, I know that. And I know what time to be home," She said in a lower tone now. Elise was so excited she could barely concentrate on anything else for the rest of the day.

Scott came to the house for Elise at 5:45. He knew he was early, but he figured that was better than being late. Besides, he wanted to have extra time in case he had a hard time finding her house. Very nervously he rang the doorbell; waiting for someone to answer, and when someone did it was a little boy. At first Scott thought he did have the wrong house after all.

"I'm Scott Parsons, I'm here for Elise," the young man said.

"Okay, come on in," Michael told him. "Elise, your date's here!" Michael yelled just as he came in the door.

"Hello, I'm Joyce, Elise's mother. Please overlook my son, we've talked about yelling through the house, but it seems like we need to talk a little more," Joyce said as she extended her hand to Scott and looked harshly at Michael.

"Hi, it's good to meet you. I'm sorry I'm a little early, but I allowed some extra time in case I couldn't find your house. I'm not too familiar with this area."

"That's alright, please come in and have a seat. This is Michael,

Elise's little brother." Scott reached out to shake Michael's hand and Michael obliged. At that moment Mark came flying down the stairs. "Wow, twins!" Scott said with wide eyes. He couldn't help but stare at the two boys who were a carbon copy of each other. "Sorry, I have seen twins before, but how does anyone tell you two apart?" he asked. Just moments after they had been seated, Elise came down the steps causing Scott's question to go unanswered.

"Hi, Scott."

"Hi, Elise, sorry I'm early."

"No problem, I see you have met my mother and little brothers, and you probably know my sister from 'Your Choice of Chicken.'"

"Yes, one of these little guys let me in, but I don't know which one." Elise giggled at Scott's confused face.

After a few moments of letting Joyce know where they were eating and what movie they were seeing, the two young people left for their first date.

Scott and Elise got a seat in the restaurant quicker than expected. It was a very nice sit down restaurant that neither one of them had been to before.

"So, how many brothers and sisters do you have?" Scott asked.

Elise giggled a little, and then answered his question, telling a little about each sibling. Scott then remembered the twin boys. "I have to ask," he said, curiosity written all over his face. "How do you tell them apart, they are so identical?"

"Well, to us they aren't because we know their personalities and their own little ways of doing things. But one way that most people haven't noticed is their faces are a little different. Mark's is a little bit fuller than Michael's."

"Aah, I'll have to remember that, of course they would have to be standing side by side for me to tell," he realized.

"What about you?" Elise asked.

Scott's family was not as big as Elise's was; he just had an older brother. He realized he didn't meet Elise's father and asked her about him.

"My dad died a little while ago."

"Oh, I am so sorry, that must be tough."

"It's alright; it was hard there for a while, especially to see how my mother was responding, but then things started getting better. We still have a way to go, but we are getting there."

When Elise returned home, Joyce was up watching TV. Elise was on time, and Scott walked her to the door, but didn't come in. Joyce lay at one corner of the sofa watching a movie that was almost over.

"Hi, how was your evening with Scott?"

"We had a great time, Mom, I like him. He's a lot of fun."

Elise told Joyce about her evening and how the waiter at the restaurant got their orders mixed up with someone else's so they ate for half price. Elise looked a little dreamy eyed, so Joyce thought she would let her daughter go on up to her room.

As Joyce watched her daughter, she reminisced about her first date with Paul. She expected she had acted about the same way, all dreamy and fascinated with the newness of someone to date. Too bad you can't look into the future on your first date and see if you should enjoy it and keep dating him, or go hide and not come out until the boy goes far away. Not that she wished she had run and hid from Paul; this thought caused Joyce's to laugh out loud just a little. She continued to watch the movie alone, and then it was off to bed.

Joyce was glad the young man didn't come in and stay, even though she did want to get to know him a little better. With the way her daughter was acting, Joyce assumed she would have plenty of opportunities for that.

"Hey, how was your date last night? Samantha asked her older sister as the two of them were sitting down to breakfast the next morning.

"Oh it was fine."

"Is he that guy you always wait on at work? The one with the 1978 red Camaro?"

"Yes, he has been in there a few times, and I usually wait on him."

"A few times! He's in there at least twice a week," Samantha said in a teasing tone. "He'll probably come in every day now."

"I hope so," Elise said with wistful eyes.

Elise wondered how Samantha knew what he drove. She found it a little odd that her sister knew this kind of information. "Sam, how did you know what kind of car he drives?"

"Aah I just notice these things, I guess. So tell me, what is his car like on the inside?" Samantha had a love for pretty looking cars. She wasn't into cars like boys were, knowing all about the engine and how fast it would run and all of that, but she knew what looked good and what didn't. It was something she must have gotten from her Grandpapa, who had been in the car business all of Samantha's life.

Joyce had worked for Don long enough now that she knew his likes and dislikes and his comings and goings almost as well as he did. She always got to work fifteen minutes before Don, so she could have a fresh cup of coffee waiting for him when he arrived. Along with the coffee, she sorted the mail so that he would not be bothered with junk mail or anything else that was not worth his time. Even the newspaper was at his desk in the mornings, just in case he wanted to read the morning news before he tore into the day's work.

Joyce, at times, helped Sean with some of his workload, but her main focus was Don. He was for whom she had been hired, and she made sure he had nothing to complain about by the way she did her duties. The Lord had given her a job she loved, and she was thankful for it.

"Good morning, Joyce."

"Good morning, Sean," she replied.

Sean had come in the office early that day to get a jumpstart on some paperwork he had somehow gotten behind on. He wondered if he would ever see the end of it. Joyce let him know if there was anything she could do to help, to let her know.

Sean went to his office and dug into the stack of papers and folders that was left on his desk from the night before. No one saw or heard from him for hours.

As Joyce sat plunging away at her own work, Don called and asked to see her and her calendar in his office as soon as she had a moment.

"Yes, sir, I'll be right there." She knew she didn't have to go right away, but she didn't want to take the risk of forgetting and Don having to remind her. To Joyce, that would not do at all.

"Joyce, have a seat, and we'll get started. First of all I need you to cancel all my appointments for this week; I will be going out of town on Tuesday and won't return until sometime on Friday. I also would appreciate it if you could get my flight arranged. I will spend the rest of today preparing for a meeting in Kansas City." Looking up at Joyce, he noticed she had written everything down.

"Joyce, have I forgotten anything?"

"Yes, you have a dentist appointment tomorrow afternoon; I can call and cancel for you."

"Oh, I had forgotten all about that. Thank you."

Joyce not only canceled Don's dentist appointment, but had lunch brought in for him. He was so deep in his work he hadn't noticed it was past noon.

When Don looked up and saw Joyce bringing his lunch to him, he looked at his watch and thanked her for being so helpful.

"What did I ever do before I hired that woman?" Don said out loud after she left the room.

Somehow Joyce got all her work done for Don, got his lunch taken care of, and ordered enough for Sean as well. After she returned from lunch, she tackled some of Sean's workload. By 3:30 she was spent. She took thirty minutes to clear her desk and headed for home.

Chapter five / 65

Joyce heard the boys wrestling the moment she got inside the house.

"Boys, that's enough."

"Mom, we're hungry!"

"Since you two are so hungry, you can come in here and help me cook supper. And," she said to cut the boys off from their complaining, "It will be done with a happy attitude."

Joyce was tired, and the kids were hungry. After everyone piled around the table to eat, Joyce asked who had kitchen duty. It was Elise's turn, so Joyce went to her room, ran a hot bath, and just soaked for a while. The hot bubbles seemed to sooth the tiring effects of the day away; she just laid back, closed her eyes, and let the hot water work its magic.

It was the middle of the night; Joyce was sleeping so good after a hard day's work at the office, but it seemed that someone was calling her name. She suddenly woke up to find Mark standing at the side of her bed.

"Mom, I don't feel good," he said to his mother very early on a Tuesday morning.

"What's wrong, Honey?" she asked as she reached for the lamp on the night side table.

Joyce saw his face and reached to feel his forehead and cheeks.

"Hum, you seem to have a fever. Go back to bed and I'll bring you something for it, with something to drink. How does your stomach feel?" She asked as she was getting out of bed.

"My stomach feels shaky and my head hurts a little."

Joyce took care of Mark's needs and got him settled back in bed. *He must have picked up a bug of some kind*, she thought to herself. She left the light on in the hallway just in case she or Mark had to get up quickly, and then went back to bed herself.

At seven o'clock in the morning, Joyce knew Leslie would be getting to the office. She called and let her know she would not be coming in; she would be staying home to take care of her sick son.

"Leslie, Don will be leaving to go out of town today, but he will be coming by the office to talk with Sean before he leaves. I won't be in today because Mark is sick with a stomach bug. Therefore, I have a few things to tell you. You may need to remind Don that I have already taken care of his needs for his trip. His ticket is waiting for him at the airport; he has a rental car waiting for him at Avis when he arrives; his hotel reservation has been made, and all of his appointments for this week have been canceled. I have already told him these things, but you might need to go over it again in case he is running late and feels like he has forgotten something."

Leslie was glad Joyce had taken care of all of Don's needs because she would not know where to begin and told Joyce as much. The two hung up and Joyce went to the kitchen where the children were gathering for their breakfast.

"Good morning, Michael, girls."

Joyce advised the children to eat light in case they got whatever Mark had. Joyce was sure it was a stomach bug and wanted to do her best to keep the rest of the family from catching it.

"It wouldn't hurt to stay clear of Mark for the day," she said as she was preparing him some tea to settle his stomach.

"Oh yuck! Mom make him stay upstairs please, I hate those stomach bugs! They make you feel awful," Samantha said with a dreadful look on her face.

"Honey, no one in their right mind likes them," Joyce replied with a bit of laughter.

"We're not sick, why do we have to watch what we eat?" Michael asked.

"If you eat light and get sick, it won't be as bad," Elise answered for her mother.

Within moments, Joyce was back upstairs in Mark's room to give him the tea she had made for him. Mark lay on his back thinking he didn't want to be in his room all day. He wished he could go downstairs and watch TV, but didn't have the strength to do so.

By the middle of the day, Mark was feeling a little better; his fever had come down, but his stomach was still not right. Joyce had cleaned house all morning and felt the need for a rest, so she sat down on the sofa and made herself comfortable. It was then she got a call from the school office, telling Joyce she needed to come pick Michael up because he was not feeling well.

"Okay, here we go." She said out loud, knowing the stomach bug was probably going to hit them all. Joyce then called her next-door neighbor, Mrs. Bailey, to see if she could watch Mark until she returned with Michael. The older neighbor lady gladly agreed.

Joyce got Michael home and settled. It was later after Elise and Samantha had come through the door that the real fun began.

"Mom, Michael is throwing up!" Mark yelled from his bedroom. Joyce went running to help her son, hoping all the way that he had made it to the bathroom.

"Mom, I feel awful," Michael cried.

"I know, honey; you will feel better now that you have emptied your stomach," she said in a loving voice.

Michael felt like the world was spinning as his mother helped him into his bed. She put a trash can near the bed just in case.

Joyce prepared a simple meal for supper for those who weren't sick: chicken soup, crackers and tea. She thought things were settling down and said as much after she, Samantha and Elise sat down to the table. Then the quiet was broken by the sound of running feet upstairs in the hallway. It was clear, whatever bug this was, Michael had it worse than his brother.

It was after eleven when Joyce finished sanitizing the bathrooms, doorknobs and anything else she could clean. She had been cleaning with a vengeance, but even with all the cleaning Joyce had done, it didn't help the situation. Michael was no longer throwing up, but now Elise was the new victim of this ugly stomach bug. Elise, being older, didn't require Joyce's assistance when throwing up like the twins did, but she mothered her just the same.

The next morning, the boys were able to go downstairs and watch TV, but food was not an option for either of them. Samantha on the other hand was staying in her room, not coming out unless absolutely necessary. She was determined not to be the next one on the bug's hit list.

After all the cleaning, special dietary needs, and running up and down the stairs, Joyce was exhausted. It was Wednesday mid-day, and she felt as if she had put in a full week at the office with no break. She decided to take a nap while all was calm, only to awaken to an aching head and upset stomach. "Oh no, not me," was her first thought.

Thursday morning, the boys seemed to be back to normal, Elise was feeling better, but Joyce felt awful and didn't look any better. Diane had called to check on things, but Joyce could not talk, she felt too bad. Joyce knew from watching everyone in the house go through it that this bug would just have to run its course.

"Good morning, Joyce. Aah, Joyce, do you feel alright?" Leslie asked on Friday morning.

"Yes, I'm fine. I may look awful, but I'm fine. I've had a stomach bug that started with Mark, and hit each of us except for Samantha," Joyce said.

"Eeww, a stomach bug, I hate those things; they make you feel terrible," Leslie said making a face.

"Leslie, honey, I'll tell you as I did Samantha, no one likes those things." Joyce then walked slowly to her office. She was no longer sick, but was a little weak and tired looking. She sat at her desk and focused on her work most of the day, and the day did go smoothly, but she was glad when it was time to go home.

The summer job for Samantha had helped her mature a little, and Joyce was certainly happy for that. The boys were about to celebrate their twelfth birthday. She had planned a big dinner of their favorite foods and, of course, cake and ice cream. A few friends and family were invited to share in the celebration.

Joyce really wanted the day to be special. Life had gotten better for Joyce and her family; it was calmer, quieter and they even managed to have fun from time to time. Joyce felt that throwing a party for her sons would be fairly easy.

As the special day arrived, Mark and Michael were up very early, before anyone else, and ready to deal with the day. The two boys were so excited about their birthday; they couldn't lie in their beds any longer.

"Michael," spoke Mark in a very hushed voice. "Let's look around and see if we can find any birthday presents."

"What! You know if we find any mom will take them back. She always says, 'If you get into your presents before it's time, I'll take them back to the store'."

"No, no, we're not going to open them, just find them, maybe shake them a little, but not open them," Mark explained to his brother.

"Well, I guess if we just *see* them it might be alright."

"Let's go," was Mark's quick reply.

Mark and Michael looked high and low and found nothing. Mark thought they would find something; he was sure of it.

"What are the two of you doing?" Elise asked.

"Aahh, nothing."

"Yeah, Elise we aren't doing anything."

"I don't know what the two of you are up to, but do you think it wise to get punished on your birthday?"

"Punished? For what? We aren't doing anything," Michael explained with large eyes.

"Whatever, just remember I warned you," Elise said as she left the two boys standing in the hallway in their pajamas.

Joyce had been running around the office all morning, trying to do her work, and get out early for the twins birthday party that evening.

"Oh, Don," Joyce called out to her boss. The two walked toward each other so Joyce could talk with him. "Just a reminder, I will need to leave about an hour early today. It's the twins' birthday, and we are having a little party."

"Oh yeah, that's right, and two at once, that's double the fun," he replied in a happy voice.

Joyce also reminded Don of his and Jennifer's invitation, and was glad to hear that they were going to attend.

Joyce planned a fun evening with friends, food, and family, all to arrive at six o'clock that evening. She would pick up the cake on her way home from work, call the pizza person at five, and hope all would go well. She had two boys counting down the minutes until party time.

Jason, Joyce's father, saw Michael looking out the window as he and Elizabeth pulled into the driveway. He could only laugh at the sight of him.

"I'll get it!" yelled Michael. He was so excited about the guests starting to arrive, he ran to the door to open it. Joyce's parents were waiting to come in and start giving out hugs and kisses to their grandchildren.

"Happy Birthday!" both Jason and Elizabeth said rather loudly.

"Hey, Mom, Dad, please come on in," Joyce said from behind her sons. "I'm glad you two came a little early, I wanted the family to have a little private time with you before the other guests arrive."

Joyce's parents came in and went into the living room, where they visited with their family.

"Mom, I have two very excited little twelve-year-olds chomping at the bit to open their gifts." Everyone laughed at the banter.

"Mark, Michael come on over here and open the gifts we have for you."

"Honestly, Jason, you're as bad as the children. You just can't wait for them to open their gifts."

"I know I'm a kid at heart; I just can't help myself. And besides, I can hardly wait to play with it myself." This brought more laughter from everyone in the living room.

"Yeah, I agree with Grandpapa on that one, let's open it now," spoke a very excited Michael.

"Wow, baby!" was Mark's response which was echoed by his brother when they tore through the paper and opened the new video games, one for each of them.

Chapter five / 71

"Thank you Grandmamma and Grandpapa, it's just what we've been wanting."

"You are welcome, boys," said each of the grandparents.

Most of the guests had arrived when Joyce went to answer the front door. To her surprise, but a happy one, it was Don, his wife Jennifer and one more person. Brandon was behind his son.

"Hello," the Millers said to Joyce.

"Hi, please come in. Jennifer, let me take your things, I'll hang them up for you."

"Thank you, Joyce."

"I hope you don't mind me crashing your sons' party," said Brandon as he peeked out from behind Don. Brandon was not a party crasher by any means; he couldn't resist the opportunity to visit Joyce.

"Oh no, not at all, you are more than welcome to come in and join the fun. Let me introduce you to my parents and some other guests." Joyce had been busy going around and making sure all her guests were not only properly introduced, but also having a great time.

Brandon was having trouble taking his eyes off Joyce; he tried getting into different conversations with the other guests so he would not be so obvious. He had even played the video games with the boys. He won one game but then Michael smoked him on the next one. He really enjoyed the boys and the game was fun, but what he really wanted was to sit down beside Joyce and just look at her. All through the evening he would glance at her, but she didn't seem to notice.

When Brandon and the other guests sat down to eat, he found himself seated almost directly in front of her at the table. Jason sat beside him. As the two of them conversed, Brandon felt as if he were being deceitful. Here he was sitting beside the father of the woman that had captured his heart, and all the while thinking about what it would be like to hold her in his arms.

"Brandon is it?"

"Yes sir, Brandon Miller."

"How do you know my Joyce and the children?" Jason asked.
"Joyce works for my sons."

The conversation went on for a little while with Jason and Brandon both talking about their work, Brandon about ranching and Jason about the car business. Brandon learned things about the car business he never knew. Still he couldn't keep his mind off Joyce.

Brandon was so distracted that on the way home he couldn't remember a word Jason had said to him for love nor money.

"Thanks for coming to my party," the twins made sure they told each guest as they left. When the evening was done, Joyce felt done too.

Everyone pitched in to clean up the mess. After the house was put back together, Joyce and her parents sat in the living room with a cup of coffee and relaxed for the remainder of the evening. Soon everyone was tired and decided to call it a day.

"Well, that was certainly some party last night. Everyone seemed to have such a good time, especially a certain guest who couldn't take his eyes off my Joycie," said Jason.

"Dad, what in the world are you talkin' about?" Joyce asked curiously as she was pouring herself a cup of coffee.

"What was his name? Aah let me think, Brad or something like that."

"Brad? Oh, you mean Brandon?"

"Yes that's it Brandon, see, you noticed it too."

"No, Dad, I didn't notice a thing, and I think you're just imagining things."

"Am I?" Jason said as he went back to his morning paper. The children were still in bed so the adults had some privacy with their conversation, serious or not.

"Good morning, everyone," Elizabeth spoke to her husband and daughter as she walked into the kitchen. "Boy, that sure was a fun party last night," she said as she kissed her husband on the cheek, and then went toward the coffee pot.

"I don't know when I enjoyed myself so much. I also noticed a very handsome man who kept looking at you. Joyce, is there anything you would like to tell us?"

"Twice in one hour," Joyce replied to the air. "I think you and dad are losing your minds. After all, who in their right mind would want a woman who had been married half her life and has five children?"

"Now, Joycie, you are a very lovely woman, inside and out. Don't sell yourself short. Any man would be lucky to have a woman like you."

"Thank you, Daddy." She said as she went over and put her arms around his neck from behind and gave him a hug and kiss on the cheek. Joyce truly thought her parents were imagining this whole thing. Brandon Miller definitely was a very nice man, but that is all there was to it, and all there ever would be. "I just work for his sons … that's all," she explained.

The conversation about Brandon Miller ended as the rest of the family made their way downstairs and into the kitchen. The children started their own conversation about the party from the previous night.

"Mark, Michael, what are you going to do with the money Diane gave you for your birthday?" Samantha asked her brothers.

"Spend it!" they replied in unison. This caused the kitchen to be filled with laughter once again.

As the family was all around the table, Joyce was thinking how it would have been different if Paul had been there. There certainly would not been as much laughter in the kitchen. He would have complained about too many people talking at once, but that was Paul. Joyce stood back, sipped her coffee, and just savored the scene of the faces that she loved, enjoying all the banter, talk and, of course, the laughter. It didn't matter to her if they were talking at the same time; it was her family and she loved them.

CHAPTER SIX

Monday morning, Don talked to Sean in his office. While the two were together, Sean mentioned the twins' birthday party.

"I heard you, Jennifer, and Dad went to Joyce's on Friday," spoke Sean.

"Yeah, and we had a lovely time. Her family is so fun to be around."

Sean went on to tell his brother how he wished that he and Susan could have been there, but had previous plans.

Don could not forget what he saw in his father that evening; it was a little surprising, but in a good way. He had to share with his brother.

"I have to tell you, Sean, I saw something I have never seen before."

"What? What did you see?" Sean asked curiously.

"I think our father is smitten with a certain lady."

"What? Who? What are you talking about?" Sean was so interested in hearing this, his eyes got really big.

"First of all, when Dad found out that Jennifer and I were going, he asked if we thought it would be alright if he tagged along, which I figured it would be, and it was. But then I kept noticing every time I saw him, he was looking at Joyce."

"Joyce? *Our* Joyce?"

"Yes, *our* Joyce. How many Joyces do you know?"

"Well, what about her? Was she looking at dad in return?"

"I don't think she noticed, or at least if she did, she hid it really well." Don went on to explain the happenings of the evening to his brother, who was all ears.

"What are we going to do?" Sean asked his older brother.

"Do? What do you mean what are we going to do? You are such a goober, Sean," Don now teased his brother, something he had done since almost the time Sean was born.

"It is best that we keep this to ourselves, and stay out of Dad's personal business. You know, Sean, to my knowledge he has never even looked at another woman since mom passed away."

"Well, I think we should keep an open mind and eye on him, after all, I for one do not want him to get hurt."

"I agree," the oldest Miller son said. Sean then took himself back to his own office where work awaited him.

―――

That day at the office, things were as normal as ever. There had not been much mention of Joyce's sons' birthday party. Don was certainly not going to mention his father's infatuation with her. Leslie and Joyce had gone to lunch that day and the talk was of sales at the mall and other general things, nothing like what had been discussed in Don's office with Sean.

Don looked up from his paperwork as he told whoever was knocking at the door to come on in. It was his youngest brother Richard.

"Richard, hey, come on in. When did you get home?"

"Late last night," he said as the two gave each other a big bear hug.

Richard had graduated from college a few months ago and the family had gone to his graduation, but he wanted to take some time and do a little traveling. Brandon had allowed him to do this and gave him some extra cash for his graduation present. Richard traveled all the way to the American-Canadian border. It was just something he and two of his friends had always wanted to do, so they did it. Richard figured now that he had it out of his system, he would never in his life regret not doing it.

Don told his brother how good it was to see him and have him home for good, and then invited him to come for supper some night soon. Richard told Don he was being taken out to dinner by their father, and invited Don and Jennifer to join them.

"I'll call Jennifer and make sure there's nothing we're doing that I've forgotten."

"Yeah, right," Richard now laughing at his brother for calling his wife to make sure he could go. Richard always made jokes at his two older brothers' expense about having the "little woman" to answer to. Of course, he was only teasing them, and they knew it. On the other hand, Don and Sean teased their little brother about anything they could. In all honesty, each gave as good as they got.

"Hey, don't laugh at me, Rich, I did that once, forgot all about us going over to some friends for dinner, and trust me, once was enough." Richard laughed out loud at this, but Don was still not laughing.

While Don called his wife, Richard slipped out in search of Sean. He walked down the hallway until he was in front of his other brother's office door, then tapped gently and opened it.

"Hey, big brother."

"Richard! When did you get home?"

"Late last night," Richard said. "Hey, dad, Don, Jennifer, and I are all going out tonight for dinner, you know a celebration of my being back home. Can you and Susan join us?"

Richard got the same spiel from Sean about needing to call the wife first. He could not let this go; he had to tease this brother as well.

"I'm tellin' ya dude. This guy is never, do you hear me, NEVER getting married."

"Yeah well, we'll see about that." In truth, Richard hoped he would find a wife one day that made him as happy as the women his brothers had married made them. They both were godly women, they made his brothers very happy, and he loved them.

At the close of the day, Don locked the office doors and headed over to Houston's for the welcome home celebration for his little brother. It was certainly good to have all the family together and around a table of good food.

"So, Richard, tell us about your trip to everywhere," Susan said.

"Yes, do tell," Sean replied.

"Well, it was very exciting; at first I thought it was just going to be a long road trip. However, when the fellas and I decided to hike it and camp out at different campgrounds, it was really fun. We met all kinds of people, some a little weird, if you know what I mean," he explained while making a crazy face. "Oh, yeah, one of my buddies found a dog, named him Alex, and Alex went everywhere we went. He still has him, he brought him home." This caused everyone to laugh.

"What did you all do about bathing?" Jennifer asked.

"The campground places had showers so we used them. Oh and Zach, one of my buddies, decided we shouldn't shave until we got home. He's just now getting a mustache." Everyone at the table laughed at the stories Richard had to tell. "I had to shave as soon as I got in the house."

"Yeah, you knew you wouldn't be able to stand the ribbing you would get if Don and I saw you," said Sean.

The waitress came with everyone's order, they bowed their heads, and Brandon blessed the food.

The talk continued of Richard's traveling adventures, there were questions about what kind of places they ate, slept, and different ways they spent their time. Richard went on to explain how they managed while out discovering America.

"We had to make sure our money lasted to the end of the trip. I believe Troy had seventy-nine cents left when he got to his house last night. I, on the other hand, had $1.42. Aren't you proud of me, Dad?" Richard said teasingly.

"Yes, Son, very." Again the laughter filled the room.

Don asked Joyce to come to his office; she was there in no time flat. He had failed to tell her of an outing for all the Lone Star Employees and their families.

"I am sorry I forgot to mention this to you, but we need to get it on the calendar for late in October."

"Alright Don, I'll get on that right away; are there any special details I need to know about?" Joyce asked.

Don filled in Joyce on the usual fall outing the office had. Last years outing had to be canceled due to some construction at the ranch, where they usually held the festivities.

Each year, the Millers invited all employees and their families to the ranch. They had games of all kinds for different age groups, delicious foods, and soft drinks.

Joyce assured her boss she would handle it; now all she had to figure out was, how she would do it.

The summer was going by in a flash; the Texas days were so hot that it was miserable at times. But then again, the summer Texas sky in the evening was spell binding, so much so, that you forgot about the heat. Joyce remembered how she always loved to be outside on the front porch looking up at that sky, sipping a glass of iced tea. On a few occasions, Paul would join her, but most of the time he was busy with his work. Some nights the kids would be outside trying to catch lightning bugs. Joyce rarely sat on the front porch anymore. It made her feel lonelier than she cared to admit.

Samantha, Mark, and Michael were spending two weeks of July with their grandparents in Athens, and Joyce missed them terribly. Timothy and Elise had pretty much been busy that whole time with work and friends, so Joyce had a lot of time to herself. A little alone time was okay, but too much alone time was not.

One evening, Joyce and Diane went out for dinner and a movie, just some fun and girl time. Both ladies decided it was time to go out and enjoying themselves. Diane made the decision that the attire for the evening was to be very laid back, blue jeans, tee shirts and tennis shoes. "Fine by me," was Joyce's comment.

The two ladies walked into the Texas Grill; all giggles and already having a good time. Suddenly, someone called out Joyce's name.

"Hello, Joyce." Joyce's head whipped around to see who called her out.

"Oh, hello Brandon." Brandon was having supper with a young man Joyce did not know, but looked vaguely familiar. She was surprised to see Brandon.

"Oh, pardon me." Brandon now spoke. "Joyce this is my youngest son Richard. Richard, this is Joyce McIntosh, she is Don's assistant at the office.

"Hello," Richard said.

"Hello, Richard, I have heard quite a bit about you. I hear you have just finished school."

"Yes, now I'm working with dad on the ranch."

"Brandon, Richard, this is my best friend Diane Harris. Diane, Brandon and his son Richard Miller."

"Hello, gentlemen," Diane spoke to both men as Brandon kept looking back and forth from Diane to Joyce. Diane thought Brandon to be very handsome, his son as well. Both men were dressed casually, almost as casually as she and Joyce, in jeans, collared shirts and cowboy boots.

"What's good here to eat? We've never been here so what do you recommend?" Joyce asked.

"Yeah, guys, what do you recommend?" echoed Diane.

"I like the half-pound steak and fries, dad always go with something lighter."

"Yeah, aah, here anything really. The food is wonderful; you can't make a bad choice." Brandon spoke, looking at Joyce.

"Well, good seeing you both. We'll leave you to your supper," said Joyce.

"Aah you ladies could join us if you would like," Brandon said with high hopes.

"Oh no, thank you anyway. Tonight is girls' night out, and you two may not enjoy that too much," Joyce spoke with a hint of a giggle.

"Well, maybe another time."

"Bye, Brandon, Richard."

"Bye ladies," Brandon said with a trace of sadness in his voice. Richard noticed how his father watched Joyce walk away until she was no longer in his view. He figured he best not say anything about what he saw, after all, he could be wrong.

Chapter six

"What was that about?" Diane asked Joyce as they sat not too far from the Miller men.

"What was what about?" Joyce asked confused.

"That!" Diane spoke with inquisitiveness as she motioned her hands toward where Brandon and his son sat. "Joyce, that man looked at you almost the entire time we were standing there."

"He did?"

"Joyce, honey, it has been too long; we need to talk, girl! When a gorgeous hunk of manhood looks at you like that, and you don't notice, you need my help, and right now."

Joyce just shrugged her shoulders.

"Now, Joyce, you mean to tell me that you can honestly say you have not noticed that man?"

"Well, I aah, I mean, he ..." Diane cut her off.

"I thought so; you had me worried there for a moment." Diane said with relief. "So, tell me what is the problem?"

"Well, Diane, I don't just go after every single man I meet."

"I know that, so does anyone who knows you. He certainly is a good looking man, Joyce, and it seems to me he is very kind and good looking."

"You already said that, Diane." Diane just smiled.

"He seems to have a good relationship with his son, and you said he attends church. Again, Joyce, what's the problem? Remember this is me, Diane, you're talking to, we know each other better than anyone on this earth."

"I just don't think the children would approve of my acting like that," Joyce blurted out.

"Acting like what ... a woman? Joyce, I'm not saying to throw yourself at the man, I'm not even saying ask him out. I'm just saying, it's okay to notice him. Maybe just have some conversation with him, that's all."

"Well," Joyce now thought and spoke. "Maybe you're right. I'll think about it."

The day of the office picnic was perfect; it was a warm fall day, with just a hint of cool in the air. The trees were starting to change colors and the landscape around the ranch house was absolutely beautiful. Joyce could have sat and looked at that scenery all day, and would have, but her time and attention was needed almost everywhere. She had to check on all the activities to make sure everything was lined up. The food was being catered, but she still felt she should check on that too.

Brandon, Don, and Richard were going non-stop as well. Finally, Sean, Susan and Jennifer drove up and helped in different areas. Brandon had given Lorna the day off; he felt that this was an office function, and she should not have to work and take care of that many people. Lorna was very happy to take him up on his offer.

Everyone seemed to be enjoying themselves. Kids were playing on bouncing blow up things while the parents watched, laughing, as their children bounced and giggled. There was a softball game that Richard coaxed Joyce into playing. She tried to tell him she was not too good at sports, but he wouldn't take no for an answer.

"Now, come on, Joyce, it'll be fun."

Joyce could not believe she had let Richard talk her into playing softball, but there she was getting ready to go out on the field and possibly making a fool of herself.

It was her time at bat; Brandon was the pitcher. He threw the ball, and after two strikes, Whack! With much surprise to Joyce, she hit the ball right to second base. She ran, giggling the whole way. For some reason, running like that made Joyce laugh almost uncontrollably. She made it to first base right before the ball was caught by the first baseman, who happened to be Mac, one of her buddies from work.

"You almost didn't make it, Joyce," Mac said with laughter in his voice. Brandon was so busy watching Joyce run that he almost got hit with the ball when it was thrown to him.

The next batter was Leslie; she also had a good hit and made it to first base. Joyce ran all the way to third, laughing the whole way. The third baseman was Sean, who wondered what was so funny. Then came the last hit. Two outs, bases were loaded, and Michael was up.

"Come on, Michael, bring your momma home!" Joyce yelled.

Strike one, strike two, whack, all the way to the outfield. Joyce ran and made it to home plate, as did Leslie. At the last second Michael slides; he was safe at home plate.

As the game went on, everyone was having such a good time; Brandon kept glancing over to Joyce at any chance he got. He never enjoyed watching someone run as much as he did Joyce. The day had been long, but a good one. Everyone was tired and had their fill of food, fun and laughter.

As the sky drew darker, the younger kids were fading fast, some already asleep in their strollers or on their father's shoulders. Older kids were still going strong, filthy with all the grass and dust, but didn't seem to care.

Joyce, tired from the ballgame, sought out the comfort of a chair with a cold Dr. Pepper.

"Yeah, I knew you could play ball, you tried to fool me," Richard said as he sat beside Joyce while she was downing her soft drink.

"Well, it helps to have those around you who know what they're doing."

"That was some hit Michael had; let me guess, he learned that from his mother."

"Yeah, right!" They both laughed.

Richard could see folks were starting to get tired and said as much to Joyce.

"Well, the adults anyway," Joyce replied.

It was then that Luke, one of Brandon's ranch hands, came and asked Richard if he wanted to shoot some hoops. Joyce couldn't believe the two young men had the energy to go play basketball after just finishing a game of softball.

"Sure, let's go," Richard answered.

"Well, the older adults that is." Joyce repeated out loud. She laughed as the two young men started to jog off to play another game. It was then Leslie came and sat beside Joyce, happy to sit for a while.

"When I get home, I'm going straight to a hot bubble bath," Leslie said to Joyce.

"Oh, me too. I may not get out until tomorrow." The two women laughed at each other.

They talked for a while, and Joyce commented on Leslie's ability to play softball, which caused the two to start laughing all over again.

Mark and Michael had run off to bounce on some play things, while Samantha joined Jennifer at the stables looking at the horses. Joyce knew the twins would not want to leave, and she felt as if she may not be able to get out of the chair.

After the senior staff pitched in and got things looking like a ranch again, everyone started to leave for their homes. The Millers thanked Joyce for all her efforts to make it a successful event. Joyce gathered her children, but not without complaint. The twins would have stayed all night. Hungry again, they looked for and found the last of the cookies, then headed to their vehicle. The boys were so dirty from the hard day of play, Joyce wondered if they would ever come clean. With dirty hands, both boys ate their cookie, not even noticing the dirt. Joyce just sighed at the sight of it.

It seemed like the year had just started, and now it was a week before Thanksgiving. Joyce and the kids had been invited to Paul's parents for the holiday. Steve and Doris McIntosh still lived in Oklahoma City where they had raised their children. Steve had paid for them to fly out for the holiday, but Joyce was not really looking forward to going. Gatherings with Paul's family with him there had been very miserable, without him were sure to be worse. The children had been to their grandparents without Joyce before, and did not want to go again without her.

Paul's mother was a little snobbish and never really accepted Joyce into the family when she and Paul married. From the time Joyce and Paul started dating, Doris just never took the time to get to know her, and Joyce never felt comfortable around Doris. Steve was a little better; he would at least sit and talk with Joyce, but at times he could be so critical.

Joyce really could not understand why Doris was like that, but like that she was. The only reason she was going was for the children. Joyce really didn't think it was fair to keep her children away from Paul's family just because she had never felt comfortable or accepted around them.

It's only three days, she kept telling herself, trying to lift her own spirits. Surely she could deal with the situation for that short amount of time.

Joyce told her in-laws that she would be renting a car, so no one would have to pick them up at the airport. She figured that way she and the children would not feel stranded.

The plane arrived on time, and it didn't take long to get their luggage or the car. Joyce was taking her time, not wanting to get there too soon. She thought any other time getting their luggage and a rental car would have taken close to an hour, but no, not this time. With each passing moment she felt more nervous about being at the older McIntosh's.

Thanksgiving Day came and went, and it wasn't too bad. There were so many people there, Joyce and the children seemed to get lost in the crowd. They stuck close together most of the day, which made her feel better, but being there made her miss her husband terribly. Joyce could tell the children were having a fair time, much better than she was, no doubt.

The day after Thanksgiving, she, Elise, and Samantha went shopping with one of Paul's sisters, Deborah, and her two girls, Tammy and Kelly. It wasn't all that bad because they went their separate ways a few times and just met up at the food court later that day. All in all, Joyce decided to not let her feelings spoil the time with her girls. The boys stayed at the house and watched a football game with their grandfather; so Joyce knew that would be enjoyable for them. Mark and Michael hated shopping, unless the item being shopped for was for them to have fun and play with.

The boys watched the game with their brother Timothy, Steve, their grandfather, and two of their uncles. There were times they sat playing a hand held video game with the sound off so as not to disturb the others. When their mother arrived back from shopping,

Mark and Michael were not only glad she was back, but had surprised her by having their bags packed and ready for the airport.

When late Saturday evening came, the goodbyes were said and Joyce had never been so happy to get on a plane in all her life.

───⁓

November fell into December, December had started off being a mild weathered month, but suddenly it turned cold two weeks before Christmas. Of course, the cold got everyone into the Christmas spirit. The kids were off from school; Timothy was home from college, and as Joyce pulled in the driveway one Friday evening, it started snowing.

Joyce loved it when it snowed and everyone was home inside safe and warm and not on the highways. By eight o'clock that evening, the citizens of Garland, Texas, had two inches of snow, and it was still coming down.

The boys, including Timothy, had to go out and play in it. It was one of the biggest snowball fights the McIntosh's ever had. Elise and Samantha joined the boys and blasted them from behind. The boys didn't even know the girls were out there. Mark and Michael took cover behind a bush and made several snowballs to hurl at Elise and Samantha. Timothy had come to where the boys were when his sisters attacked him from out of nowhere. As Joyce watched out the window, she decided she was not letting the children have all the fun, so she too joined in. After almost two hours in the snow, they were all about frozen and went inside for some popcorn and hot chocolate.

With a blink of an eye, December was gone and January about over. The air had gotten much colder, and Joyce found herself looking forward to spring. The only reason she could think of was that she was tired of bundling up every time she went outdoors. Just going to the mailbox froze a person. It was too cold for the boys to go out and play. On Sunday mornings, Joyce had to make herself get out of the warm bed to go to church. *If we could just go in our long warm pajamas,* she thought as she stood in her closet looking for a warm outfit to wear for the morning service. Yes, Joyce was ready for the spring.

Finally, April rolled around. People had begun to shed their heavy clothing and plant flowers and bushes in their yards. Joyce found herself wanting to be outdoors more.

"Mark, Michael, do you want to ride bikes to the park?" Joyce asked.

"Sure, I'll get my shoes and helmet," replied Mark. Michael decided he would ride his skateboard, and off they went. The two boys never had to be asked twice.

"Hey, Mom, want to learn to ride my board?" Michael asked.

"Sure, Michael, just take it easy on me," Joyce sort of teased. After a few times of the board taking off under her feet, she finally got the hang of it.

"Hey, this is really fun. One time Diane tried to teach me how to ride one of these things; it wasn't successful." Joyce laughed at the memory.

"Maybe she's not as good of a teacher as I am," Michael said, giggling as he watched his mother try to keep her balance.

Michael and Mark were more than ready to be outdoors on Saturdays these days. Joyce had to remind them a few times the rules for going out to have fun.

"If you boys want me to take you to the park, you had better get your chores done. I will not be reminding you again."

"Samantha what are your plans today." Joyce asked the following Saturday morning.

"Believe it or not, Mom, today I am a free woman!" Samantha said with such happiness in her voice. "No homework, I'm not scheduled to work today, nothing," She laughed.

"So what are you going to do today?" Joyce asked again.

"Well, I think I might call Shelly and talk to her; maybe she can come over and just hang out." Shelly was Samantha's best friend from school.

Joyce planned to work in the yard; she had plants that needed planting, and weeds that needed pulling. Joyce could have used Samantha's help, but knew how she felt about being around dirt. It usually turned into a very horrible time. Instead, she told Samantha she expected her to make lunch, and Samantha was happy with that decision.

Joyce took the boys to the park to ride bikes and such, Samantha called Shelly and the two of them watched movies, talked and ate snacks in the living room.

"Sam, did you know that Ted and Lacey were dating?" Shelly was referring to two of their classmates.

"No, I didn't. When did all this happen?"

"A few weeks ago. Haven't you noticed how much he hangs out at her locker?"

"No, I guess I haven't." They two girls talked of different couples in their class. Seemed like Samantha and Shelly didn't ever talk too long before the conversation turned to boys.

"Tell me, Sam, who do you think is the cutest guy at school?"

"Aah, I don't know."

"Oh come on, there has to be somebody, tell me, who?"

"Okay, okay, Andy Mason."

"Andy Mason? Isn't he a senior?"

"Yes, I followed him to class one day just to watch him walk. He has the cutest walk." Samantha said with a smile on her face, and blushing just a little.

"Samantha! I didn't know this about you." Again the giggling was in full mode.

"Hey, is he in your sister's senior class?"

"Yes, he is," Samantha replied. Shelly then asked why Elise didn't try to go out with him. Sam reminded her it was the same reason they didn't find the boys in their class good date material.

"Oh yeah," Shelly replied with a dumbstruck look.

"Hi, girls, watch ya doing?" Joyce asked as she came in and saw the two of them on the living room floor.

"Hi, Mrs. McIntosh."

"Hi, Shelly, how are you?"

"I'm fine; you look a little wind blown, Mrs. McIntosh."

"Yes, I guess I do, I have been outside with the boys. Well, I am off to a hot bath, so you two can resume your talk about boys."

"Mom! What makes you think we're talking about boys?" Samantha asked with a bit of embarrassment.

"Because believe it or not, I was once your age, and that is exactly what Diane and I used to do." Shelly and Samantha just looked at each other with their mouths hanging open.

CHAPTER SEVEN

One Tuesday morning, Joyce had to take her Jeep in to have the oil changed; there was a shop that Mac had recommended to her that was just up the street from her office. Mac worked with Joyce, only he worked in the dock area; they talked quite often and had become good friends.

Mac gave her advice about her Jeep, things like where to get her oil changed, best place in town to buy gas and tires, just little tidbits of information that would save her some money. Joyce's Jeep was getting some age on it, but purchasing a new vehicle was not in Joyce's budget at all.

This is great, I can drop it off in the morning and roller blade to the office, after all it's only two blocks away. I'll pick it up on my lunch break and hope I have time to actually eat, Joyce thought to herself as she planned the day the night before.

"Good morning, Leslie," Joyce spoke as she went rolling by Leslie's desk about thirty minutes early for work.

"Good morning, Joyce. I see you found a more economical way to work," the receptionist joked. Joyce agreed as she passed by.

Sean and Rick were in one of the offices when they noticed Joyce rolling by the open doorway.

"Sean, did I just see Joyce roll by in the hallway?" Rick asked.

"Yes, I believe it was. I'm sure there is a good explanation for why she is rolling into the office this morning." They both just chuckled. "Let's go find out what it is," Sean said as he got up and went toward the door, Rick following closely behind.

"How did the oil change go, Joyce?" Mac stuck his head in Joyce's office to ask if she had her Jeep worked on yet. She told him it should be up on the rack as they spoke.

"How did you get to work?"

Joyce picked up the roller blades that lay in the floor under her desk and wiggled them in the air at him. Mac couldn't believe what he was seeing.

"Joyce, honey, I would have given you a ride. You really didn't have to do that." Mac said with shock in his voice and on his face.

"Oh, Mac, I roller blade a lot with my kids, I didn't even think about it. It's fun and good exercise," Joyce replied, "Maybe you ought to try it sometime," She said jokingly.

"No thank you. I like my body in the one big piece it's in." Mac replied, waving his arm to her as he went on his way back to his work area.

Later that day, Joyce noticed Don's desk was covered in papers and folders. She asked him how he had gotten so behind. Don, looking at the pile, really didn't know.

"I may have to hand some of it over to Sean, after all, what are brothers for?" Don said teasingly as he was searching for a certain file.

Joyce offered to help Don and he was happy for the offer. He had called Joyce into his office to clear his calendar for the next two days so he could get all the paperwork cleared away and to send her on an errand.

Joyce grabbed a hand full of files to take to her office; she told Don she would bring them back when she had them finished.

"Thanks Joyce, but I have an errand I need you to run, and since it is so late in the day, afterward you can just go on home."

"Alright, what is it?" She asked.

"I need you to take these papers to the ranch, and give them to my father, he is expecting them today. Then I need you to go to Bill Sutton's; his place is about ten miles past our ranch. I have a few small supplies that I need to have delivered to him. I'll write out the directions just in case you need them."

"Alright, I'll clear my desk and then head on out."

"Thank you, Joyce, you don't know what a help that is for me today."

As Joyce was clearing her desk, she called Leslie and asked her to call the children and let them know where she would be. She reminded the receptionist she had her cell phone and could be reached on it. Leslie did as Joyce asked, and confirmed that she would not expect to see her back in the office that day.

"I'll see you tomorrow." And within minutes Joyce was out the door and headed to the Southern Star Ranch.

⁂

Joyce greeted Richard as she stepped out of her Jeep.

"Hi, Joyce. What brings you out here?" Richard spoke as he was dismounting from his horse. He was all dusty and dirty, but loved every minute of it. He wore his brown cowboy hat with the black band, blue jeans, a red button up shirt, and, of course, cowboy boots. His horse was a beautiful stallion, reddish brown with a light blonde mane. Richard had named this beautiful animal Rusty.

"What a beautiful horse." Joyce said as she rubbed Rusty's soft nose and face. The horse seemed to enjoy the attention. "Hey, is your father here?"

"Yeah, he's in the stables. You want me to get him for you?"

"Oh no, that's alright. I know the way, thank you anyway." Joyce said as she waved her arm toward him.

"Brandon! Brandon! Are you in here?" Joyce called out.

"Over here! Joyce, what a lovely surprise."

"Hi. Don wanted me to give these papers to you. He said you needed them today."

"Yes." Brandon said as he briefly glanced over the papers Joyce handed to him. "Can you stay awhile?" Brandon asked.

Joyce sadly declined, and told him she still had another stop to make. As the words came out of her mouth, her eyes got big, she realized she didn't get the directions to Bill Sutton's.

"Oh no, Don forgot to give me the directions to Bill's place. Brandon, can you tell me how to get to Bill Sutton's?"

"I can do better than that. I'll take you."

"No, no, Brandon, that won't be necessary, I'm sure I can find it." Joyce really didn't want Brandon to stop what he was doing to take her to Mr. Sutton's. The thought embarrassed her a little; she didn't want him to think she couldn't find her way.

Brandon had been working on a bridle for Bill and had just finished as Joyce walked in. He held up the item and showed Joyce as if to get her approval.

Bill had told Brandon he needed the bridle as soon as he finished the repairs, Brandon had planned on taking it to him the next day, but since Joyce was there and going that way, he jumped at the chance to go with her.

"Give me about ten minutes to clean up a little, and we'll go in my truck."

"Alright." She replied as they were walking toward the house. "Oh my!" Joyce said, looking up toward the sky. "Would you look at those black clouds, we'd better hurry if we want to beat that rain."

"Yeah, you're right. I'll hustle up."

Brandon ran into the house and was ready to go in ten minutes, just as he had said. The two of them headed out to the Sutton ranch as it started to rain.

As they were headed to their destination, Brandon knew this was a great opportunity to talk to Joyce about something that had been on his mind for a few weeks.

"Joyce, I wanted to ask you something," Brandon spoke. "Would your two boys like to earn a little money working Saturdays and during the summer?"

"Doing what?" Joyce asked.

"Working on the ranch," he replied. "I have some things I need a little help on if they're interested and it's alright with you," Brandon let the sentence hang.

"I'll mention it to them and let you know."

"Great," Brandon said with a smile as he looked briefly at her.

Chapter seven / 95

It wasn't so much that Brandon needed help on the ranch as it was the thought of seeing Joyce. He knew she would be the one to bring them by and pick them up. He was happy about his little plan; so far it seemed to be working.

As Brandon tried to get them to the Sutton ranch as soon as possible, he noticed the sky and how dark it looked the further they went. The news had mentioned some heavy rain, but that was all he could remember.

"Joyce, that sky looks a little angry up ahead."

"Yes, it does," Joyce replied with a little concern on her face.

Even though the sky looked angry and dark, the trees were so colorful against the darkness. Joyce thought it to be beautiful. *Only You, God, could create such beauty.* Joyce kept her thoughts to herself as they rode on.

"I heard we were to get some rain, but nothing major," she now spoke.

"Well, I'm sure it will be fine, after all, it's just rain."

Brandon and Joyce got to the Sutton ranch fine, but Bill Sutton was not there. Joyce left the supplies with his housekeeper, Ms. Price. Ms. Price instructed Brandon to take the bridle to the stables; since Brandon and Bill had known each other for years, she felt it was safe for him to do so.

Once in the stable, Joyce couldn't help but admire the horses. Mr. Sutton owned several beautiful studs, mares and fillies.

"Sutton sure keeps a nice stable, doesn't he?" said Joyce.

"Yes he does."

Before the two of them headed to the doorway of the stables, a huge clap of thunder sounded, this upset a few of the horses, so Brandon was trying to settle them down before they left. Suddenly, rain came pouring down. Joyce looked out the doorway and could hardly see anything but the rain. The truck was parked just a few feet from the door, but she could barely see it.

"I think we're going to have to stay put for a little while. Look how hard that rain is falling." Joyce said.

"Wow! You're right, but it probably won't last long." Brandon replied.

Joyce made a comment about being glad she didn't have to go back to the office in such weather, and Brandon agreed with the statement. She explained to Brandon that Don had given her the rest of the afternoon off, since he had her driving out so far on errands. Joyce looked at her watch and figured the rain should have let up by now. She wondered how the horses were doing, and asked Brandon about them.

"They seem to be fine; Sutton has a mare that is going to foal any day now. I hope all this excitement doesn't cause things to speed up," Brandon said in a concerned voice.

"Yeah, that's the last thing we need right now," Joyce replied. "I don't know nothin' bout birthin' no horsies," she said in such a silly way that Brandon just broke out in a belly laugh.

"Really there isn't anything to worry about." He said after he got his laughter under control. "Horses have their colts in barns, fields... anywhere they are at the time. They really don't need anyone to help them, unless there's a problem."

This bit of information seemed to ease Joyce's concern about the horse, but she still kept an eye on the rain. Being stranded in a stable was not her idea of the afternoon off.

"Hey, looks like the rain is slacking off; let's make a run for the truck," Joyce said eagerly.

As the two of them got to the doorway of the stables, Brandon noticed there was a lot of running water between them and the truck. He looked at Joyce and with one swift and smooth motion, he scooped her up into his arms and carried her to the truck. Joyce let out a small scream as he suddenly picked her up, wondering what in the world this man was doing and why was he doing it. As they reached the truck, Joyce opened the driver's side, scooted over and looked at Brandon with a very shocked look on her face.

"Why did you do that?" Joyce asked with eyes as big as saucers.

"Because I didn't want you to have to run though the water and mud. You could have slipped," Brandon answered sincerely.

"Thank you, but I think I could have managed." She answered breathlessly.

"No problem," Brandon said with a bit of pride in his voice.

"I really didn't mind at all." *Not at all.* This comment he kept to himself.

―――

As Brandon started the truck and tried to proceed, the rain began again. It wasn't as hard this time, but still pretty steady. They began to skid and a horrible sound came from beneath the truck. They were no longer moving, and they were no longer sitting level either.

"Are you alright?" Brandon asked Joyce.

"Yes, I'm fine, but what was that noise?"

"I'm not sure, but I need to find out," Brandon replied.

Joyce sat and watched with her mouth hanging open, as Brandon took off his jacket and shirt, leaving only his undershirt.

"What are you doing?" Joyce asked.

"I'm taking off my shirt, so when I get back in the truck I will have something dry to put on. I hope that doesn't offend you, but I don't carry extra shirts with me in my truck."

"Oh, of course, how silly of me."

When Brandon got out of the truck, he noticed the small bridge they were about to cross over was half gone, not only that, but they were safely hung up in a huge hole where the road had rutted out with all the fast rain. As he looked under the truck, he found yet another problem.

Brandon got back in the truck, took off his wet t-shirt and put his other shirt and jacket on, Joyce making sure she looked away as he did so. He asked Joyce if she wanted the good news or the bad news first. She looked at him with confusion.

"The good news is we are in a hole that has been rutted out by the heavy rains."

"And the bad news?" she asked fearfully.

"The bad news is the axle is broken. We are stuck here until someone comes and gets us."

Brandon, suddenly remembering he had his cell phone, pulled it out of the glove box and proceeded to call the ranch for help. The whole time he was thinking that he would not mind being stranded with Joyce McIntosh; the more he thought about it, the more he liked the idea.

"Well, now here is another problem," Brandon spoke with a hint of laughter in his voice. "I'm not getting any signal on my phone."

Joyce reached into her purse and pulled out her cell phone, thinking maybe hers would work. There was no signal on either of their phones. Joyce asked out loud; what was the use of having them if they didn't work in emergencies?

Brandon knew they could not stay there in the truck with it sitting in an unleveled position. He told Joyce they would have to make a run for the barn that was about fifty yards from where they sat.

"I'm afraid I will not be carrying you this time, Joyce." Brandon said jokingly.

"Why can't we just stay here? Why do we have to run to the barn?"

"The ground may give way as the rain continues; this hole is the only thing keeping us from passing over what was the bridge," Brandon explained. "Besides, we don't know how long we will have to wait for help; we will be more comfortable in the barn."

"Well, no time like the present. Let's do it," she replied.

"That's what I like, a woman with spunk," Brandon said teasingly.

As they ran, just like at the ballgame, Joyce began laughing almost uncontrollably.

"What is so funny?" He asked her with a hint of laughter himself when they made it to the barn.

"Nothing. I just can't keep from laughing when I run fast like that, especially in the rain. It's really embarrassing. Honestly, I really am a normal person," she said as she was standing inside the barn dripping wet and getting herself under more control.

"If you say so," he now joked back.

Once inside the barn Joyce tried again to use her cell phone, but it was no use, still no signal.

"My kids!" Joyce said out loud. "They will be worried out of their minds if I'm not home soon." She remembered the boys were going to a friend's house after school. Elise and Samantha would be home though, and she knew they were sure to worry, she thought as she found a nail to hang her wet jacket on.

"Come here, Joyce." Brandon said seriously, as he took Joyce's hand. She did as he asked.

It was then that Brandon took it upon himself to pray out loud for Joyce's kids. He prayed for their safety and for the children not to worry about their mother. He also prayed for his and Joyce's quick return to their families.

"I hope you weren't offended that I did that," he said.

"No, not at all, thank you, Brandon," Joyce said tearfully. It was a few seconds afterwards before Brandon let go of her hand.

Brandon had taken the two flashlights he had in his truck, along with his pistol, before they made their run for the barn. He carried a small handgun in his truck because he was in the pastures a lot; he never wanted to be at the mercy of a wild animal. Joyce saw the items he had when he laid them close to her drying jacket.

"Aah, Brandon, why do you have a gun?" Joyce asked with shock and eyes that matched.

"It's for our safety, Joyce." He kindly assured her, as he put his hands on both of her arms; he rubbed them gently and spoke to her.

"We don't want to have any surprises with any wild animals." Joyce calmed down at his touch and then felt silly for her fears.

"I keep it in my truck since I am out in the pastures a lot. I don't shoot animals for the fun of it, but I have had to protect myself a time or two.

Brandon and Joyce sat on the hay and talked about many things. They talked about the storm, their children and themselves. Joyce begin to feel more comfortable with Brandon than she ever thought possible. They continued to talk about their jobs, hers at the office and his on the ranch. Joyce found his work on the ranch to be most interesting. She never thought it took as much work to run a ranch as she had now found out. *No wonder there are so many ranch hands,* she thought to herself.

"Brandon, how did your wife die?" Brandon paused for a few seconds before answering. "I'm sorry, I was out of line just then ... really, I'm sorry."

"No, no it's okay. I don't mind," Brandon told her.

Brandon got a little comfortable as he thought about the accident Stacey was in all those years ago. "She was hit head on; the other vehicle was going way too fast. She died almost instantly." He suddenly remembered it had been over ten years.

"Oh, Brandon, I'm so sorry, that must have been a horrible time for you and the boys. I'm sorry I mentioned it," Joyce said.

"How about your husband? I understand correctly that you are a widow?"

"Yes, Paul had a major heart attack; not too long ago, but at times it seems like years and years have passed."

"I know what you mean."

As they continued to talk and get to know one another, It seemed as if they had been in the barn just a short time, when actually it had been over three hours. It had gotten dark outside, and Brandon turned on the two flashlights he brought from the truck.

"Why do you have two flash lights?" Joyce asked. "Most people have none or just one, but not two."

Brandon explained two days earlier, he went in the hardware store and noticed they were having a sale on flashlights, so he bought one. He never remembered to take the old one out of the glove box.

"Good thing, we may need them both." Joyce replied.

Brandon and Joyce seemed to not run out of things to say to one another. They both lay back on the hay, talking with plenty space between them.

Brandon arose off the hay quickly. "I thought I heard something outside, but I don't see anything, it may have been an animal looking for shelter, sort of like us." He explained with a hint of laughter.

It wasn't long after they heard the noise again that Brandon looked out and was pleasantly surprised at the sight he saw. Richard and one of Brandon's ranch hands, Luke, had come looking for them. Don had gotten a call from Elise; she was worried. When Don called Richard, he told him he would head out to find them. They found their truck and a dim light shining in the barn.

Richard laughed at the thought of them being stranded in the barn, but he took pity on Joyce's worried face.

"You daughter called Don about an hour ago. I told him I thought I knew where you two were headed and that I would look for you. I think we had better get you home and put her mind to rest."

"Thank you Richard, and you too Luke."

"Yeah thanks, fellas," Brandon said as he shook Luke's hand.

Brandon knew they would have to leave the truck until morning. Richard had parked his Bronco on the other side of the broken bridge; he and Brandon helped Joyce across to safety. Joyce was so relieved when help came; she knew it wouldn't be long until they both were safely in their own homes safe, warm, and with a hot meal, explaining everything to their families.

Joyce had never been stranded like that before in her life. She had heard of people in those types of situations, where it took days and days to be found. Of course, she knew it wouldn't take that long to get back home, but the whole incident was unnerving.

It had been a month since Brandon had been stranded in the rain with Joyce. No matter how hard he tried, he could not get that woman out of his mind. He tried throwing himself into his work, but some days he was just useless. A few of the ranch hands noticed it as well. On one occasion, Brandon left the gate to one of the pastures open; it was amazing the cattle didn't decide to walk out. His sons kept asking him if there was something wrong. When he would retire at night, he would see her face clearly in his mind ... the two of them talking in the barn in the soft glow of the flashlights.

"Brandon, old buddy, you've got it bad," he said out loud to himself as he laid in bed.

Joyce was having some of the same troubles as Brandon. She kept thinking about him at the strangest times. Later she realized it was strange for her to be thinking of him at any time. She knew just who to talk to about this.

"Hi, Diane."

"Hey, Joyce, what's up?"

"Oh ...nothing, Diane, can we meet somewhere for lunch?"

The two women met at the O.K. Café. It wasn't far for either one of them; Joyce decided to get her friends help in figuring out what was wrong with her.

Joyce didn't get anything accomplished at the office that morning. She seemed to have trouble keeping her mind on track. She had been clumsy all morning. First, she bumped her knee on her filing cabinet, spilled her coffee on her desk, and kept losing her pen. After thinking about it, she didn't know if it would be safe to go out to lunch or not.

For the past few weeks when Brandon would visit the office, Joyce found herself looking in his direction, there were even some days she would hope he would drop in. Brandon usually didn't come to the office too often, but he had been coming in more lately. Joyce had felt silly for these feelings, and had had enough of the sleepless nights and the useless workdays. She was going to talk with Diane and get a grip on the situation.

"Okay, girl, shoot, let's have it," were Diane's opening remarks to her friend. She knew what had happened several weeks ago during the big storm. She figured it took that storm to open Joyce's eyes to this very handsome, kind man, and Joyce probably didn't know what to do with her feelings about it.

"Diane, I'm a mess. I can't eat, I can't sleep, and all I do is think about Brandon. I feel like some schoolgirl; the truth is, I can't get this man off my mind. I can't wait for the next time I see him. It has to stop; I can't take it any longer," she explained with a bit of a rise in her tone. Their conversation was interrupted by the waitress who took their orders.

"I'll have the turkey club without fries and a sweet tea, please," Joyce said much calmer now.

"I'll have the same, only with fries." The waitress turned and left to get their orders.

"Diane, I am in my forties; I have five children, I was married for over twenty years. I can't be feeling like this at this time in my life."

"Why not? Is there an age limit for falling in love with someone?" Diane asked.

"Falling in love!" Joyce responded with much shock. "Who said I was in love?" Joyce spoke in a harsh whisper, leaning across the table at Diane.

"Okay, so you're not in love. Still I don't see a problem here, Joyce."

Diane then proceeded to ask Joyce question after question, she wanted to know Joyce's true feelings for Brandon, and in the process let Joyce learn of them as well.

"Has he asked you out on a date?" Diane asked.

"No."

"What about the kids?" Diane continued.

"What about them?" Joyce asked.

"Do they like him?"

"Yea ...so what's your point?"

"Listen, Joyce, I know how things were with you and Paul, and you may be afraid. But, honey, lead with your heart, not your head."

"But I loved Paul, Diane. It's been so long, I still miss him." Joyce said playing with her napkin.

"I'm sure you do. Look, Joyce, I know you loved Paul. I also believe he loved you; he just had a very different way of showing it. And that is what may have you afraid."

Diane gently told Joyce this could be the Lord giving her a second chance at love, someone special to spend her life with. She advised her to pray about it. At that moment the waitress came to their table with their food.

"Of course, you must keep me up on *every* detail," Diane told her friend jokingly. The two women giggled over the banter.

CHAPTER EIGHT

Brandon had told himself he was going to do it. He was going to ask Joyce to dinner. Today he was going straight to her office, sit down and ask her out. No more thinking about it or wondering how she would respond. His little pep talk to himself had given him enough courage to drive into town and to her office.

Mac sought Joyce out and invited her out to lunch. It wasn't a date or anything; it was just two friends going out to eat together. Mac had a coupon for a buy one get one free from Burger Palace. Two weeks prior, Joyce had helped Mac with a project he was working on, he knew he would have never finished if she hadn't helped him. Therefore, this was really a small token of his appreciation.

Mac and Joyce talked and joked with each other from time to time. When they were passing each others way, they would stop and chat for a bit. It was if they had known each other forever.

"Just two pals going out to eat?" he said with a big grin.

"Sure, Mac, I'd love to."

As Mac and Joyce were getting into Mac's car, Brandon was just pulling into the parking lot.

"Leslie did I just see Joyce leave?"

"Yes, Mr. Miller, you did."

"Was someone with her?"

"Yes sir, Mac. Did you need either one of them for something?"

"Do you know when they will return?"

"No sir," the receptionist replied. "They were headed out to lunch."

"Oh, I see. Aah no, I didn't need anything; I'll just stop in and talk to Don and Sean. Thank you Leslie."

"You're welcome, Mr. Miller."

She can't go out with Mac; she can't go out with anyone but me, Brandon thought to himself. *Are she and Mac seeing each other? This just can't be.* Brandon was so deep in his thoughts that he walked right past Don and didn't even notice him.

"Dad!"

"Oh, Don, I was just coming to see you."

"Dad, you just passed me and my office."

"Oh, so I did, I have things on my mind today I guess."

The two men went in Don's office. Brandon really didn't have anything to discuss with his son, he told Don he was hoping to meet with a friend for lunch, but it didn't work out. The two talked a little, before Brandon got up to go say hello to Sean.

"Is it me you wanted to say hello to Dad, or is it that pretty little assistant of mine?" Don teased his father.

"Is it that noticeable, Son?" Brandon looked so vulnerable at that moment. Don felt bad for teasing with him.

Don knew that his father enjoyed Joyce's company, what he didn't know was how deep his feelings were for her. Brandon hadn't meant to tell his sons of his want to see Joyce on a more serious and personal basis, but it all came flowing out, and afterwards he felt much better.

Don knew his father would never do anything like this without talking to him and his brothers first, he just imagined them all discussing it together.

"Dad, I think that's wonderful." Don said with a smile on his face. "If you and Joyce enjoy each other's company, then your spending time together is okay with me. After all, she is a very lovely person; I think you two would be good for each other. Go for it, Dad," Don said encouragingly.

Brandon started to get up from his chair to leave, however, he sat back down when Don began to tell him how Sean and Richard had

Chapter eight / 107

noticed his infatuation with Joyce. Brandon rubbed his hands down his face in frustration. "I gotta go, I'll talk to you later Son."

"Bye, Dad."

When Joyce and Mac came through the front door from lunch, she stopped at Leslie's desk to pick up any messages that she may have had. "See ya later, Joyce." Mac said, waving an arm high in the air as he continued to walk back to the loading dock. Joyce waved in return.

"No, no messages. Oh, Mr. Miller came by and I think he just wanted to say hi."

"Which Mr. Miller? Brandon?"

"Yes," Leslie answered.

Hmm, I wonder what he wanted, Joyce thought as she walked back to her office.

Joyce picked up the phone on her desk and called the ranch. She didn't normally do that, but she couldn't help wonder what Brandon wanted to see her about.

"Hello, Southern Star Ranch."

"Hi, Lorna, this is Joyce. How are you?"

"I'm fine, thank you. What can I help you with, Joyce?"

"Lorna, is Brandon there by chance?"

"No, he went into town today and I don't know when he planned on returning. Would you like to leave a message?"

"Aah, no thanks, I'll just catch up with him later. Thank you, Lorna."

"Bye, Joyce."

"Bye."

"Oh well, so much for that." Joyce said out loud in her empty office. The phone rang almost as soon as she hung it up. *Maybe that's him now*, Joyce thought to herself.

It was Sean; he was in desperate need of Joyce's help. He had misplaced an important address and phone number and asked if she could come into his office and help him locate it. Joyce went immediately and stood in shock at the condition of Sean's office. Folders and papers were everywhere a person looked. You could not see the top of his desk or any other piece of furniture.

Joyce and Sean searched his office, but the information needed was just nowhere to be found.

"Have you looked in your brief case, Sean?"

"Three times," he replied.

"Well, the only thing I know to do now is to go back in my office and see if I can pull it up on the computer."

"Thank you, Joyce, I really mean it."

"I know you do, Sean. It will only cost you a cold Dr. Pepper." Sean smiled as Joyce teased him on her way out the door.

Joyce, if you can find that number, I'll give you a lifetime of Dr. Pepper, he thought to himself as he continued to search his office for the missing information.

In less than fifteen minutes, Joyce handed Sean the information he desperately needed. She stood looking around at the mess his office was in.

"Oh, Joyce, you are a lifesaver," he replied with a big smile.

"Yeah, yeah, make sure you put it in your Rolodex this time. And, Sean, as far as this messy office goes, you're on your own."

Joyce exited Sean's office and went to talk with Leslie for a moment. When she returned to her office, she found a cold Dr. Pepper sitting on her desk with a smiley face drawn on a piece of paper beside it. Joyce just smiled as she opened it and took a big drink of the cold liquid.

Later that evening, she made her way home and thought about Brandon most of the way. Again, she wondered what he wanted. *Must not have been too important since he didn't leave a message and he didn't call*, she continued thinking. Joyce pushed the thought from her mind as she pulled into the driveway and headed into the house to now focus on her family.

It was time for supper, Joyce was ready to sit and enjoy a quiet evening at home.

"Okay, boys, wash your hands and set the table. Supper is almost ready. How was school today, Samantha?"

"Fine, nothing new; same old thing... test, homework, homework, test. Oh Mom, there's a movie coming on in an hour that I want to watch, want to watch it with me?"

"What about all that homework and test?"

"Well, I finished my homework already, and I don't have a test until Friday."

Samantha was doing well in school, and seemed to be getting her mouth under more control these days. Mark and Michael, on the other hand, were just busy little boys whom Joyce had to keep a watch on to make sure they were not being destructive.

One Saturday afternoon, the two boys were out in the garage and were very quiet. Joyce wondered where they were and what they were doing. When she opened the garage door she found the two of them trying to put the lawn mower back together. When she questioned them, they looked up at her and said they wanted to see if they could take it apart and put it back together. Neither child was happy about the punishment they received; two weeks of extra chores. They did get the lawn mower back to its original condition, but not without some help from Ron.

Ron had been very faithful in helping Joyce around the house after Paul's death. There were many times she didn't know what she would have done without him. Helping get the lawn mower back in working order was just one of those times. He had proven to be a good friend she could always rely on.

Elise asked Samantha if she wanted to go to the mall with her. Samantha told her about her plans to meet Shelly and some other friends and invited Elise to join them. Elise did want to go, but wasn't sure she wanted to hang out with a bunch of her sister's classmates. Elise gave in and went, but shopped while Samantha socialized.

While Samantha and her friends were at the mall, a very nice looking boy came over to where she and Shelly were standing.

"Hey, Shelly, Sam, what ya doin'?" he asked the girls. They both looked at him with much surprise.

"Andy Mason, hi, what brings you to the mall?" Shelly asked.

"Oh, me and a couple of my friends are here to see a movie, it starts in about twenty minutes, want to join us?"

"Aah what do you say, Sam, want to see a movie?" Oh please say yes, Sam, she mouthed to her silently.

Samantha wanted to go, but knew she couldn't just go and not let Elise know where she was. Andy offered to let her use his phone to call Elise to let her know. Samantha called and explained the situation to her sister; Elise still had more shopping to do so she figured it would be alright.

"Okay, she knows where I'll be, so let's go," Samantha answered.

"Great," Andy said as he was looking at Samantha.

As they got inside the theater and looked for seats, Samantha was again surprised by the next turn of events.

"Here, Sam, sit by me," Andy offered as he pulled out one of the seats.

"Alright," that was about all Samantha could get out. Shelly sat on the other side of her while Andy was on her right; Andy's friends were on the other side of him.

The talk between Andy and Samantha was a little awkward, mostly small talk, but neither seemed to notice. The two seemed to run out of things to say, and Samantha was glad to be rescued by the movie coming on.

"This movie may be a little scary," Andy said as the movie came on. "You can hold onto my arm if you need to."

"I usually handle these things pretty well, but thanks for the warning and the offer."

Samantha was so cool and smooth with Andy; she never let him see how nervous she was on the inside. The movie was a scary one, but Samantha never screamed, like a lot of the audience had done, nor did she grab Andy's arm. They did, however, share some popcorn.

Shelly on the other hand was down in her seat at the scary parts, asking Samantha what was happening.

"Shell, if you would sit up and watch, you would know," She whispered to her friend.

After the movie, Samantha thanked Andy for the invitation. She really did enjoy it, but she would have been more relaxed if it were just her and Shelly. Before Samantha and Andy parted, he asked if he could call her sometime, this was another surprise for Samantha. She told him yes, and wrote her number on the palm of his hand.

"Hey, Sam, there's Elise," Shelly told her.

"Oh yeah, I gotta go, thanks again, Andy."

"Bye, Sam."

Shelly and Samantha left Andy and his friends and met up with Elise, who told her it was time they went home. Samantha could hardly wait to get in the car and tell her sister all about being at the movie with Andy.

"Oh, Elise, you will never believe this one!" Samantha said with such a giggle and excitement in her voice, she could barely speak. "Andy Mason, Elise, I sat with Andy Mason at the movie." Elise knew she and Shelly were going in the movie with him and a few others they knew from school.

"Were you alone with him?"

"No, Shelly was on the other side of me. He didn't try anything or nothing like that. He asked if he could call me, I gave him my phone number."

"Sam, what will mom say about a boy two years older calling you?"

"I don't know, but I hope she says yes!" She said with a squeal of excitement.

Here we go again. My little sister gets asked out, and by an older guy, Elise thought as they were riding home.

Samantha called Shelly as soon as she got inside. Shelly wanted to know what it was like to sit by Andy Mason. Samantha was still so excited from the evening, she could hardly tell her. Shelly squealed herself when Samantha told her that Andy said she could grab his arm during the scary parts of the movie, if she needed to.

"Did you? Did you grab his arm, Sam?" Shelly eagerly wanted to know.

"No, I kept my cool, though I almost grabbed yours once or twice."

"So, what's your plan, Sam?" Shelly wanted to know.

"I will just go along as if nothing happened and see what his next move is."

"Wow, when did you get so smart about guys?"

"I don't know, I think I read that in a book once."

Shelly was happy for her friend, and when the two hung up the phone, Shelly only wished she could find someone too.

Michael and Mark arrived at the Southern Star ranch on Saturday morning at eight o'clock sharp as instructed.

"Good morning, boys." Brandon said as he looked at both of them.

"What time should I pick them up, Brandon?" Joyce said talking out the window of her Jeep.

"Around four will be fine," he answered, looking at her face. He was trying not to stare, but he couldn't seem to help himself.

"All right, boys, mind your manners and do as Mr. Miller tells you," Joyce instructed her sons firmly.

"We will, Mom, bye," they replied in unison.

Brandon was very excited about the boys starting at the ranch, but he was more excited about seeing Joyce. He couldn't help but watch her; she was so lovely.

"The first thing we are going to do today is get you familiar with the ranch," Brandon instructed his two new employees. He introduced them to the other ranch hands so that they would at least know their faces. He began his tour of the grounds at the ranch house, since that is where they would be dropped off and picked up each day, not to mention where they would eat their lunch.

Brandon was firm but kind when speaking to them about serious matters such as doing things safely, and asking for help when they needed it. He talked seriously to them about the importance of asking for help and doing the job right, versus not asking and doing it wrong or getting hurt.

"Yes, sir," the twins answered in unison.

As the two boys walked toward one of the barns and Brandon followed not too far behind, he realized a small problem. *I have no idea how I am going to tell the two of them apart,* he thought to himself, *they look exactly alike. Maybe as I get to know them I'll be able to know which one is which, but until then...* He then snapped his fingers and told the boys to wait there and he would be back in a moment. Brandon had an idea of how to solve this little dilemma.

"Boys, I'm sure you hear this a lot, I can't tell you two apart. If I am going to work with you two, I need to know who is who. So, Mark, you put this blue handkerchief somewhere on you, and, Michael, you put on this red one. Now, that way I can tell you two apart." Brandon was so proud of his little fix on this.

Brandon continued to show the boys every inch of the ranch. He showed them the stables and explained the different horses he had. Brandon owned several Thoroughbreds, a few Arabian horses, and a few Morgans.

"Will we get to ride a horse like Luke does?" Mark asked.

"Maybe, but not right now," replied Brandon. "Now boys, you must remember when you are in the stables you cannot be rowdy or it will upset the horses. Do you understand?"

"Yes, sir," they both replied looking up at the big man. Brandon told the boys other safety issues they must remember while around the horses and on the ranch; the boys seemed to take it all in.

It was noon and Lorna had made a fine lunch. Brandon had instructed her to make something a little special for the boys so she made cheeseburgers with fries and ice cream for dessert. The boys seemed to enjoy their lunch, as did the rest of the ranch hands.

For their first day of work, Brandon had Mark and Michael helping Luke feed the horses, and they both seemed to really enjoy this. Later that day, they worked alongside Richard getting some new supplies put in their rightful places. Both boys worked hard, you could tell by how much dirt was on their clothes and hands. It was hard for them to believe four o'clock had come so quickly.

"How did they do?" Joyce asked as she got out of her Jeep, and walked to the edge of the driveway to meet her boys and Brandon.

"They did great. I think you may have a couple of cowboys on your hands," Brandon told her.

"Good. Now Brandon, if you have any problem with them at all, you let me know."

"I don't think we'll have any problems, but yes, Joyce, I'll let you know. Besides, I had three of those myself at one time. I think I can still keep law and order around here," Brandon said as he smiled at the boys.

Brandon and Joyce talked a few minutes before she whisked the boys off for home. He had enjoyed being with Mark and Michael all day. It reminded him of his own sons when they were that age. For just a moment, Brandon missed those days with his boys.

All the way home and after Joyce and the twins got inside, Mark and Michael talked almost non-stop about what they had learned that day, especially about Luke, they seemed to be very enamored with this person. It was during all this talk that Joyce remembered meeting Luke at the Sutton ranch the night she and Brandon were stranded.

"You ought to see him, Mom, he can carry a calf all by himself, and he can pick up these big bales of hay. We'll be doing that in a little while won't we, Mom?" Mark asked with eyes as big as his dinner plate. Both boys talked on and on about Brandon, Luke, and the ranch.

"Oh, I'm sure it will be no time at all until you will be just like Luke," she replied with a smile to her sons.

"And Mr. Miller, Mom, he has these muscles, he can pick up more hay than Luke," Michael informed her.

"Oh, he can?" Joyce's thought of Brandon made her face flush a little.

Elise noticed her mother's face. "Mom, are you alright?" she asked.

"Yes, why did you ask?"

"Your face looked a little funny just now." Joyce felt a little uncomfortable being asked such a question when thinking of Brandon.

The boys continued their talk of the stables and horses. They told Joyce each type of horse Brandon owned. She was surprised they remembered so much in one day. She laughed a little when Mark told her they could not be rowdy around the horses. The thought of them being calm and quiet was a little humorous to her.

As the weeks went by, the boys continued to do very well. They were a big help in baling hay; of course, they could not throw the bales like Luke, Richard or Brandon did, but worked just as hard.

One afternoon, Joyce had gotten to the ranch early, and was watching the men from a distance. She saw her sons trying to imitate these men, working with their shirts off and moving the hay the best their child-size bodies would allow. Joyce felt proud of her sons, and for a moment she thought how Paul would be too. She couldn't help but smile as she watched them. She also understood now why Brandon seemed to be so well built. The boys were right, he did have muscles, Joyce couldn't help but notice as he was hoisting the bales of hay up and tossing them, it was if they weighed nothing at all. Joyce was glad she was alone when she saw him; she did enjoy what she saw.

The boys had learned to feed the horses, clean the stables, and even to ride and rope. Brandon was very proud of his little ranch hands. The boys were proud of themselves when payday came.

"Momma, Momma, we're gonna buy dinner tonight," Mark said proudly when she picked them up at the end of the day.

"You are?" She cheerfully replied.

"Yes, Michael and I got paid today, and we're treating everyone to a pizza."

Joyce couldn't help but smile at her sons. She agreed to have pizza for supper and let them pay for it. She was a little surprised when Michael invited Brandon, Luke and Richard to join them.

"Why, Mark, that is awfully nice of you. Are you sure your mother doesn't mind extra cowboys at the house?"

"She don't mind, do you Mom?"

"No, no Michael I don't mind at all. Please, Brandon, do join us," Joyce said as her eyes locked on Brandon's for a brief moment.

Brandon, still looking at Joyce, accepted the invitation for dinner. He looked at Mark and told him of Luke and Richard's plans to meet some friends in town for the evening.

"Well, we will just expect you then," Joyce replied.

At that moment, Brandon was very happy for the invitation, and could hardly wait himself.

"See you at supper, boys," he said waving his hand in the air, as they were getting in the Jeep.

"Bye, Mr. Miller."

———

Joyce made sure the house was in fine order; she was running around like a woman on a mission. She had never been a vain person, but she checked her hair three times before coming back downstairs when she heard the doorbell.

Samantha answered the door to find Brandon Miller on the other side.

"Hello, Mr. Miller, come in. Everyone is in the living room; we're waiting for the delivery guy to bring the pizza."

"Hi, everyone," Brandon said as he entered the living room.

"Since the boys were buying the pizza, I thought the least I could do was bring some ice cream."

"Did you hear that Mark? Ice cream!" Michael said.

"Thank you Brandon. That wasn't necessary, I don't want you to feel you have to come bearing gifts to be at my house," Joyce said kindly.

"No, I don't think that, I just wanted some ice cream," Brandon teased.

Mark and Michael had gotten to know Brandon pretty well and really liked being around him. They both thought there wasn't anything Brandon could not do.

"If Mark and I keep working on the ranch like you, will we grow to be as big as you?" Michael asked Brandon with big eyes.

Brandon just chuckled, "I don't know, Michael, you'll have to keep working at the ranch to find out," he said with humor in his voice. Joyce turned her head to keep from laughing.

After dinner, the boys went to the living room while Joyce and Samantha cleaned up. The phone rang just as they were getting started; it was for Samantha. Brandon gladly took her place in helping Joyce. They talked a little more about the boys until Joyce was at a loss for what to say. Suddenly she remembered the ice cream, and set the table for the dessert.

As the evening drew to a close, Joyce walked Brandon to his truck; they stood outside for a little while just talking.

"The boys sure do enjoy working with you and Luke." They both started to laugh. "I'm glad you came for supper tonight Brandon."

It made Brandon feel good inside to hear her say that. "Well, it was my pleasure. I can't say when I have enjoyed a pizza as much as I did tonight." The two adults just looked at each other as if they could not control their gazes.

The night air had a slight breeze, and it blew Joyce's hair just a little. Brandon had a slight smile on his face as he thought about reaching out to touch it. He wanted to not only touch her hair, but her face as well. Her skin looked to be soft and pretty. He was afraid that if he did so, she would think he was out of line. As they stood there, Brandon spoke to Joyce in a deep, soft voice.

"You are such a joy to be around. I have had such a wonderful evening, and I hope I'm not out of line here, but I would like for us to do this again soon." Their eyes were locked; Joyce almost couldn't find her voice.

"No, no Brandon you're not out of line," she said softly as she looked at him. "I enjoy your company as well."

The two adults stood outside in the night looking at one another, both spellbound, but neither one knew if they should proceed.

Brandon took a couple steps closer to Joyce, his hand touching her face; he bent his head down, and gently kissed her cheek. At that moment Joyce was at a loss, she really didn't know what to do or say.

"Good night, Joyce," Brandon said very low and close to her ear.
"Good night, Brandon," she replied softly.

As he pulled out of the driveway, she gave a small wave, and when he was out of sight, her hand went to the place where he kissed her while she slowly walked back inside the house.

"Mom, are you alright?" This question came again from Elise.

"Yes, Honey, I'm fine, thank you."

"You have that funny look on your face again."

"Well, I don't know what look that is, but I assure you I am fine." I don't think I will get any sleep tonight, but I am fine, she said in a low voice to herself.

Joyce felt like a teenager again, calling her best friend after a date.

"Hi, Diane, I hope you're not busy, because I have things to tell you!"

As always, Joyce told Diane all that had happened, watching the boys baling hay with the other men, seeing Brandon without his shirt, Joyce having to work hard to not think about that while Brandon was sitting at the table. This made Diane laugh out loud. She was happy for her friend, happy that she was starting to live again. When Joyce told her of his gentle kiss on her cheek, Diane was so thrilled she could hardly stand it. She told Joyce that listening to all of this was almost like reading a romance novel. It was after the two women were through discussing Joyce's wonderful evening that Diane told her about going to visit Mandy and Erin.

Her daughters were away at college; she and Ron hadn't seen them in a few months and missed them terribly. Ron was not looking forward to the drive, but wanted to see his girls more. Diane wished at times that she and Ron had more children, and told Joyce as much. Diane knew they would probably have all girls and that would just push Ron over that cliff he was on now. This caused both women to laugh out loud.

Before they hung up, Diane told Joyce to enjoy the chase with

Chapter eight

Brandon. Even if it turns out to be nothing, just enjoy it. Joyce just sighed and told her friend good night.

When Joyce hung up the phone, the conversation she just had with Diane reminded her of when they were kids, she truly enjoyed the feeling. She thought it was too bad adults forget and leave out so many fun things in their lives.

CHAPTER NINE

Sunday morning Joyce and the children overslept and missed Sunday School; they barely made it for the church service. Joyce sat with her children as normal, but kept noticing Jim Richey watching her. *Oh brother, not this again*, Joyce thought to herself.

"Good morning, everyone," Pastor Jones said to his congregation. "Today I am going to talk briefly about prayer. Of course, everyone here knows we Christians are to pray. But let's look at this in a different way, shall we. When you talk to another person, you are speaking directly to them, you are careful of what you are saying, and most times have a normal and intelligent conversation. It should be the same way when talking to the Lord. We should not get side-tracked, as we may do at times. How would you feel if someone was talking to you and, in the middle of a sentence, became side-tracked and totally forgot they were talking to you?"

Joyce herself became side-tracked because she felt someone staring at her. She missed half of the sermon, thinking about how silly, not to mention uncomfortable, it was for him to watch her all through the sermon. After all, what did he come to church for, to learn more about God or to pick up women? Pastor Jones finished his sermon on prayer by challenging the people to be mindful of their prayers, to get off alone, and spend time talking to God.

Everyone was leaving the auditorium when Jim called Joyce's name.

"Hello, Jim." Joyce wanted to run and scream, but knew that would be a little embarrassing.

"How have you been, Joyce?" he said with a grin.

Joyce thought she could just continue to walk and maybe he wouldn't pursue her. *Wrong! Here he comes*, she thought to herself. *Where are my children?* She was thinking if her kids were right with her, he wouldn't be too much of a problem.

"Joyce, I hear you're working for Don Miller."

"Yes, yes I am."

"Do you like working there; is he paying you well enough?"

Okay pal, that is too personal, she thought.

Joyce felt defensive at that moment; he was asking about things that were none of his concern. She tried to just walk away, but he continued to walk with her. He had a job opportunity for Joyce and was determined to tell her about it. He hoped Joyce would drop her job at the Lone Star and come to work for him; he was even willing to double her current salary.

Joyce was trying not to get angry. She knew that Jim was owner of a small accounting firm, and kindly told him, not only was she satisfied with her current job, and had no interest in leaving, but knew nothing about accounting. This made no difference to Jim whatsoever.

When Joyce arrived at her Jeep with Jim beside her, he gave her his business card and told her to call if she had any other needs as well. He said looking at her with a grin on his face. This really steamed Joyce, but he didn't seem to notice. The children were headed to the Jeep, so Jim went to his own vehicle.

"Thank goodness."

"Mom, did you say something?" Samantha said, thinking she heard her mother speak.

"Aah no, aah, where were you all?"

Elise and Samantha had been hanging around in the church hallway talking with their friends, Mark and Michael were running outside with theirs and didn't come toward the Jeep until Elise saw them and said it was time to leave.

"Is there something wrong, mom?" Elise asked.

"No, not really, let's just go and grab a bite to eat." Joyce was always up for something quick to eat on Sunday afternoons. To her, working in the kitchen was not resting on the Sabbath day.

Chapter nine / 123

They left the church parking lot in search of a delicious hamburger. Burger King was on their route home, and that was their quick meal for lunch.

Brandon had business to attend to in Kentucky. He really didn't want to go, since he no longer enjoyed the long trips, especially when hauling horses with him. There were many times Brandon sent Luke to make long trips to deal with the livestock, he was very good at the business end of ranching as well as the physical work. However, no matter how Brandon looked at it, he was the best one to make this trip.

"I'll be away for about a week, Richard. I have to go to Kentucky about some horses. I want you and Luke to keep an eye on things," Brandon instructed his son.

Brandon was headed all the way to Lexington, Kentucky to purchase some horses. It was a far piece, but that is where the best horses were. He also had a friend there from years back that he still kept in touch with. The two men had made a pretty good deal, but Brandon needed to go see his friend and the horses.

"Don't forget we have some calves that will be born probably this week, and don't drive Lorna nuts or she'll have both your hides," he said sternly.

"Dad, when have I ever driven Lorna nuts? Never mind, don't answer that." Richard said with a frown on his face. "We'll be good little cowboys."

Brandon had certain horses in mind that he wished to purchase; two young Pintos for sure, one for Michael and one for Mark. Brandon knew Lexington, Kentucky was like the horse capital of the United States; he knew the drive would be worth it.

Brandon was very concerned with the boys riding the horses at the ranch; they were too small to ride the horses he owned, and Brandon knew a Pinto would fit them much better.

When he returned, he planned to put in a call to Timothy for a little man-to-man talk. Timothy was old enough for Brandon to talk man-to-man about seeing Joyce on a more personal basis. All this was new territory to him, and he didn't want to make a wrong move. This was something Brandon had to push to the back of his mind until the horses were purchased, and he was back in Garland.

Brandon had gotten a good deal on three horses. Two beautiful Pintos for the boys; one was mostly white with large patches of brown, white mane, and a brown tail and the second Pinto was white with large black patches, with a white mane and black tail. While Brandon was there, he spotted a breathtaking Palomino; she had a golden coat with flaxen mane and tail. This horse seemed to be very tame. Brandon talked to his friend about this beautiful animal, and after a little dealing the Palomino was loaded into the horse trailer along with the two Pintos.

Brandon paid his friend for the horses, got them loaded in the horse trailer, settled them down and left. He knew it was going to be a long ride back, but he also knew he would never get there if he didn't get started. He called the ranch house and talked to Richard; he always checked in when on long trips, and expected his sons to do the same. While talking, he learned that the cows he expected to deliver while he was away, two of them bulls. The young bull population on the Southern Star was getting a little large, so he figured it wouldn't be long until Brandon sent Luke on a trip to sell some of them off.

"I saw Don yesterday; he came by, you know to check up on his little brother." Richard said with a grumpy voice.

"Be thankful that you have a brother to check on you. Well, I need to get on the road, son. You all take care, and I'll see you in a couple of days."

"Bye, Dad."

It was after two in the morning when Brandon arrived at the Southern Star; he was bone tired. He took a hot shower and climbed right into bed. The next morning Lorna let him sleep in, and when she heard him rattling around, asked if he was ready to eat. She had made a meal fit for a king. Most of the time Lorna made him feel like one with the way she kept his home clean, the meals she made, and never once had Brandon heard that woman complain.

Just as he was finished eating, the phone rang, Lorna answered, and gave the phone to Brandon. Any other time she would have taken a message since Brandon was still at the table finishing up his coffee, but this was Joyce and that made a big difference.

"Hi, I see you're back."

"Yes, I am," he answered with a big grin. "I'm finishing up my breakfast," Brandon chuckled a little.

"Oh, Brandon, I didn't mean to interrupt your breakfast, especially at eleven forty-five in the morning," she teased.

"Well, I didn't get in until very late, or should I say very early, this morning, so I got to sleep in."

"Poor baby," Joyce was having a good time flirting with Brandon over the phone. "I knew you were on a long trip, I was just checking to see if you made it back alright."

Brandon was very flattered by Joyce's phone call, and they talked several minutes before she had to hang up and get back to work. As he hung up the phone, he was sitting at the table smiling and he held his coffee cup up close to his face, but never drank it. Lorna noticed the silly smile on his face, but didn't say a word.

Brandon nervously dialed the phone, and waited for the person on the other end to answer. He felt silly for being nervous, but it didn't change a thing.

"Timothy, hi, Brandon Miller."

"Hello, Mr. Miller. Is everything okay?" Timothy asked, thinking it strange to get a call from Brandon Miller. He knew Brandon was the owner of the Lone Star Supply Office where his mother worked, but was surprised by his call.

Brandon had decided it was time to call Timothy and have the conversation needed about seeing his mother more seriously. He just hoped Timothy didn't take an offense to his intentions. Brandon let the young man know all was well, but just needed a little of his time.

Timothy was still at college, working hard to finish his last semester. He had a paper to write and a test the next day, but he made time to talk with Brandon. Joyce had told Timothy about Brandon, so he was not taken totally off guard with Brandon's topic of conversation.

As it was, Brandon wished he could talk with Timothy in person so he could at least read his face, but at this time, the phone would have to do. "Timothy, I'm talking to you about this because you are Joyce's oldest son, and I feel I should talk to you."

"About what, Mr. Miller?"

"Timothy, I would like your permission to court your mother." *There I said it; it is out in the open*, Brandon thought to himself as his heart was pounding almost out of his chest; he was sure the young man could here it on the other end of the phone.

"You want to date my Mother?"

"Yes... yes I do."

"I see." There was a little silence for a brief moment and Brandon thought he was going to come undone if the young man on the other end didn't respond soon.

"Mr. Miller, have you asked mom about this?"

"No, I have not asked her yet. Like I said, I wanted to talk to you first. I wanted to make sure it wouldn't be upsetting to you and your siblings."

Timothy started to answer when Brandon interrupted and told the young man he could call him by his first name. Brandon. "I think it will be fine with me, if and only if, it is fine with mom." Timothy told Brandon that he and his siblings had a very close relationship with their mother, and he let Brandon know he was the man of the house, even though he was away at school.

"I want you to know from the start we all think you are a fine Christian man, but we are very protective of our mother. I will not hesitate to take matters into my own hands if I see that she is being hurt."

Brandon appreciated Timothy's honesty and did not take any offense to his words. Brandon would never think of hurting Joyce, and he knew he would have to prove that to Timothy and his siblings. As the conversation went on, Brandon told Timothy he had respect for him, the way he handled the issue, and for his attitude toward his family.

"I just would like the chance for your mother and I to get to know one another and see where that leads us," Brandon told Timothy his intensions with a calm voice. "So, we're good here Timothy?" Brandon now asked.

"Yes, I think we're good."

As Timothy hung up the phone, he thought it strange, he had not heard of anyone asking permission to date their mother. He had several friends whose parents were divorced, and he never heard any of them mention it.

That has to be one of the hardest things I have ever done, Brandon thought, as his heart started to settle down and his breathing came a little easier. *I think that was worse than when I was a kid asking a girl out on a date. Now all I need to do is talk to Joyce.* Brandon was having a conversation with himself inside his head as he was walking toward the stable to check on the horses he had bought. He had it all planned out, when he would talk to Joyce, and what he would say.

Brandon and Joyce went out on their first date a week after Brandon called Timothy at school. Brandon was so nervous, he had gotten dressed and ready to go an hour ahead of time. His sons found this to be very amusing.

"So, dad," Richard now teased his father, "where are you going, what time can I expect you home, and do you have enough money?" Brandon's eldest son roared back and laughed at the ribbing his younger brother was putting his father through.

"Yeah, well at least I have a date," Brandon shot back.

"Oh yeah, that had to hurt," was Don's only comment, as he laughed at Richard.

Joyce seemed to be fine, very calm on the outside. On the inside however, there was a storm raging. She was hoping they were not going to be eating, because she didn't think her stomach could handle it. *I had forgotten how this could be so nerve wracking*, she thought to herself. *I'll be glad when he gets here and* – the doorbell interrupted her thoughts, and Joyce looked herself over once more in the mirror.

"I'll get it!" Mark yelled through the house.

"Hello, Mr. Miller, come on in. So, where are you taking my mom and why can't Michael and I go? Mark spoke as Brandon was sitting down on the sofa.

"Well, would you and Michael like to go?"

"Depends," was what the curious little boy said. "Depends on where you are going. Actually it's not me, it's Michael; he's worried about momma," Mark told Brandon, in a hushed tone for only Brandon to hear. But somehow Brandon figured it was Mark with the problem.

Samantha came in the room at that time and said hello to their guest. She sat down on the other end of the sofa while they waited for Joyce to come downstairs. Samantha asked the same question as her little bother about the two adults' plans. "Where were they headed?"

"I was just discussing that with young Mark here..." Brandon was interrupted by Joyce's entering the room.

"Hi, Brandon, sorry I kept you waiting. Samantha, you have my cell number if anything arises that needs my attention," she instructed as she was getting her purse.

"Yes, Mom, I do."

"Actually, Joyce, I think we may need to redirect your sitter plans."

"Excuse me, I don't understand," Joyce said with both a bit of humor and confusion.

"I was talking to Mark, and he tells me that Michael may have a problem with us going out. So, I thought if it is alright with you, we all could go out and grab a pizza together, then rent a movie."

Almost on cue, Michael came into the room. "Hey, everybody."

"Michael, honey, may I speak with you just a moment in private please?"

"No! Mom, please let me handle this... aah, really, after all he is *my* twin brother," Mark said in a hurried manner.

"What? What did I do?" Michael had that *deer caught in the headlights* look. In fact, he had forgotten his mother was even going out for the evening.

"Aah, Joyce, can I see you in private for just a minute, please?" Brandon asked. He explained the situation to Joyce, and they both realized it was Mark who had the problem, not Michael. Joyce agreed it would be best to go out all together for her young son's sake.

"Okay, everybody, let's go. We're all going out for pizza."

"Even me?" said Samantha.

"Yes, even you." Joyce said. Elise would have gone also, if she hadn't been on a date herself.

With happy faces, the boys grabbed their shoes and jackets and followed Samantha out the door with their mother and Brandon.

While at the pizza parlor, Joyce, Brandon, and the children enjoyed their time together. They laughed at Mark when he had cheese stringing from his pizza to his face. And when Michael started mocking the singer on the jukebox, they all found that hilarious. Mark and Michael loved pizza better than anything. Joyce cut them off after their fifth piece. Once they were at home, Mark put in the movie they rented. While the kids were waiting for it to start, Joyce went into the kitchen to pop some popcorn.

"Brandon, want to join me in the kitchen?" she asked.

"Sure."

"I'm sorry our first evening out 'alone' turned out to be with almost my entire family."

"No problem at all, Joyce. I would rather do that than have Mark a little uneasy with our being out. This is new for all of us, not just Mark." Brandon had the strong urge to kiss Joyce at that moment, but fought it.

After the movie, Joyce instructed Mark and Michael to go to bed. Samantha stayed downstairs with the adults for a few more minutes, and then she went on up herself. Brandon and Joyce were now alone, alone to talk and just enjoy each other's company.

They talked until almost midnight. "I really must be going, I had no idea of the time, Joyce. I'm sorry I kept you up so late."

"Nonsense, I have had a very enjoyable evening. I sort of hate to see it come to an end," she said as they looked at each other.

Brandon, Richard and Luke had cattle to herd up the next day, so he told Joyce he would talk to her tomorrow. As he was walking toward the door, he suddenly stopped and looked at Joyce, with his finger on his lip as he was thinking, but didn't speak. After a moment of silence, Brandon invited Joyce and her family to the ranch for the next weekend for a cookout. With a smile, she accepted.

Brandon stood directly in front of Joyce, his hands on the tops of her arms; he bent down and kissed her cheek.

"Good night, Joyce. I had a great time, even with the kids." He spoke in such a deep soft voice; Joyce was almost spellbound.

"So did I," she replied. "Good night, Brandon."

Brandon had been gone for nearly an hour; Joyce had readied for bed, and was doing a little light reading, when someone knocked on her bedroom door. "Come in."

"Mom, I'm sorry we all ruined your first date with Brandon," Samantha said seriously.

"You didn't, honey. I think that was the best way to handle it for your brother; he seemed to be alright and Brandon really didn't mind. Anyway, now you'll know how it will feel when I go on your first date."

"Oh, Mom!" Samantha squealed, and then went on to bed laughing down the hall.

Joyce could hardly believe she and Brandon had been seeing each other over two months. The children seemed to be doing fine with this new part of Joyce's life, and she enjoyed it herself.

"Joyce, are you free this Saturday evening?"

"Yes, I usually have a tall handsome cowboy I spend time with, but ..." she let the sentence hang and chuckled as she teased Brandon.

"Tell him you're busy with me tonight," Brandon teased in return.

Brandon had two tickets to the rodeo and hoped Joyce would like to go. Joyce hadn't been to a rodeo since before the twins were born. She loved to watch it on TV. She often wondered why those men put their lives on the line every time they got on one of those large beasts. However, she was glad they did, because she enjoyed watching it. Brandon was laughing so hard he could barely talk when she expressed those thoughts to him.

"Well, then, Joyce, I will be picking you up at five and we will go to the rodeo."

Brandon arrived at five o'clock on the button.

"Come on in, Mr. Miller," Samantha said. "Mom is in the kitchen with Mark, he fell and she is bandaging him up."

"Mom, it burns! It burns!" Mark cried out.

"I know, honey, but the medicine is cleaning out the dirt and germs."

Mark had fallen off his skateboard and slid on the pavement. In doing so he scraped his chin, hands and arms up pretty badly. Joyce was very glad he was wearing his helmet, knee and elbow pads; at least that much of him was safe from the injury.

Joyce had gotten Mark all bandaged up and his tears dried, kissed his forehead, and had given him a popsicle. She had always done that when one of the kids got hurt pretty badly; she felt it took their mind off the pain.

"Thanks, Mom," Mark said as he took a lick of his Popsicle.

"You're welcome, sweetie." Mark reached up and gave his mom a hug; this too was something the children had always done when their mother had patched them up.

All the while Joyce was working on Mark; Brandon was watching her and noticing how gentle and loving she was with her child. Brandon was very touched by the Popsicle.

"Mark, buddy, what happened?"

Mark explained to Brandon about riding his skateboard, hitting some loose pebbles, and being thrown off. He went flying one way and his board went another, he told Brandon, motioning with his hands and arms about the mishap. Thinking that had to hurt, Brandon simply replied:

"The next time I get hurt, I'll come over here to let your mom fix me up. I really like popsicles."

"Would you like to have one?"

"No thanks buddy." Brandon chuckled at the little guy.

"Brandon, I'm ready if you are," Joyce said as she came back into the room with Brandon and the children. Elise didn't have a date that evening so she was the sitter for the twins. Joyce gave Elise the speech about where she was going, when she should be home, and how to reach her if needed.

"Alright, I'll watch the little guys."

"Boys, both of you must have a bath and your hair washed before going to bed, and both of you know what time bedtime is, so I don't need to remind you. Now, give me a kiss before I go." The twins did as she bade, then she and Brandon were off to the rodeo.

―――

"Thank you, Brandon, for bringing me. I haven't been to one of these in a very long time."

"My pleasure, Joyce, now let's grab something to drink before we go in. What would you like?"

"Dr. Pepper if they have it, please." Brandon came back with soft drinks, popcorn and two candy bars.

"Well, someone is a little hungry isn't he?" she teased. Brandon only gave her a little wink.

Brandon thought Joyce looked beautiful in her cowboy hat. Then again, he always thought she looked beautiful no matter what she was wearing.

Joyce was wearing her black cowboy boots, blue jeans, a red blouse and black cowboy hat. She was not used to being complimented about her wardrobe.

"How often do you come to these?" Joyce asked as they were eating their snack.

"Not as often as I would like, for some reason or another. I just can't seem to get to the things I enjoy."

Brandon had sold some bulls to one of the bull riding companies and he wanted to see how they were doing. "One of them has never been ridden for the full eight seconds," he explained.

"Really? Which one is that, do you know his name?"

"Yes, it's Firecracker. He's a bad boy."

It was time for the show to start, and both Joyce and Brandon seemed eager to watch the event.

Starting out was a young cowboy who had been riding for about a year; he was riding a big, brown bull named Waffles. The bull had two horns that would do a little damage, if given the chance. Waffles bucked his rider off in six seconds.

Another rider, who was more of a veteran at the sport, rode Puddin'. This bull was one of the meanest and ugliest bulls they saw that evening.

"How can a bull that looks like that have a name like Puddin'?" Joyce asked with laughter.

"I know, it's funny to hear some of the names of these beasts," Brandon replied.

Puddin' not only bucked his rider off, but came charging at him; the man got up and ran before the mean, ugly beast got to him.

Finally, it was Firecracker's turn. His rider climbed on carefully and got settled, and then the gate was opened. The rider, a twenty-three year old cowboy from Oklahoma, was doing well, when suddenly Firecracker turned every which way and bucked like no tomorrow. His rider was bucked off at seven point five seconds.

"Well, Firecracker still holds his honor," Joyce said.

"That he does."

Sunday morning, Joyce and the children rushed to get to church on time. She couldn't believe this was happening again. This made the fifth time in two months they had to rush to make it to church before the services started.

"Today, my faithful friends, we are going to talk about faith," Pastor Jones said as he began his sermon. "How is your faith today?

"Exactly what is faith? In the book of Hebrews Chapter 11 verse, 1 we are told, 'now faith is the substance of things hoped for, the evidence of things not seen'."

As Joyce heard the pastor speaking, she could not help but think about her own faith. She had gone through some rough waters at the time of Paul's death, her faith, at that time, didn't feel too strong. She wanted to think she had a lot of faith, and that she would never lose her faith, no matter what life threw at her. Then she realized a person didn't really know that until they were in a personal trial. Joyce's thoughts caused her to not hear much of the sermon. She shifted herself and got her mind back in the place it belonged, and listened to what Pastor Jones had to say.

"If you, dear friend, were the only one on the face of this earth, He would have still died for just you. I hope you have faith in Jesus Christ."

After the sermon, Joyce and the children stayed around and talked with different people. Each child had their own group of friends to talk with. Joyce caught up with Ron and Diane, who invited Joyce and the kids over for dinner.

The kids had always called time at Diane's "a blast from the past." She would tell funny stories about her and their mother when they where growing up, like the time when Joyce and Diane were out riding around one Friday night. She explained back then in their hometown that was what the teens did on the weekends. On this particular night, Joyce was driving her dad's car, a small Plymouth mini station wagon. This caused the children to squeal.

The two young girls were looking at some boys that were hanging around on the other side of the street, when all of a sudden Joyce hit the curb and caused her front tire to blow out. Since Diane was spending the night at Joyce's, she made Diane stay in the room while she told her dad what had happened so as not to get yelled at.

There were always laughs at Diane's. Mandy and Erin were

home from college for the weekend so that made it even more fun.

Diane Harris and her husband Ron had been married for nineteen years; they had two girls, Mandy and Erin, who attended college at Texas A&M. Ron and Paul had not been what you would call buddies like Diane and Joyce, but the two guys learned early on in their marriages that they would not come between Diane and Joyce's friendship. It was just too strong and went back way too far. Since Paul's death, Ron had been a great help to Joyce as far as house maintenance and car repairs went, other than that he was just her friend and best friends' husband.

While they were there, Diane and Joyce had some time to talk while Ron was playing a board game with the children.

"So, how are things with you and Brandon?" Diane asked.

"It seems to be going well." Joyce replied.

"What is that supposed to mean?"

"Oh, I don't know, I guess I am a little fearful in this area." They both chuckled a little over Joyce's answer.

"Diane, do you know how long it has been since I have dated anyone?"

"Yes, Joyce, I do."

The two women talked as Diane poured them a cup of tea. Diane listened to Joyce's fears of dating Brandon. She advised her not to borrow trouble and enjoy it.

"Remember what the Pastor said this morning about faith?" Diane kindly reminded her.

Joyce felt she was being faithless again, when her friend reminded her.

Joyce had never thought she would ever be serious about another man; after all, Paul was her first love. He was a good provider and never strayed, nor did she. In all reality, Joyce was afraid of falling for someone and it not being as strong as what she had with Paul.

It was September, the summer gone, Joyce thought about how fast it flew. She felt as she got older the time flew faster. She and

Brandon had been seeing quite a bit of one another. At times the children joined them. There were even a few occasions where both families were together. Everyone seemed to enjoy themselves and was comfortable around one another.

One Saturday evening, Brandon had taken Joyce home from dinner. They sat outside on the porch swing enjoying the evening. It was still warm, with just a hint of coolness in the air. The moon was high, and the laughter from Michael, Mark and Samantha filled the air. The children went inside to watch a movie, and Samantha brought out some cake and iced tea.

"Oh, thank you, Samantha, that was very kind of you," Joyce said. It was such a lovely evening, Joyce wanted to just sit and soak it all in. She loved sitting out on the porch, only now she had someone to sit with her and put his arm around her, as Brandon was now doing. They talked about how soon the holidays would be upon them and what each of them had planned.

"My parents have given me and my sister tickets for a cruise," Joyce said.

"A cruise? Well, that sounds like fun." Brandon spoke, but was a little concerned; he tried not to show it. Did he really want this special person away on a cruise where men went to pick up women? He really was looking forward to spending the holidays with her and their families. Brandon was disappointed with his own thoughts. *I don't own her, she can go where she wants,* he thought.

"We had planned to go at Thanksgiving time, since the kids will be at Paul's parents. I don't like being away from my family on holidays, but I don't think Paul's parents really want me there, so this is the best time to go," she explained in a sad voice.

"If I know you like I think I do, you will have a lot of fun, Joyce McIntosh," he said with laughter in his voice. Then suddenly Brandon became very serious, looking deeply into her eyes as he spoke.

"But do not think for one moment that I will not miss you, because I will." As they sat looking into each others eyes, Joyce heard a noise inside and decided she had better go and see what was up.

When Joyce returned to the porch and the swing, she and Brandon continued to talk of the children and how well Timothy's graduation had gone. He was now working in town not too far from Joyce's office. Elise had started college one month earlier, and Joyce admitted to Brandon that she missed Elise something awful. Brandon comforted her and prayed with her about this time in her and Elise's lives. They also talked of Brandon's family, there was news that Sean and his wife Susan were now expecting.

"Congratulations! You're gonna be a grandpa," she said.

"Yes, well, I am looking forward to this new little person to be added to our family, but being a Grandpa will have to grow on me," he said laughing.

As Brandon stood, he took Joyce by the hand and told her he must be going. He thanked her for a lovely evening.

"You do things to my heart, Joyce." As he said these words to her, he was staring at her mouth, and then he slowly bent his head.

Joyce asked in a very low voice, "What are you doing?"

"I think you know, Joyce, the question is do you mind?" Brandon said as he paused, waiting for an answer.

"No, I don't mind," she said softly after pausing for just a second. Brandon lowered his head and gently brushed a kiss on her lips. At that moment, Joyce lost all track of where she was and who was around. She felt as if she could float.

"Good night, Joyce," Brandon said in his deep voice.

"Good night, Brandon."

Joyce actually didn't remember going back into the house.

Inside all seemed quiet. The children were in their rooms, so Joyce went to her own room and thought about the evening with Brandon.

CHAPTER TEN

The time had come, the time she was not looking forward to. Wednesday morning, Joyce took all the children and saw them safely on a plane. She was very thankful Timothy would be with them during their visit to their grandfather and grandmother McIntosh's

Timothy could feel the strain of being in his father's parent's home not only without their father, but now, without their mother. Joyce, about to board a cruise ship with her sister Karen, was missing her children already to the point she was almost in tears.

At the home of the older McIntosh's, the food was fine, but the fellowship was not so fine. Paul's family asked a lot of questions about what and how Joyce was doing these days. The kids knew not to give out much information, especially anything personal, but it was hard for the twins to determine what was not to be said, so they decided not to talk much.

At meal time, Timothy, Elise, Samantha, Mark and Michael sat close by each other. On Friday, they went to the mall, just to get out of the house for a while. Each one seemed to be more relaxed while at the mall. Elise suggested they see a movie, and then get a snack at the food court, since the twins really didn't like shopping. They all agreed that would be best.

Timothy saw to it that this visit went as well as he could manage, but it was a very strained holiday. He also made sure everyone got back home safely on Saturday evening. The actual plane ride home was more fun than being at their grandparents. When they landed and got back home everyone was in much better spirits, and Timothy was never so happy to be home in all his life. He then decided he would talk to his mother when she returned about never visiting their grandparents again without her.

Elise headed back to school on Monday morning.

"Elise, make sure you call me the moment you get in your dorm room," Timothy instructed.

"I will Tim; when did you become a mother hen?" She teased him terribly.

Samantha helped Timothy after they arrived back home, so not everything fell on him. They actually had fun together, but still missed their mother.

Elizabeth and Jason Arnold had wanted to give this gift to their children. Joyce had one sister, and two brothers; the brother's attendance was to be a surprise for their sisters when they met them at the airport.

"Doug, Chad, what are you two doing here, and where are your wives?" Karen spoke.

"Yeah, guys, where are your wives?" Joyce echoed as she hugged her two brothers.

"Where are your wives?" Doug mocked jokingly at his sisters. "We wanted to come and surprise you two; and besides, you two need looking out after so here we are."

Chad agreed with a very big smile and open arms.

"My wife cannot handle being on the ocean. The last time we came on one of these Beth was sick nearly the whole cruise," Doug said.

Chad explained that his wife Deanne was spending two weeks with her parents in Denver. Joyce took that opportunity to tease him about nobody wanting him. This brought laughter from everyone.

Joyce was indeed happy for the surprise, and teased about the boat not being able to handle all four of the Arnold siblings at the same time.

"Come on, let's find our cabins." Chad instructed.

The Arnold siblings were having a great time; the food was spectacular, and there were so many things to do. Joyce and Karen stayed up late and enjoyed a lot of things the ship had to offer. Of course, they also slept in a little later than normal; after all, that's what vacations are about.

They soaked up some sun by the pool, played shuffleboard, and a game of pool volleyball. Joyce had to admit, that she had never played volleyball in a pool before. But there were three men who asked very kindly for their help against five other women, and it did look like fun, so the two sisters agreed.

To sleep late in the mornings was priceless to Joyce since she rarely got to do it. After dressing and leaving her cabin for breakfast, she would return to find everything cleaned and the bed made. It was like having a personal housekeeper. "I could get so used to this." Joyce spoke out loud the first time she returned and found this piece of heaven. Not having to cook, clean or deal with the time of day, was so very relaxing to her as well. She had found herself thinking more and more about Brandon while on this cruise; she clearly missed him.

The ship made several stops. Joyce, Karen, Doug and Chad had seen many exciting things and tried some interesting foods as well. Chad would try anything once, but the strange looking seafood mix was one new thing too many. After trying it, he had to see the ship's doctor for a little something to settle his stomach.

"Hello, Samantha."
"Hi, Mom – hey everybody, Mom's calling from the ship."
"Hi, honey, how is everything going?"
"Fine, Diane keeps checking on us, but I guess that's okay. Are you having fun?"
"Yes I am, and guess who else is here? Your uncles, grandpapa gave them tickets too, they just surprised me and your Aunt Karen."

Joyce talked a few minutes with each of the children; Mark wanted to know if she had been seasick. She was happy to be able to tell him no.

"Oh, I almost forgot, Grandmother Doris called yesterday." Michael said.

"She did, did she want anything?" Joyce asked with a curious tone.

"No, she just called to see if we got home safe, and said she would call some other time."

Joyce told the children she missed them and said she would be home in a few days.

One day as the two ladies were relaxing in the sun, the Captain of the ship came over to Joyce and Karen and spoke with them. He had noticed the two women before and figured now was a good time to say hello.

"Good morning ladies," he spoke.

"Good morning." The two of them responded almost in unison. He didn't stay very long as he was checking with most of the passengers. He said he wanted to make sure they were enjoying themselves, and if he could be of any assistance to them, to let him know personally.

The Captain had a hard time not staring at them, two very beautiful ladies laughing and having fun. He reminded them to make sure they used plenty of sunblock; it was easy to burn out on the ship's deck.

"Thank you captain," Karen said.

The Captain then left to check on his other guests. Karen kept watching him as he walked away.

"Was it me, or did he keep looking at you Joyce?" Karen asked her sister.

"Aah it was you." She answered, giving it no mind at all.

Doug and Chad had found their sisters lying in the sun, and asked if that was all they had planned to do. The brothers had a better idea.

Doug and Chad were planning on going to one of the game rooms that evening, and invited their sisters to join them for a nice little poker game. They had learned to play as teens, but they vowed years ago to only play with family. Joyce and Karen had kept that vow, the brothers, they were not so sure of.

Brandon tried to keep busy while Joyce was away; though there was much work on the ranch to be done, his mind kept going to negative places. One day Brandon figured he would go into Dallas and hang out at the supply office. He hoped that would keep his thoughts in order. That was of little help because being at the office reminded him of Joyce's absence, and how much he missed her. He could not get the thought of her meeting another man on that ship out of his head. He kept his thoughts to himself, but Don and Sean knew he wasn't himself, but figured if he needed to talk, he knew he could.

That afternoon, Brandon went back to the ranch, and threw himself into his work. By the end of the day, he was simply exhausted; he didn't know if it was more mentally or physically.

The game had started and it was straight poker, just the four of them. As he normally did, Doug asked if everyone wanted to just hand over their money now and save themselves some time and humiliation. This caused the others to roar with laughter, and some comments in return.

The first hand went to Chad, and then Joyce won a hand. Doug couldn't stand it so he got a little tougher with his poker face, which gave him away every time. Joyce won the third hand and asked if they were ready to quit.

"Not on your life little girl," Doug replied. As the game went on things changed, and now Karen seemed to be racking up.

The Captain was strolling around the ship and came into the room. When he noticed the four of them playing, he couldn't help but go over to their table.

"I see you ladies have found a couple of gentlemen to keep you company this evening."

"No we haven't, these are not gentlemen; they are our brothers." Karen answered, and they all laughed. The Captain seemed to be relieved that these were Joyce's brothers and not just men she and her sister had gotten close to on his ship. The captain stayed for the next hand as Joyce won. He then excused himself and left.

"He did it again Joyce."
"Did what?"
"Stared at you almost the entire time he was here."
"I'm telling you, Karen, it's just you."
"No it isn't." Doug replied.

Joyce ignored the teasing and went right on playing the game. She was not interested in the Captain, or anyone other than Brandon Miller. Brandon had captured her heart as she hoped she had his.

When the poker game ended, Joyce took over half of the money at the table. "Come on Karen let's go spend our winnings," she said laughing all the way out the door.

"I hate it when those two get one over on us," Chad replied.

"Yeah, me too; so what will your wife say when she finds out how much you lost tonight?" Doug asked.

"If I have anything to do about it, she won't find out." This caused Chad to chuckle a little.

While the brothers were still sitting at the table, thinking about losing to their sister, Karen and Joyce were headed to little specialty shops for some souvenirs.

On the evening of the last night of the cruise Joyce, Karen, Doug and Chad were invited to join the Captain's table. They all gladly accepted the invitation.

Captain Will Rider was a very "Captain" looking man, if there is such a thing. His hair was gray and he wore a clean, close beard, which was the same color as his hair. He was very tall with broad shoulders. He wore a white uniform during the day, and a dark blue one in the evenings. He sat Joyce next to him at the table and spoke to her quite a bit.

"How did you do at the poker table with your family?"

"I cleaned house." Joyce said with a bit of laughter and pride. Captain Rider was careful not to neglect the other passengers, but did enjoy this fascinating person beside him.

Captain Rider never got involved with his passengers in a personal way, but he was having a hard time not doing so with Joyce.

He had noticed her all week, the way she walked, dressed and had fun at everything she did. She helped the people around her have fun as well.

After dinner, Joyce and Karen went dancing; they were kind enough to ask their brothers to join them, and they did. Captain Rider found this to be the opportunity he had been waiting for.

"May I have this dance?" Captain Rider asked Joyce.

"Aah, well, I aah, alright. The Captain was very much the gentleman; he did rather enjoy holding Joyce close to him, but not too close, he figured that would be rude of him.

"You have the most beautiful eyes," the Captain said to Joyce.

"Thank you, Captain, but isn't that a pick up line?" She sort of teased him.

The conversation between Joyce and him was light; Joyce figured he danced with all the female passengers at least once during the cruise. But Captain Rider found it disturbing to think of Joyce leaving his ship and him never seeing her again.

The music stopped; Joyce thanked the captain for the dance and returned to her siblings. Captain Rider just stood and watched her walk away.

Joyce, Karen and their brothers had the most wonderful ten-day vacation. They hated to see it come to an end, but each one needed to get back to their families and jobs. As everyone was disembarking from the ship, Joyce was headed out the main doorway.

"Joyce." She turned as she heard her name being called out. Captain Rider was calling her name and was making his way to her.

"Joyce, we'll meet up with you up on deck." Chad spoke for him and his brother and sister.

"Joyce, I'm glad I caught you, I was afraid you would be gone before I got the chance to say goodbye. Captain Rider hated to see Joyce go; he wanted one last chance to talk with her. The Captain offered her a free cruise anytime she wanted; all she would need to do is let him know. As he said these things to her, he handed her a business card with his information on it.

"Thank you so much Captain, I've had a lovely time." Joyce felt a little awkward about him offering to give her a free cruise; she just thanked him, then turned and walked to meet her family.

On the flight back to Dallas, her siblings were teasing her pretty bad about the captain, so Joyce decided to keep this bit of new information to herself.

As Joyce was walking out of the long security exit at the airport with her siblings, she was warmly welcomed by her family. Timothy, Samantha, Mark and Michael were all there. But there was another person who had come to welcome her home as well. Brandon was standing there with a smile on his face; he was so happy to have her back home. After Joyce gave out embraces, hugs and kisses to her children, and a warm hug to Brandon, she introduced Brandon to her siblings and their families.

Karen took Joyce's arm and led her a little ways away from the crowd. "Where have you been hiding him?" Karen said in a low voice, "Joyce he's gorgeous."

"Karen, honey, your mouth is hanging open." Joyce said to her sister.

"Oh, sorry; so you'll keep me posted on everything that happens between you two ... and I do mean 'everything'."

"Sure Karen." Joyce laughed at her.

Brandon was happy to see Joyce; it had been the longest ten days of his life. He gave her a long hug and kiss on the cheek. Moments later, Brandon would hear stories from the cruise that would make him doubt his future with Joyce.

As Doug and Chad were talking, they were teasing Joyce about stealing the attentions of the captain. Doug was the one who told the story of their evening at the poker table with Captain Rider. He even added a little to the story just for the added effect, not knowing that Joyce and Brandon had been seeing each other. Brandon could feel jealously rising up within him. He was not used to these kinds of feelings. The question was what he was going to do about them.

Joyce was used to her brothers teasing and gave it no mind.

Doug had a little too much fun ribbing his sister. Every one said their good-byes and gave last hugs. Once Brandon and the children had gotten Joyce home, she gave out the gifts she had bought for each of them. Joyce felt so glad to be home, the vacation was great, and she appreciated it, but she did miss her own bed.

While the kids were in the kitchen getting the dinner together, Brandon and Joyce were still in the living room. Joyce couldn't put her finger on it, but something wasn't right.

"Brandon, are you alright?" Joyce asked.

"Oh, yes, I have just had a tiring day, as I'm sure you have. I really have missed you, and I'm glad you're home, but I must be going," he said.

"Aren't you staying for dinner?" Joyce asked, clearly disappointed.

"Not this evening, like I said, I had a tiring day, and I have a few more things that need my attention before the day is over," Brandon said as he walked to the front door. Brandon bent and gave Joyce a kiss on the cheek, said good-bye and left.

Joyce wasn't sure what she felt at that moment, but something was wrong here, very wrong.

Returning back at work, it took Joyce an hour to go through the mail; she didn't even bother with the messages on the answering machine. She had not heard from Brandon since he left her living room on Friday. Brandon was on her mind a lot the last couple of days. Joyce was trying to understand what it was that she really felt for him. She knew that when she was with him, she was very happy, but what did that mean.

"Hey, welcome back," Rick said as he walked into Joyce's office. As she was talking to him about her trip, Mac came in looking for her.

"I heard you were back today, it has been boring around here without you."

"Thank you Mac."

Joyce was telling all of them about her trip until her phone rang.

It was Don.

"Well, guys, I gotta get back to work, I'm needed in Don's office."

"Later Joyce," Rick and Mac both replied.

When Joyce arrived in Don's office he asked her about her trip as well. Joyce told him all about how she was spoiled with being waited on hand and foot, and that it would take a few days to get back to reality.

"Well, it certainly is good to have you back. I for one have missed you."

"Thank you, it's good to be missed." Joyce replied.

"Don, have you heard from your dad today?" Joyce now got up the nerve to ask. Sadly, Don had not heard from him, but told Joyce that he was out of town. He and an old friend went to one of their favorite camping places with plans to do a lot of fishing.

Don was surprised Brandon hadn't told Joyce his plans. Don thought at that moment, something must be wrong with their relationship. He didn't know what to say, but on the other hand, felt he had said too much.

Joyce went back to her office; she could feel the hurt welling up in her. *This is why I didn't want to get into a relationship*, she silently told herself. *Men!* Her hurt was now growing toward anger. *They pursue you until you want them, then they pull some stupid, childish stunt.* Joyce was having a good long heart to heart inside her head and she was gettin' warm.

Relationship? What kind of relationship do we have exactly? We go out for dinner, spend time at each other's homes, talk on the phone, a little hand holding, but that doesn't mean we have to tell each other every little movement we make.

"I am not calling him; I am not, I am not! If he wants to act like a high school boy, well, then let him. I will not be a part of it." She said out loud in her empty office.

Joyce was so upset, she was slamming desk drawers, throwing files on her desk, and putting papers back into filing cabinet that she needed to be working on. Leslie knocked on the door at that moment.

"Yes, come in," Joyce said in an irritated tone.

"Joyce, are you okay?" The receptionist asked with concern.

"Yes, thank you Leslie, I'm fine, why do you ask?" Joyce replied a little calmer.

"Well, I was walking by and I heard all this noise in here."

"Oh, sorry, I'll try to be quieter."

"The noise is not the issue, Joyce; I've never seen you like this before."

"It's just a little problem that I have just solved; so it will be quiet in here, I promise."

Leslie could tell Joyce did not want to talk about it, so she let the matter drop. Leslie quickly changed the topic, hoping to help Joyce have a better day.

When Joyce got home, she felt the need to call Diane. She explained what had been going on and couldn't help but cry. She felt silly for crying over this; in fact, she always felt silly for crying over anything less than a death of someone she knew.

Her talk with Diane helped her feel better. She then went downstairs, watched the TV with her children, and pushed the whole issue out of her mind.

―――――

The following Sunday morning Brandon sat down in his usual spot for the church service. He was almost late, walking in just as the song service began. There were several announcements, then a choir special.

"Thank you choir for that beautiful music," Pastor Jennings said. Today we are going to look in God's word and see what he has for us. Please turn in your Bible to Isaiah 55 starting with verse 8, but first before we do that I want to begin with a word of prayer."

"Dear Heavenly Father, we thank you for this beautiful day. We thank you for allowing us to come freely to your house to worship you. Help me please Father, to say what you would have me to say to this congregation. If there be anyone here today that has not asked your precious Son into their heart, I ask that you send your Holy Spirit to draw them nigh unto you this hour, and give them no peace, until they get things settled. In Jesus' precious name I pray, Amen."

"Now, like I said, in Isaiah 55:8 we read, and please follow along with me. 'For my thoughts are not your thoughts, neither are your ways my ways, saith the Lord.' Don't you sometimes find yourself in a situation that you want to be taken care of not only now, but in your way? You want everything to turn out like in the storybooks, you know, happily ever after. We forget, friends, that God's ways are not our ways; we do not have the mind of God. We cannot see what God already knows, He knows the beginning, the middle and the end. Let's read on in verse nine of this same chapter. 'For as the heavens are higher than the earth, so are my ways higher than your ways, and my thoughts than your thoughts.' Our minds can't comprehend what God's can.

Brandon was having a hard time focusing on the sermon; Joyce was so much in his mind he thought he would just go mad. He did realize from the pastor's words, that he wanted things to go his way in this relationship, but he really hadn't talked with Joyce about how serious his feelings were for her.

"So, here we are told again, that God's ways are not the same as ours, and His thoughts are not the same as ours. I want you to answer this in your mind, whose thoughts are better, ours or God's? Whose ways are better, ours or God's? Let's face it folks, we are all like those little children back there in the nursery, we want our way. So, if you are struggling with how to handle a situation, ask yourself, whose way is going to be had here, yours or God's."

As everyone was leaving the church grounds, Brandon didn't stick around and talk with friends like he normally did; he just got in his truck and headed for Don's. Don and Jennifer had invited all of the family over for Sunday dinner. Usually Sunday dinner was at one of their homes, and Brandon enjoyed this time tremendously. Today he really wasn't up to it, but he went anyway, promising himself that he would not let his family know he was down and struggling with a personal matter.

CHAPTER ELEVEN

It had been a whole week since Brandon and Joyce had talked or seen each other.

Joyce took the boys to the ranch for their work day. Brandon was not in sight, so Joyce just dropped them off and left. They went straight to the stables like they had always done and found Brandon working in one of the stalls.

"Hi, boys, is your mom still here?" He asked.

"No, she's already left," Mark answered.

Maybe I can see her when she picks them up this evening, he thought to himself.

Brandon has several things that needed to be done. The boys started work in the barn; getting it all cleaned and organized. This task took most of the day.

After a long workday, Brandon realized it was time for Joyce to pick the boys up. He watched for her in hopes that they could talk. Things had been a little strained for the past few days and he was missing her; he decided he was putting an end to the strain today.

"There's our ride, Mr. Miller; we'll see you next week." Mark called out.

"Oh, is your mom here already? I'll just go and say hello." When Brandon arrived in the driveway behind Mark and Michael, it was not how he expected.

"Oh, Samantha, where is your mother?" Brandon asked with disappointment.

Samantha explained to Brandon that Joyce was at the house, in the middle of some house cleaning, but she would tell her he said hi.

"Oh, alright then," Brandon responded. The boys climbed in dusty, dirty, and hungry; within minutes they were on their way home.

As Michael was headed out the door to ride bikes with his brother, they stopped long enough to answer the phone. Joyce had talked to the twins many times about walking by the phone and not answering it when it was ringing.

"Mom, telephone," Michael yelled through the house.

"Michael honey there really isn't any need to yell, just come and get me," Joyce had to remind her son, again.

"Hello."

"Hello, Joyce,"

"Hello Doris, how are you and Steve doing?" Joyce asked out of politeness, knowing all along that Doris only called to be nosy about something. The question was what? Several times after Paul's death, Doris had called just to be nosy. It was as if Doris felt she had the right to check up on her, it infuriated Joyce.

"Oh, Joyce dear, I just called to say hello, and see how you and the children were doing."

Joyce tried to divert the conversation and get Doris to talk to the children. She was not taking the bait.

"Oh, no dear, this is long distance, besides I said hello, to Michael when he answered. I'll just talk to you and you could fill me in on everyone." Joyce just shook her head.

"Oh, I almost forgot, one of the boys told me you were dating someone, is that true?"

Now they were coming to the real reason for Doris' phone call. It was not to see how the children were doing, or how Joyce was doing. It was all about she heard Joyce had been dating.

"Aah, well, I do have a male friend that I go to dinner with on occasion, that's all, if you want to call that dating, then, yes I guess I am." Joyce really didn't want to answer, but she couldn't lie either. So she opted for the least information she could give.

"Oh Joyce, how could you?"

"How could I what Doris? Get on with my life? Enjoy an evening out? Smile and laugh every once in a while? What Doris?" Joyce was in no mood to deal with her ex-mother-in-law, and this line of questioning had made her angry.

"Joyce, my Paul hasn't been gone that long, and you have already forgotten him."

"No, Doris, I haven't forgotten Paul. I never will. But I will not sit here and mope and do nothing with my life."

"You must be careful, men are only out for one thing, and you know what I mean Joyce. Exactly what kind of a relationship is it anyway? And the children, think about the children Joyce, I'm sure they don't want a stepfather."

Joyce took a deep breath and decided to tell Doris what she really felt.

"First of all, Doris, it's not yours or anyone else's business what kind of a relationship I am having with this man; I hope you won't forget that. Is this what you called me about? Because it really isn't any of your business and I will not discuss it with you. Now, do you want to talk with the children or not?"

"I guess not; I'm really too upset to talk right now," Doris said with tears in her voice.

"Well, I guess I should let you go then. Bye Doris." As rude as it was, Joyce hung up the phone without waiting for Doris to say bye in return.

After Joyce had calmed down from her ex-mother-in-law's phone call, she called the children into the living room and explained the situation with Paul's parents. The children knew that their father's family always treated their mother a little rude and never understood why.

"It is very important not to discuss anything personal with your Grandmother or Grandfather McIntosh."

"What do you mean by personal?" Mark asked.

"Yeah, what are we not supposed to tell?" Michael chimed in.

"Anything about our money, my job, or anyone that comes to the house to see me, like Mr. Miller does. Understand?" She explained as she looked each one in the eyes.

"Okay Mom, no problem." The twins replied, as did Samantha.

"Hey, Mom, why did Grandma Doris not talk to us over the phone just then?" Samantha asked.

"I really don't know honey; she said it was because it was long distance, but then she never asked about any of you. She just wanted to know who I was seeing, or dating as she put it, and why. Basically she was putting her nose where it did not belong."

In the past Joyce had always tried to be kind when talking to the children of Paul's family, but not today, and in her mind, not any more. She decided then, she would not cover up for Paul's family any longer.

⁓

The next day, Joyce's conversation with Doris was still running through her mind, she was determined not to allow that woman to ruin another moment of her life. As she was having this thought the doorbell rang, Joyce was also not in the mood to deal with anyone.

"Mom, Diane is here," Mark yelled through the house.

"Mark honey, why did you yell?"

"I didn't know where you were."

"Well that answered that, didn't it, Joyce?" Diane said with a smile on her face.

"I just had this same conversation with Michael not thirty minutes ago." Joyce explained as she and Diane walked into the kitchen.

"I was in the neighborhood and thought I would stop in for a few minutes."

"Good, let's grab a couple of Dr. Peppers and go in the living room and talk; you don't know how glad I am it was you at the door."

The two women enjoyed their cold beverages, talked of family and work, and then came the serious conversation. Joyce told Diane about Doris' phone call and how upset it made her. Diane was curious what Doris wanted to know.

"Well, basically, she heard I was 'dating' someone, didn't know how I could do that to the children and just forget Paul. Oh, and you'll love this one. 'Joyce you must be careful, men only want one thing, and you know what I mean.'" Joyce said in a mocking tone, with a little bit of anger in her eyes.

"She said that to you?"

"Yes, she did honey, and to make things worse, Diane, I haven't heard from Brandon in over a week and honestly, I don't know why."

"You're kidding! What happened?"

"I don't know." Joyce could feel tears stinging her eyes, and tried looking away from her friend. Diane advised Joyce to call Brandon, but knew she was going to be a little stubborn about this. In all honesty, Diane could not say she wouldn't have reacted the same way.

Joyce told Diane she was not only hurt, but angry as well, and she would not be the one to call.

"I see. Well, Joyce I really don't know what to tell you, except I think we have a bit of miscommunication going on here."

"Do you? Do you really think it's that simple?" Joyce said with very sad eyes.

"Yes, I do."

The two women sat in the room and talked and laughed about many things, and as always Diane made Joyce feel much better.

"Oh look at the time, I've got to get home and put food in front of Ron, so he will feel loved." Diane said jokingly. They both laughed as Diane was headed toward the door.

When Diane left, Joyce went into the kitchen and started supper for her family as well.

"Hey Mom, what's to eat? I'm hungry," inquired Mark.

"Well, first of all, Mark, you are always hungry, and second of all we are having soup and sandwiches."

"What kind of soup?"

"Mark this is not a restaurant; you'll have the kind of soup I'm serving."

Mark realized he had said something wrong, or the right thing, just at the wrong time. No matter which it was, the truth was, if their mother wouldn't tell them what they were having for a meal, it meant it was something they didn't like to eat.

"Hey what's for supper, I'm hungry." This time Michael came through and passed his brother on his way out.

"Michael, out," Joyce said with her outstretched arm pointing to the doorway.

"Don't ask; she won't tell."

"Oh no, that means it is something we won't like." Michael said, not knowing he almost echoed his twin brother's thoughts.

Samantha came in right as the food was being put on the table. She had worked her shift that afternoon at Your Choice of Chicken restaurant.

"Am I ever tired; we were so busy this afternoon. Doesn't anyone eat at home anymore?" Samantha exclaimed as she pulled a chair out to sit at the table.

A bus load of seventh graders had come in during Samantha's shift. First they didn't know what they wanted; some of them didn't have enough money, and the mess they made was twice the work for Samantha and another crew member. She was so glad when her day at work was over.

"Well, remember it is your night to do dishes." Mark said.

"Oh man, Mark, will you trade with me just this time?" She said in a tired, begging voice.

Joyce took pity on her daughter, and said she would cover for her this time. Samantha was very glad not to have dish duty, as soon as she finished her meal; she went straight to a hot bubble bath.

Joyce remembered those days when she worked at a restaurant, the long hours, on your feet almost the whole shift; it made her tired thinking about it.

The supper dishes were done; the kitchen was put back in order, Joyce had taken a long bubble bath, and felt relaxed as she climbed into bed. She reached for her Bible, and began her daily Bible reading. She turned to the book of Ruth. While reading this wonderful story of Ruth and Naomi, she couldn't help but think about Doris.

There had been many times during Joyce and Paul's lives together, she envied those who had a great relationship with their mother-in-law. *What have I ever done to that woman? She has disliked me from the first moment she met me.* Joyce thought as she lost focus on her reading. *Please Lord, help me to never be like Doris, help me to welcome and love whomever my children marry.* She prayed silently.

Joyce got her focus back on the book of Ruth, and marveled on how Ruth and Naomi loved not only God, but each other as if they really were mother and daughter. Joyce began to think again at how people can be so different. One person can love another unconditionally; another person would not love another under any condition. This caused her to think of Paul's family and how they had been toward her.

Elise had to get home, even for a short while. Elise needed to talk with her mother and not over the phone; she needed the sights and sounds of her family.

"Elise, what a lovely surprise ... why didn't you tell me you were coming home.

"Well it wouldn't be a surprise if I told you, now would it? How I got here was through a friend. My roommate's friend was coming this way and had room in her car, and boom! Here I am."

"Well, come on in and let's catch up."

Mark, Michael and Samantha almost attacked their sister when she came in; they were so happy to see her. Timothy gave her a big bear hug when he arrived home that evening. They all talked in the living room and got caught up on Elise and she them.

The evening was filled with laughter around the table with the children; Joyce loved the sound of it.

Later that evening, the twins were already in their rooms for the night, Samantha, as she did most evenings, was talking on the phone with Shelly, and Timothy was out with Christine, his girlfriend. Joyce knew this was the perfect time to talk with her eldest daughter.

"Okay Elise out with it," Joyce asked when the two were alone.

"What?"

"Something is not right here. Now, tell me, what it is! Let me guess, grades?"

"No, calculus is making me sweat, but I'm doing fine."

"You and Scott?" Elise didn't look at her mother at that point, she looked at the floor.

"I see. If you want to tell me about it, you can, I'll listen, I may be able to help, I don't know. Or you could just rest and relax for the next couple of days."

"Thanks Mom. I really need to think right now, and I can't do that in the dorm." Joyce accepted that answer and knew there were times in everyone's life where you just needed to get away and think, right now that is what Elise needed, and Joyce would give her that.

The next morning Elise awoke and realized she was not in her dorm room, with two other girls and clothes all over the floor. She was at home in her own bed. The feeling was so welcoming she couldn't help but smile.

"Elise. Hey good, you're awake, want to go to the mall with me today?" Sam said as she entered her sister's room.

"Oh… I don't know Sam; I can't think right now, ask me later okay?" She answered with a sleepy voice.

"Oh come on Elise, I'll buy you a milkshake at the DQ." Samantha was pulling out the big guns to get her sister out of bed and off to the mall.

"Okay Sam, if you will just let me lie here for another thirty minutes, I'll go, but if not, then no!" Elise was serious; she didn't want to be disturbed.

"Alright, thirty minutes, I'll put a sign on the door… quiet, sleeping person."

Joyce went with the girls to the mall. Since it was Saturday, the twins were at the Southern Star working. The boys were doing well with Brandon and all the new areas of ranch work that he was teaching them. At the end of the day, Mark and Michael always had stories to tell about what they had done and learned, and dirt on them to prove it.

After three hours of shopping, Samantha had found many bargains. Joyce made the comment to Elise that Samantha seemed to attract sales. She had purchased two pairs of jeans, a blouse, two pair of shoes and a purse. Finally, Joyce suggested they stop at the food court and rest their feet.

"Hey Sam, where's my milkshake?" Elise asked after remembering the bribe Samantha gave her that morning.

"I'll get it. Mom, do you want anything? It's my treat."

"Well, I don't get this offer every day. I'll have a chocolate milkshake, please. Are you sure you have enough money?"

"Yes, Mom, I have a job, remember?"

As Samantha was at the counter getting the milkshakes, Elise noticed two young men talking with Samantha.

"Look Mom, it's happening again, I can't believe it. Sam can't even go buy ice cream without getting hit on; it's just not fair. I'm telling you Mom, life is not fair." Joyce then figured, this all of the sudden trip home had something to do with boys; the question was which boy. Joyce would just have to wait until Elise was ready to tell her the whole situation.

Samantha came back to the table where the other two women were sitting and handed each their treats, not noticing Elise's frustration.

"Samantha dear, who were those two boys you were talking to?" Joyce asked.

"Oh, one's name was Greg and I think the other one's Ben, anyway I told them to get lost." This comment from Samantha caused Joyce and Elise to start laughing.

"What?" was Samantha's only reply, as she looked at her mother and sister with questioning eyes.

When the women returned from their exhausting day at the mall, Joyce laid down on the sofa to watch TV. Elise came in and sat in the chair across from her.

"Mom, Scott is going out on me."

"What?"

Finally, Elise had confided in Joyce and told her what was really going on in her life. One of Elise's friends from school, who was also from Garland, was home for the weekend a few weeks ago, and saw Scott out with another girl. Now that Joyce knew what the problem was, she knew better how to help her daughter.

"Honey did you call and talk to him about this? It could all be a misunderstanding; it could have been his cousin or something."

"No, Mom, it isn't; he hasn't called me like he used to. He still calls, but not as often. I just know it's true, Mom."

"Well, you have a clear choice to make. You can either put up with it, or you can confront him and tell him to get lost. A man that cannot be faithful to his girlfriend will not be faithful to his wife. You deserve better than that Elise."

Elise was crying at the words her mother was saying; she knew she was right, but doing them was a whole different matter. That night before Elise went to bed she called Scott and told him it was over. She almost didn't tell him why; she felt if he could treat her that way, he didn't deserve to know why, but then she didn't want to stoop down to his level.

When it came to matters of the heart with her children, Joyce always tried to tread lightly. She wanted to advise them as best as she could, and she knew if she ever became emotional about their situation, she would not be able to help them as well. But, when Elise told her of Scott's unfaithfulness, she had a hard time not getting emotional. When she was alone in her bedroom that night, she had to pray about this matter; she had the strongest urge to shake that boy until his eyeballs fell out of his head.

"How are you this morning, Elise?" Joyce asked before anyone else came into the kitchen for breakfast.

"I'm okay, I hurt, but I'll survive."

"That's my girl; remember time helps us to heal." Joyce kissed her daughter on the head and started cooking her some breakfast.

Joyce hurt for her daughter. Elise would get over Scott, Joyce was sure. In the meantime, she could use some time, tender loving care, and that is what Joyce would give her.

Sunday afternoon came way too fast for Joyce. It would be another month before her daughter would be coming home again. Joyce was always thankful for the time she spent with Elise, and tried not to focus on the time she would be away. They said their goodbyes, and with an arm around her, Timothy walked his mother back to the Jeep and headed for home.

After arriving back at the house, Joyce knew she would have to dive into something to keep from being sad. The kitchen was not as clean as she normally kept it, so cleaning would be her therapy for the duration of the day.

While scrubbing the sink, her thoughts were no longer on Elise, but on Brandon. She missed him; a part of her wanted to call him, but another part was stubborn and would not allow it. She decided then and there she would put the whole situation with Brandon behind her, and never allow any man to get that close again.

As Brandon was driving through the pastures, he stopped to check on a few expectant cattle, he wanted to know where they were in case the mother to be needed help. Suddenly, his thoughts turned to Joyce.

He thought of her smile, her laugh; he really missed his friend, and the time they spent together. Brandon felt so hurt about how things had changed. If only she hadn't gone on that stupid cruise, he thought to himself. The two of them hadn't really said more than "hi" and "bye" to each other in over two weeks.

Dear Heavenly Father, Brandon began to pray inside his mind. *Why am I feeling this way about Joyce? She does things to my heart, and now I think she may be seeing other men. The only thing I know to do is just give this whole thing over to you. I have not been interested in any other woman since Stacey, you know that Lord, so why now? Lord I am just not sure what I feel for her. I know I want to see her and be with her, I love her laugh, and she is so full of life. She has told me she is one of yours Father; I just don't know what to do. Please help me to have wisdom in this area, please help us to find each other if that is your will. In Your Son's name I pray, amen.*

No matter what Brandon did that day his thoughts kept turning to Joyce. "I could call her and just ask her straight out." He said out loud to his horse Pete. "What if she tells me she doesn't want to see me? What if she just wants to be friends? I couldn't deal with that. The truth is I want her all to myself." Of course, Pete didn't have any answers for Brandon, and by the end of the day, Brandon still didn't have any himself.

⁓

Joyce was trying to watch a movie with the boys; Samantha was out with a friend, and Timothy was on a date with his now fiancée Christine. She really wasn't enjoying the movie for thinking about Brandon. *What had happened to make him change all of a sudden?* She had asked herself again, but still no answer. Joyce took that time to silently pray about the matter, and give it over to the Lord. She prayed for His will do be done. She then opened her heart and told her Heavenly Father how she truly felt about this man, to her own surprise Joyce felt more for Brandon than what she was aware of.

"That was a great movie!" Mark said. Joyce had sat with the twins watching *The Spy from Mars*, but couldn't tell anyone one thing about it.

"Well boys, go ahead and get your baths and get ready for bed, after all it's getting late, and we have church in the morning." Joyce was determined not to be running late tomorrow morning, as they were so many Sunday's in the past. They didn't seem to have this problem when Paul was alive, but now it was becoming a normal thing. She told herself it had to stop.

Joyce had trouble paying attention to the sermon on Sunday morning; she hoped that Pastor Jones did not notice. Her thoughts kept going to Brandon. *I could just call him, or just drop by*, she was thinking to herself, trying to figure out a way to end this turmoil. *No, no he needs to call me; I'm not the one with the problem. If you're not the one with the problem Joyce, why are you having this conversation with yourself instead of listening to the sermon?* The voice inside her head replied. *Ohhh!, men!* It was the only answer she could come up with.

"Diane, do you and Ron have plans today?"

"No, let's do lunch." Diane suggested, the same one Joyce was going to make.

Samantha had come up to her mother as she was talking with

Diane and Ron. Shelly had invited Samantha to go out with her and her parents for lunch. Joyce told her she could, which sent her and Shelly off with smiles and giggles.

"Well Joyce, it looks like it's you and the boys; so, boys, what will it be today?" Diane asked.

"Pizza!"

"Yeah, pizza sounds great," Ron added.

"Hey, what about Timothy and Christine?" Ron asked.

"Nah they won't come. They're in looooooove." Michael said while making a silly face.

"Yeah, they just want to talk lovey stuff to each other." Mark then began to make being sick noises, while Michael doubled over with laughter.

Joyce had been going from office to office dropping off contracts and messages. She was not paying too much attention to anything else when she heard Rick's voice.

"Is he going to be all right? What happened anyway?" Joyce heard Rick saying on the phone. She didn't mean to eavesdrop, but just caught the conversation as she was putting some things on his desk.

Wonder who he was talking about, Joyce thought. Joyce had come in late that morning due to getting the boys to the doctor's office for their check-ups. She had noticed that Don and Sean were not in their offices, and Joyce knew since she kept up with Don's schedule that he should be here.

Later when Joyce was leaving for lunch, she heard again someone taking about someone getting hurt or being sick, she wasn't for sure which it was. Maybe she would find out when she and Leslie went to lunch.

Joyce and Leslie went to the O.K. Café for lunch, as they often did, it had good food at a good price and the service was impeccable. They had given their orders and the waitress was back with their food in a remarkable amount of time.

"That was awful about Mr. Miller, wasn't it Joyce?" Leslie said.

"What? And which Mr. Miller?" Joyce replied.

"Oh, you don't know?"

"Know what Leslie? Tell me, which Mr. Miller and what?" Joyce asked anxiously.

"Mr. Miller, Brandon Miller was attacked by a bull early this morning."

Joyce gasped as her hand went to her mouth. "What! How is he? Will he be all right? What hospital is he in?" All these questions came as one long sentence; she never gave Leslie a chance to answer. "I have to see him Leslie, where is he? Is he at the hospital or at home?"

"I really don't know; I just heard about it this morning, so I really don't have all the details."

In just an instant Joyce had left money on the table to pay for her meal and told Leslie she was heading back to the office to get some answers.

"Hold on, I'm driving, remember?" said Leslie, hot on her trail. The two women were back at the office in no time flat. Joyce quickly went into Don's office, but he still wasn't there. Then on her way to Sean's office she ran right into Rick.

"Excuse me, Rick, I don't mean to be rude, but I just heard about Brandon. Where is he Rick? How is he? How did this happen?" Joyce was almost in tears.

"Joyce," Rick now spoke, as he put his arm around her shoulder, led her into his office and shut the door. "Joyce from what I understand it happened early this morning sometime, and he is in the hospital."

"Which hospital?"

"He's at Texas Memorial and they…" Joyce didn't wait for the rest of Rick's words; she was out the door and in her vehicle in no time at all. "Joyce! Let me drive you, you're in no…" She was already gone.

Joyce, driving on the highway, trying to get there quickly, and safe herself, was praying out loud the whole time that Brandon would be alive and all right. "Please Lord, I have done something, but I don't know what. He seems to be shutting me out of his life. I think I love him, but I'm not for sure. Please, heal him and help me as I go see him, and please Lord, if it be your will, help us to remain friends at least. Amen."

Rick caught Don as he and Sean were walking down the hallway of the office. "Don! How's Brandon?"

"Well, we are headed back there now; the doctor told us he was very lucky, he had a few broken bones, some stitches in several places, and he is bruised almost from head to toe. He also said he should be going home in a couple of days."

"Tell him we all are concerned and are praying for him."

"Sure thing, Rick; thanks buddy."

"Have you talked to Joyce yet?" Rick asked.

"No, we tried calling her, is she here now?"

"No, she left the office like a little storm when she heard the news."

Joyce was on the verge of tears as she waited at the information desk to get the room number. She walked briskly down the hallway, and finally approached his room. Joyce gently knocked and waited for a voice to say come in. She started to approach his bed, but her feet went faster as she got closer; it was as if they had a mind of their own, and now tears were forming in her eyes. She didn't even bother with hello or how are you; she just began speaking what was in her heart.

"I didn't know you were hurt, why didn't you call me?" He reached out his arms to hold her, she was now sobbing in his chest, and he couldn't make out what she was saying.

"Are you going to be okay? Brandon, I don't know what I have done to offend you, but I'm sorry, if you'll just tell me what I've done," Brandon cut her off and held her face tenderly in his hands, looked deep into her eyes and gave her a long, passionate kiss. A gentle knock at the door broke the kiss that left them both breathless.

It was the nurse to take Brandon's vitals and give him some medication. Joyce walked to the other side of the room to allow the nurse to do her job, but Joyce was still confused. The nurse was only in the room for a few minutes, leaving the couple to continue their needed conversation.

"Joyce, I'm so glad you came, I was afraid to tell you, because I didn't want you to worry and I was afraid ... afraid you might not come."

"Why would you think I wouldn't come? Brandon, we have to talk about what has happened between us."

Joyce and Brandon just looked very seriously at one another for what seemed to be an eternity to Joyce, but at the moment no words were spoken.

"What is it, Brandon?" As Brandon thought for a moment and saw the hurt in Joyce's eyes, he finally spoke.

"Your brother told me about you and the captain while you were on your cruise. Also, I know about you and Mac going out, I won't stand in your way Joyce." Brandon spoke with hurt in his own eyes.

"Captain?" Joyce said with much confusion. "Exactly what did my brother tell you, and which brother was it?" She demanded with fury in her voice.

"Doug, he said you and the captain had dinner together, that you two spent much time talking, and the captain was neglecting his other guests because he couldn't take his eyes off you, and ... and some other stuff."

"Let me tell you something, Mr. Brandon Miller, if the captain had difficulty spending the proper amount of time with the other passengers that was his doing, not mine. I did nothing to lead him on. I would never do that to you; I love you, Brandon. And as for my brother, he is nothing but a big joker, and I will wring his neck the next time I am in the same room with him." She said angrily

"Joyce, what did you say?" As Brandon sat there, he looked at her with his mouth hanging open and his eyes huge.

"I said I will wring his neck the ..."

"No, no, before that?"

"I forgot, what did I say?"

"Come to me Joyce." He said very sternly. "Look me in the eyes, what did you say?" Joyce stood there gazing in his beautiful dark eyes; she could no longer hold it in. The truth came spilling out like a fountain.

"I love you Brandon. I didn't think it could ever happen again, but I have fallen in love with you." He then beckoned her with his finger; she came to him willingly. As he looked in her eyes, he wrapped his arms around her, and kissed her hard and long. They broke for just a moment.

"I have waited to hear you say that for so long; I have loved you almost from the moment we met." He kissed her again, this time only to hear the clearing of some ones' throat.

"Here, here, this is a hospital," Don said with a little chuckle, as he and his brother walked into the room.

"Yeah, and it doesn't say anything on his chart about Dad's needing mouth-to-mouth resuscitation," Sean said laughing. Richard, Jennifer and Susan came in seconds after.

"Hey, Dad, how are you?" Jennifer asked, seeing all the other faces in the room.

"He's much better now that he has a private nurse to see to his face," Sean said as he continued to tease his father and Joyce.

"I guess we missed that one," Susan said to Jennifer. Jennifer and Susan talked to Joyce while the guys talked of business. Brandon and Joyce, however, kept looking back and forth to each other, their eyes locking.

"So, what is the latest on your recovery?" Sean asked now being a bit more serious.

"The doctor said I could go home maybe in two days, but I would have to be in bed for at least a week. Then take it very slowly for a time," Brandon told his family, still shooting glances at Joyce.

"That is good news, Dad. We are all very thankful you weren't hurt any worse. That bull could have killed you. I think we should take this time to thank our Heavenly Father for his protection over you." Don said, everyone in the room agreed. Everyone bowed their heads as Don began to pray out loud. "Dear Heavenly Father, we thank you for your hand of protection on our dad, it could have been so much worse. We ask that you will heal his wounds and help him, as he has to take it easy for a while. We thank you for the special friendship he has in Joyce and that you will be with the two of them. Continue to watch over all of us, in Jesus' name I pray, Amen."

"Amen", echoed voices from the other people in the room.

"Well, I think we ought to clear out and let you get some rest." Don instructed.

"Yeah, Dad, you need to rest, and we really should leave and let you do that," echoed Sean and Richard. Everyone was leaving the room when Brandon called Joyce's name.

"What it is Brandon, do you need something?" she asked.

"Yes I do, I need to make sure you will be here again tomorrow?"

Joyce assured Brandon she would be back tomorrow and the next day, and the next. She told him he would grow tired of her, but he shook his head no and told her never. He then pulled her close and gave her a gentle kiss and watched her leave the room.

CHAPTER TWELVE

Joyce spent a lot of time at Brandon's, making sure he cooperated with the doctor's wishes. He was getting tired of being in bed, and not being out on the range with Richard and the other ranch hands, especially his two youngest hands, Mark and Michael. Still, Brandon was confident that Richard and Luke could handle things in his absence.

Mark and Michael came into Brandon's room when they were done working for the day.

"Hi Mr. Miller, how are you feeling?" Michael asked.

"I'm doing better, thank you. I should be out of this bed in a couple of days." Brandon replied. Mark and Michael had worked for Brandon for six months now, and he still could not tell them apart.

"So, Mr. Miller, how did it happen?" Mark asked.

As Brandon was starting to tell the story Joyce walked into the open doorway of his room to retrieve her two boys.

"Hi Joyce," Brandon could feel his heart pound a little faster with just the sight of her.

"Hello Brandon. Boys you two aren't keeping Mr. Miller from resting are you?" She asked with concern.

"Oh, no Mom, Mr. Miller was about to tell us about the bull and how he got hurt."

"Oh, boys, please!" Joyce said as she started to scold her sons.

"No, really Joyce, it's alright."

Joyce could see the excitement in her sons' faces as they waited to hear the gory details of how Brandon got attacked by a bull.

I don't know why males like to hear of such things. She thought to herself. She let the story continue as she sat and listened herself.

"Well, it really is all my fault, and you boys can learn from this. I was driving past the east pasture as I was checking on some cattle, and I noticed a few cattle by a fence post that was leaning; I got out of my truck to fix the post. As I was working on it, the cows moved on, but I really didn't pay it much mind. Then from out of nowhere this bull came charging at me. I didn't see him at first, but heard the stomping of his hooves. When I turned to see what it was I heard, he was so close to me, I really couldn't get away from him. After he knocked me down and gored me a few times, I started to get up, and then he came at me again. He knocked me real close to my truck; while I was on the ground, I saw him scratching his hoof, getting ready to charge after me. I somehow got up off the ground and jumped into the back of my truck; I knew I would not have time to get the door open, so in the back I went. I lay flat on the bed floor, gasping for air. I laid there long enough for him to go on his way. When I was sure he was gone, I got into the cab of the truck and called Richard on my cell phone. Of course I didn't realize how hurt I was, until Richard came on the scene. The rest I think you know."

"Oh, Brandon," Joyce said with her hand to her throat. "That must have been awful."

"Wow, Mr. Miller, you must be one tough cowboy!" Mark said with his eyes almost as big as his face.

Brandon took that time to remind the boys to never be in the pasture when they know a bull might be in there somewhere. "You never know when they are going to come after you," he cautioned his young ranch hands.

"Okay Boys, Mr. Miller needs his rest; you two go on down, and I will be there in a few minutes to take you home," Joyce spoke with authority, and the boys did as she said.

Joyce pulled a nearby chair close to the bed and talked with Brandon a few minutes. She told him about her day, but what she really wanted to know was how he was feeling.

"Lonely, I miss you," he said with serious eyes. "I've done nothing but think of you all day."

"Really," Joyce asked with a hint of giggle in her voice.

"Come closer, Joyce." Joyce knew it would be best if she not go closer to him right then, after all they were in his bedroom alone. She kept her distance and giggled at him, but let him know, he must behave himself.

As Joyce was about to leave the room, Brandon caught her hand, and held it.

"I love you, Joyce McIntosh." He said seriously looking in her eyes. "I don't want you to ever be interested in a captain, or a dock loader, not anyone, but this cowboy that now holds your hand." He spoke sounding a little possessive. "Do you understand Joyce?"

"Umm hmm," she replied gazing in his eyes. It was then Joyce remembered Brandon saying something about her and Mac.

"Oh by the way, I meant to ask you, what were you referring to when you said something about me and Mac?" She asked with confusion on her face as she stood by his bed.

Brandon explained about the day he came to the office to take her to lunch, to finally speak his peace about how he felt for her. But when he saw her leave with Mac, he figured the two of them may have been seeing each other.

"Mac and I are just buddies, pals; we would never think of each other in that way." She explained. "He wanted to buy my lunch to show his appreciation for my helping him, that's all. So really Brandon, you misunderstood totally," she said with a little gleam in her eye.

By the next Saturday, Brandon was up and moving around with very little help. He felt ready to get back to the stables and the cattle, but the doctor's orders were "no". The doctor said he still could not ride a horse. This was the hardest thing for him, at times he felt he was going to come unglued, but still he obeyed. As he was recovering, he got more and more on Lorna's nerves. Everywhere she turned, he was there, asking all kinds of questions. She had even called Joyce to ask her to come over and spend most of Saturday with Brandon, just to get a break from his nagging and following her around. Joyce agreed to come and help.

"Come on, Brandon, I'm taking you outside this house and giving Lorna a break," she said with authority.

"I would love to go outside, but what I really want to do, is go to the stables," he said, looking much like a child asking to go out and play.

"All right, I'll tell you what, if you will use your cane, and go slow, I will help you to the stables. But once we are in there you must sit down and rest. Deal?" she asked with big eyes staring right at him.

"Deal," he said as he picked up his cane from off the sofa.

Once Brandon was in the stables, he had a look of pure contentment on his face. He did as he promised; he sat on a nearby bench and rested for a short while. He missed his horses, especially Pete, his thoroughbred. He had brought a piece of peppermint for Biscuit and an apple for Pete. He had missed his horses almost as much as he had missed Joyce.

The two of them sat for a while and talked until he started to feel tired. Joyce helped him back into the house, where he then reclined in his chair to rest before supper was served.

The time in the stables had done Brandon a world of good, just to be out of the house for a little while and see his horses; he knew it wouldn't be too long now until he would be totally recovered and put this whole ordeal behind him.

Lorna got a lot of work done while Joyce was there helping with Brandon.

"Please, Miss Joyce, will you stay for supper?" The housekeeper asked.

"No, I'm sorry, Lorna, I must get home and get dinner for my family, but thank you."

After Brandon had a good long rest, Don, Sean and their spouses came to visit their father; they sat around in the living room and talked and were a little silly. Richard and Luke came in around suppertime to add to the fun. Brandon silently thanked the Lord for sparing his life and allowing him to still be a part of this wonderful family.

Elise was getting things packed up to head home for the summer. She was so glad her first year of school was behind her. She honestly didn't think she could write one more paper, or take one more test, if her life depended on it. She and her roommate, Janet, had begun their packing after their last test was over. After three hours of non-stop packing, and clearing out drawers, they all had their things together and were on their way. As she looked around to her overstuffed luggage and boxes, she wondered why she had brought so much stuff to her dorm. She also promised herself she would not do that when she returned for the fall semester.

Timothy came and got her all loaded up, shaking his head as he looked at all the stuff.

"I know, I know." Elise said to her brother. "So, how are the wedding plans coming together?" Elise asked.

"I have to tell you Elise, I had no idea there was so much involved in planning a wedding," Timothy replied.

"Christine and her mom have been working on this for months and months now. I told them since I wouldn't be much help; just tell me what I need to do. Dad told me years ago, as long as I had the honeymoon planned out and ready, I would be okay."

"And you have this ready?" she asked.

"Oh yeah, have for months now. It's a surprise, but I'll let the family know where we are headed, I just won't let Christine know until we are on our way," Timothy said with a proud look in his eyes.

What Timothy couldn't figure out was why it took so long to plan the wedding. Why couldn't they just get all dressed up in rental formalwear, go to the church and get it all over and done with. Elise interrupted his thoughts when she mentioned he was about to miss their exit off the interstate.

"Hello, Joyce McIntosh's office, how may I help you?"
"Hello there." Brandon said with his deep voice.

"Well, hi." Joyce replied with a smile on her face and a twinkle in her eyes. "Are you behaving yourself today?" Joyce asked teasingly.

"I felt I needed a little rest, so I thought I would give you a call, and as for behaving myself, I'll not answer that one."

Brandon's doctor had told him it may take awhile to get back to one hundred percent, Joyce sweetly reminded Brandon of this. She was glad he had been released from the doctor and could go back to work, but was concerned that he would overdo it.

"Yeah, he did; I feel like I am at about ninety percent. I get aggravated when I think about that bull, after all, I feed him, give him a place to stay, give him all those cows for his pleasure, and what does he do; he tries to kill me," Brandon said with irritability in his tone. "I honestly don't know what I did to alarm him." Joyce couldn't help but laugh a little.

"There is something I want to talk to you about; are you free for dinner tomorrow night?" asked Brandon.

"I think tomorrow sounds good. Elise gets home tonight, and that will give me some time with her," Joyce explained.

"Great, I'll pick you up at seven."

"I'm looking forward to it."

"Bye, Joyce."

"Bye, Brandon," she said with a hint of a giggle.

It was then Leslie came in Joyce's office to hand her some papers, and made the comment that she must have been talking to Brandon, because she had that look on her face. This made Joyce blush a little. The receptionist just went out the door and about her business.

Samantha heard a thump at the front door, and cautiously looked out the window to see what the noise was. She then called her mother to come quickly.

"Oh, sweetie it is so good to have you home. I can't tell you how much I have missed you." Joyce said to her eldest daughter, as she gave her a big hug and a kiss on the cheek.

"Hey! Elise is home." This came from Michael and then Mark. Everyone was so thrilled to have Elise home for the summer. They all ran to her to cover her in hugs and kisses.

Elise enjoyed all the attention, and let them all know how glad she was to be home, and how much she had missed everyone in return. With all the attention, she forgot Timothy was bringing her luggage in all by himself.

"Mark, Michael, can you help me get these things in please; if you two help me, we will be done by August, I'm sure." Timothy teased. Mark and Michael did as their big brother asked, and wondered why girls took so much stuff with them to college. When they helped Timothy unload his stuff he only had one big duffel bag, a large suitcase and one box of books. The twins gave a big sigh when they finally got the luggage in Elise's bedroom.

Joyce ordered Mexican takeout for dinner so they wouldn't have to spend their first evening with Elise back at home cooking and cleaning the kitchen. Elise told them all about her roommates, Janet and Emily, and the fun they had. She also told all kinds of stories about classes, professors and the cafeteria. She, like her roommates, had gained a few pounds during their first year; she just didn't know why. Her eating habits hadn't seemed to change, but the size of her hips and backside had. Was it the cafeteria food, or the fast foods outside the cafeteria? Either way Elise had told herself, during the summer break she was going to lose those few extra pounds. She wasn't banking on Joyce serving Mexican the first night she was home. Joyce only thought her daughter looked wonderful; she was starting to look more like a young woman and less like a teen.

Joyce and her children stayed up laughing and talking much later than they should have. Elise's siblings had stories to tell her as well, things that happened at their schools. Samantha couldn't wait to tell her sister of the high school gossip. Of course, she waited until they were alone in Elise's room, because Joyce didn't like them gossiping about anything or anyone. After many hours of family time everyone made their way to bed, and Joyce slept a little better that night knowing her daughter was in her room down the hall.

Brandon waited patiently for someone to answer the door.

"Hello, Mr. Miller." Samantha said as she answered the door. "Come on in; Mom will be down shortly. Mark will you tell Momma that Mr. Miller is here?"

"Sure Mom! Mr. Miller is here!" He shouted at the top of his lungs.

Brandon turned to speak with Samantha when he heard Joyce coming off the last step of the stairway.

"Thank you, Mark," Joyce said, holding Mark's chin in her hand. "It wasn't necessary to yell, all you had to do was come to the top of the stairs, knock on my door and say, Mom, Mr. Miller is here." She kindly, but firmly explained.

"But Momma, my way is much faster." Joyce kissed his brow and Brandon turned his face away to keep from laughing. *The little guy has a point,* he thought to himself.

"Brandon, are you sure you feel well enough to drive?"

"Yes, I feel very well and rested today."

"Well, if you're ready, shall we go?"

Joyce gave instructions like usual when going out for the evening. Both girls were going to be there with Mark and Michael, so she knew things would be fine, but old habits die hard.

"Joyce, I want to talk about our relationship." Brandon spoke after finding his voice at the dinner table. He had taken Joyce to Harvey's. Harvey's served some of the best beef and pork in all of Texas. They also served a chocolate soufflé he figured Joyce would love.

"Okay Brandon," she replied feeling a little uncertain about the subject.

Brandon looked into Joyce's beautiful face, the face he wanted to look at forever. He reached for her hand and gently held it as he began to speak

"Since my accident, I feel you and I are at a new level in our relationship." Brandon went on to ask Joyce if she would not date anyone but him. He was a little afraid of her answer, but he needed to put all of his cards on the table and hope he didn't lose. "And of course, I would not see anyone but you."

Joyce looked at Brandon sitting across from her; he was so handsome, and she loved to be near him.

"There is no one I want to see but you, Brandon," she replied seriously. Brandon, now able to breathe again, continued with what was on his heart.

"I have talked to my boys about us; of course, they seemed to know how I felt about you long before I was sure myself," he said with a little humor. Joyce chuckled at this information.

Brandon's sons were fine with their father seeing Joyce on a personal level. They couldn't help but wonder what had taken him so long to ask her out.

"I think you should talk to your children as well," Brandon said.

"Well, I didn't want to mention anything that I wasn't sure of. They know I have special feelings for you, and of course you are coming around quite often. I will talk to them this weekend." She said grinning at him.

Brandon asked Joyce if she wanted him to be there when she spoke to the children. She felt that was very sweet of him, but knew it was something she would have to do on her own.

"I think I should do this myself, that way everyone will be more at ease to say what is in their heart."

"I see, I think you're right, it would be best if you did this without me there."

Brandon paid the check; the two of them went for a walk, and returned to sit on a bench right outside the restaurant they were eating at earlier. The night was lovely, the sky clear, and the half moon shining.

"What a lovely evening, I wish we could just sit here forever." Joyce said out loud, not really meaning to. Brandon gently took her hand, kissed the back of it, and sat very close to her as they enjoyed the scenery and the time alone together.

Joyce invited Brandon in for a cup of coffee after he brought her home. Elise then came in and began to talk with the two of them.

"Momma tells me you were attacked by a bull, Mr. Miller."

"Yes, I was, and I'm still recovering, but I am almost there," he replied.

"Has it made you fearful of your cattle now?" Elise asked.

"Not really fearful, but more cautious at times I think."

Elise talked with Brandon for about an hour, then excused herself and went on up to her room.

"Well, I really must be going, thank you for the coffee and wonderful evening Joyce."

"Thank you." Joyce said with a little grin on her face. Since the kids were all upstairs for the evening, Brandon was not going to let this opportunity go by. He took Joyce's chin in his hand and placed a soft kiss on her lips. As she looked up at him with loving eyes, they said good night.

As Joyce said she would, that Saturday morning she talked to her children about her relationship with Brandon.

They were all sitting around the kitchen table, eating breakfast; Joyce knew this would be the best time, since Samantha and Elise would be leaving soon to work their shifts at Your Choice of Chicken. The twins were to be at the ranch by 9:00 a.m. and, of course, Timothy would be with Christine later in the day.

"Children, I need to speak to you all this morning; I wish to know what you think of Brandon and me dating more seriously. We have begun to see each other more, and I want each of you to speak your own mind about this matter, because it affects all of us." Joyce instructed.

"Mom, are you and Mr. Miller getting married?" Samantha asked in a worried tone.

"Marriage has not come up." She assured her daughter. "But, if it does come up, I want to know what each of you think about it; I don't want this to be upsetting to anyone. I will tell Brandon that we can no longer see one another if it's going to be upsetting to anyone in this household; do I make myself clear?" She said very sternly. Heads begin to nod.

"Right now Brandon and I are just dating, and I must tell you honestly, I care very deeply for him. When your father died, I thought my heart would break. Even though it wasn't always a cheerful time around here, we truly loved one another. I honestly thought I would never date, much less care for anyone ever again. I just want to know how you feel about Brandon, our dating, and if he were to ask me to marry him; I need to know your true feelings." She said as she looked each one of her children in the eyes.

"Well, I think Mr. Miller is a fine Christian man, and he did ask me if it was okay if he dated you. Personally I was impressed." Timothy then chuckled a little and I certainly have never heard any of my friends speaking about their mother's dates asking their son for permission."

"I like Mr. Miller," Michael said.

"Yeah, so do I," echoed Mark. "He is the toughest cowboy there is; he isn't afraid of anything, not even a big ol' ugly bull." Joyce chuckled at this confidence that came from her sons.

"I don't have a problem with it. I mean he seems to be nice. He has been coming around here for well over a year. My question is how come this has taken so long," Elise said.

"Well, I don't want you to marry Mr. Miller," Samantha seriously said. Everyone was a little stunned by her words. "What about Daddy, how can you just forget him Mom?" Samantha said with tears in her eyes. As Joyce went to her daughter and hugged her, she looked her in the face, with tears starting to form in her own eyes.

"Samantha, honey, Daddy is gone, and he is not coming back," she said very tenderly. "We all have to go on with our lives. I still have a love for your father, and always will." Joyce tried to explain, but felt she was doing a pitiful job. "I see your father and the love we had for each other in each of your faces. I have not forgotten him; please believe that. Do you all understand that?" she asked. They replied yes verbally, and one or two heads nodded.

Samantha still did not like the idea of her mother possibly marrying again. They continued to talk for a while longer, and Joyce found out that Samantha had a lot of fears that Joyce was never aware of. Some of those fears came from her classmates in school; several children that Samantha knew had parents that had been remarried several times. Joyce thought, *no wonder she had fears, but the question is, what were she and Brandon going to do about it?*

Monday, Brandon took Joyce out to lunch. He brought a picnic basket filled with several goodies in it. He had packed roast beef sandwiches, fruit, cheese, iced tea, and two large brownies for dessert.

"I know this quiet little place we can go and be alone." He told Joyce.

"Oh, I see," she said smiling up at him. There was silence for a few moments before she spoke. "I talked with the children Saturday morning, and we are good, except for Samantha," she said with sadness in her voice.

"What seems to be the trouble?" He asked with much concern as he was laying the food out for their lunch.

Joyce assured Brandon the problem was not him personally, it could have been any man and Samantha would still have a problem with it. She was not ready for her mother to be with anyone, but her father, and possibly never would be.

"I feel it will be best if we go slowly, and she sees that things will be all right. She will need to see for herself how you treat me. I think she needs to know you will be around forever and not for just a little while and then move on, like some of her classmates parents have had done to them." Joyce told Brandon that one of Samantha's classmate's parents had been remarried six times.

"I see, you're right. We will need to take it slow, and I honestly do not want to hurt any of your children, Joyce. You must believe that," he replied seriously.

"I do... I do, but remember my children are younger than yours with the exception of Richard, and I haven't been alone as long as you have; so it may take a little getting used to." Brandon kissed Joyce on the forehead, and they continued to eat their lunch.

"Well, I guess I had better get you back to the office; I hear you have a big, mean boss."

Joyce laughed at Brandon's silliness. But before they got up to leave, Brandon pulled Joyce a little closer and put his arm around her. He gave her a gentle kiss on the lips. Joyce automatically put her arms around his neck, and it felt so right to her; she allowed him to kiss her for as long as he wished.

Brandon walked Joyce into the office, then said hello to his sons before he went back to the ranch. Sean was in a moment of a crisis when Brandon dropped by, so he stayed longer than intended. It seemed one of the suppliers that the Lone Star had work with for many years, had all of a sudden decided to drop them as a customer. Sean had spent many hours on the computer and the phone trying to clear up this problem, and was about at the end of his patience when Brandon walked in.

Seeing his son's frustration Brandon offered his help, and Sean took it gladly. After fifteen minutes of Brandon talking with Jason Harper, the man in charge of that company, the matter was settled and all was well. The problem had simply been a computer error. After Sean thanked his father for his help, Brandon left and headed back to the ranch. He knew he would not get much done with the lateness of the hour.

Pastor Jones had known Timothy since he was a very small boy. He spent several weeks counseling Timothy and Christine before their wedding; he did that with every couple that came asking him to perform their wedding. Pastor Jones felt that all couples should have counseling before they committed their lives to each other; he wanted to be sure both were prepared and serious about their future together.

"You should go into a marriage with your eyes wide open, and after the wedding, close them just a little," he kindly advised. "Mrs. Jones and I have been married for forty-three years now, and there are times, few but still times, we are not on the same page, and may not feel too kindly toward one another. Still, we have stayed together and weathered the storms that life has thrown our way, and there will be some thrown at you as well. You both will have to commit to love each other no matter what life throws at you."

Pastor Jones answered all their questions and guided them to scriptures that would always be a help to them in their marriage. His wife Libby counseled with Christine privately about her role as a wife, while he spoke to Timothy privately about his role as a husband. Both Timothy and Christine came away from their time well spent with the older couple and with truth they hoped they would always remember.

"There are a lot of things I never thought about," said Christine.

"Neither did I, but Christine, I truly love you, and I'm willing to commit to you for the rest of my days." He then kissed her on her forehead, hoping his words would calm any fears she may have.

It was the day of Timothy and Christine's wedding. Everyone was running around trying to get dressed and to the church early. Pastor Jones was performing the ceremony and the church was decorated beautifully. All the flowers were beautiful and carefully arranged and the reception hall was decorated with flowers. Wedding bells were behind the table that held the wedding cake. Everything was ready for the big day, including Timothy's nerves.

The bride was a little nervous, but holding up well. Joyce knocked on the dressing room door where Christine waited until time to start. Joyce wanted to see how she was doing and if she could be of any help.

"How's Timothy?" Christine asked as soon as she saw Joyce.

"He's doing fine, dear. He did seem to be a bit nervous this morning, but has since calmed down. Poor thing, he put on two different shoes, I am so glad his sister noticed before he left the house." Everyone in the room laughed at Timothy's behavior.

"How are you?" Joyce asked with a hint of laughter. Right before Christine answered, her mother came in.

"Hello, Helen."

"Hi, Joyce." Helen replied in a bit of a rush.

"Doesn't Christine just look beautiful?" Joyce asked.

"Oh, yes, she does," Helen replied as she gave her daughter a hug. "And I think I just may make it through this day as well." The two mothers chuckled.

"Is Daddy ready, Mom?" Christine asked her mother for the third time.

"Yes dear, he and Timothy's little brothers are sitting out on the front steps talking."

"Now that could be interesting," Joyce said. "I'm sure William will learn a lot."

The music started, and all the guests were seated, Pastor Jones took his place down front as did Timothy and his groomsmen. Then all stood to see the bride as she came down the aisle on the arm of her father. Timothy thought she's the most beautiful woman I have ever seen. At that moment, all seemed to slow down for Timothy. He felt his day had been a bit rushed and too busy. As he took Christine's hand he mouthed the words, 'I love you'. Christine smiled at him, and the service continued.

Timothy and Christine made it through the wedding vows without any problems; it also didn't last as long as they both thought it would, but it was wonderful. There were a few tears from both mothers, but that was to be expected.

Joyce was happy her son had found a young woman like Christine; she refused to think she was losing a son, but gaining a daughter. Joyce had prayed that she would be another mother to Christine, and not just an in-law.

"After the first child gets married, it gets easier," Brandon told Joyce as he walked up behind her.

"Oh please, Brandon, I don't think that is helping me right now, I don't even want to think about going through this again anytime soon." Brandon just smiled at her.

The reception was a fun party, everyone eating and laughing. The new couple had their pictures taken and then opened their gifts. Everyone was so amused to see that Christine and Timothy received three toasters, two blenders, and only one set of towels.

When it came time to cut the cake, Timothy being in a playful mood, put his finger in the icing, without his new bride knowing, then mischievously wiped it on her nose. Of course, she could not let this action go without reward. Timothy was just about to put a big bite of cake in his mouth, when Christine shoved the whole thing in his face. Feeling she had gotten even with her groom, he then grabbed her and gave her a big kiss.

Michael and Mark found this most amusing, looking at each other and softly mouthing the words food fight. Samantha quickly read the look on their faces, and told them firmly it was only for the bride and groom.

Timothy and Christine made their way around the room and took time to speak with each of their guests. Finally Timothy had the opportunity to thank someone privately. He sat down beside his mother and spoke where only she could hear.

"Thank you, Mom."

"For what?" she asked.

"For accepting Christine into our family."

"Oh, honey, it was so easy; she is a very lovely person. She seems to love you very much, and as long as she makes you happy, I'm happy." Joyce gently kissed her son on the cheek and then rubbed his face with her hand.

"Speaking of Christine, we are leaving shortly; we're headed to the Executive Hotel for the night and then off to the mountains where I have rented a little cabin for the next five days. She doesn't know where we are going, but I wanted to let you and her parents know where we would be."

Fifteen minutes later, the newest Mr. and Mrs. McIntosh were off to their honeymoon.

CHAPTER THIRTEEN

Brandon and Joyce had been taking things slowly for Samantha's sake, but it didn't seem to be working. On Thursday evening Joyce came home from work with good news for the whole family.

"Hey everybody, come into the kitchen please, I have something to tell you."

As Elise, Samantha, Mark and Michael sat around the table; Joyce told them they were all invited to go camping with Brandon and his family.

"Wow," "Yessss!" "Alright, when do we go?" "Tim and Christine too?" were the replies.

"Yes, Tim and Christine too, all of us," Joyce answered.

Samantha didn't say too much, but seemed to be only a little happy about going camping.

"We leave tomorrow early afternoon and return Sunday night late."

The boys were so excited they could hardly sleep that night; both were packed before going to bed and even helped their sisters roll their sleeping bags. Joyce was sure sleep would be hard coming for the two of them.

Joyce and the children pulled up to Brandon's ranch house at two that afternoon. Brandon was still loading his gear, so Mark and

Michael ran to help him. They figured if they helped out they could get to the campsite a lot faster. This was the largest group Brandon had ever taken: Brandon, Richard, Don, Jennifer, Elise, Timothy and Christine, Samantha, Mark and Michael. "I hope we brought enough food," Joyce said to Brandon as she counted all the heads that were coming.

"We did, besides there will be plenty of fish to catch." Brandon said as he kissed Joyce on the cheek.

"Quick everyone, gather around; come on everyone." Brandon was like a mother hen gathering her chicks. "Before we leave I want us to have a word of prayer for our safety and just to have a good time together. Don would you please lead us?"

"Yes, sir." Don did as his father bade; he asked the Lord's blessings and safety on both families and thanked Him for his goodness.

At last it was time to pile in and take off. Joyce and the twins rode with Brandon. Samantha and Elise rode with Timothy and Christine. Richard rode with Don and Jennifer. No vehicle was overly crowded.

Mark and Michael couldn't wait to get there. When they finally arrived the excited boys both quickly jumped out of the Bronco ready to start the fun.

The boys had their tent up in no time and then helped Joyce get hers up. She, Elise and Samantha were sharing a tent, but neither of them really knew how to put the thing together, so the boys were a very big help.

After all tents were up and standing correctly, the men were headed toward the wooded area to get some wood to make the fire. While the men were gone, the women set up the tables and then sat around talking. When the men returned, they had enough wood for the entire weekend. Don and Richard got the fire started, while the women did some food preparations.

The food could not have been any better. There were pork chops, baked potatoes, side salads, breads and cookies. Don and Brandon had cooked the meat to perfection; the pork seemed to be so tender and juicy it almost melted in your mouth; there really wasn't a need for a knife.

Chapter thirteen / 187

Samantha was sitting by the campfire away from the others when Mark asked her to come with him.

"Mom, Sam and I are going to the lake," he yelled. Joyce walked to where the two of them stood.

"Mark, honey, you didn't have to yell; all you had to do was come to me and ask. Now all the little critters in these woods are running from this awful noise they have just heard." Samantha and Mark just laughed at this.

"Don't be long and don't get wet," Joyce said kindly to both of her children.

Once at the lake destination Mark had a very important conversation with his big sister.

"Come on Sam, don't be a wet blanket on this camping trip. Everyone seems to be having a good time except you." Mark said with a pleading voice. "You're just being a lump on a log, and you know Mom will not enjoy herself if one of us is not enjoying ourselves."

"I know, but I'm really afraid Mom and Brandon will get married," she said to her little brother.

"Sam, Michael and I work with Brandon every Saturday, if he was a bad person, we would know it by now. And in case you haven't noticed, when he looks at Momma, he has this goofy look on his face." Silence was between the two siblings for just a moment, when Mark spoke again.

"Sam, did Daddy have that look on his face when he looked at Momma?"

After Samantha thought for a moment, she replied, "I can't remember."

"Sam, I really don't think you have anything to be afraid of."

"You're probably right Mark. Thanks, let's go back and see if it's time to eat, I'm starvin', and I will try to stop being a lump on a log."

"Great, let's go," Mark said as he jumped up.

The rest of the camping trip Samantha seemed to be more at peace with the relationship between her mother and Brandon, and she had her little brother to thank for it.

After the meal was over and the cleanup was done, everyone sat around the campfire.

"Hey, I have a game we can play," said Michael. "I am going to start a story and when I stop, the next person has to pick up where I leave off and continue the story; they stop and the next person goes," he explained.

Michael started the game; everyone played and laughed. As the story got longer it also got sillier and sillier, the laughter seemed to go on and on as well. The hour had gotten late, and the adults decided it was time to turn in.

Brandon began to walk Joyce to her tent, talking the whole way.

"If you need anything, just let me know. I'll come to your rescue," he joked.

"What if you need anything?" she teased back.

"Then you can come to my rescue." This caused them both to laugh out loud.

With a quick good night kiss the two turned into their separate tents.

After getting settled into her sleeping bag, sleep came easily to Joyce; the outdoor air and sounds were so relaxing.

"Mom?" Samantha spoke.

"Hmm," Joyce said in a sleepy sound.

"I think I may be all right with you and Brandon seeing each other more seriously." This shocked Joyce and woke her up.

"What happened? What made you change your mind?"

"Oh, I don't know, something Mark said," she told her mother.

"Mark?"

"Yep, Mark," she simply replied.

"I'm glad you told me honey, thank you." After that little bit of news, Joyce went from about to fall asleep to being wide awake. She silently thanked the Lord for the peace he had given Samantha, along with being together with her children, Brandon, his family and enjoying God's beautiful creation.

Saturday morning, Joyce was working at preparing the coffee; Don had begun cooking the meat. The smell of bacon cooking on the open fire seemed to empty the others from their tents.

"Good morning." Brandon said to Joyce in a rough, deep, just got out of bed voice.

Chapter thirteen

"Well, good morning sleepyhead," she teased. Brandon gave Joyce a kiss on the side of the head as she handed him a cup of coffee.

"This mountain air just puts me out like a little baby; either that or I was more tired than I thought," Joyce just chuckled at him and the way he looked in the morning.

After their morning breakfast, everyone got themselves put together; their bedrolls were put away, and they were ready for the day's activities. Don had planned a whole day of fun for the group. The first thing was a hike, not a long one, but he felt everyone would enjoy it. There is a waterfall at the end of the hike that was sure to be a fun activity itself, not to mention refreshing to play in.

"Aah man! Mark did you hear that? A waterfall!" Michael said with much excitement.

When the group got to the waterfall, it was so beautiful. The sun danced off the water that was falling from the top of a mountain, it was so inviting. Everyone seemed to echo each others one sound. Aah! They were all hot and tired from the hike and needed a moment's rest.

Mark and Michael were the first ones to run right through the waterfall and then jumped in the small lake. Joyce was only happy to know they took their shoes, shirts and socks off first.

The water was cold at first, but after you got used to it, it felt wonderful. Timothy and Christine sat to themselves for a while stealing a kiss from time to time; they were still honeymooning. As the laughter was swept away on the wind, it could be heard for miles.

Brandon took Joyce behind the waterfall; she was amazed at its beauty and the noise that it made. It was just as beautiful from behind as it was in the front.

"I've never been behind a waterfall before." She said as her eyes were drinking in all its wonder and beauty. Brandon, never missing an opportunity, put his hands on Joyce's waist, pulled her close and gave her a very tender kiss that lasted several seconds. They quickly returned to the outside of the waterfall; after all they were not at the falls alone.

"I think I could get used to those kisses," Joyce said to Brandon before they got in earshot of anyone else.

"Good, I was planning on that," he replied with a big smile. After playing in the water, everyone sat or laid on the big rocks and let the sun's warm rays dry them before they headed back to the campsite. They were so happy when Joyce pulled out a backpack filled with snacks. She figured they all would need a little something before they started on their way back.

As the day moved on, Samantha couldn't help notice how much attention and care Brandon took with her mother. He seemed to be very watchful, making sure she was safe and happy. *Did Dad treat Mom like that; did he look at her like Brandon is looking at her now?* These thoughts came to Samantha, but no answers. She also noticed how protective Brandon had become of her mother. He held her hand, made sure she didn't fall while on the hike. *Maybe it was because it is all new to them. Maybe Daddy never was really attentive and we just didn't know any difference.* Thoughts and questions kept flooding Samantha's mind, but still no answers.

Elise came and sat beside Samantha as she continued to allow the sun to dry her. "Hey, Sam, having a good time?" Elise asked.

"Yeah, how about you?"

"Oh, it's great, I was afraid I wouldn't like this camping thing at first, but I do, it's so much fun." Elise said excitedly as she lay back on the rock, allowing her body to dry in the warm sunshine.

"Elise, can I ask you something?"

"Ask away."

"Did Daddy look at Mom like Brandon looks at her? I mean, did I just never notice, or did he not do it? Did he ever act toward her like Brandon does?" Elise looked at her sister and saw that she was serious about her questions, and needed some answers.

"Well, Sam, I know this will sound awful, but I can't really remember. I have noticed when Brandon is around, Momma seems so happy and they both seem to be attentive to each other. I have also noticed a silly grin on Brandon's face from time to time when he is around her. I'm sorry if I haven't helped you with your questions, I mean maybe Daddy was just not the lovey-dovey type. Everybody's different you know. I know it may seem hard to understand right now, but you have to remember, Dad loved Mom and us, and we still love him. He just showed it differently, that's all." Elise tried to explain.

"Thanks Elise."

"No problem, hey, what are big sisters for anyway, now let's go and push the twins in the water," Elise teased. They then both laughed and sought out their little brothers.

The hikers returned to the campsite, hungry and tired. The boys had enough energy to keep going without a problem. After a bit of a rest, all the men took off to the lake to do some fishing. Michael was thrilled when he caught a four pound trout. They returned to the campsite, got the fish cleaned and ready to go on the fire.

Brandon didn't know which part of camping he liked the most. There was something about sitting around the campfire that made him feel good all over. When the cleanup was done, and dark was closing in, that is when everyone gathered.

Richard played his guitar while the others sang. While this was going on, Joyce and Brandon brought out marshmallows, chocolate, and graham crackers. The twins looked at each other and said at the same time. "S'mores!"

Everyone got a long stick that Don had made just for this event, and got their s'mores made. They ate them with much enjoyment. Jennifer made the remark that the weekend was going to add about three inches to her waist. "You're not the only one honey," was Joyce's response.

"Coffee?" Joyce offered to Brandon. "Thank you, s'mores and coffee, yum yum." Joyce just smiled at him as she handed him a mug.

Once again, the campers headed to their tents, and the night air lulled each one to a very comforting slumber.

Sunday morning as everyone gathered after breakfast, Brandon gave the devotion. Even though they were not in a church building, he felt that was no excuse for not taking time for the Lord on His day.

"I'm going to read from the book of Genesis, so those of you that brought your Bible can turn there; if you didn't, well, shame on you." Brandon said teasingly.

"Genesis 1:1 'In the beginning God created the heaven and the earth.' So, we know before there was anything, there was God, He has always been. Never a beginning, and never will He come to an end. God's beautiful creation is all around us here in these mountains. As we look all around us, we can see God's creation, and some beginnings of our own. Timothy and Christine have started the beginning of their lives together as man and wife. It is good that we not only think on new beginnings as a blessing from God, but thank God for them.

Everywhere I look here at this campsite, I can see God's hand in it. In the mountains, the water and trees, the faces that sit around this campfire. I'm very happy to be up here enjoying God's creation with each and every one of you. I hope you all have had as much fun as I have, and I hope we can all do it again soon."

Brandon led the group in a prayer of thanksgiving. Afterwards everyone seemed to go in different directions, enjoying the last few hours of their camping trip that remained.

Each one packed up and got ready to head out of the campsite. Joyce and Brandon were the last to leave, making sure everything was left clean and nothing left behind.

"Thank you for inviting me and my children to this lovely place. I wasn't sure how everyone would do; after all, the girls have never been camping before. I think this has been a weekend of new beginnings as you said, and none of us will ever forget it."

"You, my love, are very welcome," he responded as he kissed the top of her head. "Shall we head out?"

Brandon and Joyce were alone traveling back in the Bronco. It really wasn't planned; it just seemed to turn out that way, but neither one complained.

"Brandon," Joyce spoke. "I have news for you."

"What is it?" He replied with curiosity.

Joyce let Brandon know about the conversation she had with Samantha the first night in their tent. When Brandon heard that Samantha was okay with him; seeing Joyce more seriously, he was so thrilled; he could hardly keep from singing at the top of his voice. Brandon laughed out loud when he was told that Mark had been the one to calm Samantha's fears. As Brandon was driving he was making sure that in his excitement he didn't run off the road.

There had been one thing Brandon wanted to ask Joyce, and he felt now was the best time.

"Joyce, would it be uncomfortable for you to tell me about Paul?" Brandon asked. Looking at him a little oddly, she answered.

"Well, I hadn't really thought about it, but what would you like to know?" she replied.

"I don't know; just tell me, what kind of man he was, what did he do for a living, things like that."

Joyce thought before she began, not really knowing just what it was Brandon wanted to know. As she thought her mind went all the way back to their beginning, when Paul had started working for an engineering office right after college graduation. Two years into the marriage Timothy was born; it had been an exciting time for the young couple. Paul worked a lot, Joyce was not aware that his job would cause him to have to work so many hours. He didn't seem to mind though; it seemed all the time they were married he never finished with his work; there was always a new project, and he loved it. At times Joyce thought he loved his job more than her and the kids.

A couple of years later; Elise was born, then Samantha. The years seemed to be flying by; Paul had gotten a promotion, then a different job, doing the same line of work, just for another company, and then the twins were born. Paul was good to Joyce; he didn't run around on her; he didn't drink or do drugs; he took his family to church. He was not a patient man though, the smallest things got on his last nerve, and then the yelling would begin. Once Paul got started, look out, everyone was going to get his or her share of the yelling, and in Paul's eyes it was their "fair" share."

Paul and Joyce didn't go on too many vacations because he could never be away from work very long. A weekend here and there, mostly close to home. He held a few positions at church, people from church thought a lot of him. They were a happy couple most of the time.

"But, isn't that what marriage is mostly?"

"What do you mean?" Brandon asked.

"You know, it all starts off wonderful, fireworks and all, but as life goes on and the babies and bills come, the gentleness sort of goes away," Joyce explained.

Brandon didn't know how to answer that one, so he just kept silent. This information was a little unsettling to him.

"What about Stacey?" Joyce asked of Brandon. "What kind of person was she?"

"I met Stacey at a church function; she was eighteen and I was twenty-one. At first she didn't like me; can you imagine that?" Brandon laughed out loud. "One of our mutual friends was having a party and we both were invited. We spent a lot of time talking and then, next thing I knew, we were dating; then a year later, we were married."

"Stacey was always real attentive and loving to me and our boys. She didn't like the outdoors all that much, but she played along for our sakes. She worked in many different church programs, mostly with the children's programs. She had a temper though, and it was best if you not get on her bad side. I guess everyone has that type of thing in their personality, after all no one is perfect. She was a good wife; we had a good marriage, but like you and Paul we too had our fair share of a little rough water."

Brandon never dated anyone after his wife's death, until he met Joyce. He never met anyone that he was attracted to; at one time he figured that part of his life was over. Then when Joyce came into Don's office, Brandon thought he had to be dreaming. It had been so long; he really didn't know what to do with those feelings.

The conversations in the other vehicles were not as serious as the one Brandon and Joyce were having, but they were meaningful and fun as well. Mark and Michael kept everyone in Don and Jennifer's vehicle in stitches with laughter most of the way back home. Jennifer had not been around the twins much, but found them to be a real hoot.

Finally, the caravan of campers pulled up to the ranch house to be greeted by Luke and Lorna. Everyone got out and stretched when they got both feet on the driveway at the Southern Star; several campers made a mad run for the bathrooms.

The men unloaded the vehicles and then loaded up Joyce's Jeep. By nine o'clock that evening, the McIntoshes headed for home and hot baths.

Elise thanked her mother for taking them camping. She admitted, at first she thought it would be hard sleeping outdoors, but after getting there it was fun, and she wanted to do it again. Samantha agreed with her sister, but added she really was looking forward to soaking in a hot bathtub.

It was fall in Texas once again; the children were back in school, the twins still worked for Brandon on Saturdays. Joyce said as long as their grades stayed up they could continue.

Elise was back at school, her second year. She did as she promised herself; she lost those few pounds and did not take more than was needed back to her dorm room. Samantha would be in college come the next year. Joyce could feel the time fly by, but tried not the think on it too much because it made her sad.

Sean and Susan had a healthy baby girl, Victoria Jane Miller. Sean's feet didn't touch the ground for two weeks. Brandon was so excited to be a grandfather and, of course, having a little girl around was going to be a new and exciting thing for him.

"So what is your title going to be to this little girl?" Joyce asked with a hint of laughter.

"Well, I don't really know, I guess I'll let the parents come up with that one, but I do get veto power," he said as he chuckled, "Probably just granddad."

"Well, let me just say, you're the best looking "granddad" I've ever seen, and that's no lie." Joyce told him for his ears alone.

"Well now, that is nice to know," he said with a big grin on his face.

Sean brought the little bundle to let Brandon hold her. She was so tiny and had the smell he remembered from his own newborn babies. She was wrapped in a warm pink blanket and a little pink cap. She looked so small in his large hands; Brandon fell instantly in love with this little person.

"I must admit, she is the prettiest little thing I have ever laid eyes on. I don't know what to do with little girls, but it is going to be fun learning."

Brandon then bent his head down and kissed the baby, and told Sean, his mother would have been so proud and beside herself with joy over this little one. Sean just smiled at the thought.

Back at the office, the buzz was about the birth of little Victoria. Sean had more photos of his daughter than anyone could imagine, he was very proud of his little family.

When Sean finally got back into work mode, things were back to normal, with one exception. Joyce hobbled into the office.

"What happened to you?" Leslie asked with a shocked look as she watched the way Joyce was walking. Her left arm was wrapped up; her right ankle and foot were wrapped up, a bandage on her chin, and scrapes on both of her arms.

"Well, it isn't as bad as it looks." She said with a little bit of unbelieving humor. "I was riding my roller blades with my boys, and this little, and I do mean little toddler came from out of nowhere and darted right in front of me. It was either crash or hit him," Joyce explained to Leslie and now Mac who had come into the lobby to drop off some mail. Both Mac and Leslie made an awful face as they heard her story.

"Can I get you anything, Joyce?" The receptionist asked in a pitiful tone.

"A cup of tea would be great, Leslie, thank you. I'll be in my office and hope and pray no one needs me today," she said as she hobbled down the hall. Once inside she let out a loud sigh as she sat down in the chair thinking how good it felt to let her body rest from the walk.

"Here's your tea and your mail, Joyce."

"Oh, thank you Leslie; you are a gem," Joyce replied.

"What did your doctor say about all those 'boo–boos'?" Joyce just looked up at Leslie as she looked in her purse for something for pain.

"You haven't been to the doctor have you?"

"No, it really isn't that bad."

"To me, it looks bad enough to see a doctor, but hey, I'm just a receptionist," she teased.

"Mr. Miller is here this morning, right now he's in Sean's office."

"Do you mean Mr. Miller as in Brandon?"

"Yes ma'am."

"Thanks Leslie," Joyce replied.

After giving Joyce her needed items, and receiving needed information, Leslie was out the door and back to her desk.

It was a little while before Joyce saw Brandon; he had several items of business to discuss with his sons. Since Joyce was sore and stiff from just getting to work, she was going to stay put and be in misery all alone in her office.

"Knock, knock," Brandon said as he entered the half open door. "Busy?" but before Joyce could answer, Brandon cut her off.

"What happened to your chin ... and your arm?" He then walked around the desk and took inventory of the rest of her, and saw her foot propped up on another chair.

"Joyce, what in the world happened to you?" He asked shockingly.

"Well, to make a long story short, it was me, my roller blades and a two year old running from his mommy." There was a few seconds of silence as Brandon stared at her. "Funny, Mac and Leslie made that same face when I told them as I hobbled in this morning."

Brandon stood looking at Joyce wondering why she came in to work. He asked if Don had seen her, thinking he would tell her to go home. And as if right on cue, Don was walking past Joyce's office and heard his name mentioned, he stuck his head in the door.

"Has Don seen what? Wow, Joyce, what happened?" Joyce explained for the third time her incident with the roller blades and the toddler. Brandon was correct, Don tried to get Joyce to go home and rest, but she would not have any of it. Joyce felt these men were being silly over a few scrapes and bruises. They just looked at each other with disbelief.

"Honestly guys, I'm fine. I'm sore and stiff as a rod, but I'm fine."

While Don was in Joyce's office, she figured she could get some things to him without getting up. She had his itinerary for his upcoming trip next week, and his reservations at one of the best hotels in Nashville. "So, behave yourself," she teased.

"I've never been to Nashville; I'm really looking forward to it." Don said with his eyes dancing. Brandon couldn't help chuckling at his son; he was like a child going on a school trip.

At this time Sean came in the room and asked the same question to Joyce when he saw the shape she was in; this time Brandon filled his son in on what had happened.

"Wow, that had to hurt!" was all Sean said.

Joyce was glad Sean came in her office; she had things for him as well.

"Here is the letter you wanted typed, the contracts you needed ready to be signed, and the phone numbers of the two business prospects you asked for."

"You are absolutely priceless, Joyce."

As Don and Sean left the office, Brandon stared at Joyce. He wasn't sure she was as okay as she was telling everyone. Joyce told Brandon she had taken something for the pain and was feeling pretty good at the moment.

"Maybe you shouldn't be on roller blades anyway, Joyce." He said with a stern look.

"I love doing things with my kids," she explained. "Don't you?"

"Well, yes, but not when I know I'll break parts of me." They both just laughed a little.

Joyce explained this was her first crash since she was a kid herself. Brandon had a look of surprise when she told him all the activities she and her children did together and always had skateboarding, skiing, biking, and ..."

"Okay I get the picture; you're wearing me out just listening to you."

"Well ... for what good it is, I don't play tennis, I refuse to chase that little ball all over the court." Brandon couldn't keep from laughing out loud.

Brandon had other business in town and told Joyce he would check in on her around lunch. He gave Joyce a soft kiss on the lips, hoping he wouldn't hurt her. She looked as if she could just break at the slightest jar.

"I'm not in that bad of shape," she said as she looked at him with a frown on her brow.

"I don't know about that," he said chuckling as he left the room.

Joyce made it through the day with care. Brandon had checked on her mid-day as he said he would, to find her working away. She was very thankful he had brought her lunch; she had wondered how she was going to manage that one. Instead of going to people's offices, she called them to her. This little system was working out very well; she was glad she thought of it. Getting to the bathroom was a different story; she was so stiff from sitting she could barely walk down the hall. She tried not to dwell on the stiffness or the pain, but it was getting harder. When she returned to her office and her comfortable chair, she looked at the clock and realized she had four more hours before she could go home.

Joyce thought four o'clock would never arrive. Mac walked her to her Jeep and carried her briefcase. "Thanks Mac, I'll be fine now." Joyce told her friend and co-worker.

When she got home, she asked the children if they would make supper. They gladly agreed since they knew their mother wasn't feeling well. Mark helped her with her things and began to tell her of his day at school. Joyce stopped at the entryway by the front door, picked up the mail from the table and started to proceed to the stairway.

"I'm just going to lie down for a little while; call me when supper is ready please. Aah, on second thought, I'll just lie down here on the sofa. That way when supper is ready, I won't have that far to walk."

Samantha helped her mother to the sofa, while Michael got her a pillow for her foot and a light blanket. Not ten minutes later, Joyce was sound asleep.

The children were discussing what they were going to prepare for the evening meal when the phone rang.

"Hello."

"Hi, Mark, it's me Brandon."

"Hi, Mr. Miller."

"How are you today?" Brandon asked.

"Fine, we are about to start supper cause Momma got hurt and doesn't feel like cookin'."

"I see. What is your mother doing now?" Brandon asked.

"She's lying down. Do you want me to get her for you?"

"No!" Brandon said very quickly. "No, not at all, instead I would like for you all to stop making supper, and I will be there shortly with some burgers; how does that sound?"

"Hey, that sounds great to me, thanks Mr. Miller."

After hanging up the phone, Mark told his siblings the conversation he had with Brandon.

"Hey, hey, burgers are on the way," he now sang out.

Samantha gave instructions of what was needed to be done before Brandon arrived. Everyone worked to get the table set and drinks poured; it wasn't long until burgers were being delivered.

As Mark opened the door for Brandon, Samantha started to help Joyce off the sofa and into the kitchen. "Oh, here, Samantha, please let me do that." He quickly went to Joyce, giving the food to Mark to put on the table.

"Brandon what are you doing here?" Joyce asked in a confused tone. "I mean, I'm always glad you're here, I just didn't know you were coming, I must look awful."

"I was concerned about you so I called to find out that you were lying down, the kids were about to start supper, and I told them I would bring some very nutritious food over. And you look beautiful with your blow out patches." He teased her, making her laugh a little. He chuckled at his own joke as he was bodily carrying Joyce to the kitchen.

"So, what do you think? Burgers alright," he said as he was standing at the table holding Joyce.

"I think burgers are fine, and you may put me down now." She said with a smile.

"Oh, yeah, right." The children started placing the food on the plates, thinking these two adults had lost their minds.

After the meal was eaten, the children were cleaning the kitchen; they usually didn't make a fuss about chores when their mother was hurt or sick. Brandon carried Joyce back to the sofa and gently laid her down and propped her foot on a pillow.

"Joyce, maybe you ought to have that foot looked at by a doctor. Here, let me take a look at it."

"Oh, are you a doctor in your spare time now?" she said chuckling at him.

"Yes, I am as a matter of fact," he replied.

"Brandon, I have seen more sprains than you could imagine, and I'm telling you it's only a sprain."

"Well, humor me; I want to see your 'sprained' foot." Brandon gently lifted her leg and laid it on the pillow on his lap. He proceeded to carefully unwrap her ankle and foot.

"Honey, can you move it?" He seriously asked, noticing it didn't look too good.

"Yes, I can move it, just not much."

"Does it hurt to touch it?" As he asked he gently touched her foot, and Joyce almost came off the sofa from the pain.

"I'm sorry, I am so sorry. But I barely touched you. I think tomorrow you need to have it looked at."

"No, Brandon, really it will be fine in a few ...," Brandon cut her off.

"Joyce, honey, I seriously think you need to have it seen by a doctor. I'll be here early in the morning to take you, and that's the end of it."

"Well, I don't think I have much choice now, do I?" Samantha just stood there watching the two adults, discussing Joyce's hurt foot and wondering which one was going to win.

"No, my love, you don't." He said as he kissed her on the nose.

The next morning as Brandon said, he was there to take Joyce to have her foot checked out by a doctor. He helped her as she hobbled to his vehicle parked in the driveway.

Joyce was lying on the examining room table when Brandon came in; she looked as if she might cry.

"Joyce honey, are you alright? You look like you're about to cry." Brandon thought his heart would break at the sight of her.

"It's not a sprain after all," she now explained. "I have two torn ligaments and may be looking at surgery. I don't like the sound of that Brandon."

"Oh, honey, it will be okay, I'll be right here. Of course, you know this would have never happened if your feet weren't so small," he teased, which made Joyce laugh a little.

The doctor came in with Joyce's x-rays in his hands.

"Well, after looking over your x-rays, we are definitely looking at surgery," the man in the white coat said. Joyce really looked like she was about to cry now. "It's no emergency right now, so we can schedule it for some time in the next week or so."

Joyce explained to her doctor that her boss was out of town on business, and it really wasn't a good time for her to be away from work. When Brandon heard this he had to speak up.

"Joyce, honey, the office can manage; you need to deal with this now."

Her doctor saw the conflict in the timing of this surgery, so he simply told Joyce that she could put it off a few weeks, but no longer.

"It isn't going to get better on its own," he explained.

After little debate, Joyce agreed to have the surgery done as soon as Don was back from his business trip; she wasn't happy about the whole ordeal at all.

"Joyce, are you sure you don't want to come to the ranch to rest? Lorna will be there to fix your meals, I'll be there, and the children certainly will be coming too." Brandon asked as he was sitting on the side of the examining table holding her hand.

"No, thank you Brandon, we'll be fine at home, and it would probably be better for the children as well, after all it will only be a few days, I'm sure we can manage."

In all reality, Joyce was planning on working up until the day of her surgery. Dr. White talked her into at least cutting down her hours.

"I'm gonna have to keep an eye on you, aren't I?" Brandon said to her in a low, deep voice close to her face. Joyce didn't have a response.

"Okay," Dr. White said. "You're free to go home for now, but I will see you in seven days for surgery, bright and early. I have written out a few instructions for you and a prescription for pain if needed ... and no roller-blading," he said with a smile.

"What about work?" She now asked with uncertainty in her voice. "You may return to work one week after surgery."

"Joyce, I'm sure Don and Sean can handle everything," Brandon said.

It is really important you give your foot plenty of rest, not to mention, you yourself could use it as well."

"Yes, I guess your right. I'm just not used to being down, that's all."

"I'll see to it that she follows your instructions, Doc." Brandon said.

It was the morning of Joyce's surgery; Brandon got her to the hospital bright and early just like the doctor instructed. Samantha and the twins along with Tim and Christine were waiting in the family waiting area. The surgery took only about an hour, and Joyce found herself in the recovery room, feeling very groggy, and out of sorts.

Dr. White talked with Brandon and the family about how well the surgery went, and that Joyce would only need to stay overnight in the hospital. He had his nurse write down the instructions Joyce was to follow to help with her recovery and went over them with Brandon and Timothy. After receiving the good news, the family waited until the nurse told them they could see Joyce, before Timothy took them home.

"I feel like I've been hit by a bus," Joyce said in a very sleepy voice.

"It's the medication, honey; it'll wear off." Brandon explained to her.

"Yeah Mom, you'll feel better as the day goes along." Timothy replied.

The family didn't stay long since Joyce kept drifting off to sleep. The nurse explained to them that she would probably sleep most of the day. Tim and Christine took Samantha, Mark and Michael back to their house, while Brandon stayed with Joyce.

Brandon took a chair next to Joyce's bed and sat quietly. He couldn't keep from looking at her sleeping face; this was the face he had fallen deeply in love with. He wanted to take care of her, protect her from everything, even a hurt foot. As he sat there, he silently prayed for the Lord's wisdom and timing for Joyce and him to be married; he wanted that with all his heart, but he knew he would have to wait. He would have to wait on the Lord and the woman he loved.

Joyce followed the doctor's instructions to the letter; Brandon watched her like a hawk. At times he seemed more like a mother hen. She did appreciate his help, but felt the need for a little time alone; she was careful not to hurt his feelings.

"I do appreciate all your help Brandon, but you need to get back to the ranch."

"Richard and Luke can handle things while I'm gone." He replied kindly.

"I know, dear, but I can take care of myself. I have all the things I may need right here in my reach."

"Joyce, honey, are you trying to get rid of me?" he said in a taunting manner.

"No, I just don't want you to get behind on your work, and to be honest with you, I could use a couple of hours alone," she said with a big smile to not hurt his feelings.

"Alright, but you behave, and stay off that foot."

"Yes, Brandon," she said like an obedient child.

"And call me if you need anything."

"Yes, Brandon."

"I'll be back later." He bent over and gave her a gentle kiss and left the house.

After a week at home and off her foot, Joyce thought she would come completely undone. She was never so glad to be back to work in all her life. The children had been very helpful; Timothy and Christine had come over a few times and made dinner and helped with some household chores. Samantha had done the shopping and took care of most of the boys needs. Elise called several times, and the twins kept her entertained. Diane was over every day checking on her friend making sure all was going well. Brandon also visited every day and made several phone calls during the day while he was working.

During the day Joyce had so much time on her hands; she caught up on her Bible reading. She had started in the book of Genesis at the beginning of the year, but had gotten so far behind; she had been thinking it would take two years to make it through all the books, which was not as she had planned. By the end of the week she was now one book ahead of schedule.

Joyce missed her co-workers and was glad to see them. They let her know they missed her in return. When she walked in her office, on her desk sat a big bouquet of yellow roses. The card read 'welcome back' and all the employees of the Lone Star Supply had signed it.

Don told Joyce about his trip to Nashville, Tennessee. The business meeting went very well, and they actually got done a little early, so Don got to see a lot of the Nashville area. He was eager to tell Sean of this exciting place he had seen.

"Now that's a beautiful place, Sean; we will have to go there on vacation sometime. They have almost everything you could imagine there. The food was great, the hospitality superb. There is this restaurant called Demo's Steak and Spaghetti; oh Sean, I can't tell you with words how delicious the food was. Plus you can take a horse and buggy tour of downtown. When I saw that, I couldn't help but miss my wife.

CHAPTER FOURTEEN

Joyce had been working nonstop in her office when she received a phone call from Brandon. She then leaned back in her chair to talk to him, as if she had all day.

"Well, hello there, why aren't you out in the stables or somewhere?" She teased him.

"Because I had to make an important phone call to a certain lovely lady."

"Oh, anyone I know?" She joked, and they both laughed.

"Are you free for dinner Saturday evening?"

"Well, let me check my date book." She was still teasing him. "Yes, I do have an opening, shall I pencil you in?" They both laughed at the banter.

Brandon told Joyce he would pick her up at five; the dress would be casual and the children were invited to come along with them. He assured her everyone would enjoy their evening out.

Leslie walked in as Joyce hung up the phone; she laid the mail on Joyce's desk, but could not pass up the opportunity to tease her. "You were on the phone with Brandon again, weren't you?" This seemed to snap Joyce out of her trance.

"Aah, yes I was; how did you know?"

"Really, Joyce, the look on your face; it isn't hard to tell." The two giggled and Leslie left the room.

Brandon had a cook-out for his and Joyce's family. Luke and Lorna were invited as well. Lorna figured if she stayed she would work, so she took the evening off with Brandon's blessing. The food was great, steaks cooked on the grill to perfection. As Sean had said long ago, 'Dad could burn water in the kitchen, but on the grill he is the master.' Steaks, baked potatoes, corn on the cob also cooked on the grill; Lorna had prepared beans and salad before she left for the evening. There was tea and soft drinks. Joyce had made three different types of desserts to go with the ice cream she knew would be there; black forest cake, two apple pies, and Brandon's favorite... homemade chocolate chip cookies with nuts.

The boys rode their horses close to the stables where they could be seen by the adults. These were the horses Brandon bought in Lexington, Kentucky just for them. Brandon and Joyce went on a ride of their own.

Richard had brought out a card table; he, his new female friend, Lou Ann, Luke, Samantha, Don, Jennifer, Sean, and Susan all played cards until it got too dark to see. Their laughter could be heard all over the ranch.

Brandon and Joyce rode their horses to the south side of the ranch and enjoyed not only the beauty of the land, but being alone. They stopped at a little creek and let the horses graze. Brandon picked a rosy-petal wildflower and gave it to Joyce. He then pulled her close and kissed her. Her lips were soft, like the delicate petals of the flower he gave her. They stared into each others eyes and held hands. Brandon hated to have to get back to the house, but he realized since it had begun to get a little dark, they should get back.

Brandon's heart was so full of love for Joyce; he didn't want the evening to end. But end it did; that night as he lay in bed, he prayed silently.

Dear Father, I love her. You have brought us close together, and my heart just explodes when she is near me. If it is your timing dear Father, I would like to ask her to be my wife. Help us both in this decision and give us wisdom, in Jesus' precious name I pray, Amen.

After praying, it took a little while, but Brandon drifted off to sleep.

All the while Joyce was sleeping comfortably in her own bed. After returning from their evening at Brandon's, she took a long bubble bath, while she soaked she allowed her mind to recall the events of the evening; this brought a smile to her face. After her bath, she climbed into bed, even with Brandon on her mind, sleep came swiftly.

───

The weeks had passed and it was now late November. It was a little late in the year for Brandon to take Joyce to his favorite camping place, but he wanted the best place for such a special occasion.

"Joyce, my love, how are you?" He asked as they talked on the phone while she was at the office. "Are you free to go somewhere with me on Saturday?"

"Yes, do you have something planned?" she asked.

"I would like for us to spend the day together, up at the waterfall, I know it's too cold to get wet, but it's pretty up there this time of year. We will just spend the day and drive back in the evening."

"Yes, that sounds lovely. I'll pack us a lunch; how does that sound?"

"Sounds great, I'll see you Saturday morning at nine."

"Bye Brandon."

Brandon was at Joyce's house at nine like he said he would be. She was ready with a cooler of food and some soft drinks.

"Samantha dear, what are your plans for today?" Joyce asked.

"Well, I have to work until two, then some friends and I are meeting at the mall; you know, Shelly, John and maybe a few others," Samantha replied.

"Now that sounds like fun," Brandon replied.

Brandon had made arrangements with Richard to have the twins stay at the ranch until he and Joyce returned. Joyce wanted to make sure Samantha was not left with a full day of nothing on her hands.

"Okay, Brandon, I'm ready if you are," Joyce said.

"I'm ready."

"Now, Samantha, I should be home by the time you are, Brandon and I will pick up the boys on our way back. I have my cell phone and you have yours, so we should be in good shape."

"Okay, Mom, have a good time; and I'll see ya' later."
With that Brandon and Joyce were on their way.

Brandon prayed in his mind as he and Joyce drove toward his favorite camping place. It was there, Mark helped Samantha put her fears of her mother's and Brandon's relationship to rest.

Help me dear Lord not to go too fast, I don't want to rush her, I'm nervous, but you know my heart Lord, I truly love her. Brandon prayed silently as they drove toward his favorite camping place.

The drive was beautiful with the sun brightly shining, the look of winter coming. With such beautiful scenery, neither of them felt the need to talk continually.

When they arrived they had the place almost to themselves. Brandon felt this was absolutely great; there were a few people around, but none too close by. He took Joyce by the hand and kissed the back of it, as he led them on a walk, not far from where they parked.

Since the air was much cooler now, getting close to the waterfall was not an option, Brandon simply took another route. The two of them sat on a huge rock that overlooked the lake; the view was breathtaking. With the sun dancing off Joyce's hair, Brandon had to slow down and enjoy the view. After gaining a little more control of himself, they began to talk about different things. How their families got along, and how the children were doing with their relationship. They had sat there for over an hour when Joyce asked, "Hungry?"

"Yeah, I'll get the cooler and bring it over to this area where we can be in the sun."

Brandon carried the cooler, and Joyce took care of spreading out the blanket for them to sit on. She had brought fried chicken, raw vegetables, fresh bread, soft drinks, and Brandon's favorite, chocolate chip cookies with nuts.

"This is a fine meal; it may make me a little too lazy for a walk to the waterfall," Brandon replied as he continued to eat. Joyce laughed at the way Brandon enjoyed his meal and the sun making him relaxed.

After they finished their meal, they sat, talking, laughing, Brandon moved closer to Joyce and with one finger, gently rubbed the side of her face. Her skin was so pretty and soft; he gently raised her chin and kissed her tenderly. Brandon then decided they would go for their walk to the falls after all; he realized he could not come to such a wonderful place, with the woman he loved, and not walk to the waterfall.

When they arrived at the waterfall, it was just as lovely and welcoming as it was when they were there back in the spring. The water was cold, but the beauty was just as lovely. The sun glistened off the water; it was such a breathtaking place. The sounds of the rushing water made you want to sit and take in all its wonder and beauty. Brandon knew this was the perfect spot to bring the woman he loved with all his heart.

"I love to listen to the waterfall. It's a powerful sound, but in a soft way. If that makes any sense?" she said suddenly looking at Brandon.

Brandon standing next to Joyce put his arm around her. They were standing as close to the falls as they could without getting wet from the spray. Looking around, he found a spot for them to sit, and he took her hand and gently rubbed the back of it. He tried to ignore the fast pounding of his heart, but Joyce had that affect on him.

"Joyce, I'm truly, deeply in love with you," he said as he looked earnestly in her eyes. "I want to spend the rest of my days with you." He paused only a few seconds. Joyce looking in his eyes with wonder, "Will you please be my wife?" Joyce, being lost in Brandon's words, had to mentally shake herself. She sat and looked at him; her mouth almost flew open, but she controlled it. Her heart started to beat as if it were coming out of her chest.

"Oh, Brandon," she replied looking with all seriousness. "Yes, I will."

He took her in his arms and kissed her long and passionately. When the kiss was broken, Brandon reached into his pocket and pulled out a beautiful diamond engagement ring. He gently slipped it on Joyce's slim finger and kissed the back of her hand.

They stood in each others' arms in silence for a few moments;

savoring the moment and the scenery. Brandon was full of love and happiness; he was ready to marry Joyce right then and there. If there had been a preacher or justice of the peace at the campground, he would have suggested they say their vows right then.

"When Joyce? When can we be married?"

"I don't know, how long did you want to wait? I mean ... we will need to plan." She began to think more clearly as she continued to answer his question.

"Hey, it's fine with me if we go to the justice of the peace right now and get married, but it wouldn't be fair to the children," he said with love in his eyes.

"Yeah, we won't do that," Joyce said giggling.

"There is one request I have," she said.

"What? Name it and it's yours."

"That we have a small wedding, just our family and a few friends."

"Okay, that sounds like a winner to me."

"Afterwards we can have a big reception with food, friends and so on."

"For you my love, anything," He then pulled her close to him, and the two kissed again and again.

When they returned to the house, they didn't tell the children, because it was late, and Joyce wanted all her kids to be there for the announcement. Elise was coming home in two weeks that would give her and Brandon time to pick a date and make plans for both families to be present. How they were going to keep this hidden until then was a mystery to her.

Two weeks later, Brandon had reservations at one of the finest hotel restaurants in Garland for both their families. He had reserved one of the smaller dining halls so there would be plenty of room. All the children were there; they all enjoyed the food and fellowship together as always. Between Richard and the twins, the laughter kept going.

The laughter started to die down when Mark told of the day at school coming back from the library; it was raining and all the boys were trying to dodge the rain drops, and in doing so, one of the boys ran right into the flag pole ... knocked him right off his feet. This brought the room to laughter once again.

The food was wonderfully prepared. They had their choice of roast beef, ham with potatoes, baby carrots, green beans, salad, dinner rolls and corn bread, iced tea, and for dessert, a delicious chocolate cake with vanilla ice cream.

Everyone ate their fill; little Victoria was starting to get sleepy, so her mother took her in her arms and held her until she fell asleep.

Brandon took his knife and gently tapped the side of his glass. He got everyone's attention as he stood at the head of the table and spoke.

"I see everyone is through eating, and I hope everyone got plenty. However, I do have something to say to you all, an announcement that is. A few weekends ago, I asked Joyce to be my wife, and believe it or not, she said yes."

Claps and cheers were heard from the entire family. Don stood and hugged his father and started to cry.

"Dad, I am so happy for you, I know you and Joyce will be so happy together; I mean look at you, you already are."

Brandon's other sons came and hugged him as well, then hugged Joyce after her children were through hugging her. The twins just sat and watched as they continued to eat their cake.

Joyce never got out of her chair because so many had come to her to bend down and hug her.

The news was very well received by the family, even Samantha, who at one time was very worried about her mother and Brandon. She was afraid her mother had forgotten her father, and didn't want Joyce and Brandon to become close. Now after months of Brandon and Joyce going slowly in their relationship, and wise words of wisdom from her little brother, she was happy for her mom and Brandon.

"So, are you okay with this Samantha?" Joyce asked.

"Oh, yeah, what took you so long anyway?" Samantha said laughingly. The two of them broke out in laughter all over again.

Joyce couldn't wait to call Diane and tell her the whole story; after all she had kept this to herself for a couple of weeks, and thought she would explode before the announcement was made. Diane was so happy for Joyce she nearly cried. The two women spent hours talking about the day up at the waterfall, how Brandon proposed, weddings, colors Joyce wanted and who would be attending.

"Joyce, honey, it may be difficult keeping the wedding small, if you both invite your families." Diane simply explained. This caused them both to laugh out loud. Joyce asked Diane to once again be her matron of honor. Of course she agreed.

After two and a half hours on the phone, Diane and Joyce felt as if they had covered everything there was to cover. Having something to say was never a problem for the two of them, but they did finally hang up the phone.

CHAPTER FIFTEEN

Brandon had a little surprise for Joyce when he talked to her that evening. He was excited and was for sure she would be too.

"Joyce, I want to take you to meet my parents. I've told them so much about you, and they want to meet you." This news was exciting to Brandon, but not to Joyce.

Oh my! I knew this day would come. *Lord, please help me; please help me not be anxious or just plain scared out of my mind.* Joyce was praying silently when Brandon broke into her thoughts.

"Joyce, I think – are you with me?"

"Oh, I'm sorry I think I drifted there for a minute … what where you saying?"

"I want to take you to meet my parents."

"Oh, yes, aah when did you want to go?"

"Next weekend we'll drive up on Friday afternoon. I'm sure Don will give you the afternoon off. We'll stay until Sunday and drive back. How does that sound?"

"Oh, great, it sounds great."

You are such a liar Joyce McIntosh; you know you are scared to death to meet that man's parents. Joyce sat scolding herself inside her mind.

⌒

Friday came way too soon for Joyce. She had made arrangements for Timothy and Christine to stay at the house with Mark, Michael and Samantha. For some odd reason that Joyce could not explain, her work at the office was all done much earlier than ever before. Don told her to take the whole day off if needed; it really wouldn't be a problem. Joyce refused and stayed until after lunch.

"Hey Sean," Joyce said as Sean laid some files on her desk.

"So, I hear you are going to meet the folks." He started to tease Joyce, but then decided against it.

"I remember meeting Susan's parents for the first time. I thought I was going to be sick," He told her. "It all turned out fine, but I wouldn't want to go through that again for all the tea in China. My grandparents are great people, Joyce; you'll love 'em. See ya' when you get back."

"Thanks Sean," she said half heartedly as she stared at the door he walked out of.

Brandon arrived to pick Joyce up and got her bags loaded into his truck. Brandon was so excited about seeing his parents, it showed on his face.

Samantha and the twins were looking forward to watching movies and staying up late with Tim and Christine. Joyce almost wished she could too.

Joyce tried talking herself into things going well with the Millers, and she almost had herself convinced when doubt and fear once again crept into her mind.

Larry and Barbara Miller had lived in Sweetwater, Texas for over twenty-five years. Both were retired now, but at one time Larry worked as a sports writer, and Barbara stayed home with the children and took care of their home. She had a passion for decorating and now did a little part-time work for one of her decorator friends.

"When was the last time you saw your parents, Brandon?" Joyce finally asked.

"Almost a year ago, it's been too long; I try to see them a couple of times a year. I was planning a visit, and then that bull attacked me. Well, that set me back a few months, so I really want to go now. You'll love my mother; she is such a sweet woman."

"Yeah that's what I hear." Joyce said with a half smile.

"Joyce, are you alright?"

Chapter fifteen / 217

"Yeah, just a little nervous that's all." *Boy is that the understatement of the year,* she said to herself.

"We'll stop here for some gas, and on down the road there's a great little place to eat."

The restaurant was a little truck stop that was full of truckers and other hungry travelers. The place was very clean and smelled of meats and vegetables. The tables were decorated with red and white checked table cloths, with a small vase of flowers in the middle of each table.

"What can I get you?" The waitress asked kindly.

"I'll have the turkey club, with a salad, no fries, and a sweet tea."

"And for you ma'am?"

"I'll just have sweet tea, thank you."

"Sure thang, I'll get this right to ya'." The woman responded in her laid back Texas drawl.

"Joyce, honey, are you not hungry?"

"No, right now I truly don't think I could eat a bite. The tea will be fine, thank you."

Joyce figured the tea would help settle her stomach, but food was not an option at this time.

As the two of them sat, they talked and laughed; Brandon flirted shamelessly with Joyce, and she enjoyed it.

"You love to flirt, Brandon Miller, I will have to keep my eye on you," she said teasingly.

"I only flirt with you; I can't help it. You bring it out in me."

"Mmm-hmm." They both chuckled and composed themselves, as Joyce noticed the waitress coming with Brandon's food.

Brandon ate his fill, paid the check, and they were once again back on the road.

After driving for almost an hour, Brandon let Joyce know they only had another eight miles to go; he was looking forward to seeing his parents and introducing them to Joyce. He had noticed Joyce had gotten quiet, but figured she was just nervous. He knew when they got there everything would be fine.

"Aah Brandon would you mind pulling over please, I think I may be sick."

"Sure, Sweetheart."

As Joyce got out of the truck and let the cool air hit her in the face, Brandon came quickly to her aid. "Are you okay? Maybe you should have eaten lunch."

"Oh no, if I had eaten a bite I would have definitely been sick." She informed him. "Brandon I have to confess, I am so scared about meeting your parents."

"Why?"

Joyce stood outside the vehicle, with the air helping her feel a little better; she took the time to explain the reason for her nerves.

"It's very simple really," she began.

Years ago when Joyce met Paul's parents, they immediately took a dislike to her; she never did figure out why. She and Paul discussed it several times, and all he would ever say is, 'Yes, they like you Joyce.' But in reality, they didn't.

"Brandon, I want your parents to like me for me. I am just afraid it will be Paul's parents all over again. I'm sorry Brandon, but I honestly can't help it."

Brandon wondered how anyone could feel that way about this sweet, wonderful woman.

"Joyce, it's alright that you are afraid, but I telling you honey, I really think you are going to hit it off just fine with mom and dad. Let's just stay here for a few minutes and let your nerves and stomach settle down, and then we'll move on."

Brandon took that time to pray with Joyce about her fears of meeting with his parents. It amazed her that at every difficult time, Brandon would pray about it. No wonder he seemed to be so together, she thought to herself.

After about ten minutes or so, Joyce seemed to settle down. Brandon gave her a loving kiss on the forehead, and they were again on their way.

Within a few minutes they were in the driveway of Larry and Barbara Miller.

Brandon opened the truck door to get out, when a man and woman from the front door of the house came quickly toward him. Brandon opened the passenger door for Joyce and before he could make the introductions a big man had his arms around Joyce.

Larry Miller was a loving soul. He was as kind as his son. Joyce was a little surprised that he hugged her before knowing who she was.

"You must be Joyce; we are so glad to have you in our home." He let go of Joyce and looked at his son, to whom he gave a huge embrace, the two hugged unashamedly. Barbara came right to Joyce and did just like Brandon's father had. She then turned, hugged and kissed her son.

Larry said, "well, let's go inside, your mother has made a cake, and I for one, have been waiting too long to get a piece of it."

"I'll get the bags and be right in, Joyce." Brandon told her. He worked quickly at gathering the bags; he knew how nervous Joyce was about the weekend, so he didn't want to leave her alone too long.

Barbara wanted to hear all about Joyce and her children. She had been waiting for months to meet her, now finally, here she sat at the kitchen table, as lovely as Brandon had described.

"Brandon says you have five lovely children." This was a relief for Joyce, she never had a problem talking about her children and after talking in the kitchen for about an hour, Joyce was feeling more and more at ease.

"This cake is wonderful, Mrs. Miller. I love chocolate more than anyone you have ever met." Joyce said with a hint of laughter.

"Thank you, Honey, and please call me Barbara."

"Okay, Barbara it is." She replied as she lifted her cup of coffee.

The four adults sat at the table, eating cake and drinking coffee as if they had all day. Joyce listened as the Millers spoke of Brandon's siblings. She wondered if she would meet them at this visit.

Joyce commented about how lovely the Miller's home was decorated. That was all it took for Barbara to get started on that subject. She took Joyce all through the house showing and explaining some of her decorating techniques. Joyce quickly learned Barbara knew her stuff when it came to decorating.

That evening, Barbara made a wonderful meal, fried chicken, green beans with new potatoes, fried corn, homemade bread, and sweet tea. For dessert, there was more of the cake they had enjoyed earlier that day. Joyce and Brandon offered to help with the cleanup.

"Oh, Brandon, honey, go ahead in the living room with your father. It will give me more time to get to know your Joyce." Barbara said.

'Your Joyce,' that sounded so good to Joyce's ears, as it did to Brandon's.

"Aah well, okay. Mom, if you and Joyce don't want my help, then I guess I will just go away," Brandon teased his mother.

"Oh silly, I didn't say go away hurt, just go away," now she laughed, Barbara Miller gave as good as she got and she and her children joked all the time.

While Brandon was sitting in the living room talking with his father, his mind was in the kitchen.

"Dad, can I get you anything to drink?"

"No thank you, Son."

The two men sat, talking while the evening news was on.

"I'm going to get a glass of water, I'll be right back." As Brandon walked into the kitchen his mother and Joyce were laughing and talking like old friends.

"Yes, Brandon, did you need something honey?" His mother offered.

"Just a glass of water, Mom, that's all." He said as he winked at Joyce. Brandon got his water and when his mother's back was turned, Joyce mouthed to him the words; "thank you." Then he knew all would be fine.

⁓

"Joyce, honey, you'll be sleeping here in the guest room, and Brandon, you'll be down the hall in your old room. Now Joyce, if you need anything, just let me know, but please make yourself at home." Barbara explained.

"Thank you Barbara, I think this room will be just fine, and I will probably be asleep as soon as my head touches the pillow."

"Okay, Brandon, you have to go down the hall now." Joyce teased him.

"I know, I know, but I just wanted to make sure you will be fine and don't need anything."

"Just a good night kiss will do."

"Oh, I think I can handle that request just fine."

Joyce lay in the big, soft bed, replaying the day. So relieved of the outcome; Brandon's parents were different from Paul's. Joyce thanked the Lord for answering her prayers and allowing everything to go well, for calming her nerves, and letting Mr. and Mrs. Miller like her for who she is. Somewhere after praying for her children, Joyce drifted off to sleep. Brandon, on the other hand, was doing some praying of his own.

The next day Brandon drove Joyce around the little town his parents lived in. They stopped at a local grocery store that had been there since the nineteen-fifties. They still had a coke machine where you pulled the bottle out of the slots. Larry and Barbara met up with them for lunch and afterward did a little antique shopping. Barbara knew all the best places to go; it seemed as if she knew everyone who worked behind a counter.

Late that afternoon, the adults enjoyed the outdoors on the patio. Joyce was sitting in a lounge chair talking with Larry.

Joyce wore a tan cowboy hat, to keep the sun off her face, a white blouse, blue jeans and cowboy boots. Brandon's heart just melted; she looked so beautiful to him as he watched her from inside the house, his mother came up behind him and spoke.

"She's a lovely woman, Brandon. You should keep a hold on her." Barbara kissed her son on the cheek and opened the door for him.

Brandon gently sat beside Joyce, looked at her with a grin and spoke.

"Well, I guess now would be a good time to tell them, don't you think so Joyce?" Brandon asked.

"Tell us what, Honey?" Barbara asked as she sipped her tea.

"Joyce and I are getting married," Brandon said smiling widely.

"Oh that is wonderful; Larry, did you hear that ... they're getting married!"

"Of course I heard it, I'm sitting right here,"

As Joyce hugged Larry, Barbara hugged Brandon, the parents switched, and Joyce was hugged by both parents.

"Now Joyce, honey, tell me all the details, date, and so forth." Barbara said. She was so happy for her son and for Joyce; it took her almost an hour to settle down.

Larry talked seriously to Brandon about how he and Barbara wanted to get them something special for a wedding gift. He also said they couldn't wait to meet Joyce's children.

Later, Brandon's siblings that lived near by came to meet Joyce; they fell in love with her just as Mr. and Mrs. Miller had. The adults talked and laughed until the time got late. Joyce had so much fun learning about Brandon's childhood. It was hard for her to picture Brandon and his brother as little boys, strapping paper wings to their arms and jumping out a tree to see if they could fly. She then made a mental note to make sure her mother and father didn't tell Brandon stories of her childhood.

The church the older Millers attended was a small church; the walls and ceiling were of cedar; the pews were also made of cedar, but with beautiful blue cushions. Fresh flowers were placed directly in front of the podium the pastor stood behind. It gave the room freshness and added to the beauty of the room.

Everyone was so friendly. The congregation seemed to be an even mix of older and younger people. Mr. and Mrs. Miller couldn't wait to introduce their new soon to be daughter-in-law.

"Joyce, please sit here by me." It seemed Barbara went out of her way to make Joyce feel at ease; she felt so accepted by Brandon's parents. She recalled Sean's words just then, 'you'll lov'em.' He was right; they were great people and she loved them already.

After the service, Brandon and Joyce were swept away for lunch with his family.

After the noon meal, Joyce and Brandon had to say their goodbyes.

"Joyce, please have Brandon bring you back again, it has been so much fun having you here."

"Thank you, Barbara, I've had a lovely time, and I would love to come back."

With big hugs and a few wet eyes, Brandon and Joyce left for home.

"You were right; your mother is a lovely person; I just love her." Joyce said to Brandon.

"She thought a lot of you too," he replied.

The ride home was much more pleasant than the drive there. When stopping to get gas and eat, this time Joyce was able to eat and enjoy the time with the man she loved.

"I just can't get over how much fun it was to be at your parent's home. Thank you for taking me Brandon," she said as she leaned over and gave him a kiss.

"Well, if that's what I get, I think I'll take you there a lot more." She chuckled at him as the waitress came over to take their orders. This time, Joyce ordered the roast beef and steamed vegetables, Brandon ordered a burger and fries.

While on the drive back to Garland, Joyce thought back over the weekend; she felt silly for her fear of meeting Brandon's parents. She thanked her Lord for the peace she now had and that her children would never have the fear that she experienced; she also prayed they would never have in-laws that didn't like or accept them.

It was the fifth of April; spring was coming up everywhere, trees were budding, grass was beginning to turn green and flowers were poking their heads out of the ground. Everything seemed to be richer in their color at the beginning of spring. Joyce loved this time of the year; it made her feel so alive.

Brandon and Joyce had spent several hours with Joyce's pastor for counseling over the past month. Pastor Jones had spent a few hours talking about Stacey and Paul as well as their new lives together.

"Stacey and Paul will always be in your past, but the two of you must not allow them to come into your present or your future. It doesn't mean you have forgotten them, or no longer love them, but that love for them has to be left with them, put in a special place, you might say," he kindly explained. "God has given both of you a second chance at love, and what appears to be a deep love. My advice to you, Brandon, do not expect Joyce to do things like Stacey. Joyce, do not expect Brandon to do things like Paul."

Pastor Jones continued to talk about the two families becoming one, and firmly cautioned them against using terms such as: 'his' children' or 'her' children. Pastor Jones said these things in a kind and loving way so that neither felt bad about their feelings for Paul and Stacey. Pastor Jones also knew that Joyce and her children would be joining Brandon and the church he attended. He felt no ill will toward either of them, but felt it was right for them to do so. Joyce, however, wanted her pastor to perform the wedding service. The children weren't too happy about changing churches, so Pastor Jones felt it wise to talk to them about this matter.

"The woman is to follow her husband," Pastor Jones explained to Samantha, Mark and Michael. "When two families are joining together, it can be hard at times; both sides will have to do their share to make it one family instead of two families being slammed together."

Pastor Jones took as much time as needed with the children; he congratulated them for handling this situation very well. There were some kids from school that went to Brandon's church, so they felt it wasn't going to be all bad; at least they would know someone.

Mark and Michael were not happy about leaving their friends behind. The pastor kindly explained there wasn't any reason for them to lose their friendships; he also added they would be adding more friends to their lives.

"Hi, Diane, come on in; how are you? Joyce asked as she closed the door behind her best friend.

"Fine, aah Joyce, are you free this afternoon?"
"I think so; what did you have in mind?"
"I really want a slice of pizza; let's go to the mall."
Joyce took about fifteen minutes to get ready to leave the house, she checked with Samantha to make sure she was free to watch the boys, and instructed her to make sure they didn't destroy anything.
"Sure, Mom, I'll get the duct tape and tape them together in their rooms as soon as you leave." Joyce just looked at her daughter.
"Just kidding, Mom, we don't have any duct tape." Joyce turned back around to look at her daughter again. Samantha laughed out loud as she left the room.
"Joyce we'll take my car, I'll bring you back home." Diane said.
"Alright, let's go."
As the two women headed for the mall, they talked and giggled like always. Some things never change, no matter how many years go by.
"So, how are the wedding plans going?"
"Oh, Diane, I had forgotten what all goes in a wedding. At times running off to a justice of the peace looks pretty good. Put on a nice dress, have the rings, the license, and you're good to go. Say your vows ... bing, bang, boom! You're done." Diane laughed so hard she thought she would cry. She couldn't help but think how funny it would be to see her friend's face if one of her children came home and told Joyce they had just gotten married at the courthouse.
Once inside the mall, the women didn't go straight to a store, they made a bee line to the food court. Diane got her pizza, and Joyce got in line at the Dairy Queen for a chocolate milkshake.
"Diane, after this little mall run, I may not be able to fit in my dress."
"Well, you won't be alone. Joyce I need to tell you something..., I'm pregnant." Joyce just stared and looked at her friend, sat her shake down and just starting smiling.
"Diane, that's wonderful, oh, I am so happy for you. When did this happen, I mean how far along are you?"
"Six weeks, and Joyce, I haven't told Ron yet."
"What? So, now we know just how important I am, don't we?"

This caused Diane to chuckle. "Why haven't you told him?"

"Well, remember awhile back I said something about; in a way I wished we had more children, but if we had one now, Ron wouldn't be too happy about it?"

"Yes, I remember."

"Well Joyce... he is not going to be too happy, I mean after all Erin will be nineteen in three months. Joyce we are in our early forties and starting all over again."

"I see. Diane, honey, just tell me you will tell the man before you go into labor. Ron's a pretty smart guy; he just may figure something's up." Joyce always made Diane laugh, and today was no different.

While the two women sat, ate and talked, Joyce could see the turmoil Diane felt over this situation. Joyce really didn't know what to say, after all, she was going to have a baby and that was that.

"So what am I to do Joyce?" Diane asked after downing a few bites of her pizza.

"Diane, you have only one choice here. You will go home, cook a nice meal for Ron, and while he is enjoying it just say, 'Oh by the way sweetheart, I'm pregnant.'" Joyce chuckled, as did Diane, but to Diane it wasn't as funny.

"Seriously, Diane, if he gets upset, remind him, you didn't get like this by yourself." After pausing a few minutes to take a few sips of her shake she spoke again. "So, I'm the only one that knows?"

"Yes, well, you and my doctor. I took that home pregnancy test four times, I knew it had to be wrong, but noooo that silly stick turned blue every time, each time it got bluer."

Joyce threw back her head in laughter.

"So after that I went to the doctor, and he confirmed it. Oh Joyce, what will the girls say; this will be so embarrassing to them!"

"Sweetie it will be alright. They may find a new baby at home fun, besides with the two of them being in college, they won't be around all that much."

"That's all you could come up with on that one wasn't it?" Diane asked.

"Oh yeah," now both women were laughing again.

"If they're embarrassed, they will just have to get over it."
"Yeah, I guess you're right."
After Diane had eaten her slice of pizza and a milk shake, she felt better, and ready to go home and face her husband.
"You realize we didn't shop for anything." Joyce said in a light tone.
"I know, I just wanted to talk to you without any distractions, and I thought the mall the best place; besides there was pizza." The two started the laughing all over again.
"Like I said, I am happy for you, and I think when Ron regains consciousness, he'll be happy too." Joyce couldn't help but tease her friend.
Diane dropped Joyce off at her house, and Joyce went inside and was greeted with two little boys who complained about their sister not letting them watch a certain movie while their mother was away. Joyce just sighed.

⁕

Joyce saw Diane at church the following Sunday, after the service she took her by the arm as they walked to their cars, whispering all the way.
"So what did he say? Tell me; tell me I'm dying to know." Joyce whispered.
"I haven't told him yet." Diane said with eyes that were like a child's dreading to tell her mother something.
"Diane, why not?"
Diane looked at Joyce with frustration in her eyes and explained. After she had cooked a special dinner for Ron, she was just about to tell him when Erin and Mandy walked in.
Neither parent knew the girls were coming home for the weekend. It was going to be hard enough for Diane to tell Ron at age forty-three he was going to be a new daddy, she was not about to try and face all three of them at once.
"I chickened out." Diane replied, feeling silly about the whole matter.

"When do the girls go back?"

"This afternoon."

"Tell him as soon as they leave, Diane. Putting this off isn't helping anything. Diane I want to ask you something, are you happy about this baby?"

"Yes, Joyce I am; I have fallen in love with this little person already."

"Shhhh, here comes Ron and the girls." Diane said to Joyce.

"Hey Ron, Erin, Mandy, I hear you girls go back to school this afternoon?"

"Yeah, time flies when we come home, but it drags the rest of the time. Oh, congrats on your upcoming wedding Joyce," Mandy told her.

"Thank you, I'll be glad when it's over; I get more nervous as the days go by." They all chuckled.

Joyce said goodbye to Diane and her family; she knew they had things to discuss and little time to discuss them. She then gathered her own family, and their discussion was about where to go eat. They decided on Tex-Mex, and Tex-Mex it was to be.

Ron and Diane saw the girls off; it reminded Diane of how much the girls had grown to be more independent. She missed them ... missed them needing her and wished she could see them more often.

She poured herself a glass of iced tea and decided it was time she had a talk with her husband; no matter what the outcome, it had to be done now.

"Ron, would you come in here please; I need to speak with you."

"Want something to drink?"

"Yes, please. Do we have any cookies, or did the girls eat them all?" he replied.

Ron loved it when the girls were home, but when they left, the cupboards were pretty much bare. He then went to Diane and put his arms around her waist and kissed her lips and then her neck. "The good part is we have the whole house all to ourselves," he whispered in her ear.

Ron suddenly remembered Diane wanted to talk to him about something, not letting her go he asked what she wanted to discuss.

Chapter fifteen / 229

"Now, what did you want to talk to me about? Or can it wait?"

"Well, aah... Ron... I... aah, I can't think when you do that, so sit down please." Diane said thinking she needed to put some space between them.

Ron could not figure out what in the world was the matter with his wife; she appeared to be so baffled at something. Ron took a drink of his coffee, all the while looking at his wife. Diane sat playing with her glass, trying to get up the nerve to tell her husband they would not have the house to themselves for much longer.

"Ron, sweetheart, I have something to tell you; you may find this shocking at first, but..." Ron cut her off.

"What Diane? Just tell me, just spit it out."

"Okay. Ron, I'm pregnant." There was silence as Ron just looked at his wife, his eyes were glazed and he sat there as if he were in complete shock.

"Ron, Ron did you hear me?" Diane was getting a little frustrated with him, after all, it had taken her all this time to tell him, and now he just sat there, staring at her.

"Uh huh." His mouth hung open, but no words were forming.

"Ron, I know we didn't plan it, but it happened anyway ... Ron, would you say something please?" Diane was about to cry.

"Aah what?" Ron's face looked a little pale, his eyes glassy. "We're having another baby?" Ron finally replied, "At our age?"

"Yes, and I don't think we will make any world records at 'our age'."

It was as if Ron was coming around; he drank a few sips of his coffee and began to speak in complete sentences again. "Diane, are you sure? I mean you could be mistaken couldn't you? Maybe you're just late."

"It's no mistake Ron, I've been to the doctor and he confirmed it." Silence fell at the table once again.

"Well, I guess we're having a baby then." Ron got up and took his wife by the hand, they both stood and faced each other; he kissed her gently.

They continued to talk, and after Ron seemed to accept the fact, Diane felt better.

"I need to eat or I'm going to be sick." Diane said, as she was looking in the cupboard for something to eat.

"Now that you mention it, I have noticed you eating more snacks lately; I just never thought that…" Ron let the word hang.

"We need to tell the girls; they will be excited," Ron said.

"They will be embarrassed." Diane said matter-of-factly.

"We need to tell them soon, so they don't hear it from anyone else." Ron then realized as he watched his wife eating, they would need to tell Mandy and Erin soon, or they will know by looking at their mother's mid-section.

CHAPTER SIXTEEN

It was the morning of Brandon and Joyce's wedding. Brandon was up earlier than he had planned, but he could not lay there in the bed when he had such a big day ahead of him.

"Dad, are you going to make it?" Richard laughed.

"Of course, why do you ask?"

"Well, for one, you poured orange juice over your cereal."

"Oh my, I did, didn't I? I guess my mind is in another place."

"Yeah, I bet it is," Don replied with a grin. This action over the cereal caused Don to remember his own wedding day and how nervous he had been. Sean came into the room and gathered what the conversation was about.

"You know all this wedding hoopla is for the women; we men could have just the preacher on the basketball court, and it would all be just fine. Say I will, I do, and be done with it." Laughter filled the kitchen.

"Yeah, well, just don't let a woman hear you say that or she'll rip you apart," Brandon advised his son.

Brandon looked ever so handsome; Lorna had pressed his suit and had his clothes all laid out for him, and he was dressed and ready to go two hours early.

Don took that time to let Brandon know he and his brothers were happy with his choice to marry Joyce. They had grown to love her and were glad she was being added to their family.

"Hey Richard, what happened to your girl friend, Lou Ann, was it?" Sean asked.

"Aah well, she was getting too serious and I just wasn't in that same place, so we thought it best to stop seeing each other."

"Too bad, I doubt there's another female out there that will have you," Sean teased. This caused all the men to laugh at Richard's expense. The Miller boys always had fun ribbing each other. They took it all in stride, but never missed the opportunity to zing the other when it occurred.

When Joyce arrived at the church, she didn't appear to be nervous at all. Later, Timothy knocked on the door and came in.

"How are you, Mom?"

"I'm fine, I honestly thought I would be nervous, but I seem to be just fine. Have you seen Brandon?"

"Yes." Timothy said with a little grin on his face.

"What? What is it?" She asked.

"Well, Richard told me, this morning Brandon was a little off his game, and he put orange juice over his breakfast cereal," Timothy said, bursting out with laughter.

"Oh!" Was all Joyce said as her hand went over her mouth, trying to hold back the laughter.

"Weddings can do that to a person," Diane said as she was thinking of her own wedding all those years ago.

"I remember Ron's father had to give him a comb to comb down his hair right before the service started. Why the man didn't look in a mirror before he left the house, I just don't know." Joyce and Diane started laughing at the memory of that day.

Joyce wore a beautiful light blue mid length dress with matching shoes. Diane had done her hair and her make up was done lightly. Elise, Samantha, and Diane wore dresses that were complimentary to Joyce's. Timothy, Mark and Michael wore dark gray suits with light blue ties.

Brandon wore a smoke gray suit with a light blue tie and black cowboy boots. His sons wore suits and ties matching Joyce's sons. Everyone looked elegant for this special event.

As the music began, Timothy walked Joyce down the aisle. Only the family, Lorna, Diane, Ron, and family were in attendance. Joyce wanted a small wedding, which was fine with Brandon. She had done the big wedding thing over twenty years ago and felt it wasn't necessary today. Diane stood up with Joyce as she did many years ago; Don stood up with his father.

The ceremony was not lacking for anything; it was very simple but also very precious. The girls had decorated the church auditorium with flowers and candles. Jennifer played several pieces of music on the piano, along with the wedding march. Samantha made little decorative bags with bird seed inside, to later throw at the bride and groom.

The pastor stood before the couple, welcoming the guests who came to witness this special occasion. He asked Brandon and Joyce to face each other and hold hands. As Brandon looked into the face of this woman, he thought his heart would beat out of his chest. He had waited for her, and now the time had come to make her his own. He gave Joyce a quick wink and made her smile right before the pastor had them repeat their vows.

Within minutes, the vows were made and Pastor Jones told Brandon he could kiss his bride, and he gladly did so. They turned and Pastor Jones introduced the congregation to Mr. and Mrs. Brandon Miller.

The reception was held at the ranch. Friends from work and church, along with family attended the celebration.

"I'm so glad you are in my family now, Joyce; you do wonders for my son, which does wonders for me," the older Mrs. Miller said. "Now, after you get back from your honeymoon, and get all settled in at the ranch, Larry and I want to come for a visit. You and I can go shopping and other girl outings." Joyce was excited by this invitation from her new mother-in-law.

"That sounds wonderful, Barbara, I look forward to it."

"Son, you sure are a lucky man. Your first wife was a good woman, and we loved her; now God has blessed you with a second wife that is absolutely wonderful. Your mother and I love her dearly; yes, Son, you're a lucky man." Brandon's farther spoke as he patted Brandon's shoulder.

The reception was very large; a band played music almost the entire time. Flower decorations were in several different places; a wedding bell with satin ribbon was the center piece at the bride and groom's table. Joyce had a friend of hers make a four tier wedding cake.

Many varieties of finger foods were served at the reception. Mark and Michael especially liked the tiny baked ham sandwiches.

"Having a good time, Richard?" Elise asked.

"Yes, I am, I love parties even if they are weddings." They both laughed over his silliness. "How about you?"

"Yes, I am; I hope our parents will be very happy."

"I don't think you have anything to worry about; after all, I can't think of anyone who looks at each other the way those two do."

"Yeah, I guess you're right."

"I look forward to having sisters, and your little brothers are so much fun, I love 'em." Richard's words were very comforting to Elise; Brandon's sons seemed to be very kind, but she was still a bit nervous about the big move.

Mark and Michael were with Jason and Elizabeth, Joyce's parents. From a distance you could tell that all four of them were having a great time. The laughter was contagious. The music playing once again, and people were going out on the dance floor, and Mark and Michael looked at each other.

"Oh no, dancing! Quick Michael, let's get out of here now before some old lady makes us dance with her." The boys made the most awful face to one another and ran off to safety.

"Joyce my love, will you dance with me?"

Joyce giggled as she gave Brandon her hand, and he led her to the dance floor. The first dance was for the bride and groom; then after a few bars of music others joined in on the fun.

"Don, where are you headed?" Richard asked.

"I am going to ask one of my new sisters to dance. Samantha, may I have this dance?"

"Aah sure, if you don't mind getting your toes stepped on."

As the music played Don danced with Samantha, finding her to be a very sweet young lady, his heart was filled with wanting to protect her. Sean was dancing with Elise; sure he was finding out the same thing. Timothy danced with Jennifer and then Susan, and then sought out his own wife for the remainder of the evening. Richard not only danced with Christine, but his sisters-in-law as well, no one was left out, except the twins who were in hiding as far from the dance floor as they could get.

Joyce could not keep her eyes off Brandon during the reception. He was so handsome in his suit and tie. *Very handsome and all mine.* She thought to herself.

Diane walked up to Joyce and sat beside her, while she was alone. Brandon had gone to get them both something to drink. Diane noticed how Joyce watched her groom walk across the way; it was as if Joyce were in a daydream.

"Hello, anybody in there?" Diane asked, joking at Joyce for being off in another world.

"Oh Diane, I was somewhere else just then."

"I bet you were, and I bet I know where and with whom?" The two giggled.

"Hey, how are you feeling?" Joyce asked, changing the subject as quick as she could.

"I'm hungry constantly, and when I'm not eating, sleeping or throwing up, I feel fine." Joyce could not help but laugh; it was so much fun to watch her friend during this pregnancy.

"And how about Ron, how is he dealing with this new little one on the way?"

"He's doing fine too, he has become so attentive to me, and making sure I'm fine and not overdoing. He went out last night at ten-thirty to get me a banana popsicle. I can't remember him ever doing that when I was expecting with the girls."

"Honey, enjoy that one; Paul never got me anything I was craving, I had to get it myself. All he would say is 'you don't need that'. So enjoy it girl."

The day was drawing to a close; Brandon was looking for his

wife and saw her from across the way speaking to her parents. "There is my vision of loveliness," he spoke out loud. How long he had waited for her to be his. He went from being afraid to ask her out, to her now being his to have and to hold. With thoughts of the rest of the evening on Brandon's mind, he didn't want to rush her, but it was getting rather late in the day.

"Joyce, my love, it is time we were on our way."

"Yes, I guess it is, isn't it." She said as she gave Brandon a small smile for him alone.

Brandon and Joyce went inside, changed into casual clothes, but before they left, Joyce threw the bouquet and all laughed when Richard caught it. The newlyweds said their goodbyes, and as always Joyce gave some instructions for the children; then they were off for their honeymoon.

Brandon and Joyce arrived at one of Dallas' finest hotels for the first night of their married lives. Once inside Joyce looked around the spacious room. There was a beautiful flower arrangement sitting on the coffee table. Joyce gently took the card and read it.

"Congratulations, we love you both. Timothy, Elise, Samantha, Mark, Michael, Don, Sean and Richard." Joyce just smiled at the thought.

The room was one of the honeymoon suites, and it was simply beautiful. The decorations were done so carefully. The prints that hung on the wall were breath-taking. The bathroom alone could be used as a day spa; Joyce thought when she first saw it. His and her matching bathrobes; along with long thick matching towels, two sinks, a large mirror, and a very large whirlpool tub and shower.

In the bedroom sat a large flat screen TV, king size bed that looked so inviting, Joyce couldn't help but accept the invitation. She sat gingerly on the side; it felt so soft she was tempted to lay back and just let the softness of the mattress surround her. Someone placed chocolates carefully on the pillows, which Joyce couldn't keep from having one right then. Joyce loved this room, even the sitting area along with wet bar stocked with snacks and soft drinks was beautiful.

The newlyweds had a light snack brought to their room, neither one was too hungry, but a little snack of fruits, crackers and cheese was just enough. Brandon took Joyce's hand and led her to a chair, then sat her on his lap, gave her a kiss and held her. For the first time since meeting Joyce, he allowed his thoughts to be where they were now headed.

Brandon woke before Joyce did, so he lay there watching her until she awoke.

"Good morning." Brandon said to his sleepy new wife.

"Umm good morning," she replied, her eyes not yet open.

"How did you sleep?" He asked as he gently rubbed his finger along side her face.

"Umm, very well."

"Oh, me too, no complaints here," he said with a grin.

"What are our plans today, Brandon?"

"We're doing them." He said softly.

"What do you mean we're doing them?"

"Well, I called room service before you woke, so a delicious breakfast should be arriving any minute now. I hoped we could just spend the day right here, in this magnificent room. Our plane leaves at two, so we have all morning to laze around."

"Well, I guess I don't need to decide what I will wear then do I?" They both just laughed and snuggled together.

Joyce loved the way she fit into his arms, she felt so safe and secure. She never wanted to leave that spot, that room, or his arms.

That afternoon the Millers checked out of their hotel suite, caught a plane headed for Hawaii, where they would spend the next ten days. Brandon had rented a little chalet in a fairly secluded area.

The sky was so perfectly blue; the water was simply an echo of the sky. The air was so warm and inviting, Joyce thought this had to be the best place on earth. Their chalet was a little hut type cabin that contained a small sofa and chair, television, and an eating table with a small kitchenette and powder room. The bedroom was a little larger than the rest of the cabin; it contained a large bed, dresser, a closet, and one bathroom. It was nothing like the honeymoon suite in Dallas, but it was lovely ... a very romantic place to spend their honeymoon.

Brandon and Joyce had their choice of the beach or a swimming pool that was just a little walk from their chalet. One evening as it was getting late, the other guest in that area were leaving the pool, Brandon thought that was the perfect time for Joyce and him to play in the water alone.

Brandon was having a little too much fun splashing, so Joyce had to return fire when he was off guard.

Neither Brandon nor Joyce had ever been to Hawaii. Brandon wanted to go some place that was new to both of them, so Hawaii was the perfect choice, and neither one of them regretted it for a moment.

"Oh it's perfect alright, everything, Brandon is just lovely, I could not ask for anything more. I have you and that really is all that matters." This got Joyce a kiss.

They enjoyed the beach as much as the pool. They had it to themselves most of the time; the two of them were getting a good tan, but being careful not to burn. They did some shopping and went to a luau. There were many different sites to see; they tried to see as much as they could without overdoing it. "This is such a wonderful place Brandon, thank you."

"You are welcome, my love, we must plan to come back, anytime you wish."

"I don't know, I may not want to leave," She said as she put her arms around his neck and gave him a kiss.

When the newlyweds returned home to the ranch, they were greeted warmly by their family; both adults could tell they were definitely missed. The children had millions of things to tell them, but when the mentioning of gifts from Hawaii was said, of course, the boys couldn't wait.

A few days after arriving home, Joyce decided she had put it off long enough; it was time to tackle her house and get it ready for the next owners. There really wasn't any major work needed, just some spiffing up.

Joyce, Brandon, Ron, and Diane worked diligently on getting everything in Joyce's house moved out and ready. She gave some unneeded furniture to charity, some to Timothy and Christine, had carpets cleaned and walls painted. Timothy arrived later than he had planned, but he was ready to do some work to help the cause.

"Sorry I'm late," Tim said as he came through the door.

"Hi, Timothy."

"Hi, Mom."

"Where is Christine?" Joyce wanted to know.

"Her sister came in from out of town last night, they haven't seen each other in months, so they went shopping, and Christine said to tell you she was sorry, but her sister was only going to be here for a day."

"Well, I can understand that; tell her I missed her."

"I will. You four have been on the stick," Timothy said as he looked all around. To him it looked a little funny with most of their stuff gone. While standing in the living room with his hands on his hips, he tried to remember what it looked like when they moved in all those years ago. He was pretty young so he really couldn't remember it.

Ron was helping Brandon move some larger items out to the truck.

"I think that is the last of the furniture," Ron said. "The rest are boxes."

"Hey, what's for lunch? I'm starved." Timothy asked his mother as he brought out two boxes stacked on top of each other to the truck.

"I don't know, son; ask the pregnant lady what she would like to eat."

"Diane, Mom wants to know what you would like for lunch."

"Eeww, I would love to have some cold chicken."

"Mom, Diane wants cold chicken." Timothy yelled through the house.

"Well, cold chicken it is, but I would like mine warm. Brandon, what about you?"

"Oh… I don't know, cold chicken sounds pretty good right now, put me down for cold." He answered as he was carrying boxes out of the house.

"Brandon honey, do you have something you need to tell me." Joyce giggled at her new husband.

"Yes, I love you deeply." Brandon said as he gave Joyce a quick kiss while still carrying the boxes.

Ron felt Diane needed a break, so he volunteered to go get the food. Diane went along, not only to get a break, but to take a nap, one she didn't realize she needed, until they were on their way.

"Now, Timothy, I have something very important to discuss with you." She told her son when he came back in the house from loading some boxes.

Joyce's house was completely paid for. She remembered how hard it had been for Paul and her to get out of their apartment and into a house. She told Timothy she wanted to give the house to Christine and him. This caused her son to stare at her with his mouth open. "I really would like for it to stay in the family as long as possible. I want you and Christine to have it … that is if you want it."

"What?" Timothy said with eyes as big as saucers.

"You heard me, I want you and Christine to have this house, I really don't want to sell it, and since you and Christine are still in your apartment, what do you think?"

"Well, I would need to discuss it with Christine first, but I think it will be no problem."

"Good, after you talk to …" Timothy cut her off with a big kiss on her cheek.

"I have to go find Christine, right now." Joyce smiled at her son as he dashed for the door.

Brandon came in the room as soon as Timothy left, Joyce still looking at the door.

"So, what did Timothy say when you offered him the house?"

"He was very happy, so happy he left to go find Christine at the shopping mall," Joyce replied in a small laugh.

"Oh which reminds me, I need to tell you something, now that we are all alone. Joyce, you do understand you may decorate the ranch house any way you like? It is your home as well as mine, and the children's also."

"Thank you Brandon. I think we are all going to love living at the ranch. You know, you never realize how much stuff you have until you move." She said as she looked around at all the things that still needed to be boxed.

"How long did you live in this house?"

"Seventeen years," she replied. Brandon made a low whistle. "My, that's a long time."

"Yes, a lifetime to the children," she said as she sat and looked out into the rooms that were being torn apart and emptied.

Joyce and Paul moved into the house right before Samantha was born. Only two weeks into their new house, Joyce's labor started, and they had their little Samantha. Elise was so enamored with her, she kissed her almost constantly. Joyce remembered how she could hardly feed the child alone. So long ago, but just like yesterday. Joyce was standing and smiled at the memory.

"It's good that Timothy and Christine will live here now. This will be a great start for them," Brandon said. "Who knows each one of your children may start off in this house with their husband or wife. It was a great idea and gift, Joyce."

Ron and Diane came back with chicken; they sat down on a few remaining chairs and ate while they rested. Ron kept a constant check on Diane in her delicate condition, making sure she didn't overdo.

"Ron, I'm alright, really; I can stay a while longer and help." Diane tried to explain to her over-protective husband.

"I think I should take you home; you have done enough for today." Ron said as he got a little stern with his wife.

"Joyce, I'm taking Diane home to lie down for a while, I'll be back in about an hour to help finish up."

"Sure that's fine, I'm sure Timothy will be back soon, so really you don't have to come back, you can stay with Diane."

"I'll be back." Ron said waving his arm as he and Diane were leaving.

At the ranch house, things were a little bit in disarray. Brandon and Joyce took the master bedroom that was on the lower level. Previously, Brandon had used it as a guest room. All the children's rooms were upstairs. Samantha had her own room, the boys shared a room. Richard had talked Brandon into letting him move into the small bunk house that had originally been built for a foreman for the ranch. Elise took Richard's old room for when she was home from school. The master bedroom upstairs that was Brandon's was now a guest room. Lorna still had her room and would be staying on at the Southern Star ranch. Brandon and Joyce both would not hear of her even thinking of leaving.

"Did you mean what you said about decorating things here at the ranch, Brandon?" Joyce shyly asked.

"Yes, I did, you may decorate and make our home look like a woman lives here. I know things are mostly masculine, but after all, it was just me and the boys living here for many years," he kindly replied.

"Your mother and father will be coming for a visit soon, I may get some ideas from her on what to do with some of the bedrooms, and I feel the rest of the house is just fine." Joyce said as she looked around the master bedroom.

Joyce and Lorna had always gotten along very well, and neither one got in the other's way. When Joyce felt like she could be of help, she just went to work doing whatever was needed. Joyce also made sure the children didn't take advantage of having a housekeeper. They were to make their own beds, keep their rooms neat and clean, and pick up after themselves. Joyce explained this to Lorna kindly, and then very firmly to the children, and also let them know what the punishment would be if the rules were not followed.

After several hours of work, Lorna and Joyce enjoyed a cup of tea on the patio. It was a place where the two women would in the future come to sit, relax, and enjoy each others' company.

"It is so wonderful having you here with me." Joyce said to her new friend.

"Well, I must say, I do enjoy your company Joyce, and this delicious tasting tea." They both drank tea giggling.

Finally night fell, all the moving in and rearranging were mostly complete, now the job of finding things was a task for tomorrow. Joyce fell back on the comfortable bed right before Brandon walked in; he looked down at her and smiled.

"Now, that's what I am looking for," he said with a mischievous look on his face.

"What are you talking about?" she sheepishly asked.

"Oh, just that it has been a long day, and I was looking for something soft and warm to cuddle up with."

"Oh you were, were you?" Joyce asked as she was giggling just a bit. "Well, come a little closer and I'll see if I can help you."

Brandon's parents arrived for a visit several months later, Brandon and Joyce knew they were coming, but not the exact time of day.

"Mr. and Mrs. Miller, hi, come on in," Samantha said to the waiting couple at the door. "Brandon is in the stables, and Mom is at the office. Please, come in, and make yourselves at home."

"Thank you, Elise is it?" Larry asked.

"No sir, that's my sister, I'm Samantha."

"Oh, I'm sorry, it may take me a while to get everybody's names right."

Samantha smiled at the couple; she was used to people getting her and her sister mixed up.

"Samantha dear, tell me everyone's names again please." Mrs. Miller asked as they walked in the living room to sit down.

"Okay, Timothy is the oldest, he is married to Christine. Then Elise, she is in college, then me, then Mark and Michael the twins."

"Oh yes, I remember twin little boys at the wedding reception."

Samantha filled the Millers in on the boys being in school. She told them happily about it being Christmas break week and went on to tell how many days she had until she would be a 'free woman' as she put it.

"Oh, how fun. I remember those days, of not being able to wait until Christmas break, or summer break, or even Graduation. And now look, it has been forever." Mrs. Miller now laughed at herself. She then touched Samantha's arm, "Don't rush it, honey."

Samantha was the kindest hostess; she offered the couple something to drink, but they declined.

"No, thank you, we'll just sit down and rest awhile, then later, Larry you may want to go find Brandon, oh, and speaking of our son, here he comes." Mrs. Miller said.

"Hi, Mom, Dad," Brandon said as he gave each one a big hug. "I'm sorry I probably don't smell too pleasant, I have been working in one of the stables today. Can I get you anything?"

"No Son, this lovely young lady has been a very gracious hostess and has already offered us something," his father said.

"Oh, thank you Samantha." Brandon said to her kindly.

"No problem." Samantha now was off to her room to call her friend Shelly whom she hadn't seen or spoken to in at least two hours.

"So, how long can you stay? I hope a while. I know Joyce will be happy to see you both, as I am."

Brandon excused himself as he went to clean up. Larry and Barbara made themselves at home out on the patio. Lorna brought out some coffee and cookies. Even though it was mid-December, the air was not too cold. If you were sitting in the sun and dressed accordingly, it was quite enjoyable. Brandon quickly joined his parents and thanked Lorna for the cookies.

As the aroma of the cookies arrested the noses of ranch hands, up came Richard and Luke. "Hi Grandma, Grandpa," Richard said to each of his grandparents. "I would hug you, but you wouldn't like the smell," they all laughed.

"Hello, Mr. Miller, Mrs. Miller," Luke said as he shook their hands.

"We thought we smelled Lorna's cookies, so we just gave ourselves a little break so we could come and sneak a few," Richard said to the older adults.

"Umm, I thought I smelled cookies ... oh, and my favorite too."

The aroma of chocolate chip cookies made its way to Samantha's room and lulled her down the stairs and out to the patio.

"Hi Richard, hi Luke," Samantha said as she was biting a cookie.

"These are so good, how does she do that?" Samantha was speaking of Lorna and the magic way she had with cookies.

"Hi, Sam, didn't you have school today?" Richard asked.

"Yes, I did, but I'm done with all of my tests, and I'm a free woman until after the New Year."

Luke didn't say anything other than hello to Samantha; he seemed to be at a total loss. To Luke, Samantha was such a pretty girl, he would love to sit and just stare at her, but he didn't think she would appreciate that too much.

The ranch hands went back to work, and Samantha went back to her room. The three adults sat and visited for a while, before making plans to meet Joyce for dinner.

"Barb, are you up to going into town tonight?" Larry asked his wife.

"Sure, I just need to freshen up a little."

"I'll find Richard, and let him know, the boys will be home from school in about an hour. I'll just go up and tell Samantha, oh yeah, and Lorna, I need to tell her our plans as well," Brandon explained.

"Surprise," Brandon said in a soft tone to his wife as he poked his head in the door. As he came fully in and closed the door behind him, Joyce got up out of her chair and met him half way.

"Oh Brandon, what a lovely surprise," she said right before she wrapped her arms around his neck and kissed him.

After a few moments when they finally broke apart, Brandon still with his arms around Joyce's waist, told her of their guests' arrival.

"Your parents are here? Now, where are they? Oh Brandon, you didn't leave them out at the ranch alone did you?"

"Of course not, they are in Don's office talking to him and Sean. I just wanted to come in here and see you. I like it better in here," he said mischievously.

"Well, let's go in Don's office so I can say hello." Joyce said as she tried to break from Brandon's embrace.

"In a few minutes, I need to talk to you." Brandon said taking a seat and leading Joyce into his lap. "I have to go out of town next week; I have some cattle to sell. I'm taking Luke with me; he is pretty good with buying and selling livestock." Brandon explained. "I should be gone three, four days at the most."

"Well, I don't like it, but I guess it will have to be that way. How long are your parents staying?"

"Until Friday, then Luke and I leave on Monday." Brandon told her. As the conversation of Brandon's travel plans ended, there was a soft knock on the door.

"Come in," Joyce said as she rose off Brandon's lap.

"Barbara, Larry, hello, come in, it's so good to see both of you!" Joyce hugged both her in-laws and invited them to sit down. "When did you get in?"

"About three hours ago," Larry answered.

"I hope there was someone at the house to greet you."

"Yes, your daughter, now wait a minute, let me see if I get the name right this time, Samantha?"

"Yes, Dad, that was Samantha." Brandon replied.

As the adults were talking, Mark and Michael came in; Michael took the seat behind the desk.

"Hey, when are we going to eat I'm hungry."

"Yeah, me too."

"Brandon, we'd better get these boys some food; I don't think they'll make it much longer," Barbara said teasing with the twins.

Sean came in and asked if anyone had decided where they were eating. Mark took it upon himself to answer his question.

"No, you'd better decide Sean, 'cause they're taking too long."

"Mark." Joyce said sternly. That was all it took for Mark to understand he had said the wrong thing at the wrong time. Mark just looked down with a frown on his face.

Don called Jennifer asking her to pick up Susan and meet them at 'Johnson's Steak House.' New in the area, and on top of that, a four-star restaurant, Don had wanted to try it.

"Sounds good," Larry said.

"Hey, where is Samantha?" Joyce asked.

"She had plans with Shelly and a few other girls, so she won't be joining us. She said she had mentioned it to you." Brandon replied.

"Oh yes, I forgot."

"I'll call Timothy and see if he and Christine would like to join us."

"Honey I already called them, Christine isn't feeling well, so they can't join us," Brandon explained.

With this information, everyone left Joyce's office and headed for the restaurant.

CHAPTER SEVENTEEN

Samantha and Shelly met some other classmates at Pete's Pizza Parlor. Pete's was a local pizza place where a lot of younger people ate. The food was good and decently priced; Samantha and her friends ate there quite often.

"Ma'am, we need a pretty large table, we have six other people joining us." Samantha told the waitress.

The two girls sat at the large table, and waited only about five minutes when the others joined them. "Are you all ready to order now?" The waitress asked.

"Yes, I think so," Shelly replied. "We will have four large pizzas, two ham and pineapple, two meat lovers, and soft drinks all around please.

As Samantha sat there with her friends, Luke walked in. She spotted him as soon as he came in the door. Samantha thought Luke to be so good looking. He was with some friends of his own, three other guys. As they were walking to their table, they passed Samantha and her friends.

Luke said hello to Samantha, and she said hello in return. They exchanged a few other pleasantries and then Luke went on to his table.

"Hey, who's the pretty girl, Luke?" one of his friends asked.

"Just someone I know."

"Wow, I wish I knew her, hey Luke can you introduce me?"

"No James, she's too young, leave her alone."

"Alright, alright," James said dropping the topic. Luke did not want to discuss Samantha with anyone. What he really wanted to do was to sit with her and just stare into her pretty face.

"Hey Sam," Donna whispered to Samantha. "Who's that guy that spoke to you?"

"Oh, that's Luke; he works on Brandon's ranch. He's cute isn't he?" Samantha said with gleaming eyes.

"You can say that again." Donna replied.

As the night went on, Luke and his friends were getting up from their table to leave, while Samantha and her friends were still at their table. Samantha watched him pass by, and noticed him looking at her, but neither one spoke. Luke gave her a small wave with his hand. Samantha smiled at him and wiggled her fingers toward him in return.

"Brandon, your mother and I are going shopping, oh and Samantha is going with us. I don't know how long we'll be, but I am sure you and your father will keep busy," Joyce said to her husband as she gave him a gentle kiss on the cheek.

"Well, yes, actually we are; Dad has invited me to go play golf, so we will be gone most of the day ourselves. Try to have fun without us," he teased.

Joyce giggled.

Joyce then went into the kitchen to speak with Lorna, she wanted to let her know of everyone's whereabouts and how many to prepare lunch for. Lorna thanked her for informing her, and with that the women were on their way.

"Let's ride ladies." Joyce instructed.

The women shopped for fabric, drapes, and before returning home made a quick stop at the hardware store for paint samples. Joyce really wanted to get as much done while her mother-in-law was there to help her as she could.

Samantha could not go on a shopping trip and not shop for clothes, while the other two women were looking at drapes, Samantha found the cutest blouse, a pair of jeans and some shoes all on sale. Sales were like a magnet to that girl.

Barbara had a great time with Joyce and her daughter; she couldn't remember when she laughed so much. As usual, when at the mall they ate at the food court. Joyce had to have her usual chocolate milkshake from Dairy Queen. She figured she would be walking it off anyway, why not splurge a little? After about five hours of the stores, they decided to call it a day.

"Well, Samantha, you made out pretty well, you got several new things, didn't you?"

"Yes, I did, and they were all on sale."

"I don't know how she does it Barbara. Every time we are at a mall, she finds good sales."

"It's a gift." Samantha replied.

The night before Brandon's parents were to leave, Samantha sat in the kitchen having a little late night snack. It was then when Barbara came into the kitchen.

"Oh, hi, Samantha, I hope I'm not intruding. I just came in to get a glass of milk."

"No, it's fine! Have a piece of Lorna's apple pie; it's to die for." Samantha told her.

"Is that what you're having?"

"Um Hmm, I just don't know how she does it, it is so good."

"Maybe you should ask her to show you sometime."

"Maybe," Samantha replied. "Mrs. Miller, I want to thank you for today."

"Today, what? Did I miss something?"

"I mean, the way you are with Momma. Daddy's parents were never that way with her; she was always so on edge when they were around. And now with you and Mr. Miller; well, it's as if you all have been the best of buds for years. I know it means a lot to her."

"Well, dear, it's so easy to be 'buds' with your mother; she is such a fun-loving person. She loves my Brandon, and we love her, we also have fallen in love with her children too." Barbara said as she took Samantha's chin in her hand. "Good night, sweetie."

"Good night."

When Barbara left the kitchen, Samantha finished her pie, and thought about Mr. and Mrs. Miller. They really were nice people, and they had accepted her mother with open arms into their family. She thought about how family functions at her father's family had always been. Samantha hoped that when she married, she would have in-laws like the Millers.

⁓

As morning arrived, Brandon's parents headed back to their home. Brandon went on to the pastures to get some work done. There were fences to mend, hay to bail, and two bridles that needed repairing. The kids were enjoying their time off from school; the boys played video games, and Samantha talked on the phone with Shelly. Joyce thought this would be the perfect time to go for a ride on Millie, since Don insisted she take the day off.

Millie was a young filly Brandon bought for her while in Kentucky when he purchased the pintos for the boys. She was a very gentle horse, and Joyce adored her.

"Going for a ride?" Brandon asked as he put his arms around his wife's waist.

"Yes, I miss your mother already, so I thought I would ride Millie. She needs some exercise anyway."

"I would love to come with you, but I am a little behind on my work. You won't be long will you?" He asked.

"No, not very, I'm planning to ride in the direction of the pond, just in case you need to know where I'll be."

"Alright, enjoy."

Joyce took off on a small trot, then a full run. She was out with Millie for about two hours and enjoyed the ride tremendously. The day was sunny, a bit of a chill, but Joyce was dressed warmly and didn't seem to mind. She enjoyed riding out in the open space, with the sun on her face and the wind in her hair. Joyce then slowed Millie down to a slower walk while she talked to her Lord from her heart.

"Lord, you did it; you not only gave me a husband that loves and cherishes me and loves my children, but also gave me a mother-in-law that loves me as well. Now, I know some of what it was like for Ruth and Naomi. I thank you Lord from the bottom of my heart."

Michael came running into the stables, looking for Joyce. It didn't seem to be urgent, but he had something to tell her.

"Mom! Mom! Are you in here?"

"Yes Michael, I'm here, I'm over here brushing down Millie, I just finished with a ride. Did you need something dear?"

"Tim and Christine are here."

"Oh, alright, tell them I'll be right there." Joyce finished up her work with Millie, gave her some oats, patted her on the neck and told her good-bye.

"Timothy, Christine, what a lovely surprise, can you stay for supper?" Joyce asked of her son and daughter-in-law.

The two of them looked at each other and shrugged, "sure."

"I'll just let Lorna know there will be two more for supper, then I am going to take a quick shower, I just finished a ride with Millie, and I'm sure I smell like a horse. I'll be quick."

"That's fine, we'll be fine," they assured her.

Timothy and Christine made themselves comfortable on the sofa, when Mark came in and asked his big brother to play a video game with him. Timothy agreed, and after a few games, Christine played also; she beat Timothy twice.

Timothy loved to play with his twin brothers. Since their father died he tried to do that more and more when he could. It was a little harder now, with being married and living in a different house, and not to mention work. Timothy promised he would never do what his father had, and work almost non-stop. He would enjoy God's blessings each day.

Joyce entered the room as her three sons were stretched out on the floor playing the video game. "So, Christine, how are you, dear?"

"Oh, I'm fine, I wish we had come a little earlier we could have ridden horses together."

"Yes, that would have been so nice; let's plan on that next

week." Timothy gave Christine a strange look. Joyce noticed it, but kept her thoughts to herself.

About that time, Brandon and Richard came in.

"Hi, everybody," Brandon said as he kissed Christine on the cheek and shook Timothy's hand. "I'm going to clean up for supper, and I will be right down. Please don't think me rude, but I probably smell like a horse."

"Funny how everyone smells like a horse around here," Richard said, causing everyone in the room to laugh.

"Speaking of smelling like a horse, Richard dear ... hit the shower." Joyce teased him. Richard and Joyce teased each other quite often; they found each other to be very humorous when others didn't.

Lorna served a delicious meal as always: pork chops, salad with a light vinaigrette dressing, scalloped potatoes, snow peas, bread, and iced tea. For dessert Lorna had baked a chocolate raspberry cake. As everyone filled their plates and ate, Timothy made a most interesting announcement.

"Aah, I have a bit of good news for everyone; I think you all might find this a little interesting... Christine's expecting. We're having a baby!" Timothy exclaimed looking at his wife lovingly.

"Oh Timothy, Oh Christine," Joyce didn't know who to hug first. The room filled with good wishes and excitement and everyone rushed to hug Christine and Tim. Everyone except Mark and Michael; they kept right on eating.

As all this was happening, Elise slipped in among all the commotion; she was finally home from college for the winter break. Her arrival was somewhat a surprise; she wasn't expected until the next day.

"Elise! Hey! Look everybody, Elise is here!" said Mark, "Elise you are just in time for the news."

"What news?" She asked, very confused.

"We're having a baby." Mark explained.

"What? Mom, you're having a baby?" Elise asked her mother with a stunned look on her face. "Oh, goodness no! Joyce replied shockingly. "Christine is having a baby."

"Oh, congratulations Christine; big brother, you're going to be a papa. Wow, now that's deep."

Elise sat at the table and enjoyed cake with the rest of the family. The talk at the table was mostly of babies. Mark and Michael asked to be excused after finishing their cake and were allowed to do so. Joyce sat and listened to the noise around the table, enjoying every sound of it.

Brandon was up early Monday morning; he and Luke had business in Abilene. Brandon knew some ranchers there who traded livestock, and he had livestock he needed to trade. He was hoping to get the business at hand done as soon as he could and get back home to Joyce. The two of them hadn't been away from one another since the wedding, and Brandon hated the separation. He did enjoy Luke's company, but it just wasn't the same.

Joyce decided she would keep busy in Brandon's absence, thinking it would help the time to pass. Don insisted she take another day for herself.

She decided it was a good time to go through the twins' closets and clear out what they no longer could wear. Joyce was knee deep in clothes when she heard the doorbell ring.

"Diane, hey, come on in, I am so glad you stopped by today." Forgetting all about the clothes laying in the middle of the boys' bedroom floor, Joyce took Diane into the kitchen for coffee and cake.

"You have to try a piece of Lorna's cake, 'It's to die for' as Samantha says." The two women chuckled.

"Umm that is good, how does she do that?"

"Honestly Diane, you sound just like Samantha, she says the very same things when she bites into her cakes, pies, or cookies."

"Joyce you don't seem to be yourself, are you feeling alright? Are things going well with Brandon gone and you on this big ranch without him? I can't say alone because there are too many people here for you to be really alone."

"Other than missing Brandon terribly, I'm fine."

"Oh, Joyce this cake is delicious!" Diane said for the second time. Joyce just shook her head.

"I'm sure you do Joyce, after all you two haven't been married very long, and he has to go out of town, and as much fun as cleaning out closets can be ...," Diane just let the sentence hang.

"Yes, you're right, but I don't like sleeping in that big bed alone."

"When does he get back anyway?"

"Friday night, if all goes well; or Saturday morning sometime."

The two women sat around the kitchen table, talking and giggling. Joyce told Diane she was going to be a grandmother. Diane was happy for not only Joyce, but the young couple as well.

"We never even thought for once that one of us would be having a baby at the same time as one of us would become a grandmother now did we?" This caused both women to just laugh out loud. Diane was doing well in her pregnancy, but at times she couldn't help but feel a little too old to be doing this.

Several weeks later Joyce drove home from work slowly due to the heavy rains. She could barely see the road. As she pulled up into the garage, Brandon was waiting for her.

"I was starting to be concerned that you weren't home yet." He gave her a kiss and took her brief case as he put his hand at the small of her back and guided her inside.

"That rain is coming down so hard. Sort of reminds me of the night we were stuck in that barn," Joyce giggled and looked up at Brandon with a grin. He chuckled.

"Yes, I remember very well, Mrs. Miller," as he spoke low to her ear. Joyce giggled even more.

The children were very glad to see their mother home. They weren't prone to worry, but Brandon found Mark and Michael looking out the window several times watching for her.

Lorna prepared a comforting meal, perfect for rainy days, and had just begun to put it on the table as Joyce walked in. They all sat down, bowed their heads and thanked the Lord for the food He provided, and then engaged in conversation about everyone's day.

As Samantha was telling about an event that happened at school that day, the phone rang.

"I'll get it." As Mark answered the phone, the rest of the family was still listening to Samantha while eating their meal.

"Mom, it's Christine, she wants to talk to you." Mark told his mother on the way back to his place at the table.

"Hi, Christine, how are you? What's wrong honey?" Joyce's hand went over her mouth and she listened with much fear. "I'll be right there!"

"Brandon, Brandon we have to go, come on we have to go now, everybody we need to go."

"Joyce, honey, go where? You're not making any sense, what's happened?" Brandon asked, standing up and putting his hands on both sides of Joyce's arms looking down into her face. He could tell something was wrong, very wrong.

"Timothy, it's Timothy. He's been in a bad accident and they are rushing him into surgery," she said frantically. "Brandon, please, we need to go."

Everyone grabbed their jackets, purses and whatever else they needed that was close by; they were out the door in no time flat.

All the way to the hospital Joyce prayed in her mind and heart that this was all a bad nightmare, that it wasn't as bad as Christine had made it sound.

"Joyce." Brandon's voice called her out of her own thoughts. "What all did Christine say?"

"She just said he was in an accident, it looked pretty bad and they were getting him ready for surgery; he was barely coherent."

Brandon got them to the hospital in record time. They flew into the emergency room waiting area; Joyce could not get to the information desk quickly enough.

"Miss, my son has been brought in and he's…" The woman behind the desk very calmly started asking Joyce questions before she could give the woman all the information.

"Your son's name ma'am?"

"Timothy McIntosh, he was in an accident; they're getting him ready for surgery now, and can you tell me where my son is?" Joyce pleaded with the woman.

"Joyce, honey, please let me handle this." Brandon had his arms around his wife, while he tried to get information out of the woman behind the desk.

"Timothy McIntosh was brought in here a little while ago, he was in a pretty bad accident from what we were told, this is his mother, we need to find him and his wife; can you help us?"

"Christine!" Joyce heard one of the children call out. "Mom, there's Christine." Christine ran to Joyce and wrapped her arms around her.

Christine cried in Joyce's chest as she tried to explain what she had been told. She tried telling her that Timothy was being prepared for surgery, and that she had briefly spoken to the doctor. She continued to tell what had happened as they were heading toward the surgical patient waiting area.

Tim had been hit broadside by an on coming car. The rain was so heavy the other guy couldn't stop. He took the full brunt of the hit. The doctor that examined Tim, said there was injury to the spine, and he was bleeding internally. Joyce hugged her daughter-in-law as tears came down both their faces.

⁓

Christine was now about four months along in her pregnancy, Joyce knew the importance of keeping her calm as possible.

"Sweetie, I'm here, we'll pray and just deal with things as they come. Now, first of all, have you eaten anything this evening?"

"I had a small snack around four then I got the call about Tim."

"Samantha, will you and the boys go see if you can find Christine a little something to eat, and bring some milk for her to drink."

"Sure, come on boys." Samantha said as she tried to think where a snack machine would be.

Christine, Joyce and the rest of their family waited in the waiting area for over four hours before the doctor came out. When he finally came through the double doors, Christine stood up, thinking that her legs were going to fold, afraid of the news she was about to hear.

"The surgery is over; we got the bleeding stopped; he has damage to the spine. We will have to wait and see exactly how much damage was done when the swelling goes down. He's in recovery right now, Mrs. McIntosh you may go in for a few minutes."

As Christine took off toward the recovery room, Joyce continued to ask the doctor more questions.

"How long will it take for the swelling to go down?" Joyce asked.

"With an injury like this one ... usually several days. After that we will do some other tests and find out whether or not he will be able to walk."

"Walk? You mean he might not be able to walk?" Joyce asked fearfully.

"I can't really say for sure; it may be a temporary paralysis. Again, we will have to wait and see. The nurses will keep a very close eye on him tonight, and I will be checking him again in the morning."

"Thank you, doctor," Brandon said. As the doctor walked away, Joyce looked in shock. Her son had been in an accident and now may never walk again.

"Joyce, honey, you can't let your mind go there." Brandon knew his wife so well; he knew she was thinking of Timothy never walking again. "He said it may or it may not be any permanent damage, we have to be strong right now for Christine."

These words seemed to pull Joyce back into focus; she continued to hold Brandon's arm, thinking she had to get herself together and help Christine and her son.

Samantha called Diane, then Pastor Jones. His wife, Libby called and started the prayer chain at their church. Brandon called Don and had him tell the rest of the family. Richard and Luke were sitting in the waiting room with the other children, Diane, and Ron. The waiting room was full of Timothy's family and close friends.

"Joyce, honey, do you want to go back there and see him now?" Brandon asked

"Yes, if they will let me." Joyce being so tired and worried didn't notice that a nurse had just come and told them they could have a short visit with Timothy.

Brandon held Joyce's hand as they walked to the recovery area. The nurse had said they could not stay long. As soon as Timothy woke up they would be putting him into a regular room.

"Timothy, Timothy honey, it's Momma; can you hear me?" Timothy only flickered his eyes; he couldn't speak, but squeezed her hand. "Honey, everything is going to be alright, you just rest and do what the doctor tells you; we're taking care of Christine. You're going to be fine; do you hear me, Timothy?" Timothy did not respond at that point.

Christine, with Joyce's arm around her walked back to the waiting area with Brandon. The hour was very late, and she looked like she was dead on her feet.

"Christine, honey, we need to get you home and in bed so you can rest."

"I doubt I can sleep with all this, I need to be near Tim," Christine replied.

Joyce told the family about Timothy's condition that he was in recovery, but still not fully awake. Brandon asked Richard and Luke to take the others home and have Lorna make Christine as comfortable as possible, while he and Joyce stayed a little while longer.

It was one in the morning before they got Timothy into his own room, Joyce stayed by his side constantly, since Christine was not able to be there. Joyce was now worried not only for her son, but also for her unborn grandchild.

"It would be best if you go home now. He needs lost of rest, and he may be able to respond to you in the morning." The nurse told them kindly.

"She's right, Joyce, let's go home, get some sleep, and we'll come back first thing in the morning." Brandon replied. Somehow Brandon talked Joyce into leaving, just as she had talked Christine into leaving just a few hours before.

Christine, however, was up by four, getting dressed and making a little breakfast, when she heard Lorna come in the kitchen.

"Here, Christine, let me help you," said Lorna.

"Oh no, Lorna, please go back to bed; it's too early for you to be up. I'll fix myself a little something and go on out to the hospital."

"Honey, it's too early for anyone to be up. Let me ask you something." Lorna said leading Christine to one of the kitchen chairs to sit down, "Can I get you to lie back down for one more hour? Then, you can eat and be a little more refreshed and maybe you won't be so tired by noon. You're not going to do anyone any good if you exhaust yourself.

"I need to be with him, Lorna, I'll be alright, and I feel fine." She said as Lorna noticed the dark circles under her eyes.

"Christine, just one more hour, that's all and you will feel much better." Lorna begged, gently holding both Christine's hands.

"Just one more hour and then I am going out there."

Two hours later, Christine still hadn't risen. Joyce was now in the kitchen dressed and eager to get to the hospital.

"Is Christine still asleep?" Joyce asked Lorna.

"Yes, she was up at four, and I talked her into laying back down. She finally gave in; I don't know if we should wake her or not."

"Let's give her a little more time." Joyce suggested.

Samantha had called Elise early in the morning to break the news. She knew being so far away at school was going to be hard, but Elise needed to know what was going on back in Garland. Samantha promised to call her often throughout the day even if there wasn't any news to report.

Brandon got the boys ready, and Samantha met her mother in the kitchen. Christine had awakened and was drinking some tea. Within ten minutes they all were out the door and on their way to the hospital, each one of them praying in their minds for Timothy's quick recovery.

CHAPTER EIGHTEEN

The doctor was right; the swelling went down in a little over one week. Timothy had begun to remember what had happened to cause him to be where he was. Christine was still tired, but doing much better. Joyce had seen to her needs as much as possible. The twins came in to see their big brother; they hadn't seen him at all during the intense time after the surgery.

"Hey, guys, how are my buddies?" Timothy held out his arms to hug his two little brothers. Just with a little conversation Timothy seemed to be tiring already.

"I guess I'm just weak from being in this bed and from all that has happened," Timothy said.

"It has only been a little over a week, Tim." Christine told him as she rubbed the side of his face. The doctor came in at that moment, and most of the room cleared out. Joyce stayed with Christine to hear the news.

"Timothy, we're going to release you, maybe in two days. If things continue as they are now, you'll be doing a lot of physical therapy, but your family can bring you in for those, three days a week."

The doctor started to leave the room when Timothy asked if he could speak to him privately. Everyone left the room and found the others down the hall.

"Alright, Doctor Williams, why are my legs still numb?"

"Timothy, I have been straight with you and your family from the start. You have some spine damage, but it is not as bad as we were afraid it would be. You are doing better, but you will have to work at getting your legs to function again; right now we can't risk you taking a fall. Next week you will start therapy, and the therapist will have strong people there to keep you from falling. It will be hard; I'm not going to lie to you. You will work and you will work hard 'if' you want to walk again."

"Thank you, Doc. I did ask, and that's what I needed to hear," Timothy replied.

Timothy was not too happy with what the doctor told him. Dr. Williams did give him some hope of walking again. He lay on his back looking at the ceiling, feeling anger swell within him. He was not going to spend the rest of his life in a wheel chair if he had anything to do with it.

The weeks crept slowly by; Timothy was doing well at his physical therapy, but it wasn't going as fast as he wanted it to. He quickly grew impatient and at one point he had overdone it; instead of taking it slow like he had been told, he tried to speed up the process by doing more exercise than he should have. This caused him a setback in his recovery.

Timothy had become cross with everyone in his life. He yelled at Christine over every little thing. Samantha had gone to Christine and Timothy's to help out. Christine called and asked if she would keep Tim company while she went to the grocery. What Samantha heard as she was leaving was very upsetting.

"Why did you have my sister come here?" Tim asked angrily.

"Tim, I needed to go to the grocery, and I didn't want to leave you alone."

"So, you think I can't take care of myself, is that it?"

"Tim, no that's not it, I just thought…" Tim interrupted her in the middle of her sentence. "I'll do the thinking around here Christine!" He yelled in her face. Christine left the room, went in the bedroom, locked the door and began to cry.

"Great! That's just great!" He yelled after her.

Being pregnant and Timothy injured, she didn't know how much more she could take. It seemed like he got so upset at everything she did or didn't do.

Samantha was so upset at the way Timothy reacted to her being there. She thought he enjoyed spending time with her she told her mother. Joyce hugged her daughter and reminded her that Timothy was not himself lately, and they all would have to be patient with him.

"Mom, you should have heard him; it was awful," Samantha exclaimed. "I didn't mean to hear it really, but the yelling was so loud, I couldn't help it. I didn't know Tim was like that," Samantha said as she looked down at her hands.

Joyce was at a loss; she didn't know what to do for Timothy or Christine. She prayed for them daily, but in her weakness, she felt the Lord was not hearing her. Suddenly, she decided to talk to Brandon about Timothy's behavior; maybe he would know what to do.

Sam left the house, took a walk, and found herself at the stables. "Well, hello there, what brings you down to the stables?" Luke asked.

Samantha looked up to see him standing by one of the horses.

"Oh, hi Luke, I didn't see you, I just came down here to pet the horses."

"Well, you are always welcome and besides they love to be rubbed down, even it if it's just on their faces. Take Biscuit here, he's a pushover for pretty girls." Samantha laughed a little as she stroked Biscuit's face.

Luke was always so kind spoken and gentle, Samantha thought to herself, *or is it just for now? Later on when he's married he will probably yell at his wife too.*

"Well, thanks Luke, I'd better be going; I'm sure you have work to do."

"Anytime Sam, anytime," Luke couldn't help but turn and watch her walk away, wondering what had her sad today.

Joyce had been waiting for Brandon to come in the house so she could talk with him about Timothy, when he suddenly came in the kitchen.

"Brandon, I need to speak with you please."

"Sure, what's up?" They sat at the kitchen table while Joyce filled Brandon in on what happened at Timothy and Christine's that morning. Joyce felt she really should go to them and try to help somehow.

"I need to go to Timothy and Christine's; is that alright with you?" Joyce asked.

"Why do you feel you must?" She continued to explain how Timothy had been yelling at everyone, especially at his wife. For Joyce it brought back many unpleasant memories of her and Paul.

"I just need to talk to him; he's not treating Christine fairly, and I just need to speak with him and explain what he's doing and how much damage…" Joyce stopped talking at that moment and put her hands on her forehead.

"Joyce, honey, you can't do that. You have to let them stand on their own."

"Brandon, they're not standing on their own right now. He is over-working himself to recover, and it's setting him back. He's taking it out on everyone, especially Christine. It's not good for their marriage or their baby." She explained with a little tension in her voice.

"I understand you want to take care of him and them, but you can't, Joyce. He is a grown man, and if you go over there and try to fix this he isn't going to listen to you." Brandon paused as he looked at Joyce, knowing he had to tread lightly here. "No, Joyce, I don't want you to go."

"Excuse me!" Joyce looked at him with anger in her eyes. Brandon had never seen that look on his wife's face before. He was shocked, but still stood firm on his decision.

"Joyce, I do not want you to go over there; I honestly feel it will be a big mistake."

"What is it with you men?" Joyce stormed out of the room, went to the bedroom and slammed the door. Brandon stood up and stopped himself from going in after her; he paced around the kitchen for a few minutes, hoping she would cool off a bit.

Brandon quietly opened the door to their bedroom; Joyce was

sitting in the chair by the window, looking out at the scenery.

"I guess we just had our first argument, didn't we?" Brandon said in a soft voice. "You know, Joyce, the way we handle this right now, will set the tone for how we will handle any and every argument we have in the future." Joyce didn't respond in any way.

Brandon sat on the bed where he could see her, but she continued to look out the window not speaking or looking at him.

"Joyce, neither one of us is leaving this room or turning in for the night until this is settled," He said softly, but firmly. Joyce kept looking out the window.

"Honey, I know this is hard on you. I will talk to Timothy if you want me to; believe it or not it will have more power coming from another man than coming from his mother. You must believe that. Besides, you are way too emotional over this whole thing right now." Joyce finally looked at Brandon, he continued looking at her, and the two of them sat staring at one another.

"You would do that? Talk with Tim?" She asked, after breaking the silence.

"Yes, I will." Brandon got up went over to Joyce, took her by the hand and pulled her up from the chair; the two of them stood facing each other.

"I love you with all my heart, Joyce; I don't like watching you hurt. I also love your children as if they were my own."

"I'm sorry I ran out and slammed the door." Joyce replied.

"Can we make up now?" Brandon asked with a low voice as his face was so near hers.

"Maybe," Brandon gave Joyce a soft kiss, and the two went back out to the kitchen. All the while Brandon was thinking of how he could approach Timothy without making him look like the enemy.

Brandon took Timothy to his physical therapy on Monday morning. Timothy was in a horrible mood. He made Christine cry, again, this time over the upkeep of the car. What he didn't know was the response he would get when he returned.

"Timothy, are you alright?" Brandon asked as they were driving to the hospital.

"I'm fine."

"I'm here if you want to talk."

"Thanks, I'll keep that in mind." Timothy replied coldly.

As they pulled up to the entrance door, Brandon helped Timothy get inside. "I'll pick you up at noon, right?"

"Yes, noon," when Timothy got inside he could manage getting to the physical therapy room on his own. His instructor, Randy, was waiting for him to begin the days exercise.

"Hey, Tim, ready?"

"Ready as I'll ever be; the question is will it matter," Timothy mumbled.

"Excuse me?" said Randy.

"Nothing, let's get started."

Brandon returned at noon just as Timothy was coming out the door. Brandon helped him into the truck, took him home and went inside to say hello to Christine, when he and Timothy got inside, it looked as if Christine were ready to go somewhere, so Brandon thought it best if he leave.

"I'll see you two later, call if you need anything."

"Brandon, I'll walk you out." Christine said. She continued to follow Brandon out to his truck so she could talk to him privately.

"I want to explain to you, and you can explain to the family. I'm leaving for a while, I just can't take all this any more; it isn't good for the baby; I can't be upset all the time. I don't know how long I'll be gone, but you can reach me at my parent's home, here's the number." Christine then handed Brandon a small piece of paper. "I'll be calling you and Joyce to check on Tim, but this is something I have to do for our baby and for myself and to be honest with you, I think it may be helpful for Tim as well. This way I won't be around to upset him so much."

"I do understand Christine, and honestly, I can't say I wouldn't do the same thing if I were in your shoes. We'll keep you informed, you take care of the two of you," Brandon said as he gave Christine a hug. "Please, take this; you never know when you may need it."

Brandon said as he pulled cash out of his wallet. Christine didn't want to take the money Brandon pressed into her hand, but Brandon was pretty adamant about it.

Once again, Timothy began to shout at Christine as she told him of her plans. She had come to expect that type of reaction from him about almost anything she did, but it didn't stop her. She was determined to get away from the yelling and stress their lives had become, the question was; would she ever come back?

Christine told Timothy she couldn't handle living like this any longer. The yelling, stress, and fear of setting him off over the least little thing, of course, this only made Timothy angrier.

"Yes, Christine let's not forget about you, little Christine. At least you can walk!" he yelled, "You're not going; I forbid it!"

"Just like that, I'm not going? Let me remind you something Timothy McIntosh, I married you to be my husband; not my boss; not you or anyone else will forbid me to do anything!" Those words and the slamming of the door was the last Timothy heard from her.

"Christine! Christine!" Timothy yelled, but got no response. "Fine, run to mommy and daddy, I don't need anyone! Do you hear me?"

Brandon came back about an hour later; he figured things might be calmer then. He needed to have a man to man talk with Timothy, and it was going to be now whether Timothy liked it or not.

Brandon let himself in and took a chair at the kitchen table. Timothy sat in his wheelchair in the kitchen as well.

"Timothy, if you don't stop this, you're going to lose that woman."

Timothy never said a word. He just sat there staring at his hands.

"Remember when I called you and asked if I could date your mother? You told me that you would not hesitate to take things into you own hands if I hurt her. Remember that?"

"Yeah, I remember, what of it?" he asked coldly.

"What about Christine? Are you hurting her? What will her

father do when he finds out how you've been treating her? He may want to take matters into his own hands."

"I have not done anything to my wife, Brandon, and by the way, you are way out of line here. With a non-family member yes, you would be right, but you and Christine are a part of my family. My wife is so upset at watching you turn into your father that she cries in her sleep," Brandon continued.

"I'm not like my father, what do you know about my father any way," the young man said with gritted teeth.

"In case you have forgotten, I'm married to your mother, and she has told me some things about Paul. How he would yell at Joyce, his temper at times toward you kids. Now, your mother and I will help you in anyway possible, Timothy, but we cannot make you treat Christine right, you either do it with the love that you feel for her, or you don't, but Tim, she doesn't deserve this." Timothy just sat looking out into space while Brandon continued.

"Have you looked at her face lately, Timothy? Have you noticed the dark circles under her eyes? You've put them there. This is too much stress for her in her condition; she is not the cause of your accident ... that woman loves you, but the way you've been treating her is awful. She will only respond to your actions, good or bad. You're in the lead here whether you act like it, or not. That's what women do; you treat them right, they respond in a good way, you treat them badly, they respond in a way to survive."

Timothy didn't respond to Brandon, nor did he look at him. He just sat there with anger filling his heart.

"Are you done now with your little marriage counseling Brandon?" Tim said smartly.

"Yes, I am, but the question is; are you done? Done or not son, you had better get your act together, walking or not walking, or be prepared to live without Christine and your child," Brandon said as he got up and walked out the door.

―――

Sunday morning, Brandon and Joyce picked up Timothy for

church. Christine had been gone for six weeks, and Timothy was feeling the effects of his wife's absence. He wasn't in the mood for church and hadn't been going, but he let his mother talk him into it.

The well-wishers at church only frustrated Timothy; the music that was sung did nothing for him. He was just getting out of the house and his mind off his troubles, or so he thought.

"Today's lesson or sermon, if you will, is on loving our spouses. For some reason this message has most always, from the beginning of time, been directed to the women, but not today."

"Now, most of us have been taught how to treat others, have we not? We know how to be polite and use our manners, do we not? What about how we treat our spouse? After all spouses are people, too." The pastor joked and the congregation responded with light laughter.

"Believe it or not, but there are times my sweet, loving wife, would love for me to put my neck right there in her pretty hands, so she can squeeze ever so tightly." This caused the congregation to laugh out loud.

"Let's look into God's Word, shall we? Turn to Ephesians Chapter 5, Verse 23. Now, many of us men have this verse memorized, don't we? Oh yeah, we got this one down. We have brought it up to our wives, over and over. We 'Amen' the preacher when he preaches on it, don't we men? Let's read."

"'For the husband is the head of the wife, even as Christ is the head of the church: and he is the Savior of the body, Verse 24. Therefore as the church is subject unto Christ, so let the wives be to their own husbands in every thing, and here is where we are going to camp out for awhile, so don't check out on me, I need you all to listen here. Husbands, love your wives, even as Christ also loved the church, and gave himself for it."

"Let's say you come to church every week, everything seems beautiful on the outside; you're smiling, your wife is happy, the kids are happy. Everyone looks good, you have a nice car, nice home, and you're the perfect family. People in the church respect you, they listen to you speak intelligently about spiritual matters. Then you go home, you take off the nice clothes, the smiles, and you are yourselves. At times you don't even get home before the real you comes out. The kids are bickering; the dinner is burned, and the dog bit you. Laundry is piled high you have no clean socks to wear. The checking account is overdrawn because your wife didn't balance it; because she was too busy having your fifth child. Did any of that sound familiar? You yell at your wife, you scream at your kids. You're being a not nice person. If we men were women, how would we respond to us?"

"Men, remember back to your wedding day. Your wife's father gives his little girl whom he loves so dearly to you, a man who doesn't see a little girl, you see a woman. We promised men, didn't we? We promised to take care of her, provide for her, love and cherish her. What part of screaming at her and making her do all the things around the house is loving her and cherishing her?"

"What part of yelling at her because she spent a little too much on a blouse is cherishing her? We are commanded to love our wives, even in the hard times, the bad times. Does Christ show his love to the church by yelling and screaming? Does he show his love by ignoring the church's needs, not only for things, but for growth? Men, what about it? I want each married man and each man thinking of marriage to think on this today."

"Let us pray."

Timothy was about to come undone. *Christine! What have I done to my Christine? It was all he could think about, he kept seeing her face in his minds' eye. She may not come back; I can't blame her if she doesn't. She has to come back to me. Her pregnancy is almost over and I have missed most of it because of this stupid accident. Why Lord, why did you allow this to happen? Why now, this was supposed to be a very new and special time for both of us, and look at us. We're apart and it's my fault, all my fault. Brandon was right, I have become the very man I said I would never be.* These were the thoughts that ran rapidly through Timothy's mind as the Pastor prayed.

Timothy couldn't get out of that church fast enough; he had things to figure out; he didn't want anyone to be kind and shake his hand, or stop and speak with him; all he wanted was to go home.

Chapter eighteen / 273

"Timothy, would you like to come out to the ranch for dinner?" Joyce asked.
"No thanks, Mom, I'm feeling a little tired, I think I just need to go home and lie down for a while."
"Are you sure, honey? You could rest at the ranch."
"No, I need to go home, thanks anyway." He said with his usual cold face.
Brandon and Joyce took Timothy home, but he didn't lie down as he said he was going to. Instead he picked up the phone to call his wife.

Timothy sat with his hand on the phone, trying to think of just the right words to say to Christine. It took him several minutes.
"Hello, Mrs. Bradford, it's Timothy, how are you?"
"Timothy, hello, I'm fine, how about you?"
"I've been better, but I am also getting better. Aah Mrs. Bradford is Christine there?"
"Yes, she is, hold on just a moment." Mrs. Bradford interrupted Sunday dinner to get Christine to the phone. Christine was really not sure she wanted to talk to her estranged husband, but took the phone from her mother's hand anyway.
"Hello." Christine said rather softly.
"Christine, hi, how are you?"
"I'm okay."
"I miss you Christine, I want you to come home."
"I'm sorry Tim; I can't do that right now."
"Why Christine? Why can't you come home where you belong? You belong here with me."
"I'll come home when I think the time is right, and now the time isn't right."
"We need to talk Christine, and we can't do that if you're not here." Timothy was working hard to keep his voice even and not yell.
"Seems to me we're talking now. Or actually, you're just telling me what to do. I'm not coming home now Tim and that's that."

"Well, I guess there isn't anymore to say right now is there?" He said firmly.

"No, I'm afraid not."

"Bye Christine."

"Bye."

Christine hung up the phone, but didn't return to the dining table with her parents, instead she went to her room, laid down, and cried.

Timothy had found that being alone was not fun; he missed his wife in so many ways. He missed her smile, even though she had not been doing much smiling before she left. He missed her cooking and hated being in their bed alone. Everywhere he looked he saw her, and it was about to drive him mad.

He had come to terms that her leaving was his fault, and if he wanted to get her back he was going to have to work at it. He was going to have to prove to her that he was still the man she had married. But how, how could he do that with all the hurt he had caused, and with her miles away from Garland. Each day he longed for his wife's return. Finally, Timothy had his total fill of this mess he had created. He lay in bed one morning, dreading facing another day. It was then he decided it was past time to call on the Lord.

"Lord, I have acted awful toward my family, especially my wife. I'm so sorry, will you please forgive me? Would you please bring her home, safe to me Lord? I don't want to be hard toward her, please help me each day to be the man you would have me be. Amen."

Timothy had shown progress in his physical therapy. It was a long time coming for him, but come it did. Joyce had taken him to his therapy on Wednesday morning, as she usually did.

"I'll pick you up, Timothy, at the regular time." She said as she was letting him off at the front door to the building. Joyce noticed he had not said much as they rode together. She didn't want to upset him, so she allowed him his silence. She just silently prayed for her son as she drove away.

Timothy worked hard at his attempt to regain the use of his legs.

Chapter eighteen / 275

He had been working hard all along, but now it was with a new attitude. He was no longer yelling or being cold toward others, and it seemed to make a difference. Randy, his therapist, noticed it and said as much to Timothy.

Since Joyce got to the hospital early to pick Timothy up, she went in to where he was and silently watched. With a hand to her mouth she watched as tears started to form in her eyes. She thought she would shout. Timothy had taken his first step.

When he turned around he noticed his mother, she ran to her son and hugged him. Tears filled in both of their eyes. He was tired and almost out of breath; sweat beads were on his brow from the hard work.

"Ready to go again?" the instructor asked.

"Yes, but let me catch my breath."

"Sure, that's the key to this thing, Tim, keeping at it without overdoing."

After a while he started at the end of the bars again. He walked four whole steps this time, taking a total of eight steps that day. Joyce prayed silently in her heart.

Thank you Lord, I watched Timothy take his first steps as a baby, he was all giggles and smiles then, and I'm watching him take his first steps again now, with pain and excitement in his eyes. Thank you, Dear Lord.

CHAPTER NINETEEN

It was Saturday afternoon, and after many weeks of being away, Christine had agreed to come home. Timothy asked Samantha and Joyce if they would come and help him get the house ready. The two women were only too happy to oblige; Lorna had prepared a meal to be taken to them as well.

"Son, I think you should be here alone when Christine gets here, so we're going to take off now, unless you need something."

Timothy thanked his mom and sister for their help, and agreed it was best if they left. He wanted things to be just right when his wife came home. The house was clean, and there was a warm meal waiting for her. Timothy laid down on the sofa while he waited for the sound of her vehicle to pull in the driveway. He needed the rest, and the comfort of the sofa caused him to relax a little.

As he lay there, his body relaxed, his mind was running in all directions.

Will she be the same? Will she want to stay, or is she coming to collect the rest of her things?

The baby is due in three weeks; maybe she is coming just to be closer to her doctor.

"Aah stop it, stop it Timothy!" He spoke out loud in the empty room.

Should I shave? He thought to himself. Timothy went in the bathroom, looked himself over a few times, washed his face, combed his hair, checked his clothes, and walked out to the living room where he sat in the chair and waited.

After what seemed like hours, he heard the car pull into the garage, and he waited patiently for Christine to come through the door. Timothy had a surprise waiting for his wife, but it seemed it was taking her a long time to come in, and then finally she walked through the door.

Christine just stood staring at Timothy, her mouth hung open and she began to cry.

Timothy had not only stood waiting at the door for her, but took five steps toward her. They both cried in each others arms. He felt a little unstable and sat back down in a nearby chair.

"So, how long have you been able to do that?" Christine asked wiping the tears from her eyes.

"About three weeks, I wanted to surprise you."

Timothy stood again and looked at his wife; he gently put his hand on her stomach that was very large with their child.

"It isn't going to be long now, is it?" He said with amazement.

"No, it isn't."

"You look beautiful, Christine, really you do."

"Thank you, Tim," was all she could manage to say. For the brief moments she was home, Timothy seemed to be more of his old self.

Timothy took his wife's hand and the two went into the living room where they sat side by side on the sofa.

"Christine." He took her hand and lifted her chin for her to look at him. "I'm sorry, I have treated you awfully, I will never do that again, none of this was your fault and I had no right, no right at all. If you never forgive me and leave me you would have every right to. Please Christine, never leave me, I need you and our baby, you're a part of me."

This was Christine's undoing. She sobbed in Timothy's chest. He lifted her chin and gave her a gentle kiss.

Timothy told Christine how he had started taking steps and how hard it was, how Brandon and Joyce kept an eye on him while she was gone.

"Mom and Brandon made me do quite a bit of things alone, tough love and all that. You should have heard the things Brandon said to me."

Timothy wasn't aware that Brandon and Joyce talked with Christine each week and told her how he was doing. Christine felt it best to keep that between the three of them for the time being.

The two talked while they ate the meal Lorna had prepared for them when Christine began to frail, she looked tired. Tim was tired as well and thought it best they both rest.

"Come on, let's both go lie down, we have had an emotional, tiring day."

Once in their bedroom lying beside one another, Timothy leaned over and gently kissed his wife, and thanked the Lord silently for bringing his family home.

Joyce and Brandon were reading in bed, Joyce couldn't help but think about the past events – all the turmoil, tears and fears. She outwardly sighed.

"What was that for?" Brandon asked.

"The Lord has brought us through another storm, Brandon."

"Yes, he has, life has a lot of those; some are small, some are bigger than life itself, but God takes care of his children."

"I was afraid Timothy and Christine were done. It scared me to watch and not be able to do anything about it. I'm just glad they worked things out."

Joyce and Brandon heard a noise upstairs in the boys' room. "Speaking of storms I think one is blowing in right now," Joyce grinned at her husband.

"I'll go, you stay." He gave Joyce a very tender kiss.

As Brandon was checking on the boys upstairs, Joyce's mind went to many different places. She remembered the trials she and Paul had early in their marriage, how he made her feel when he would yell at her for something so unimportant, or forbid her to do something. She didn't want any of her children to live like that.

When Brandon returned he asked her of her thoughts. She kindly told him...

"Marriage doesn't have to be that way; it should never be that

way." She said as she looked at the man who loved her to distraction, she then thanked him and gave him a gentle kiss.
"What was that for?"
"For treating me like a queen."
"You, my love, are certainly welcome."

⁓

Christine was pretty much on the money for her delivery date. Three weeks later, at two thirty in the morning she woke Timothy.
"Tim, Tim wake-up."
"Huh, what is it?"
"Tim, I think my labor has started."
Timothy woke immediately; he was out of bed in no time flat.
"I'll call the doctor." He said to his wife, as he noticed she had a very strange look on her face.
"Tim, we're supposed to time the contractions, remember? When they get about fifteen minutes apart, then we call. It could be this time tomorrow before anything happens."
"Oh, Christine! Don't tell me that! But you're right; we need to time the contractions. When was the first one?"
"About twenty minutes ago. I think maybe I will just get up and go to the bathroom."
"Why? What will you do in there, is there something we need to be doing?" He said frantically.
"Tim! I need to go potty, that's all; I'll come right back. You'll have to calm down or we both are not going to make it." Christine couldn't help but laugh at her husband when she got behind the closed door of the bathroom.
At six o'clock that morning, Timothy and Christine left for the hospital. Timothy's foot got a little heavier on the gas pedal at each contraction. As soon as they arrived, a nurse took Christine to the delivery area while Timothy signed papers that seemed to go on forever. When that was finished, he sought out his wife and they both waited patiently. His body was getting tired from all the walking, so he sought out a chair and sat while he could.

After many hours of labor, at midnight, Christine delivered a healthy baby boy, Nathan Daniel McIntosh. He was red and screaming at the top of his little lungs, but he and his mother were fine and healthy and that was all that mattered to Timothy.

Timothy sat in the hospital room holding his son. Looking him over, cooing at him and just enjoying holding him in his arms.

"Christine, he's so perfect, look at him, honey; he's just beautiful. I can hardly wait to have another."

Christine was taking a drink of juice when Tim made that comment and nearly choked.

"Tim, please, Nathan isn't even a day old yet."

"I know, but we do want more. But I guess we can wait if you insist." This caused the two to laugh out loud.

The nurse came in to check on Christine, noticing Timothy, and how at ease he held the baby.

"Well, look at you; most new fathers don't know what to do with a new baby. You look like an old pro."

"I'm the oldest of five, so I'm kind of broken in already," he said proudly looking at his son.

When Joyce came in and saw her grandson, she couldn't help but fall in love.

She held him gently, and kissed the top of his little head; she felt so overjoyed at the way her grandson felt cradled in her arms.

It wasn't long until Samantha, then Elise had their turn at holding little Nathan. Mark and Michael didn't want to hold him; they only looked at him and then visited with their big brother. After everyone else had a turn holding Nathan, Brandon cleared his throat, and instructed Joyce to hand the baby to him, it was now his turn.

Two weeks later, everything had settled down some. Christine's mother had come to help with the baby; Joyce had helped some and couldn't seem to get enough of her grandson.

"You know tomorrow we are on our own," Christine told her husband.

"Yes, I know, I'll be glad in a way. I mean I love your mother Christine, but with your mother and my mother in and out, well, that is just a little too much mother right now." Christine couldn't help but laugh. Christine had thanked the Lord many times for giving her back her Timothy, the man she fell in love with and vowed to love always and for their healthy baby boy.

Samantha went in search of her mother. She knew she was getting ready to go out with Diane, but it seemed to be taking longer than it should have.

"Mom, Diane is waiting, what seems to be the problem?" Samantha called out to her mother. "I'm coming, I'm coming." Joyce responded.

Diane and Jace were waiting in the living room for Joyce; the three of them were spending the day together. Joyce loved Jace dearly; as she did Diane's other two children. She couldn't help but hold and kiss him, and in return he would light up with smiles and giggles when he saw her.

Diane was handling being a mother of an infant again just fine. The only problem was when the girls were home and out with Jace, sometimes older women would think he belonged to one of them and not Diane. "That aggravates me and the girls to no end." Diane told Joyce.

Joyce and Diane shopped and bought things for both babies. Joyce had to make herself not overspend for Nathan, but it was hard, especially when she saw the little teddy bear sitting on the shelf in one of the baby stores they were in.

"Isn't this the cutest little teddy bear you've ever seen?" She said to Diane. "Nate will love it. Look at his face, I've gotta get this." Joyce exclaimed. After spending almost ninety dollars in one store, she figured she had better call it done for the day.

Joyce and Diane enjoyed themselves as they always did. Even through major changes had occurred in their lives, Joyce marrying Brandon, Diane having another baby, they still remained the best of friends, and spent lots of time together, if not on the phone, then with one another. Brandon and Ron had become friends as well, and neither tried to interfere with the life long friendship their wives had, it became stronger as the years went by.

Joyce asked the Lord many times to give her children a 'Diane' in their lives like she had. There was something about having a friend that had always been in your life.

⁓

That evening Joyce had planned a surprise for Brandon.

"Lorna, Brandon and I will not be eating here this evening; I'm going to surprise him with a little picnic for just the two of us. Oh, and make sure the children don't come looking for us unless we are gone over eight hours," she said teasingly.

"Yes, Ma'am." Lorna and Joyce chuckled together.

Joyce had one of the ranch hands saddle Millie up for her and rode out to the area where Brandon was working. She and Millie strode quietly up to Brandon.

"Well, what do we have here?" Brandon asked, "A good lookin' woman with a basket. Whatever could this mean?" Joyce dismounted Millie, and walked to where he stood.

"I thought it would be nice to eat out here, just the two of us."

"That depends on what's in the basket," he teased.

"Brandon Richard Miller, you can march right up to the house and eat with the children if that is your attitude," she teased back.

Brandon only laughed. "What did you bring me?" he said as he grabbed her around the waist, trying to apologize without saying the words.

"I don't know if I should show you or not," she teased again.

"Sure you should, after I get my kiss, that is."

Joyce laid out a blanket, and opened a basket with some of Lorna's leftovers. Lorna's cooking was so good; there was hardly ever anything leftover. Joyce had brought roast beef, dinner rolls, raw veggies, and some sweet tea. Brandon told her it all sounded delicious. "And for dessert…" Brandon cut her off. "I think I know what I want for dessert." Brandon said pulling her close and talking very close to her face.

"Brandon, now you will behave," she giggled.

"For dessert we have some apple pie, I took the last two pieces; the boys will be hurt, but hey, all is fair in love and Lorna's apple pie."

Brandon and Joyce had their horses tied closely together on a bush, as they sat under an oak tree and ate their meal. Joyce noticed that Pete, Brandon's horse stayed real close to Millie.

"Brandon," Joyce spoke and caused him to look up. "I think Pete is getting fresh with Millie." Pete was one of Brandon's stallions, beautiful horse with a reddish brown color with black mane and tail.

"Well, would you look at that, sure seems like it. It isn't her mating time, but he sure does seem to like her, smart horse." He and Joyce continued eating their food when she noticed Brandon staring at her.

"Why are you looking at me like that?" She said with raised eye brows.

"I just enjoy having time alone with you; don't get me wrong, I love the full quiver we have, but times like these are precious to me.

"I love you, you know?"

"Yeah, I had heard that," he teased.

"Now eat your pie, before I take it." she teased in return.

Brandon and Joyce enjoyed the quiet time they spent out of doors; it was like a boost of energy to both of them.

Timothy, Christine and Nate had come to visit. As soon as they entered the door the squeals started from Nate.

"Come here Nate, come see Aunt Sam." Samantha said as she hugged and kissed her nephew.

"Hey where are Mom and Brandon?" Timothy asked.

"They are somewhere on the property having a dinner all to themselves, they should be getting back. It's starting to get dark," Samantha replied.

Christine talked with the twins and found their conversation informative. She now knew all about the latest video game that was just out on the market. Christine loved her little brother's in-law, but after all this time with this family, she still had the hardest time telling them apart.

Timothy and Christine had been at the house for about thirty minutes when Brandon and Joyce walked in.

"It must be a day for surprises. Hello, Tim, good to see you."

Joyce went to hug her oldest son, and then her daughter-in-law. "Now, let me have my grandbaby," Joyce playfully demanded.

Everyone sat around the living room and talked and played with the baby. The twins had even started playing more with Nathan.

"Coffee, anyone?

"I'll have some, Mom."

"I'll just have something with no caffeine; here let me help," offered Christine.

The two women went into the kitchen and talked while the coffee was brewing. After just a few minutes the men followed while the twins and Samantha played with Nate.

Joyce was happy to see him continue to recover from his accident. Timothy's doctor had told him and Christine that Timothy should make a complete recovery.

While Joyce took Christine upstairs to show her the new bedspreads she had bought for the boys' room. Timothy took that opportunity to talk to Brandon about a private matter.

"Brandon, I want to thank you for all you did, not only for me, but for mine and Christine's marriage. I feel so horrible when I think back to it, I acted like a monster. I still don't know how I could have ever done that. Again, thanks."

"You're welcome, son. I knew you weren't yourself, and I didn't want that to become you; I'm very happy for you, Timothy, really, I am."

The two women came into the room and didn't sense there had been any serious talk between the men.

"Christine, I think Nate is hungry. He's getting a little fussy, or maybe he's wet, or sleepy, but something is wrong, he's not a happy camper right now." Samantha said as she handed Nate with his little poochie lip over to his mother. Nate dug his head into Christine's chest and began to cry a little.

"I need to feed him, Samantha, may I borrow your bedroom a few minutes while I feed Nate? Sure, just close the door, no one will bother you."

"Thanks, come on Nate, let's go eat."

Joyce talked to her son while Christine was feeding Nate. Timothy told her they had gotten a little behind on some bills, but were doing fine. He had been back to work for two months and they were still playing 'catch up', but were dealing with it.

"I'm still working to prove to Christine I'm not that monster she was living with several months ago, and the doctor says I'm improving more each time he sees me. I still do my physical therapy, so all in all things are better."

"You really scared me there for awhile, son." Joyce said.

"Yes, I think I scared everyone including myself, and especially Christine. I don't want to ever see that look in her eyes again. The look of fear – afraid to tell me anything and afraid to be around me. Mom, I realized you lived in that fear didn't you? All those years with Dad."

Joyce told her son yes, but she never thought about it affecting her children. She admitted she should have put a stop to it when it started, but for some reason she could not recall, why she didn't.

Christine came back in the room with Nate who looked sleepy. Timothy took the baby and held him gently.

"It looks like old man Nate here has his belly full and needs to go home to bed." Timothy said as he put his forehead to Nate's.

Christine got the diaper bag put back in order and the once again happy couple headed for their home.

"Boys, in thirty minutes you two head for bed yourself."

"Yes sir," the twins replied in unison.

"Oh man! Mark, I wanted to watch that new cop show."

"Oh, yeah I forgot about that. When does it come on? Michael asked.

"Let me check the TV listings. Here it is, comes on at ten."

"We can't stay up that late, we have school tomorrow, Mom and Brandon will never let us do that."

As Mark and Michael headed for the upstairs to take care of their personal hygiene needs before going to bed, Michael had an idea of how to see that show.

Mark and Michael had seen previews of the new cop show; 'Jake and Norman', and could hardly wait to watch it. Jake and

Chapter nineteen / 287

Norman were two rookie cops working the beat in New York City. Each episode would introduce them to new experiences as cops and teach them the hard life of New York rough necks.

Neither Mark nor Michael realized the show would be on so late, so now they had to come up with a fail proof plan to get downstairs and watch the show without anyone knowing.

"Hey Mark! Hurry up, come here." Michael said in a hushed voice. The two went into their bedroom and closed the door.

"Okay, here's the plan, at ten o'clock Mom and Brandon are usually in their room, and Samantha is usually in hers and on the phone. All we have to do is quietly go down the stairs and watch the show."

"Michael, they'll hear the TV, we'll get caught."

"No, we won't, we'll keep the volume down so no one will hear." Michael had already thought about Lorna, and put Mark's worries of her to rest. He knew the housekeeper would also be in her room, probably watching 'Jake and Norman', Lorna loved cop shows.

"At ten o'clock I'll go down; I'll just go get a drink of water, look around and make sure no one is up." Michael explained his plan with bright eyes.

"What if you get caught?" Mark asked with eyes as big as his fear.

Michael had planned the whole event. If he got caught being downstairs, he would simply tell whomever caught him, he was getting a clean cup for the bathroom. Mark thought this was a brilliant idea, and was all for it.

"Good, that's a good idea." Mark replied.

At ten o'clock on the button, Michael looked out the door and into the hallway to make sure Samantha was in her room.

"Great, I can hear her talking on the phone, so the coast is clear. Now, give me five minutes to get downstairs and check the area. If I don't come back, you come on down," Michael instructed quietly.

"Right."

Michael carefully went down the stairway; there was a dim light on in the kitchen that usually stayed on. He slowly stepped off the bottom step looking all around as he did. He carefully looked around, no one was there, as a matter of fact, the whole downstairs was completely quiet and pretty much dark.

Mark waited the five minutes as instructed and then started slowly down the hall going down each step carefully into the living room.

"Great! We made it," Mark said. Michael turned the TV to where the reflection would not be toward any room in the house. The two boys sat on the floor with the volume down very low and began to watch "Jake and Norman', the new cop show that all the kids at school would be raving about.

Brandon watched the news and Joyce read a book. Brandon broke the silence causing Joyce to look up from her reading.

"It was good to see Timothy back to his same old self again wasn't it Joyce?"

"Yes, it sure was, I don't know what scared me the most, his not ever walking again, or his yelling at Christine. It was all I could do to not shake him when he did that."

"I know, when they are babies, it's hard to watch them fall down and cry. But I think it's harder to watch them fall down as young adults, because you know you can't pick them up and kiss it better."

"Brandon that was awfully deep," Joyce teased. "Maybe you should write a book on parenting," she now giggled.

"Alright, you've been teasing me all day, and I'm going to have to do something about it."

Brandon turned off the TV, went closer to Joyce and took her book from her, and began to tickle her. Joyce was ticklish on every spot of her body, Brandon knowing this, took full advantage.

"Oh, stop, Brandon; you know I can't stand that." She begged and laughed. After her surrender things got quiet in their room.

"Brandon do you hear something?"

"No, I don't here something." He said mocking her.

"I thought I heard something. After a few minutes Joyce thought she heard the noise again, this time getting Brandon's attention.

"I'll check, maybe one of the kids is in the kitchen." Brandon quietly walked out of their bedroom and looked to the direction of the noise. It was dark, but he did get a glimpse of two small people walking toward the stairs.

"Hold it boys!" Michael and Mark almost came out of their skin at the sudden sound of Brandon's deep voice.

"What are the two of you doing up at eleven o'clock at night?"

"Aah, we aah, both boys trying to evade the question, but having no luck. We wanted a drink, so we came down to get one." Michael said.

"Yeah we came to get a drink, and now we are headed back to bed."

"Now, that's funny that both of you needed a drink at the exact same hour." Brandon replied, knowing the whole time Mark and Michael were up to something, the question was what?

"Well, aah, being twins you see, we have needs at the same time."

"Hmm, I've never noticed this about you two before. Brandon replied, "Both of you in the living room, now." He said in a very firm tone.

Joyce could hear voices, so she put on her robe and joined Brandon. She was surprised to see her sons sitting on the sofa looking up at Brandon.

"Boys, what are you two doing up? It's after eleven o'clock; you'll never want to get up in the morning." Joyce said to her two sons.

Brandon filled Joyce in on his suspicions about the boys.

"Well, I suspect that young Mark and young Michael were doing something they weren't supposed to be doing. Now boys I am waiting for an answer, and I do expect the truth this time." Brandon said in a very stern tone.

"We were watching TV" Michael said looking down at the floor.

"What were you watching?" Joyce asked.

"A new cop show; all the kids in our class get to stay up and watch it, and we wanted to watch it, too," Mark explained.

Brandon explained to the boys what the punishment for this type of offense would be. He told them watching a television program without their mother's or his approval was not permitted. That cost them one month with no television. Brandon then got sterner with the boys; he had never had any trouble with them before and was shocked by it now. He knew he would have to get their attention, and make them understand they would follow the rules he and Joyce set for them.

"And," Brandon said with emphases.

"For not telling me the truth about why you were downstairs, you both will be spanked. I will not allow lies being told to your mother or myself. Boys! How could you?" Joyce said with a disappointed look on her face.

"Now both of you go into our room and let's get this over with right now, go on," Brandon instructed.

Joyce stayed in the living room and let Brandon handle the two offenders. When in the master bedroom, Brandon took the paddle he at one time used on his own sons to discipline the two boys. "Now boys, the Bible tells us 'spare the rod, spoil the child,' so it is my responsibility to do this in this way. Do you understand?"

"Yes sir," they replied in unison and in a low voice.

Joyce could hear vaguely the sounds that went on in the bedroom. She didn't like it, but it did need to be done, and it had to be done by Brandon. After a few minutes the boys and Brandon came out, the boys didn't look too happy and went on upstairs like they were instructed. Joyce and Brandon went back into their bedroom as well.

"Did you hear their reason for their coming downstairs?" Brandon asked his wife.

"No," Joyce replied.

He told her the same story the boys told him, but with a half smile on his face, as he watched his wife's face break out into a laugh also.

"I hope they learned their lesson," Joyce said.

The next afternoon when the twins came home from school, Richard and Luke needed a little help, it had been a rough day. One of the cows had gotten her head stuck in a fence; it took both Richard and Luke to free her, Luke then had to repair the fence.

Biscuit threw a shoe, and Brandon worked to get Richard's horse ready to be ridden. There were new cattle that needed to be tagged, this process took several hours, and with two ranch hands out sick, it made more work for Richard, Luke and Brandon.

When Richard saw the boys heading into the house, he followed them.

"Hey guys, do you have any homework this afternoon?" Richard asked.

"No, we got it done at school," Mark answered.

"In that case, Luke and I can use your help. We're tagging some cattle, so change your clothes and meet us in the north pasture," Richard instructed.

After changing their clothes and getting a small snack, the boys went to help Richard and Luke. Mark and Michael were still too small to help with the larger cattle, but when it came to the calves, the two of them together could handle the job.

Brandon, still working on Biscuit, saw the boys when they came for their horses.

"Hey, boys."

"Hi, we're going out to help Luke and Richard with the tagging." Michael said.

Brandon let the boys know when he was done with Biscuit, he would join them.

As soon as Mark thought of the shows he would be missing over the next month, not to mention the uncomfortable feeling when sitting on his horse, he gave Michael a little instruction.

"Michael, the next time you have a stupid idea, keep me out of it, will ya?"

"Oh, you wanted to see that show as much as I did."

Richard noticed the boys seemed to be arguing and couldn't keep from asking what was up.

"Hey, what's up with you two? You seem in a bad mood," Richard asked.

"We got a whoopin' from Brandon last night for telling a lie," Mark replied, "And no TV for a month."

"Aah, been there! I got caught too, so don't feel bad. But that was nothing like the time dad caught me and Sean smoking a cigarette; he made us eat one."

Mark and Michael's eyes got as big as the calf they were trying to tag.

"What happened then?" Michael asked.

"We both got sicker than a dog. I thought I was going to die. Sean was lying in his bed praying to die. I have never been that sick, ever. To this day the smell of a cigarette just about makes me sick to my stomach."

"Wow, Richard, I guess you won't ever smoke." Michael said.

"No, I guess I won't." Richard replied as he laughed a little.

The boys and Richard got all the little calves tagged before it was time for supper. The boys were glad Richard told them of his experiences and felt better about their punishment.

The boy's punishment with no TV seemed to drag, but Joyce would remind them every time they mentioned it, it was their choice to break the rules, it was their choice to lie. So, they would take it like little men. This only made the two boys groan with displeasure.

School was to be out in just two weeks. Samantha could hardly wait; after all she would be graduating from high school in eight days. She and Shelly had dreamed for as long as she could remember what they would do after graduation.

The two had registered at the University of Chicago to study for their choice of degrees. Samantha was hoping to get a degree in culinary arts. She had watched and learned under Lorna's hand for the past couple of years and really enjoyed cooking. Shelly on the other hand was interested in having a business of her own. She wanted to be the boss of whatever business it was going to be. The two cooked up the scheme that they would own their own restaurant. Samantha would be the head chef, and Shelly would run the business end of it. When they spoke of it, it was such a done deal, except the little minor detail of getting the degrees.

One afternoon Samantha had a conversation with Luke that surprised him a little. She told him of her and Shelly's plans for college; they would be leaving the third week in August, and she sounded so excited just talking about it.

"College can be great fun, if you don't forget why you're there," Luke said.

"I don't think we'll forget; we have a plan, and it involves hard work, good grades, oh, and aah no guys."

"No guys uhh?" Luke was trying not to grin at Samantha, she looked so adorable.

"Yes, we figure if we have guys hanging around, we may end up with a boyfriend, and if we end up with a boyfriend, we may wind up getting married, and if we wind up getting married, we can kiss our plans goodbye," she said very confidently. Samantha had learned from her mother's experience; Joyce met Paul in college, fell in love, and got married, then dropped out of school. Then Timothy was born, and before long, she was the mother of five.

Luke found this to be a very interesting way of looking at the future. He was glad Samantha didn't have any plans for any guys while away at school.

"Why did she never go back and finish her degree?" Luke asked.

"She says she's too old and there is no need for it anymore. So, no guys," she said with a small smile to Luke.

"No guys." Luke repeated with a grinning look.

"Well, Samantha sweetheart, that sounds like a very good plan, I hope you stick to it, and if any guys bother you, you just give me a call, and I will handle it personally."

―――――

Elise had worked hard and actually graduated early. She was tired of textbooks and classes, but mostly she was tired of being so far away from her family. She had taken summer classes, full loads and now it was paying off, she was tired, but she was done. She had plans to rest and enjoy herself a little before she hit the job interviews.

"So, what now?" Timothy asked his sister as she visited him and his little family.

"Well, first of all, I'm taking a few months off, off from every thing. I am doing nothing but lie around the ranch and let my brain rest."

"Sounds like a smart idea, Elise," Christine told her.

One of Elise's professors told her about a job opportunity in Colorado, but she didn't want to be that far away from home ever again. "It's too tough," she said as she was playing with her nephew.

Elise told her bother and sister-in-law to pick a night to go out and she would stay with Nathan. She loved her nephew and wanted to spend time with him. Christine didn't want to take advantage of Elise, but Timothy was ready for some time alone with his wife.

Joyce enjoyed having her daughter home; she shook her head when she thought abut one child coming home, and one leaving in a short while.

Elise told her mother about her staying with Nate while Timothy and Christine were away. Joyce thought it a wonderful idea.

Friday evening, Elise arrived at Tim and Christine's a little early. Tim was ready to go, but Christine was a little nervous for some reason Tim could not understand.

"Come on Christine, let's go, Elise can handle Nathan, besides Mom is not too far away. If she needs help, she knows where to go."

"I know, it isn't that I don't trust you Elise, it's just that I have never left him over night before."

Finally, with a kiss on Nathan's little head, the two were out the door.

"Alright, Nate, my little man, it's just you and me." Elise said as she shut the door and walked with Nate to the living room. It wasn't too long until Joyce called to check on the two of them. Joyce felt better just checking, and reminded Elise to make sure the doors were locked. Children grow older, that's true, but mothers are always mothers, and that was a fact, too. Joyce sweetly explained to her daughter.

Elise fed and bathed Nathan and rocked him to sleep, then went downstairs and called one of her friends from high school that she still kept in touch with, and knew was in town for the weekend.

Tyne invited Elise out to eat, but Elise explained to her, she was babysitting her nephew, but would love to Saturday evening. The plans then were to meet at Pete's Pizza place and do a little catching up.

The two girls laughed and talked like they had done so many times before, but Elise had to cut the conversation short.

"Oh, I hear Nate, I gotta go Tyne, and I'll call you tomorrow when I know when we can meet."

The two girls hung up from talking, and Elise saw to Nathan's needs.

Joyce had just pulled up in the driveway when she spotted Brandon getting off his horse, Pete, and headed her way.

He greeted her with a kiss and asked her about her day. Brandon opened the kitchen door for his wife, only to find a mess on the floor.

"What's all this?" Joyce asked when she tried to step into the kitchen door.

"Boys!" Joyce called out.

"Is Tim here?" The two boys said as they ran down the stairs to the kitchen.

"Oh, is that tonight? I had forgotten."

"Is what tonight?" Brandon asked.

"Timothy is taking the boys camping with the church group. He felt he hadn't spent enough time with his brothers so he signed them up. They will be back tomorrow evening," Joyce told Brandon.

"I can't believe Lorna didn't make them move their things from the kitchen door."

Brandon had forgotten to tell Joyce that Lorna had asked for this weekend off a few weeks ago, she and her sister were visiting an aunt that lived nearby. Lately it seemed everyone was running in so many different circles, it was getting hard to keep up.

"Hey, who's going camping?" Richard asked as he almost tripped over the sleeping bags.

"We are!" Michael said with excitement.

"Hi, Richard, how was your day today?" Joyce asked.

"Fine, I just came in to get a cold drink and to let you know Luke and I will be gone the rest of the evening; we are going into town to get some pizza with some other friends, and maybe pick up a basketball game, so I don't know what time we'll be in."

"Well, that was nice of you to let us know," Joyce said.

"I can't help it, I'm the nice son, remember?" Everyone laughed at Richard.

"Later ya'll." He said in a silly drawn out tone.

"Boys! Tim's here! Take your things to the truck," Joyce said as she went out to say hello to her son.

Joyce gave Tim a hug and then got a quick run down on Christine and Nathan. He was looking forward to this camping trip as much as Mark and Michael. Joyce could not help but laugh a little at him. Timothy made the comment to Joyce that he and the boys would be fine sleeping under the stars and eating off the land. As he finished his sentence, Mark asked about the cookies Lorna had made for their trip.

"Yeah, eating off the land," Brandon said laughing.

All three waved as they pulled out of the driveway.

"Well, Brandon, you will have to suffer through my cooking tonight, but I think I can keep you from starving." Joyce teased. Just as the two entered the house, they were met by Samantha who then told them her plans for the evening. She was spending the night at Shelly's and would be back by noon the next day.

"Brandon, I have an idea, instead of me cooking, why don't we order a pizza and rent a movie?"

"Sounds good ... what does Elise like on her Pizza?"

"Elise is not here, she is in town, remember? She and Tyne are looking for apartments to rent?"

"Oh, I did forget." Brandon stood there for a moment staring at his wife. It was as if a light switch had just been turned on.

"Joyce, my love, do you know what's happening?"

"No, what?"

"Joyce we have the entire house to ourselves."

Joyce put her hands to her mouth that was now hanging open.

"You're right!" she exclaimed. "We could not have planned this if we tried."

"So, what do you want to do?" He said as he came closer to her and put his arms around her waist, and began to nuzzle on her neck.

Joyce giggled. "I'm sure you'll think of something."

This weekend alone had not been planned; the family had all gone in different directions. Brandon knew this did not and would not happen often, so he planned on making the best of it.

Brandon and Joyce did something they did not allow the children to do. They ate in the living room in front of the TV. When they had finished their pizza, Brandon put in the movie he had rented. Joyce decided to put on a little something more comfortable.

As she went back into the living room, Brandon dimmed the lights and the two of them sat together on the floor with a bowl of ice cream, sharing the spoon. They were enjoying their time alone, when all of a sudden, there was a knock on the front door. The sound surprised both of them; the children were all in different places for the evening, and no one was expected at the ranch for a visit.

"You've got to be kidding me!" Brandon said in disgust. Joyce just looked toward the door, then back to Brandon. The person on the other side knocked a second time, and Joyce decided she should go into the bedroom and dress more appropriately.

"Hi Dad, Susan, Victoria and I were out for the evening and in this area, so we thought we would stop by and say hello." Sean said to his father.

"Come on in. How's my beautiful granddaughter this evening?" Brandon asked as he held out his hands for Victoria, who went gladly to her granddad.

"Where is everyone?" Sean asked.

Brandon explained the whereabouts of everyone, and that he and Joyce were puttering around the house alone.

"Joyce will be out in a minute, sit down." The adults sat on the sofa, and Brandon started to play with Victoria.

"What did you eat for supper Victoria?"

"Peeesa," the little one said, trying to say Pizza.

"You know what? That's what I had too. I love pizza, do you love pizza, Victoria?" The little girl with her blond curls nodded her head up and down.

"Well, what a lovely surprise!" Joyce said to her company. "Hello Victoria, how are you this evening?"

"I'm mine." The adults laughed as the little girl told Joyce she was fine.

"I drink," Victoria told her mother.

Brandon gladly took Victoria to the kitchen to get her a drink.

"Susan, what can she have?"
"Milk will be fine."
Brandon sat the little girl in her booster seat, and gave her a cup of milk; he also asked Susan if she could have a cookie. Brandon couldn't let his granddaughter eat alone, the two of them sat in the kitchen eating cookies and milk.

While Brandon and Victoria were in the kitchen, Susan, Joyce and Sean were talking in the living room. Sean soon left the women alone, and joined his daughter and father. Once again there was knocking at the door, this time it was Don and Jennifer.

Brandon was glad his sons had come for a visit, but he was really looking forward to this time alone with Joyce. It reminded him of his college days, when some guys would have a girl in their dorm room, they would hang a neck tie on the door knob, so others would know not to disturb.

After a few minutes of talking, Don asked if either of them wanted to go out to eat. It was then that Brandon suggested the five of them go out, he and Joyce had already eaten and were looking forward to a quiet evening at home.

"Well, even though we have already eaten," Sean said. "We'll go, maybe have a little dessert."

The younger Millers all said good night to Brandon and Joyce, as they walked to their car Susan got the strangest feeling they had interrupted a quiet evening for Brandon and Joyce.

"Sean, I think we may have interrupted your father and Joyce."
"What makes you think that?"
"I don't know for sure, but think about it. We show up unannounced, the whole household is out for the evening or longer, even Lorna. And most of the house was dark. I feel a little embarrassed."
"That's silly. I mean, us coming by gave them something to do."
"Sean!"
Susan could not believe her husband could be so blind to some things.

Brandon and Joyce made their way back to the living room again. After they had gotten comfy cozy again, Joyce couldn't help but laugh out loud.

"What are you laughing at?" Brandon asked with a total confused look on his face.

"Here we didn't plan anything for this evening; all the kids are out doing something that will keep them out until tomorrow, even Lorna. So we're excited about having all this time alone in this big house, and what happens? The adult children show up, and don't think anything about it."

Now they both were laughing out loud. Brandon sat down beside his wife and gave her a big hug and kiss.

By afternoon the next day most of the ranch residents were back and doing their normal things. The twins came in dirty and happy, they had major fun with their big brother. Tim looked like he had a good time as well, but was not as dirty. The boys were instructed to go and bathe.

Everyone had a good weekend with their family and friends, but Joyce was glad to have her house full with her children and hear the sounds of life that each one made.

Before Joyce was really ready, it was time for Samantha to pack up and get off to begin her first year of college. Joyce thought she would be better at this by now, after all this was her third child to go away to school, but she continued to fight back tears all that day.

"Do you think we can get all this stuff in that little dorm?" Timothy was asking Brandon when the two men looked at the containers, boxes and luggage Samantha had ready for them to take down the stairs and out to be loaded. The two men shook their heads, and then Timothy mentioned that Shelly would probably have just as much.

Once Samantha and Shelly were at the school, they got their room location; the two girls had the look of utter happiness on their faces. Shelly's father and mother had brought her, and now thinking the same thoughts as Brandon and Joyce. The sadness of their daughter leaving home and wondering how in the world that little dorm room would hold all her stuff.

After all the unloading and lugging up to the third floor, Brandon and Charles, Shelly's father, looked at one another, both thinking the same thought. Where was it all going to go? Joyce and Vicki, Shelly's mother, couldn't help but laugh, not at their tired men, but at all the stuff the girls felt they had to have. Finally after all was in the tiny room, the adults decided it was time to go. Brandon took Samantha to one side and kindly spoke to her.

"He told her not to forget to call home often," as he hugged her tightly. "I feel happy for you Samantha," he said as his arms were tightly around her. "Happy for you because I know you will be fine; you will learn a lot; you have your best friend with you, and the two of you will have fun. But, honey, don't forget who you are, and where you come from. Don't forget to keep God in your days, or your days will not be good ones. Many opportunities will come along that will look good, sound great, but will be very wrong; you must pray about each one. Read the word every day, and keep going to church even though your mother and I will not be here to see that you do. You will have to be a responsible young woman now, the one we know you are."

Brandon then kissed Samantha on the top of the head and then reached into his wallet and gave her some extra money. Joyce hugged her daughter tightly as well, but she had told her all she needed and wanted to before they left the house, because she knew she would not have the voice to tell her when this moment came.

"I miss you already." She kissed Samantha on the cheek hugged her again tightly, and with Brandon's help left the dorm and went to their vehicle. Brandon held his wife close as she cried as if her heart was breaking, just as she felt with Tim and Elise when it was their turn to leave home and start college. When she settled down, he gently kissed her forehead, started up the Bronco and headed for home.

Even though her children were mostly grown up now, she still had two teenage boys at home, boys that needed her time and attention. She was sad about the missing people around her table, but knew it was a normal phase of life to go through; with her families' and the Lord's help, she knew she would make it through.

Chapter nineteen / 301

One Saturday morning, Joyce felt the need for a ride. She had been so busy at work during the week that she couldn't find the time to take Millie out. Joyce dressed, and headed for the stables, after letting her family know where she could be found if needed.

"Hi, Luke, how are you?"

"I'm fine, are you headed out for a ride today Miss Joyce?"

"Yes, I thought I would take Millie out; we both can use the exercise and fresh air."

"I'll try to get her away from Pete; he likes her you know." Luke explained.

"I told Brandon Pete had a thing for Millie. I hope he won't get angry at us." The two began to laugh.

Within ten minutes Luke had Millie saddled up for Joyce and she and Millie were on their way.

Joyce rode for about an hour, the ride not only felt good physically but mentally as well. Something about being in the wide open spaces with the wind going through her hair made Joyce feel good all over. She had thought back to a time she didn't live on a ranch, didn't have a horse to ride. Riding seemed to do her so much good, it cleared her mind and made her feel so alive. She always talked to her Lord when out in those open spaces.

Joyce really enjoyed living on the Southern Star Ranch; it was peaceful and she found beauty everywhere she looked. She loved every part of ranch living, especially the ranch owner. Joyce couldn't help but think of the few years she and her children had been on this ranch, in reality, it hadn't been all that long. At first, she wondered how she would like living on a ranch; now she couldn't think of living anywhere else; this ranch had become her home.

After her ride, Joyce went inside and cleaned up before Jennifer and Don came in.

"Dad, Joyce, I have news for you. Jennifer's pregnant." Don told the family with a big smile on his face as he looked at his wife.

"Well, now that's good news." Brandon got up hugged and kissed his daughter-in-law on the cheek, and then gave his son a big bear hug.

"We are so happy for the both of you, another little one to run around here, that's so great." Joyce replied as she hugged the happy parents to be.

The twins seemed to not even notice anything was being said.

"Boys," Joyce spoke to them as they both looked up with food in their mouths.

"Did you hear what Don said?"

"Umm hmm," the look on their mother's face let them both know they were supposed to say or do something.

"And do the two of you have anything to say?"

"Oh, aah congratulations on the happy arrival of the upcoming baby," Mark replied.

This caused the whole room to burst out in laughter.

Two weeks later, Timothy, Christine and Nathan walked onto the front porch where Lorna had just finished sweeping. The two adults stopped to talk to Lorna, before going inside.

"Hello, Nate sweetie, grandmomma is really glad to see you." Joyce said as she picked her grandson up and kissed his soft cheek. Nate was getting harder to pick up; but Joyce couldn't resist as Nate toddled to her.

The boys came down the stairs at that moment, said hello, and then went to Nate to play with him; Nate loved to play with his uncles.

"Come on into the kitchen, can I get you some coffee or a soft drink, either of you?"

Brandon just walked into the kitchen himself, and asked the same question as Joyce.

"Yes, but sit down, Brandon, I'll get it myself; soft drink, Christine?" Tim asked.

Tim got everyone a drink, Elise came in and got her own and asked if either one of them wanted a piece of Lorna's chocolate cake.

"Eeww Lorna's Chocolate cake, I'll have some of that." Timothy said with eyes big as a plate.

"Nothing for me thanks Elise." Christine said.

Timothy took it upon himself to explain that Christine was watching her weight.

"Christine, honey, you don't need to watch your weight, you look wonderful," Joyce kindly told her.

Christine explained it wasn't the weight she now had, but the weight she was going to have.

"Christine?" Joyce said with her eye brows raised in question.

"Yes, Joyce, I'm expecting again. I'm about two months along.

"Oh, Honey," Joyce went and hugged her daughter-in-law, then her son. It was the same scene played a few weeks earlier with Don and Jennifer.

"Wow!" Elise said as she was putting her fork to her mouth, "First Jennifer, and now Christine."

The boys came through the kitchen with Nate. They too wanted cake; Elise gladly told the boys the good news.

"Oh brother, more babies, when is this all gonna stop?" Mark asked out loud as he was getting a piece of cake.

The adults just laughed at him and Brandon rubbed the top of his head. Joyce had told Tim and Christine about Jennifer's pregnancy; they were happy for Don and Jennifer as well.

"So, who will come first I wonder." Both women were due pretty close together.

"We could have a baby pool, you know, see who guesses right." Brandon said as he sipped his coffee causing the adults to burst out into laughter again.

"Of course, he's teasing." Joyce said as she poked her husband in the ribs.

Looking rather seriously at his wife, Timothy spoke.

"Seriously, I missed most of the wonder and specialness of Christine carrying Nate; I don't plan on missing this one." He then leaned over and gently kissed his wife.

It was almost Joyce's undoing, as she suddenly remembered the hard times of those months, how she had wondered if her Timothy would ever be himself again. She quickly made her thoughts come back to the happy time of the present.

Christmas Day had been one of many hours of enjoyment. The family had come in and out all through the day. Since the married children also had in-laws they were expected to visit, Brandon and Joyce told them to go ahead, it was understandable they couldn't be at two and three places at once and Joyce said she would not be a part of making the holidays a hectic time for her family. They each were told they were welcome to stop by when they could.

Joyce, Samantha and Elise made a big dinner for the family, Brandon had given Lorna a week off for the holidays, and she was spending it with her sisters.

After the meal, Brandon read the Christmas story from the Bible; all who were there listened with much attentiveness, even though they all had heard it many times before.

The boys were so excited with the dirt bikes Brandon had bought for them; it wasn't clear who was more excited by this gift, the boys or Brandon. The other children were equally happy with their gifts, as Joyce sat in Brandon's arms in the big overstuffed chair in the living room and watched. Later that evening it was much the same scene as they watched their grandchildren and their adult children open their gifts.

As Joyce sat in Brandon's arms secure in the love he had for her, and feeling the love she had for him, she bathed in that love and the joy that these two families had for one another. Joyce almost started to cry when the children all exited the room to get some of Samantha's Christmas pudding she had made earlier that day.

"I love you with all my heart, Joyce, I hope you know that." Brandon said as he gently turned her chin up so she could see his eyes.

"I know, and I love you with all mine; I can't think of when I have been happier, even when storms come our way, no matter how strong or how long, we have our God, our family and we have each other."

The two shared a gentle kiss, comfortable in the chair in each others arms.